A Philosopher, a Psychologist, and An ExtraTerrestrial Walk into A Chocolate Bar

"Jass Richards is back with another great book that entertains and informs as she mixes feminism, critical thinking, and current social issues with humour ... The wedding intervention was hilarious. ...." James M. Fisher, *The Miramichi Reader*

"I found myself caught between wanting to sit and read [*A Philosopher, a Psychologist, and An ExtraTerrestrial Walk into a Chocolate Bar*] all in one go and wanting to spread it out. I haven't laughed that hard and gotten to spend time with such unflinchingly tough ideas at the same time. ... [And] the brilliance of the Alices! ... I can now pull out your book every time somebody tries to claim that novels can't have meaningful footnotes and references. [Thanks too] for pointing me to the brilliant essay series 'Dudes are Doomed.' I am eagerly watching for *The ReGender App* ...." C. Osborne

CottageEscape.zyx: Satan Takes Over

"A hilarious take, based in reality. You know Jass has lived this life. It is way too familiar. I laugh ... as much as I cry ...." Jennifer Jilks, mymuskoka.blogspot.com

TurboJetslams: Proof #29 of the Non-Existence of God

"Extraordinarily well written with wit, wisdom, and laugh-out-loud ironic recognition, *TurboJetslams: Proof #29 of the Non-Existence of God* is a highly entertaining and a riveting read that will linger on in the mind and memory long after the little book itself has been finished and set back upon the shelf (or shoved into the hands of friends with an insistence that they drop everything else and read it!). Highly recommended for community library collections, it should be noted for personal reading lists." *Midwest Book Review*

"We all very much enjoyed it—it's funny and angry and heartfelt and told truly … " McSweeney's

"If you're looking for a reading snack that has zero saccharine but is loaded with just the right combination of snark, sarcasm, and humor, you've found it." Ricki Wilson, Amazon

"What Richards has done is brilliant. At first, I began getting irritated as I read about a familiar character, or a familiar scenario from our time living on the lake. Then, as the main character amps up her game, I see the thrill in the planning and the retribution she undertakes for pay back." mymuskoka. blogspot.com/2016/07/ book-review-turbojetslams.html

The ReGender App

"This book is brilliant. …. The scene at the airport had me laughing out loud. …" Katya, Goodreads

"A book I really recommend to any book club and to people who are interested in gender differences and gender discrimination." Mesca Elin, Psychromatic Redemption

License to Do That

"I'm very much intrigued by the issues raised in this narrative. I also enjoy the author's voice, which is unapologetically combative but also funny and engaging." A.S.

"I love Froot Loup! You make me laugh out loud all the time!" Celeste M.

"A thought-provoking premise and a wonderful cast of characters." rejection letter from publisher

The Blasphemy Tour

"With plenty of humor and things to think about throughout, *The Blasphemy Tour* is a choice pick ...." *Midwest Book Review*

"Jass Richards has done it again. As I tell anyone who wants to listen, Jass is a comedy genius, she writes the funniest books and always writes the most believable unbelievable characters and scenes. ... I knew this book was a winner when ... a K9 unit dog kind of eats their special brownies ... and dances Thriller. ... Rev and Dylan are not your ordinary guy and girl protagonists with sexual tension and a romantic interest, at all. They both defy gender roles, and they are so smart and opinionated, it's both funny and made me think at the same time. ... They tour around the USA, in their lime green bus that says 'There are no gods. Deal with it.' Overall, I highly recommend anything by Jass, especially this one book, which is full of comedy gold and food for thought." May Arend, Brazilian Book Worm

"If I were Siskel and Ebert I would give this book Two Thumbs Way Up. ... Yes, it is blasphemy toward organized religion but it gives you tons of Bible verses to back up its premises. And besides, it's pure entertainment. There's a prequel which I recommend you read first. *The Road Trip Dialogues*. ... I only hope there will be a third book." L.K. Killian

"Wretchedly funny." C. Mike Rice, Realworldatheism.com

The Road Trip Dialogues

"I am impressed by the range from stoned silliness to philosophical perspicuity, and I love your comic rhythm." L. S.

"This is engaging, warm, funny work, and I enjoyed what I read. ..." rejection letter from publisher

"Just thought I'd let you know I'm on the Fish'n'Chips scene and laughing my ass off." Ellie Burmeister

"These two need stable jobs. Oh wait, no. Then we wouldn't get any more road trips. Fantastic book which expands the mind in a laid back sort of way. Highly recommended." lindainalabama

"Watched *Monty Python and the Holy Grail* last weekend. Could only think of Jass Richards and *The Road Trip Dialogues* ...." May Arend, Brazilian Book Worm

Dogs Just Wanna Have Fun

"Funny and entertaining! I looked forward to picking up this book at the end of a long day." Mary Baluta

"... terrifically funny and ingeniously acerbic ...." Dr. Patricia Bloom, My Magic Dog

"... laugh-out-loud funny." M.W., Librarything

This Will Not Look Good on My Resume

"Ya made me snort root beer out my nose!" Moriah Jovan, *The Proviso*

"Darkly humorous." Jennifer Colt, *The Hellraiser of the Hollywood Hills*

"HYSTERICAL! ... There are really no words to describe how funny this book is. ... Really excellent book." Alison, Goodreads

"This book is like a roller coaster ride on a stream of consciousness. ... Altogether, a funny, quirky read ...." Grace Krispy, Motherlode: Book Reviews and Original Photography

"Brett has trouble holding down a job. Mainly because she's an outspoken misanthrope who is prone to turn a dead-end job into a social engineering experiment. Sometimes with comically disastrous results, sometimes with comically successful results. (Like pairing up a compulsive shopper with a kleptomaniac for an outing at the mall.) I don't agree with everything she says, but I will defend her right to say it — because she's hilarious!

"My favorite part was when she taught a high school girls' sex ed class that 70% of boys will lie to get sex, 80% won't use a condom, yet 90% are pro-life. She was reprimanded, of course. I think she should have gotten a medal.

"You will likely be offended at one point or another, but if you are secure enough to laugh at your own sacred cows instead of just everyone else's, this is a must read." weikelm, Librarything

"Wonderful read, funny, sarcastic. Loved it!" Charlie, Smashwords

"I just loved this book. It was a quick read, and left me in stitches. … " Robin McCoy-Ramirez

"First, let me just say I was glad I was not drinking anything while reading this. I refrained from that. My husband said he never heard me laugh so much from reading a book. At one point, I was literally in tears. Jass Richards is brilliant with the snappy comebacks and the unending fountain of information she can spout forth. … The quick wit, the sharp tongue, the acid words and sarcasm that literally oozes from her pores … beautiful." M. Snow, My Chaotic Ramblings

Substitute Teacher from Hell

"I enjoyed reading "Supply Teacher from Hell" immensely and found myself bursting out laughing many, many times. It is extremely well-written, clever, and very intelligent in its observations." Iris Turcott, dramaturge

Too Stupid to Visit

"Your material is fabulous! It reminds me so much of George Carlin." *Gemini Rising*

Jane Smith's Translation Dictionary of Everyday Lies, Insults, Manipulations, and Clueless Comments

"Oooh, awesome!" C. Osborne

more at
jassrichards.com

·

Writing as Peg Tittle

Fighting Words: notes for a future we won't have

"'Men Need Sex' is terrific!" An ovarite from ovarit.com

"Love. Just reading 'What Sane Man' was satisfying." Anonymous, ovarit.com

Jess

"[Jess'] perspective on being a girl and woman while having memories of being a man offers an understanding I'd never thought of. Really interesting book." Poolays, LibraryThing

Gender Fraud: a fiction

"A gripping read ...." Katya, Goodreads

Impact

"Edgy, insightful, terrific writing, propelled by rage against rape. Tittle writes in a fast-paced, dialogue-driven style that hurtles the reader from one confrontation to the next. Chock full of painful social observations ...." Hank Pellissier, Director of Humanist Global Charity

" ... The idea of pinning down the inflictors of this terror is quite appealing ...." Alison Lashinsky

It Wasn't Enough

"Unlike far too many novels, this one will make you think, make you uncomfortable, and then make you reread it ...." C. Osborne, moonspeaker.ca

"... a powerful and introspective dystopia .... It is a book I truly recommend for a book club as the discussions could be endless ...." Mesca Elin, Goodreads

"Tittle's book hits you hard ...." D. Sohi, Goodreads

"*It Wasn't Enough* punches well above its weight and straight in the gut ...." Shefali Sequeira, 4w.pub

Exile

"Thought-provoking stuff, as usual from Peg Tittle." James M. Fisher, Goodreads

What Happened to Tom

"This powerful book plays with the gender gap to throw into high relief the infuriating havoc unwanted pregnancy can wreak on a woman's life. Once you've read *What Happened to Tom*, you'll never forget it." Elizabeth Greene, *Understories* and *Moving*

"I read this in one sitting, less than two hours, couldn't put it down. Fantastic allegorical examination of the gendered aspects of unwanted pregnancy. A must-read for everyone, IMO." Jessica, Goodreads

"Peg Tittle's *What Happened to Tom* takes a four-decades-old thought experiment and develops it into a philosophical novella of extraordinary depth and imagination .... Part allegory, part suspense (perhaps horror) novel, part defense of bodily autonomy rights (especially women's), Tittle's book will give philosophers and the philosophically minded much to discuss." Ron Cooper, *Hume's Fork*

Just Think about It!

"An excellent collection of thought-provoking essays and short pieces. *Just Think about It!* (2nd edn) covers an amazingly wide range of topics that really made me think ...." Karen Siddall, Amazon

Sexist Shit that Pisses Me Off

"Woh. This book is freaking awesome and I demand a sequel." Anonymous, barnesandnoble.com

"I recommend this book to both women and men. It will open your eyes to a lot of sexist—and archaic—behaviors." Seregon, Goodreads

"Honestly, selling this in today's climate is a daunting challenge— older women have grown weary, younger women don't seem to care, or at least don't really identify as feminists, men—forget that. All in all a sad state of affairs—sorry." rejection letter from agent

Shit that Pisses Me Off

"I find Peg Tittle to be a passionate, stylistically-engaging writer with a sharp eye for the hypocritical aspects of our society." George, Amazon

"Peg raises provocative questions: should people need some kind of license to have children? Should the court system use professional jurors? Many of her essays address the imbalance of power between men and women; some tackle business, sports, war, and the weather. She even explains why you're not likely to see Peg Tittle at Canada's version of an Occupy Wall Street demonstration. It's all thought-provoking, and whether or not you'll end up agreeing with her conclusions, her essays make for fascinating reading." Erin O'Riordan

"This was funny and almost painfully accurate, pointing out so many things that most of us try NOT to notice, or wish we didn't. Well written and amusing, I enjoyed this book immensely." Melody Hewson

" ... a pissed off kindred spirit who writes radioactive prose with a hint of sardonic wit .... Peg sets her sights on a subject with laser sharp accuracy then hurls words like missiles in her collection of 25 cogent essays on the foibles and hypocrisies of life .... Whether you agree or disagree with Peg's position on the issues, *Shit that Pisses Me Off* will stick to your brain long after you've ingested every word— no thought evacuations here. Her writing is adept and titillating ... her razor sharp words will slice and dice the cerebral jugular. If you enjoy reading smart, witty essays that challenge the intellect, download a copy ...." Laura Salkin, thinkspin.com

"Not very long, but a really good read. The author is intelligent, and points out some great inconsistencies in common thinking and action .... may have been channeling some George Carlin in a few areas." Briana Blair, Goodreads

" ... thought-provoking, and at times, hilarious. I particularly loved 'Bambi's cousin is going to tear you apart.' Definitely worth a read!" Nichole, Goodreads

"What she said!!! Pisses me off also! Funny, enjoyable and so right on!!!! Highly recommended." Vic, indigo.ca

Critical Thinking: An Appeal to Reason

"This book is worth its weight in gold." Daniel Millsap

"One of the books everyone should read. A lot of practical examples, clear and detailed sections, and tons of all kinds of logical fallacies analyzed under microscope that will give you a completely different way of looking to the everyday manipulations and will help you to avoid falling into the common traps. Highly recommended!" Alexander Antukh

"One of the best CT books I've read." G. Baruch, Goodreads

"This is an excellent critical thinking text written by a clever and creative critical thinker. Her anthology *What If* is excellent too: the short readings are perfect for engaging philosophical issues in and out of the classroom." Ernst Borgnorg

"Peg Tittle's *Critical Thinking* is a welcome addition to a crowded field. Her presentations of the material are engaging, often presented in a conversational discussion with the reader or student. The text's coverage of the material is wide-ranging. Newspaper items, snippets from *The Far Side*, personal anecdotes, emerging social and political debates, as well as LSAT sample questions are among the many tools Tittle employs to educate students on the elemental aspects of logic and critical thinking." Alexander E. Hooke, Professor of Philosophy, Stevenson University

What If?...
Collected Thought Experiments in Philosophy

"Of all the collections of philosophical thought experiments I've read, this is by far the best. It is accessible, uses text from primary sources, and is very well edited. The final entry in the book— which I won't spoil for you—was an instant favorite of mine." Dominick Cancilla

"This is a really neat little book. It would be great to use in discussion-based philosophy courses, since the readings would be nice and short and to the point. This would probably work much better than the standard anthology of readings that are, for most students, incomprehensible." Nathan Nobis, Morehouse College

Should Parents be Licensed? Debating the Issues

"This book has some provocative articles and asks some very uncomfortable questions ...." Jasmine Guha, Amazon

"This book was a great collection of essays from several viewpoints on the topic and gave me a lot of profound over-the-(TV-)dinner-(tray-)table conversations with my husband." Lauren Cocilova, Goodreads

"You need a licence to drive a car, own a gun, or fish for trout. You don't need a licence to raise a child. But maybe you should ... [This book] contains about two dozen essays by various experts, including psychologists, lawyers and sociologists ...." Ian Gillespie, *London Free Press*

"... But the reformers are right. Completely. Ethically. I agree with Joseph Fletcher, who notes, "It is depressing ... to realize that most people are accidents," and with George Schedler, who states, "Society has a duty to ensure that infants are born free of avoidable defects. ... Traditionalists regard pregnancy and parenting as a natural right that should never be curtailed. But what's the result of this laissez-faire attitude? Catastrophic suffering. Millions of children born disadvantaged, crippled in childhood, destroyed in adolescence. Procreation cannot be classified as a self-indulgent privilege—it needs to be viewed as a life-and-death responsibility ...." Abhimanyu Singh Rajput, Social Tikka

Ethical Issues in Business:
Inquiries, Cases, and Readings

"*Ethical Issues in Business* is clear and user-friendly yet still rigorous throughout. It offers excellent coverage of basic ethical theory, critical thinking, and many contemporary issues such as whistleblowing, corporate social responsibility, and climate change. Tittle's approach is not to tell students what to think but rather to get them to think—and to give them the tools to do so. This is the text I would pick for a business ethics course." Kent Peacock, University of Lethbridge

"This text breathes fresh air into the study of business ethics; Tittle's breezy, use-friendly style puts the lie to the impression that a business ethics text has to be boring." Paul Viminitz, University of Lethbridge

"A superb introduction to ethics in business." Steve Deery, *The Philosophers' Magazine*

"Peg Tittle wants to make business students think about ethics. So she has published an extraordinarily useful book that teaches people to question and analyze key concepts .... Take profit, for example .... She also analyzes whistleblowing, advertising, product safety, employee rights, discrimination, management and union matters, business and the environment, the medical business, and ethical investing ...." Ellen Roseman, *The Toronto Star*

more at
pegtittle.com

•

Writing as chris wind

This is what happens

"An interesting mix of a memoir and a philosophical work, together with some amazing poetry. ... *This is what happens* won't only be the book of the year for me, but it ranks high, top 5 on the best books ever read." Mesca Elin, mescalime.wordpress.com

"*This is what happens* relates how women are hamstrung by patriarchy ... the sexism both insidious and glaring that profoundly shaped Kris's life from its beginnings ... An incisive reflection on how social forces constrain women's lives. ... Great for fans of Sylvia Plath, Doris Lessing's *The Golden Notebook*." *Booklife*

Thus Saith Eve

"Short, but definitely entertaining ... and serious between the lines." Lee Harmon, A Dubious Disciple Book Review

" ... a truly wonderful source of feminist fiction. In addition to being an extremely enjoyable and thought-provoking read, the monologues can also be used for audition and performance pieces." Katie M. Deaver, feminismandreligion.com

Snow White Gets Her Say

"Why isn't anyone doing this on stage? ... What a great night of theater that would be!" szferris, Librarything

"I loved the sassy voices in these stories, and the humor, even when making hard points." PJ O'Brien, Smashwords

Deare Sister

"You are clearly a writer of considerable talent, and your special ability to give expression to so many different characters, each in a uniquely appropriate style, makes your work fascinating and attractive. ... The pieces are often funny, sometimes sensitive, always creative. But they contain an enormous load of anger, and that is where I have problems. ... I know at least one feminist who would read your manuscript with delight (unfortunately she is not a publisher), who would roar with laughter in her sharing of your anger. ..." rejection letter from Black Moss Press

Particivision and other stories

"... your writing is very accomplished. ... *Particivision and other stories* is authentic, well-written, and certainly publishable ...." rejection letter from Turnstone Press

"... engaging and clever ...." rejection letter from Lester & Orpen Dennys, Publishers

"As the title indicates, this collection of stories is about getting into the thick of things, taking sides, taking action, and speaking out loud and clear, however unpopular your opinion may be. ... refreshingly out of the ordinary." Joan McGrath, *Canadian Book Review Annual*

dreaming of kaleidoscopes

"... a top pick of poetry and is very much worth considering. ..." *Midwest Book Review*

Soliloquies: the lady doth indeed protest

"... not only dynamic, imaginative verse writing, but extremely intelligent and intuitive insight. ... I know many actresses who would love to get their hands on this material!" Joanne Zipay, Judith Shakespeare Company, NYC

"'Ophelia' is something of an oddity ... I found it curiously attractive." *Dinosaur*

UnMythed

"... A welcome relief from the usual male emphasis in this area. There is anger and truth here, not to mention courage." Eric Folsom, *Next Exit*

"... With considerable skill and much care, chris wind has extrapolated truths from mythical scenarios and reordered them in modern terms. ... Wind handles these myths with and intellect. Her voice suggests that the relationship between the consciousness of the myth-makers and modern consciousness is closer than we would think." Linda Manning, *Quarry*

"Personally, I would not publish this stuff. This is not to say it isn't publishable—it's almost flawless stylistically, perfect form and content, etc., etc. It's perverse: satirical, biting, caustic, funny. Also cruel, beyond bitter, single-minded with a terminally limited point of view, and this individual may have read Edith Hamilton's Mythology but she/he certainly doesn't perceive the essential meanings of these myths. Or maybe does and deliberately twists the meaning to suit the poem. Likewise, in the etymological sense. Editorial revisions suggested? None, it's perfect. Market potential/ readership targets: Everyone—this is actually marketable—you could sell fill Harbourfront reading this probably. General comments: You could actually make money on this stuff." anonymous reader report for a press that rejected the ms

Paintings and Sculptures

"You know that feeling—when you read the first page and you know you're going to like the book? That happened when I read the first poem. ... I loved 'Mona' and I could picture the scene; it might have happened that way, we'll never know ...." Mesca Elin, barnesandnoble.com

Satellites Out of Orbit

"*Satellites Out of Orbit* is an excellent and much recommended pick for unique fiction collections." Michael Dunford, *Midwest Book Review*

"... I also love the idea of telling the story from the woman's perspective, especially when the woman is only mentioned in passing in the official story, or not mentioned at all. ..." Shana, Tales of Minor Interest

"Our editorial board loved it. Our readers said it was the most feminist thing they've read in a long time." rejection letter from publisher

As I the Shards Examine / Not Such Stuff

"*Not Such Stuff* challenges us to rethink some of our responses to Shakespeare's plays and opens up new ways of experiencing them. ..." Jeff, secondat.blogspot.com

"This world premiere collection of monologs derive from eight female Shakespearian characters speaking from their hearts, describing aspects of their lives with a modern feminist sensibility. Deconstructing the traditional interpretations of some of the most fiercely fascinating female characters of all time, the playwright is able to "have at it" and the characters finally have their say. And oh, what tales they have to weave. ..." Debbie Jackson, dctheatrescene.com

Let Me Entertain You

"I found 'Let Me Entertain You' very powerful and visually theatrical." Ines Buchli

"I will never forget 'Let Me Entertain You.' It was brilliant." Kate Hurman

ProVocative

"Timely, thought-provoking, dark, and funny!" Kevin Holm-Hudson, WEFT

"... a great job making a point while being entertaining and interesting. ... Overall this is a fine work, and worth listening to." Kevin Slick, *gajoob*

The Art of Juxtaposition

"A cross between poetry, performance art, and gripping, theatrical sound collages. ... One of the most powerful pieces on the tape is 'Let Me Entertain You.' I sat stunned while listening to this composition." Myke Dyer, *Nerve*

"We found [this to be] unique, brilliant, and definitely not 'Canadian'. ... We were more than impressed with the material. *The Art of Juxtaposition* is filling one of the emptier spaces in the music world with creative and intelligent music-art." rejection letter from a record company

"Controversial feminist content. You will not be unmoved." Bret Hart, *Option*

"I've just had a disturbing experience: I listened to *The Art of Juxtaposition*. Now wait a minute; Canadian musicians are not supposed to be politically aware or delve into questions regarding sexual relationships, religion, and/or sex, racism, rape. They are supposed to write nice songs that people can tap their feet to and mindlessly inebriate themselves to. You expect me to play this on my show?" Travis B., CITR

"Wind mixes biting commentary, poignant insight and dark humor while unflinchingly tackling themes such as rape, marriage (as slavery), christianity, censorship, homosexuality, the state of native Americans, and other themes, leaving no doubt about her own strong convictions upon each of these subjects. Her technique is often one in which two or more sides to each theme are juxtaposed against one another (hence, the tape's title). This is much like her *Christmas Album* with a voice just as direct and pointed. Highly recommended." Bryan Baker *gajoob*

"Thanks for *The Art of Juxtaposition* … it really is quite a gem! Last Xmas season, after we aired 'Ave Maria' a listener stopped driving his car and phoned us from a pay phone to inquire and express delight." John Aho, CJAM

"Liked *The Art of Juxtaposition* a lot, especially the feminist critiques of the bible. I had calls from listeners both times I played 'Ave Maria.'" Bill Hsu, WEFT

"Every time I play *The Art of Juxtaposition* (several times by this point), someone calls to ask about it/you." Mars Bell, WCSB

"The work is stimulating, well-constructed, and politically apt with regard to sexual politics. (I was particularly impressed by 'I am Eve.')" Andreas Brecht Ua'Siaghail, CKCU

"We have found *The Art of Juxtaposition* to be quite imaginative and effective. When I first played it, I did not have time to listen to it before I had to be on air. When I aired it, I was transfixed by the power of it. When I had to go on mike afterward, I found I could hardly speak! To say the least, I found your work quite a refreshing change from all the fluff of commercial musicians who whine about lost love etc. Your work is intuitive, sensitive, and significant!" Erika Schengili, CFRC

"Interesting stuff here! Actually this has very little music, but it has sound bits and spoken work. Self-declared 'collage pieces of social commentary'. …very thought-provoking and inspiring." *No Sanctuary*

more at
chriswind.net
and
chriswind.com

Also by Jass Richards

fiction

CottageEscape.zyx: Satan Takes Over
TurboJetslams: Proof #29 of the Non-Existence of God

The ReGender App
License to Do That
The Blasphemy Tour
The Road Trip Dialogues

A Philosopher, A Psychologist, and An Extra Terrestrial
Walk into A Chocolate Bar

Dogs Just Wanna Have Fun
This Will Not Look Good on My Resume

stageplays

Substitute Teacher from Hell

screenplays

Two Women, Road Trip, Extraterrestrial

performance pieces

Balls

nonfiction

Too Stupid to Visit
Jane Smith's Translation Dictionary

Writing as Peg Tittle

fiction

Fighting Words: notes for a future we won't have
Jess
Gender Fraud: a fiction
Impact
It Wasn't Enough
Exile
What Happened to Tom

screenplays

Exile
What Happened to Tom
Foreseeable
Aiding the Enemy
Bang Bang

stageplays

Impact
What Happened to Tom
Foreseeable
Aiding the Enemy
Bang Bang

audioplays

Impact

nonfiction

Just Think About It!
Sexist Shit that Pisses Me Off
No End to the Shit that Pisses Me Off
Still More Shit that Pisses Me Off
More Shit that Pisses Me Off
Shit that Pisses Me Off
Critical Thinking: An Appeal to Reason
What If? Collected Thought Experiments in Philosophy
Should Parents be Licensed? (editor)
Ethical Issues in Business: Inquiries, Cases, and Readings
Philosophy: Questions and Theories (contributing author)

Writing as chris wind

prose

This is what happens
Thus Saith Eve
Snow White Gets Her Say
Deare Sister
Particivision and other stories

poetry

dreaming of kaleidoscopes
Soliloquies: the lady doth indeed protest
UnMythed
Paintings and Sculptures

mixed genre

Satellites Out of Orbit
Excerpts

stageplays

As I the Shards Examine / Not Such Stuff
The Ladies' Auxiliary
Snow White Gets Her Say
The Dialogue
Amelia's Nocturne

performance pieces

I am Eve
Let Me Entertain You

audio work

ProVocative
The Art of Juxtaposition

A Philosopher,

A Psychologist,

and An ExtraTerrestrial

Walk into A Chocolate Bar

Jass Richards

Magenta

A Philosopher, A Psychologist, and An ExtraTerrestrial
Walk into A Chocolate Bar
© 2024 Jass Richards

jassrichards.com

Originally published in 2018 by Lacuna,
an imprint of Golden Orb Creative

978-1-990083-06-8 (print)
978-1-990083-08-2 (pdf)
978-1-990083-07-5 (epub)

Published by Magenta

Cover design by Jass Richards
Formatting and interior book design by Elizabeth Beeton

Library and Archives Canada Cataloguing in Publication

Title: A philosopher, a psychologist, and an extraterrestrial walk into a chocolate bar / Jass Richards.
Names: Richards, Jass, 1957- author.
Description: Second edition.
Identifiers: Canadiana (print) 20230565727 | Canadiana (ebook) 20230565735 | ISBN 9781990083068 (softcover) | ISBN 9781990083075 (EPUB) | ISBN 9781990083082 (PDF)
Classification: LCC PS8635.I268 P55 2024 | DDC C813/.6—dc23

Originally published in 2018 by Lacuna Publishing; this reprint contains a few changes.

Regarding the stories described in chapter one—I found all three on the internet. I think the first one is a true story and the last one is fiction; the second one, I can't remember. And I really didn't want to go looking for them again.

Thanks to Robert J. Sawyer for the quip about men wanting guns.

Crime stats are based on FBI information, as reported by Richard Wrangham and Dale Peterson in *Demonic Males.*

Regarding the Jean Luc Picard poster, there's another amusing one here: http://theimmoralminority.blogspot.ca/2014/11/misogynistic-quotes-from-christian.html

Thanks to J. Neil Schulman's *The Rainbow Cadenza* for the light synthesizer idea and Stephen Leigh's "Staying Still" for putting into my head ways to describe it.

What I imply about the wives of the men at Alamo, Christa McAuliffe, and Judith Resnik—*pure fiction.*

The parts per million carbon dioxide mentioned in chapter 16 as 404? That was when I first wrote the novel in 2015–2016. It's now at 422.

Thanks to Geoffrey A. Landis, NASA John Glenn Research Center, for taking the time to respond to my emails and, especially, for the poster title.

Jane's translation dictionary (*Jane Smith's Translation Dictionary of Everyday Lies, Insults, Manipulations, and Clueless Comments*) can be downloaded at jassrichards.com. (And feel free to send additions for a subsequent edition!) Her *And here's something else that would never happen to a man* list appears at the end of the dictionary. (Also open to additions!)

1

Spike walked into the polished, marbled, and columned lobby of Manus Industries, Inc. carrying two bright-red five-gallon containers. Despite that, she was ignored by Security. Duh. She was wearing grey cotton cargo pants and a grey sweatshirt. And she had short spikey hair. Besides which, she had no boobs. *And* it looked like she forgot to put her make-up on. She probably didn't even shave her legs. Let alone you know. The one Security guy shifted his overflapping belly. The other one scratched his armpit.

Once she reached the corporate goldfish pond, she set down the containers, then shrugged off her knapsack. She took out a little fish bowl and a long-handled net, then put the knapsack on a nearby overstuffed leather chair. She carefully leaned her phone against the knapsack, set to record. Returning to the goldfish pond, she filled the bowl with its water, then scooped up the five goldfish that were swimming about, transferring them into the bowl. She noted that another seven were not swimming about. It was disturbing, for more than one reason, but convenient. She left them floating belly up.

Next, she up-ended the five-gallon containers, putting into the pond chlorine compounds, dyes, solvents, adhesives, coatings, inks, and oils. She'd spent her week as a temp doing on-site research, watching what went down the drains, comparing existing paperwork with regulations and best practices. Then she'd done the math. Parts per million and all that. Her action was not an exaggeration.

She'd thought about announcing her action—she was particularly fond of bullhorns—but thanks to the out-of-control advertising industry, anything duller than strobing neon and deafening sound, which was pretty much everything that was real and true, failed to make an impression. So, she acted in silence. *That* might be noticeable.

And indeed, a small crowd had gathered. Though probably only because this was the most interesting thing that had happened all day, maybe even all week.

As a result, the two guys lounging at the Security Desk finally paid attention to her, and headed her way.

She left the five still-alive fish in their bowl, their new but considerably more constrained living space, perched on the ledge, on the edge, between the emptied containers, each thoughtfully labeled like a granola bar with its Nutrition Facts.

After zooming in for a close-up, she pocketed her phone, grabbed her knapsack, then, seeing the approaching guards, broke into a trot for the door, slaloming, just for the hell of it, between the pedestalled busts of past presidents—odd to call them busts, as surely none of them were women—to make a nicely coordinated exit through the heavy revolving doors. She crossed Bloor Street, moving from the shadow of one skyscraper into the shadow of another.

Meanwhile, in the other skyscraper, on the fourteenth floor, in cubicle 20371-b, the one with the pathetically inept sound-absorbing divider covered with bright orange fabric that had a tear near the top corner and leaned in perilously because one of its shiny silver supports was broken, Jane Smith was focused on the screen of her laptop. Not the screen of her desk computer.

It was a dark and stormy night, she'd typed. *Which meant that the program had failed again*, she added. Then stopped. Don't storms, by definition, necessitate dark? Or at least cloud cover? Is there any kind of storm that happens on a sunny day? A wind storm. Wind happens without cloud, doesn't it? And magnetic storms. And solar storms. No, they'd happen in outer space, where it's—no, wait, the sun's right there. Always shining. So why is it dark in outer space?

She pondered that for a while, then moved on. 'Night' by definition necessitates dark. That was the bigger problem.

No, the bigger problem was that such sloppy work, work that *opened* with such obvious redundancy, got published. Life was so not fair.

Though of course 'dark' could just mean there was no moon.

It was a relatively dark and stormy night. She retyped the first sentence. Then totally changed the second one.

"Ready to go to lunch?" Spike bounced into Jane's cubicle.

Jane jumped a little, because she hadn't seen or heard her coming, grinned, because she was always happy to see her, then looked pointedly at a huge clock hanging on the wall. Because it was 10:00.

"Good point," Spike said. "So we'll go in ten minutes."

"Much better."

Spike cast about for something to do for ten minutes—

But then it occurred to Jane. "Hey, why aren't you—" she looked at her intently. "You did something, didn't you." Spike was always staging 'Moments of Truth'. She'd record them and then upload them to YouTube.

Spike shrugged, then perched herself on the corner of the desk.

"What did you do," Jane asked, in the tone one uses to reprimand an incorrigible terrier whose tail was wagging.

"Oh, nothing."

She waited.

"I turned the corporate goldfish pond into a reflective pond."

Jane thought about that. "In all three senses of the word?"

Spike thought about that. "Yes."

"Good for you!" They high-fived. Jane would watch the video later.

"So who are you today?" Spike changed the topic, looking for a nameplate somewhere on the desk. Then realizing that only desks in corner offices have nameplates. Hm.

"Cynthia Lewis," Jane said. Not that it mattered.

"And what does Cynthia Lewis do?"

"I haven't figured that out yet. It's only ... 10:05."

"But it's only 10:05 on Thursday. Haven't you been Cynthia Lewis since Monday?"

"Good point." Jane thought about that. A little.

"Maybe she just sits here," Spike suggested. "In which case, you're doing an excellent job!"

Jane grinned again. "But it wouldn't necessarily be 'just'. Being can be doing."

"You've been reading Sartre again. Or Heidegger."

"Chodorow,"[1] she corrected. "And Rachels. You know ... if you give someone a lethal injection and they die, that's *active* euthanasia, because you've *done* something, but if you withhold food, that's *passive* euthanasia, because you're *not* doing anything. Supposedly."

"But they still die."

"Exactly. So even by not-doing, by just *being*, you've done something."

"Cool." Spike liked that.

She looked at the clock then. It was not yet 10:10. "So is Cynthia a pregnancy or a nervous breakdown?"

"*Or?*"

"Good point."

It still wasn't 10:10. "How's the novel coming?"

Jane grimaced as she turned her laptop so Spike could read the screen.

It was a relatively dark and stormy night. Even the Jell-O was scared.

Spike laughed. "I like it!"

"Ah!" A Very Important Man had appeared at the cubicle, looking friendly and patronizing. "Just the girl I'm looking—"

"Excuse me?" Spike said to him, surreptitiously reaching into her pocket to record. "Does she look like a child?"

---

1 http://swbplus.bsz-bw.de/bsz004743032inh.htm

Jane grinned at Spike, then looked at the man, waiting for his answer. It was a very good question.

"I beg your pardon?" The man turned from Jane to Spike, surprised to be addressed, let alone interrupted, in that way. Especially by someone who looked like Spike.

"Not my pardon you should be begging," Spike replied. Then repeated, "Does she look like a child?"

The man didn't understand her point. So he ignored her. Go figure.

"Look," he turned back to Jane, "I need those financial reports—"

"If you can't tell a child from an adult," Spike commented, "you should *not* have access to financial reports."

"What?" The man was confused.

"The word 'girl' means 'female child'."

"Oh *excuse me*," he said insincerely. "You're just the *woman* I'm looking—" He knew as soon as he said it that that was worse. No, wait a minute, how could that be worse than a grown man looking for a girl? Okay, now he was really confused.

"Who *are* you?" he said to Spike, even more irritably.

Jane grinned.

"I'll tell you who *I* am if you tell me who the hell you think *you* are!"

"I need those copies by 10:30," he turned back to Jane.

"No," Spike corrected him. "You *want*—better yet, you *would like*—those copies. *Please.*"

The man left, clearly angered. But he'd be unable to articulate why exactly.

"Ten-thirty!" he shouted back.

Spike waited a moment.

"So have you found the photocopier yet?"

"No," Jane replied, ruefully.

"Have you looked?"

"No!" she replied, indignantly.

Spike grinned. Then looked at the clock. 10:09.

"You know," Jane said, thoughtfully, "I don't even think he's my supervisor."

"He's a man, you're a woman, by definition ..."

"Yeah," Jane said. Sadly.

"Okay, time for lunch!" Spike announced and popped off the desk.

Jane saved her work, backed it up to the permanently-plugged-in mini flash drive, then closed her laptop and put it in her bag. She took two steps after Spike, then stopped and went back to her desk. She moved everything from the inbox into the outbox.

"Time for lunch!" she agreed.

And the two of them left the building.

"Hey, Jane, Spike." Bridgit greeted them with a broad smile as she placed two glasses of water onto their table. "The usual?"

"Yes, *please.*" They settled into their favorite booth in the corner of the dessert café, then casually looked around. Most of the customers were, as usual, women. It was nice. It was one of the reasons they were regulars.

"So are you going back to Manus?" Jane asked. Probably unnecessarily.

"Don't think so."

"Got anything else lined up?"

"I hear Riverdance is holding auditions."

Jane took a sip of water. "You'd be able to use your psychology degree."

Bridgit returned with two cups of tea and two different, but equally decadent, chocolate desserts. And that was the other reason.

"Thanks, B," Spike said.

"Yes, thank you, thank you," Jane said, immediately forking off a huge piece of her Chocolate Divinity Cheesecake and mumbling "need this, need this ..." Of the two, she was a little more ... addicted.

"Mmmm," she leaned back, as the ecstasy travelled from her tongue to her brain. "The pure pleasure that is chocolate." She lovingly licked her fork.

"Mr. I-Need-Those-Financial-Reports should just chill and have some chocolate," Spike said, taking a bite of her own euphoria.

After her second, more leisurely, forkful, Jane commented, "Men don't seem to have the capacity for pure pleasure."

Spike thought about that, then nodded agreement. "Their so-called pleasures are really just victories, aren't they. Which means they derive pleasure only through competition. What's the philosophical term for pleasures like that? Pleasures that aren't pure."

Jane gazed off in deep thought, crinkling her forehead, searching for the obscure and technical word ...

"*Im*pure pleasures," she announced.

"Yeah, that's it," Spike grinned.

They continued to enjoy their lavish desserts. Slowly.

"Yesterday he called me Janey."

"Who?"

"Mr. I-Need-Those-Financial-Reports."

"Billy? Ricky? Bobby? Do you know?"

"Do I care?" she responded. "Wish I had a name, though, that didn't have a diminutive version. What do people call you when they want to reduce you?"

"Ezzie-the-Lezzie."

Jane looked at her. "Oh. Right."

For a while, Jane had envied Spike, née Esmerelda, her community. For a while, ten years ago when they first met at a Women's Issues group that had formed when they were both in their second year, she had accompanied her to the lesbian bars, thinking that politics surely trumped sexual orientation, but she felt like such an imposter. She simply wasn't physically attracted to women.

'Course, now, she wasn't physically attracted to men either. At some point in her mid-twenties, she faced a mind-body problem not addressed by Descartes: the dissonance between the two had become too great to ignore. And, apparently, too great to reconcile. She was delighted, therefore, when she realized, a short year later, that her body had opted for asexuality. She was completely comfortable with complete celibacy.

Furthermore, she quickly discovered that just as people were mistaken to assume that all straight women performed femininity, she had been mistaken to assume that all lesbians were politicized. As Spike had pointed out, one's sexual orientation had nothing to do with whether one thought about shit. So maybe she wasn't missing out on community after all.

Then again, as a straight woman who *didn't* buy into the feminine mystique—either the make-up and heels thing, *or* the male attachment thing, *or* the kids thing—she was some sort of freak (where *were* the post-70s straight women who'd said goodbye to all that?) who didn't fit in anywhere. She couldn't even claim a hyphenated-Canadian status based on skin colour or ancestry. So she *was* missing out on community. It's just that she just didn't envy Spike anymore for that. Especially since *The L Word*.

She still thought lesbians more *likely* than straight women to reject male domination in any of its forms, but she recognized now that that could be an accident of sociocultural practice rather than the result of conscious recognition and analysis of the patriarchy. That gay men were as likely as straight men to subordinate women seemed to prove Spike's intriguing point: same-sex orientation didn't necessarily entail rejection of sexism, despite the latter's basis, and embodiment, in heterosex.

"I shouldn't have quit teaching," Jane said after a while.

"You didn't quit. You were fired."

"I was a sessional," Jane protested. "Sessionals don't actually get fired."

"They get not-asked-to-teach-again."

"Well, yeah."

"And why did that happen?" Spike reminded her. Clearly they had spoken about this before. "Because you criticized the students' opinions."

"It was a Critical Thinking course!" She protested again. "The whole point of the course was to teach that not every opinion is equally acceptable."

"Even so. That was *disrespectful*," Spike was clearly quoting. "The students were *offended*. Especially what's-his-name who went running to the Chair of the Philosophy Department. Who, in turn, felt compelled to mention it at the national philosophy conference. To everyone he met."

"Little prick."

Spike flagged Bridgit to their table.

"She's going to need another one of those."

Jane slouched into the bench seat.

"Remember the students' evaluations?" Spike asked. "She made it perfectly clear that she knew more than any of us. She—"

"I was their professor!"

Bridgit appeared with another slice of Chocolate Divinity Cheesecake.

Jane took a large forkful.

"At least I was in the company of my intellectual peers," she mumbled.

"You mean the faculty, right?"

Jane gave her a look.

"As I recall, you weren't too impressed with them either. And I quote, 'Inquiring minds don't give a fuck.'"

A long few minutes passed before Jane spoke again.

"I hear that in Paris, they have chocolate bars."

"They have them here too. At the 7-Eleven."

"No, I mean chocolate *bars*. Not *chocolate* bars.

"Oh, well then."

"Like instead of serving beer and ... beer, they serve, like, a hundred different kinds of chocolate."

"Yeah?"

Jane licked her spoon. She also licked her plate.

"We have to go to Paris then."

2

This is a bad idea," Jane said from the passenger's seat. It was Jane's car—Spike just had her motorcycle—but Spike liked driving and Jane did not.

"Going to Paris?"

"Going to Paris on our lunch hour."

"And by car," Spike suggested.

"That too."

A while later, once they finally seemed to be out of Toronto, which really, in their minds, included North York and Scarborough, Jane got out her laptop.

"Going to work on your novel?" Spike asked.

"Yes. No. Maybe." She looked over at Spike. "Apparently it's turned into Schrödinger's Cat."

A few kilometres went by.

"Hey," Jane said, staring at her laptop, "did you know that Plan B is now available at drugstores without a prescription?"

"The morning after pill? When did that happen?"

"And why didn't we know about it?"

"I think I can tell you the answer to that one," Spike said. "Check out the major papers at the time it became available. Without a prescription."

Jane found one of the national papers, clicked on its archive, then on a specific date. She looked carefully through the entire news section, found nothing, then flipped past the section—an entire section—on sports, ditto cars, ditto stock market prices, before she finally found it. It had been given a few inches of column space at the bottom of page five.

"In the Lifestyle section!" Jane was amazed. "*Lifestyle*!"

"I think," Spike ventured, "a man probably made that call. And didn't consider rape."

"Or, worse, did."

That required a moment of silence. And more chocolate. From the bag full of bars they'd gotten at the 7-Eleven.

"If I ran a newspaper," Spike said then, "I'd have all the politics, sports, cars, and stock reports on just one page. At the back. The Men's Page."

"The Men's *Lifestyle* Page."

"And wars," Spike added a few moments later. "They'd have to fit on the Men's Lifestyle Page too."

"I don't think there'd be room for them," Jane said. "They'd have to get cut."

"But then no one would know about all those heroes fighting to save us from—"

"Whatever they're told they're fighting to save us from."

Jane stared out the window.

"They should advertise it," she said after a while. "Plan B."

"They probably tried. Magazines and television stations probably refused to run the ad. Like that *Adbusters* thing, remember? We prepared all those cool ads,[2] and no one would run them because they were *too controversial.*"

"Like endorsing alcohol and big cars isn't?" Jane asked rhetorically.

"*We cannot accept any ad that criticizes or might offend other advertisers,*" Spike had the response memorized. "Especially the big ones," she added, probably unnecessarily, "because if they pull their ads, the magazine or whatever loses all that revenue."

---

2 http://www.adbusters.org/spoofads/

"But what 'other advertiser' would be offended by Plan B?" Jane understood the policy, but was having trouble with its application to this case.

"Take your pick," Spike said. "*Any* conservative, right wing, fundamentalist— Can't you hear it? *Plan B is murder!*"

"But it's not! It just stops ovulation. And if perchance ovulation has already occurred, Plan B just stops fertilization. Which is like a guy ejaculating, I don't know, *not* in a vagina. Is *that* wrong?"

"Plan B: just like jerking off." Spike grinned.

"And if fertilization has already occurred," Jane continued, "it just prevents implantation. Thus making abortion unnecessary!"

"*You* know that," Spike sighed, "and *I* know that—"

"And if the papers actually gave it decent coverage ..."

They drove on in silence for a bit.

"You know what would make a good ad?" Spike started singing. "It's my body, and I'll choose if I want to, choose if I want to ..."

"... choose if I want to," Jane joined her. "You would choose too if it happened to you!"

Then, since the chorus was all that mattered, they sang it again.

"That is *so* good!" Jane was furiously typing away. "And I'll bet—"

"What are you doing?"

"Sending it to them! The Plan B makers."

"They won't accept it."

"Sure they will! It's a *great* idea! Don't you think Lesley Gore would give permission? It'll catch on, women everywhere will start singing it ... *It's my body* ..." she started singing it again as she typed.

"No, I mean they won't even consider it. Their marketing department won't consider unsolicited ideas."

Jane looked up, then over. "Well, how do we get it solicited?"

"Haven't figured that one out yet."

Jane stared at her laptop.

"And Lesley Gore probably didn't even write the song," Spike added. "Some guy probably did. Because if it happened to *me*, at *my* party, I wouldn't give a flying fuck."

"Are you sure?" Jane asked a bit later. Then clarified. "About them not even considering it?" Something had suddenly become very clear. "Remember my *Boston Legal* script? Are you saying— Do you think—"

"They didn't reject it," Spike said gently.

"They didn't even read it." Jane sighed.

"That was the one about some kid playing cops and robbers or something, and he jumps out at a man passing by, right? And the guy shoots him, thinking the kid's toy gun was real?"

Jane nodded.

"It's their loss they didn't read it. It was *good.* And you had Alan Shore's lines—they were *so* Alan Shore."

Jane nodded again.

"Maybe we could send the idea to some Riotgrrls who do covers."

"Preaching to the converted. Fun, but ..."

"Speaking of Lesley Gore," Spike said a short while later, "remember that video[3] by the Clichettes? 'You Don't Own Me?' They start all cutesy and sexy, and by the end, when they're singing the 'Don't tell me what to do' and 'Don't tell me what to say' lines, all four of them are on their knees, just banging away, pounding their fists into the floor in frustration, and the audience just cheers like crazy?"

"Oh yeah!" Jane smiled, thinking about it. "Must've hit a nerve."

"Ya think?" Spike grinned.

A while later, Jane mused aloud, "I wonder how many inches Viagra got."

---

3 https://www.youtube.com/watch?v=NHrJo8bsZxY

"Surely, you don't."

"Column inches," Jane mentally poked Spike. "In the news-papers. When it was released."

"Ah. But as I recall, we found out about Viagra not so much because of the news but because of the ads."

"Hm," Jane thought about that. "So do you really think the men who dominate the advertising industry made a conscious decision—"

Spike glanced over with her eyebrows raised.

"—*not* to give Plan B the same attention? Why? I mean, if you were a man, wouldn't you *want* to have ..." she trailed off, seeing where her reasoning was going to take her: to men against abortion. Men weren't responsible, didn't take responsibility, didn't *have to* take responsibility, for the kids they created. So they didn't look past the principles, to the consequences. Or didn't include the consequences in their principles. Having a kid was a testament of their virility. Replace 'Do you want to have kids?' with 'Do you want to *look after* kids?' and see how many say 'Sure, okay.'

"If they'd thought about it at all," Spike said, understanding that Jane had come to a dead end, "they wouldn't've named it Viagra."

"I think it's supposed to sound like Niagara."

"But it's Niagara *Falls*," Spike held up her hand, then let her fingers fall over. "Better to have chosen Geyser. 'Course that sounds too much like Geezer."

"Better to have avoided that line of imagery altogether," Jane suggested, "and gone with something like Hamburger Helper."

Half an hour later, they slowed to pass through a town. Which was to say, they slowed to pass by a Walmart, a Sobeys, a McDonald's, and a Tim Horton's.

"That squeak is getting louder," Jane observed. She'd noticed it a couple days prior, and had mentioned it to Spike, because she liked fixing things, but then they'd both forgotten about it.

"It just needs a bit of WD-40."

"There," Jane pointed, as a Home Hardware came into view.

Spike pulled into the parking lot.

A few minutes later, they entered the store, passed the check-out, then wandered around the aisles a bit. Unable to find WD-40, Jane went to the Customer Service counter at the back, while Spike continued to look. No doubt intending to yell 'FOUND IT!' as soon as she found it.

There were three men standing at the counter, leaning onto it and over it, talking with each other and with Gus, the name-tagged Customer Service staffperson.

"And he says, 'Gimme a Phillips,'" one of the men was saying. "And I says, 'You don't want a Phillips. What you want is a Robertson.' And he says, 'Gimme a Phillips.'"

"Excuse me," Jane said. She didn't want to wait while they validated their masculinity. More to the point, she didn't want to watch.

They ignored her.

"He didn't know the difference? Between a Phillips and a Robertson? What kinda—"

"All I knows is he keeps askin' for a Phillips." Yeah, yeah, so the guy kept asking for a Phillips.

"Don't know why," the man spoke slowly, taking up as much conversational space as possible. "'Gimme a Phillips, he says.'"

"Excuse me," Jane repeated, a little more loudly, then shifted from one foot to the other. Many animals don't notice something until it moves.

A fourth man approached the Customer Service counter. "Hey, Gus, did those ratchet tie-downs come in yet?"

"Yeah, I got 'em right here," Gus started to reach under the counter.

"HELLO," Jane said more loudly still. "I believe I was here first," she turned to the newly arrived man, and then to Gus.

Spike paused as she passed by, WD-40 in hand, took in the situation, then kept walking.

Gus looked at Jane, but didn't bother to say 'Yes?', let alone 'I'm sorry, what can I do for you?' What he did say was "We thought you were with him."

Jane looked at the fourth man. Who had arrived *after* her. "Why would you think that?" She was genuinely puzzled.

"Well, you're not with me," one of the three men said, "and you're not with him," he nodded to the second man, "and you're sure not with Bob here!" They all laughed, as if he'd told a good joke. Jane didn't get it. Was there something funny about a woman not being with a man? Or was the joke about none of the men being with a woman?

Spike appeared again, a can of pink spray paint in her other hand. She calmly added FOR MEN ONLY to the CUSTOMER SERVICE sign. The men gasped and went running—for a tin of turpentine, a gallon of black paint, a 600-pound-capacity-high-pressure-power-sandblaster-that-delivers-a-deep-penetrating-abrasive-at-125-pounds-per-square-inch—*some*thing—because the colour pink— Well, Spike may as well have sprayed menstrual blood. Onto the sign.

The two of them headed back to the front of the store to the check-out. Leaving the can of pink paint on the counter where, they knew, it would sit ... Until one of the men found a pair of heavy-duty titanium gloves.

"Well, look at that," the cashier said, as she rang up their purchase. "WD-40 is free today." She grinned at them. "Seeing as you had to deal with the assholes at the back."

Spike and Jane grinned back.

"Oh, and we're giving these away—today!"

She picked out an X-acto knife from the plastic bin on the check-out counter and handed it to Spike. They were clearly marked with a price.

"Why, thank you!" She put it into her pocket.

"Anything else I can get for you today?"

"Might you also be giving away battery chargers? Today?" Jane asked.

"'Fraid not," she smiled. "But nice try!"

As soon as they were back on the highway, they heard the squeak again.

"Oh yeah," Spike said.

"We need gas anyway," Jane said, nodding to the gas station a few blocks ahead.

While Spike popped the hood, squirted some WD-40 onto the thing that was making the noise, and filled the tank, Jane went into the convenience store and paid for the gas, a couple fudgesicles, and another bag full of chocolate bars.

They moved the car away from the pump, enjoyed their ice cream, then carried on their way, Spike again at the wheel.

A few minutes later, Spike noticed Jane staring at the chocolate bar in her hand.

Finally, she had to ask.

Jane replied. "Why would you need re-sealable packaging on a chocolate bar?"

"So are we really going to Paris?" Jane asked, once she'd proved that re-sealable packaging on a chocolate bar was indeed unnecessary. "I mean, lunch ends at … well, lunch ends."

"And if you still had a job, that would be relevant."

Jane looked at her.

"It's three o'clock," she explained.

"Good point." And then Jane smiled.

"You remember that credit union I temped at for a while?" she said a moment later.

"The one that happened to be a women-only place of employment?"

"Yeah. If I could find a full-time job like that— It was so … easy. So comfortable. Everyone was friendly, respectful, efficient. That's all. That's everything. There was none of that 'This is serious' shit, conveyed by that perpetual male Scowl of Importance. And the hierarchy wasn't shouted at you, it wasn't in your face all the time. And there was no pressure to perform, to perform better, always better."

She stared out the window for a while.

"Men have a deadening effect," she summarized. "On everything. Whenever they're present, it's not fun anymore. Or even enjoyable. Let alone easy."

Spike didn't have to express her agreement.

"We'll need our passports," Jane said a moment later, lazily, still not really ...

"Check." Spike nodded to her well-worn and ever-present knapsack, tossed into the back seat. It contained everything she'd ever need. "You?"

"No," she said sadly, "I don't normally— Wait!" She leaned forward, then reached under the seat. "I don't think I unpacked from that trip to the conference ... Yes!" She pulled out a Ziploc bag containing a slim wallet. "Passport *and*—" she waved a shiny, new credit card in the air, "as yet unused! Introductory offer of a $10,000 credit limit!"

"Seriously?"

Jane nodded. "They knew I was unemployed."

"All set then," Spike grinned at her. "Do you need to buy anything?"

"No. I was so depressed when I figured out what had happened, why my interviews were so—not, my travel bag is still in the trunk. Though all I really need is in here!" she nudged her laptop.

"Okay then!"

"We're on our way to Paris," Jane sang, "We're on our way to Paris ..."

"What say we check in to a motel or something?" It was a couple hours later, and starting to get dark. Spike didn't enjoy driving at night. And Jane hated it. More to the point, neither of them wanted to deal with Montreal's rush hour traffic. Despite it being considerably better than Toronto's rush hour traffic.

"Good by me."

The room was pretty basic. Jane put her laptop and travel bag onto one of the beds, then headed for the bathroom, happy to see towels and a little wicker basket of soap, shampoo, and toothpaste. She'd belatedly suspected, rightly, that her own supply was somewhat depleted.

Spike tossed her knapsack onto the other bed, flipped through the many take-out menus on the nightstand between the two beds, then made a call.

"Yeah, I'd like a large, double cheese, pineapple, and sun-dried tomatoes."

She waited.

"And one of your dessert specials."

She waited.

"Chocolate milk. Two."

She waited.

"Mozey's Motel. Fifteen."

She waited.

"Okay, thanks."

Sometimes it was nice when conversations followed a well-defined script. She pulled her tablet out of her knapsack and quickly uploaded the Manus video and the Just-the-girl-I'm-looking-for audio-only recording she'd made, then she opened the nightstand drawer, looking for the remote, and—just stared.

When Jane came out of the bathroom, considerably refreshed, she saw her standing there, still staring into the drawer. Curious, she walked over to see what she was looking at. A book and a magazine. *The Holy Bible* and *Fuck the Bitches*.

"It's perfect," Jane said.

"It is, isn't it," Spike agreed.

"In a purely juxtapositional way, of course."

"Of course."

"But the relationship isn't oppositional," Jane continued her analysis, "or even complementary ... It's like the one is a distillation, a—"

"A *Reader's Digest* version of the other."

Jane considered that. "I think 'reader' is pushing it."

After Spike took a picture, Jane picked up the *Bible*, settled onto one of the beds, and merrily began deconstructing it. She ripped out the entire book of Genesis: Abraham pimped his wife, twice, and Lot offered his daughters to rapists. I Corinthians was next: Woman was created for Man. Then Ephesians, wherein women were told to submit to their husbands. Then Colossians. Romans, Titus, 1 Peter, and Acts. 'A woman should learn in quietness and full submission. I do not permit a woman to teach or to have authority over a man'—the book of Timothy got tossed into the garbage. Then Deuteronomy: women who have sex before marriage should be stoned to death. And Leviticus: men are worth fifty shekels; women, thirty.

Had she taken a Bible Study class? In a manner of speaking. She'd read *The Woman's Bible*.[4] Shortly after, she and Spike had been amazed, and horrified, to see fifty copies of the book on the remainders table in a bookshop. Not a bestseller, apparently. Because who the hell was Elizabeth Cady Stanton? Not Beyoncé, that's for sure. They'd thought the book was out of print. They'd also thought any remaining copies would go for $100 each. Not $1. The box was still in the trunk of her car. Now full to the brim with other books they'd since added. In case of emergency.

"Besides which," Spike endorsed Jane's deconstruction by quoting an off-script Jean Luc Picard[5] poster, "'How the fuck did Jesus find guys named Peter, John, James, Matthew, Andrew, Philip, Thomas, and Simon *in the Middle East*?'" She couldn't help grinning.

---

4 https://archive.org/details/WomansBibleElizabethCadyStanton
5 https://s-media-cache-ak0.pinimg.com/736x/7d/60/15/7d6015379ad9b5a
299d3e0db22e24f6e.jpg

"Do you want to leave?" she asked Jane a few moments later. *Fuck the Girls* was still in the drawer.

"Yes. Would a black person be comfortable staying at a motel in which the nightstand contained a copy of *Let's Lynch 'Em!?*"

"Such a magazine would be illegal."

They both sighed. For Dworkin and MacKinnon[6] and ...

"Regardless," Spike added, "black people wouldn't even be *allowed* in whitey's motels."

Jane looked at Spike, oddly. Smiling. As if she'd just seen a posting for a job she could apply for. A job she might even get. "Imagine a chain of women-only motels, owned and fully operated by women, accepting only women as guests ..."

"Such a motel chain would be illegal."

"Yeah," Jane acknowledged. Sighed again. Then added, "I'm too tired to find an alternative."

"Should any other motel actually *be* alternative."

"Yeah." Sighed yet again.

"Pizza'll be here in half an hour. Does the shower have actual hot water?"

"It does." There was that, at least.

Spike took her knapsack off the bed then, and headed for the bathroom.

Jane tossed what was left of the *Bible* into the trash can, then opened her laptop.

"Nine out of ten young men[7] now use pornography," Jane read the stats[8] out loud when Spike came back into the room. *Fuck the Bitches* had motivated her to check the current pulse of misogyny.

"So not all young men," Spike said with a weird grin.

6 http://www.nostatusquo.com/ACLU/dworkin/other/ordinance/Hill SilverOrd1.html
7 https://fightthenewdrug.org/porn-consumption-rates-among-young-adults-underreported/
8 http://www.internetsafety101.org/Pornographystatistics.htm

Jane knew what that grin was about. "No. Not all men. Just nine out of ten." She continued reading. "Every second, three thousand dollars is spent on pornography. Every second almost 30,000 people are viewing pornography online." She looked up. *"30,000 each and every second!"* She looked back at her screen. "Half of it contains verbal aggression, and almost all of it—88%—now contains physical aggression. The researchers[9] of this study had intended to use men in their 20s who had never used pornography as a control group."

"But they couldn't find any," Spike anticipated.

Jane nodded. Things had certainly changed since— Well, since whenever they'd last read the stats. Which couldn't've been too long ago.

"That was all in the UK. In Canada," she clicked a few keys, "40%[10] of boys in grades 4 to 11 view porn. One-third[11] of them, every day." She looked up, opened her mouth, then just closed it. "Another third say they've viewed porn videos 'too many times to count'."

"Well, that could be anything more than five," Spike said. "Given."

Jane grinned.

"There are now over 100,000 websites[12] featuring child pornography," she'd clicked to another site. "116,000 searches per day.[13] For child pornography." She clicked to another site and went silent. Very silent.

Spike got up to look over her shoulder, to see what she'd found.

She read a story about a young woman who'd died of internal bleeding and infection because of anal penetration. Her bowel had

---

9 http://www.telegraph.co.uk/women/sex/6709646/All-men-watch-porn-scientists-find.html
10 http://www.business-standard.com/article/news-ians/watching-porn-sexting-on-rise-among-canadian-teenagers-survey-114060301350_1.html
11 http://www.covenanteyes.com/2013/02/19/pornography-statistics/
12 https://wsr.byu.edu/pornographystats
13 http://gizmodo.com/5552899/finally-some-actual-stats-on-internet-porn

been perforated. Her rectum torn all to hell. She and her friends had been kidnapped, taken to a boat, then blackmailed into 'participating': if you refuse to do whatever the however many men tell you to do all day, or if you jump ship, or kill yourself, I'll just go get your little sister. "Wreck the bitch," one man had instructed another. Another story was about a girl forced to run up and down the stairs wearing some sort of clip on her clitoris that had weights attached. Another was about girls who had been conditioned to be 'cunts'—animals trained to race like greyhounds, their nipples and clits chained in some elaborate way to their wrists and ankles. The winner got fucked by several men.

"This is ... fiction?" Spike asked, quietly. Because she'd read about a case in Australia[14] in which an infant girl about two years old had been held down by two adult men while she was fully penetrated by a third. Pictures had been taken and a video made. During an interview, the man who had penetrated the toddler told a female detective, "There's nothing quite like hearing that crack." The crack he was referring to was the child's pelvic bone breaking.

"Does it matter?" Jane replied, also quietly. "I mean, it *does*, of course. But if this is what excites men—a lot of men—most men ..." She didn't finish her sentence. How could she? What do you say when you find out that porn has become less about bikini-clad centerfolds or even sexual intercourse and more about humiliating, degrading, and torturing women? That for nine out of ten men—*almost all* men—seeing women being hurt is met not with horror, but with *pleasure.* That men constantly demand to see new ways of hurting women and girls, that new ways of hurting women increases men's excitement and pleasure, that yesterday's aberration becomes normalized, and today's aberration is *never enough.* That men, and boys, *need* to see women and girls being hurt. By them.

---

14 https://liberationcollective.wordpress.com/2012/03/11/big-porn-inc/

"Even if white people *did* have magazines, and movies—a whole industry—showing the degradation of blacks," Jane tried again, "do you think they'd claim it as *entertainment*?"

"They sure as hell wouldn't say they *needed* it," Spike said. Far too quietly.

There was a knock at the door. It would be the pizza guy. They froze for just a moment, then forced themselves to relax. Living in an occupied country required a constant ... pretense. How else could one ever answer the door, knowing it was a man on the other side? A man who was, in all probability, one of the nine in ten. How else could one eat, and enjoy, a pizza?

Especially a chocolate fudge brownie pizza.

Next morning, they packed up their stuff and left. But not before Jane put a copy of *The Woman's Bible* into the nightstand drawer.

Spike left a copy of the *SCUM Manifesto*.[15]

---

15 http://www.versobooks.com/books/196-scum-manifesto

T he next day was relatively eventful. Spike didn't see the point in having any other kind.

"So what are we doing in Montreal?" she asked about half an hour from the city limits. She knew Jane would've googled and prepared a list.

"We're going to Sophie's Croissant Café. Apparently she has 'the best ever pain au chocolat'. A logically indefensible claim, of course, but—"

"Because of the definitional problem, right?" That's what happens when you hang out with a philosopher.

"No, that can be solved easily enough, by establishing some arbitrary definition of 'best'."

"Or you could just appeal to God."

Jane looked over at Spike, her eyes squinted with suspicion. And concern.

"What? Just sayin'. If there was a god, surely she'd know what 'best' means, as it applies to pain au chocolate." She slowed down a bit to accommodate the increasing traffic.

"True," Jane conceded. "But more likely, she'd just make a proclamation, willy-nilly, about her pain au chocolat preference, which we would then accept and call 'best'. Unable, being god-believers, to think for ourselves, but, and this is more likely, unwilling to die an infinite, and infinitely horrible, death. You see the problem, right?"

"Yes." But she suspected it wasn't the same problem Jane saw.

"The willy-nillyness is critical, of course."

"Of course."

"Because if, as you say, she just *knows* what's best, as it applies to pain au chocolat, because, supposedly, she's omniscient, then she must be appealing to some higher standard, beyond herself. So she wouldn't, then, be god. In the conventional sense of the word. You know, 'the supreme being above which there is no other' or some such."

"Ah."

"And if she declares 'best' willy-nillyly, then we're at the mercy of a supreme being who makes pronouncements ... willy-nillyly."

"I see."

"Which, also, doesn't make her very godlike. The willy-nillyness. Not our being at the mercy of."

"But wouldn't that also make her ungodlike? Putting people at her mercy? Regarding pain au chocolat quality?"

"Hm." Jane hadn't thought of that. "I think it would. Good one!"

A moment later, Jane picked up the other thread. "The reason Sophie's claim is logically indefensible is because 'best ever' necessarily implies that all instances of pain au chocolat that have ever existed have been sampled. And there's no way to be sure, to be conclusively certain that ..." Jane trailed off, no doubt thinking about sampling every instance of pain au chocolate ever to have—The scream of a siren tsunamied her reverie.

Spike looked in the rear-view mirror, then pulled over. A white van went by, lights flashing, but it had BERT'S CAR LOT written on it. Not AMBULANCE. And the siren gave way to "COME DOWN TO BERT'S CAR LOT TODAY! RIGHT NOW!! BERT'S CLEARING THE LOT! COME DOWN TO BERT'S CAR LOT TODAY! RIGHT NOW!!"

"It's a frickin' ad!" Spike said, with, surprisingly, surprise. She pulled back onto the road and sped after the van.

"And I am so frickin' tired of advertising!" she shouted at the moving white chunk of crap that obliterated her view of anything beyond itself. "You can't go for a walk, you can't listen to the radio, or watch tv, or check your email, and half the time when you answer your phone it's someone wanting to sell you something—"

She broke off to concentrate on safely passing the several cars that had, like them, pulled over.

"What gives them the right to be so frickin'—"

"Intrusive?" Jane had her hand on the dashboard to brace for impact. Not that that would make any difference. At the speed they were going.

When they caught up to the van, Spike pulled into position beside it, and Jane rolled down her window. "PULL OVER!" she commanded in a voice she didn't know she had. She was frickin' tired of advertising too. The constant assault on the senses, on the mind, the imposition of someone else's interests, that, worse, will eventually *replace* your own— And no doubt the interruptive nature of advertising was single-handedly responsible for the two-second attention span that was now, apparently, the norm. She figured she'd shoot herself in the head when marketing companies discovered holograms. The very thought of ads popping up in front of her wherever she went—

"What?" the driver looked across at her in confusion.

"*PULL. OVER.*" Spike boomed across Jane.

The van pulled over, and Spike pulled over in front of it. She and Jane got out of their car, Jane thoughtfully setting her phone to record. As back-up.

"What the hell are you doing?" Spike stomped over to the man, who had also gotten out of his vehicle. Unwisely.

"I pulled over!" he replied. "I thought you were, whatchama-callit, unmarked cops."

"Yeah, and I thought you were, whatchamacallit, an *ambulance*!

He chuckled. "Yeah, that gets 'em every time. People hear the siren, they pull over."

"And why do you think that is?" Moron.

"What?"

"Why do people pull over for an ambulance?" Spike asked, barely containing her impatience at such stupidity. Despite having had a great deal of experience with it.

"Because it's the law, I guess."

Jane groaned. Legal moralism is the source of all evil. Discuss.

"Or maybe it's because they think it's on its way to save someone's life," Spike suggested.

His face lit up triumphantly. "And my siren fools 'em!" He chuckled again.

"You think it's funny?" Jane took over. Before Spike hauled back and decked him one. "If it happens often enough, people won't pull over anymore when they hear a *real* siren."

The man started to get the idea that they weren't too supportive. Despite their being women.

"Yeah, well, not my problem." His smile was gone.

"Moral Excuse #1," Jane said quietly. To no one in particular.

He turned to get back into his van, but Spike grabbed him, whipped out the X-acto knife the hardware store cashier had given her, and held it across his throat.

"It could be," she said to him. Then to Jane, "Better call 9-1-1."

Jane pretended to make the call.

"If I slit your throat, how long would it take you to bleed to death? A minute? Two?" She turned slightly to Jane. "I don't hear an ambulance, do you?"

"No. That's odd." She pretended to make a second call.

"They did dispatch an ambulance," she reported, "but no one's pulling over. So it'll be at least an hour. Because *it's stuck in traffic. That won't pull over*," she added. Necessarily.

"Gee, you'll be dead by then," Spike observed. "Oh well, not our problem."

She shoved him away. Having *not* slit his throat.

"Look, you got no call to— I'm just minding my own business here—"

"Moral Excuse #1b," Jane said.

"That other stuff you're talking about, it's not my concern!"

"#1c."

"Not your concern?" Spike repeated. "What, if it doesn't affect *you*, right here and right now, it's not your concern?"

He stared at her, the look on his face saying, 'Yeah. What's wrong with that?'

Jane turned to Spike. "That's what, stage one of Kohlberg's moral development?" She knew very well what stage it was.

"Two. Late childhood."

"Hey gimme a break here," he protested. "I'm just doing my job. My boss tells me to do something, I do it."

"Moral Excuses #2, #3a and b."

"Yeah, well, get another frickin' job!" Spike all but screamed at him. "You can do that in this country, you know."

"It's not that easy! I got a wife and kids to support."

"#4."

"What, and that justifies—"

"I'll bet the guys at the nuclear weapons plant say the same thing," Jane offered.

"Whose decision was that?" Spike asked the man.

"What?" The question was clearly a reflex response. Perhaps initially intended to give him a few seconds to come up with something that didn't require him to actually process what had been just said.

"*You* decided to keep a woman. And *you* decided to make a couple kids. Why should *we* make allowances for *your* choices?"

"Look, lady, I don't know what you're talking about. Mr. Reynolds, he's got a business to run."

"Moral Excuse #5." For pretty much everything. When people say 'business', the red carpet rolls out. Business gets special treatment. It gets right of way. Literally. We are to step aside and let business proceed unimpeded, unchallenged. 'I've got a business to run!' can legitimize, and prioritize, almost anything. But there was simply no justification for the desire of one person, let alone the desire of one person *for money*, to be imposed on everyone. Let alone granted immunity from morality.

"So?" Spike was relentless. "That gives him the right to *kill* people?

"Look, I don't mean no harm!"

"#6," Jane said. "The one favoured by people too stupid or too lazy to consider the consequences of their behaviour."

"What did you *think* would happen," Spike screamed, "when you put a firecracker into a dog's mouth—and then lit it?"

Jane turned to stare at her, eyes wide.

"A couple kids—boys—*male* kids—did that," she explained, quietly. "Saw a picture of the poor thing on YouTube."

They were both silent. What the hell is *wrong* with them?

The one standing before them had had enough. There's only so much self-examination a man can take. Only so much blame. So he drove off. That's why men love cars so much.

"Quite apart from," Jane wasn't done, even though they were back in the car and on the road again, "there are enough alternative venues for advertising—radio, tv, newspapers, magazines, websites, malls. And *every single one of them* is preferable to the use of public space because one can choose, at least to some degree, whether or not to be a target.

"Advertising in public space is *especially* reprehensible when that public space is otherwise beautiful." They passed an impossibly ugly billboard sign smack in the middle of a long stretch of forest. Possibly the only remaining such stretch within fifty kilometres of Montreal.

"Would those of us who can hear allow a deaf person to make a clamour with cymbals all day long?"

"We would not." Spike thought she'd get a word in.

"Then why do those of us who can appreciate beauty allow aesthetically impaired CEOs to do just that?"

"I don't think 'allow' is quite the right word ..."

"You know," Jane still wasn't done, "the internet could make advertising totally unnecessary. Whenever you want to buy something, you could just look it up in a complete directory with a really good search engine that could provide a shortlist based on your preferences. The shortlist would have product information and customer reviews.

"Then instead of spending $500 billion to make their products *look* good, companies could spend the $500 billion to make products that actually *are* good. And to clean up their messes."

"Like *that's* what they'd do with it," Spike muttered. Mostly to herself.

"Did you know," Spike added a moment later, "that drug companies spend more on marketing than on research and development?"

Jane looked over, horrified, but said nothing.

"Twice as much more."[16]

Five kilometres later, Jane was revisiting the scene of the crime. "And you know, there's something objectionable about a perfectly-capable-of-working adult being 'kept' by another adult. It seems to me the epitome of laziness and immaturity to be supported by someone else, to have someone else pay your way through life."

"Worse," Spike agreed and went one further, "we subsidize their keep. The price for a couple is typically less than the price for two singles, which means that hers is cheaper—"

"Or his," Jane pointed out what she knew would be an exception, then continued with a stronger point. "In fact, it doesn't even have to be a mixed-sex couple."

"No, but I'll bet that was the initial idea."

She looked over at Spike. "What, to financially reward men for keeping a woman? To *encourage* them to do so? Why? Oh." She knew very well why. Sigh.

"Either way," Spike continued the discussion, "it means the rest of us pick up the slack. We have to pay extra income tax so what's-his-name's wife can pay less. We also subsidize her discounted car

---

16 http://www.who.int/trade/glossary/story073/en/

insurance. Her discounted club membership. Should either of us ever belong to the same club. Hell, even her discounted airline ticket. If he wants to pay her way, fine, but her way should cost the same as ours. It's not like she's making some huge contribution to society by being married."

"Yeah. Why should a professor's wife get health and dental, when she's not even teaching *one* class!" Jane had often taught three classes. With no health or dental.

"So, you've got directions to Sophie's Croissant Café?" They both needed chocolate.

"I do. But first we're going to the last remaining feminist bookstore in the country." Almost better than chocolate.

"Cool." Spike looked forward to spending an hour in such a haven. It was so relaxing, to be surrounded by validations rather than challenges. To not be compelled to say something, to do something, about the otherwise ever-present sexism.

"Remember the Montreal massacre?" Jane asked. As they passed the "BIENVENUE!" sign.

"Of course."

"I was subbing at a high school at the time. And the next day, all the male teachers at the school vehemently denied that it was a crime of misogyny, a reflection of the so-ordinary-it's-normal misogyny in our society. Even though the guy had killed only women. And had said—*said*—that women were ruining his life. They all insisted that what he did was symptomatic of mental illness. 'Yes!' I agreed. But they didn't get it."

"Men are mentally ill." Spike got it. "As a norm."

They took the next exit, found the last remaining feminist bookstore in the country, and were astounded to discover that the place was so busy, they could barely get inside the door, let alone browse the shelves. They'd thought feminism was dead. Morphed into something recognizable only as Deluded Princessism.

"Hey, you're here for the SlutWalk?" A cheerful young woman greeted them.

Oh. That explained it.

"No," Jane replied. "We didn't know there *was* a SlutWalk. Today. Here. We're just on our way through."

"Oh, you should hang around then. The speeches are about to begin, and then we're walking through downtown, along Rue Sainte-Catherine."

Before she'd finished her sentence, Spike had located, and confiscated, a bullhorn. Jane grinned. And reached into her pocket for her phone. They made their way back outside and around to the small empty lot behind the store, where a platform had been set up.

"... and we can dress however we want!" The speeches had apparently already begun. "We have the power! To choose! We're *proud* to be SLUTS!"

Cheers rose from the gathered crowd, most of whom were, indeed, dressed as sluts. That is to say, they wore their boobs and butts on the outside, accentuated with bustiers, fishnets, and stilettos.

Oh dear. Jane stumbled, horrified to have heard her grandmother's voice in her head. Or at least her colloquialism.

"Seriously?" Spike addressed the speaker from their position on the fringe, then started moving through the crowd to the stage. "*Proud* to be *sluts*?"

Jane followed in her wake.

"Prude!" Someone called out.

"Another fat and ugly feminist who thinks we should all wear Birkenstocks!"

"Yeah, get with the program, sister! The new feminism is sex-*positive*!"

Spike reeled. Jane didn't think she'd ever seen her reel. She was also speechless. Call 9-1-1!

Where to begin, Spike was thinking. *Not* with the obvious fact that she wasn't fat. Or ugly. Or that she was wearing Doc Martens.

"WE ARE *NOT* SLUTS!" Jane jumped into the silence, leaning toward Spike's bullhorn and raising her fist to punctuate her shouts. "WE ARE *NOT* SLUTS!"

"But we are," Spike had put her hand over the mouthpiece of her bullhorn. "At least, we *were*. Didn't you have sex with guys you weren't married to?"

"Well yeah. Given." Jane hadn't ever been married, hadn't ever intended to *be* married. And certainly hadn't intended to remain a virgin all her life. Ergo. "That doesn't make me a slut."

"Guys who weren't even your boyfriend?"

"Well yeah, but—"

"Guys you just met."

She considered that.

"WE *ARE* SLUTS! WE *ARE* SLUTS!"

"Wait a minute," she stopped suddenly and turned to Spike. "I wasn't *completely* indiscriminate. The guy had to use a condom, he couldn't have any STDs, and he had to be my type. I mean, I didn't have sex with just *any*one."

It took just a moment.

"*MEN* ARE SLUTS! *MEN* ARE SLUTS!"

That caught on.

Until a young woman close by grabbed Spike's bullhorn. "What are you doing? We've *reclaimed* the word 'slut'!"

"Are you sure?" She nodded at a man standing at the perimeter. He was grinning at the young woman and making vigorous jerking off motions with his hand.

"Have we also reclaimed 'skank', 'ho', 'beaver', 'cow', and 'cunt'?" Jane asked. Innocently.

"Bitch!"

"Another word we've apparently reclaimed," Spike noted dryly as the woman strutted off.

They'd reached the stage. Bereft of her bullhorn, Spike leapt up and stood at one of the two microphones. "Part of you smiles to think of yourself as a slut. You're a bad girl, a wild girl, you're dangerous, you're taking risks. But that's exactly what they want. Sexual access. No-strings-attached sex. We fell for that too. In the 60s. In the 70s. Free love, we're *not* prudes, we're okay with our bodies, we're okay with sex. We're 'with it'.

"But they never took us seriously. They never considered us part of the movement. Behind our backs, they'd snicker and say the best position for a woman is prone."

"Stokely Carmichael." Jane shouted out the citation. For anyone who wanted to know.

"It's either/or for men," Spike continued. "If you're sexually attractive and/or available, you can't possibly be anything else. Intelligent, competent—"

"Actually," Jane interjected, "even if you're *not* sexually attractive and/or available— Maybe *especially* if you're not sexually attractive and/or available—" she broke off again. So sexuality *did* give women power? Attention, at least? But ... No, they *still* didn't take you seriously. As Spike had said.

"And okay," Spike continued, "you're accusing me of being anti-sex. But you know what? I am. I *am* anti-sex. *As it typically occurs.* As it is *expected* to occur. Which is primarily for men's pleasure, often via women's pain. Sex for *women's* pleasure wouldn't even *involve* the penis!"

"SlutWalk isn't *about* dressing like sluts—" another woman had taken the stage, and the other microphone.

"Then why call it *Slut*Walk?" Jane muttered, truly perplexed.

"It's about victim-blaming," she continued, to scattered applause. "Women shouldn't be blamed for sexual assault. They're the victims. We need to hold *men* responsible. For their actions."

"But there are conventions, symbols, uniforms," Spike responded. "You'd be an idiot to wear gang colours—*your* gang's colours—into some other gang's territory. And then whine when they beat you up."

A sharp intake of breath hissed through the crowd.

"Dressing like a hooker indicates that you're available for sexual service," Jane tried to help. "'Hooker' by definition ..."

"If you look like bait and act like bait ..."

"But it's *not about* dressing like a hooker," someone called out.

Spike looked around. Pointedly.

"And anyway, what's wrong with being a hooker?" This from a transvestite, wearing shiny black hotpants, fuchsia feather boas, and little else.

"Yeah, the new feminism is *inclusive!*"

Jane and Spike exchanged looks. Confused looks. Inclusive of what, exactly?

"So are you saying that if we wear a short skirt, we should expect to be raped?" A woman shouted out to Spike from across the crowd.

What? No—

"A couple years ago," another woman had gotten up onto the stage and taken the second microphone, "when I was waiting for my boyfriend outside a record store, a guy came up to me, just a boy-next-door kind of guy, not a drunk perv or anything, and he asked how much I charged for a blow job. I was wearing jeans, a t-shirt, a jean jacket, and a knapsack." She paused. "It didn't quite sink in at the time. That as a woman, I would always be considered available for sexual service."

The crowd had the good sense to applaud that.

"And dressing like hookers reinforces that!" Spike added.

But then, "We have the right to dress however we want!" someone in the crowd insisted.

Yes! Jane thought. Even if you're an office temp. Because god knows, she was sick of not getting assignments because she wore comfortable shoes.

"But you also have the responsibility to consider the message you're sending," Spike replied. "If dressing like a hooker isn't an invitation, what is?"

"The word 'YES'." The other woman on the stage still had the mic. "Clearly spoken, voluntarily. Anything else is just a 'maybe'."

"Oh, I like that," Jane said.

"Except that it ignores the communicative value of non-verbal signals," Spike muttered. As she jumped down off the stage.

"And anyway what's *wrong* with having sex with more than one person?" Jane asked as they walked back to their car, bookless. She'd obviously leap-frogged backwards a bit. Spike didn't mind. She'd kind of collapsed in the middle of a cartwheel.

"Men are willing to support only their own biological offspring, so if a woman has sex with anyone other than him, he'll never know which of her kids are his."

"Oh, right. I forgot for a moment that men define everything."

"No, wait a minute," she said a moment later, "we have paternity tests."

"Emasculating. To have to have one done."

"Ah. Better to shame the woman for perfectly acceptable behaviour."

They got into their car.

"Did you know that spouses are the leading cause of death for pregnant women in U.S.?" Spike asked as she turned the ignition. "That is, men make women pregnant and then kill them for being pregnant."

"Maybe they're thinking they weren't the one who made her pregnant." While Jane thought about the grammar of what she'd just said, Spike considered the implication.

"So better to just *kill* the woman than get a paternity test," she said.

Jane thought about that. Because it was way more interesting than grammar.

"They *want* us to be sluts," she said. "And then they kill us for *being* sluts."

4

Half an hour later, they parked on a side street off Rue Saint-Denis and walked a couple blocks to Sophie's Croissant Café.

"Women have no idea," Spike said as they walked, already trying to figure out how the SlutWalk Moment of Truth had gone so wrong, "how much men fail to see them as anything but sexual."

Jane agreed. "Though, to be fair," she said, "most men see themselves that way too. Physical strength, financial wealth," she nodded toward the two young men who had just walked past them, "visible underwear. They're all just proxies for sexual prowess."

"Wow," Jane said as soon as they entered. Scattered throughout the café were a dozen little tables, all white marble and gold filigree, each with two little chairs just as ornate. Jane walked toward the first grouping, fascinated with the intricate detail. It was so ... baroque. Spike drew her attention upward then, to the three chandeliers, all crystal and gold and somehow lace. Jane circled each one, absolutely amazed.

They claimed a table, eventually, in the corner by the window. A bit private, a bit watch-Montreal-while-we're-here.

Jane struggled with her high school French to place their order. Two plain pain au chocolat, one for her, one for Spike, then another one, with chestnut cream, for her, and two cups of tea. She was perfectly aware that the waiter's English was probably much better than her French, but she wanted to make the gesture. It was appreciated, judging by the smile playing in his eyes. Either that or she'd ordered a horse in a hat.

"So," Jane opened, "we really need to figure out what we think about Slutwalks." They'd avoided the issue to date. Like many second-wavers, they'd assumed that the young fun-femme faction would become fringe, not mainstream, feminism.

"Yeah," Spike said.

She waited until their tea and pain au chocolat was in front of them. And Jane had taken her first bite. No point in starting before then.

"I blame Beyoncé," Spike opened. "Remember that one song she does, while behind her, projected on the backdrop, are quotes from—actually, I don't know—"

"Chimamanda Ngozi Adichie."

Spike gave her a look. "How do you *know* this stuff?"

Jane shrugged, and took another bite of her pain au chocolat.

"Anyway, one of the quotes is something like 'Girls are raised to see each other as competitors, not for jobs or accomplishments, but for the attention of men.' And *while* it's projected, Beyoncé struts across the stage clearly primped *for the attention of men.*"

Jane nodded. "It's like those ads for pick-up trucks, where the greenhouse-gas-emitting and fracking-motivating, hence groundwater-contaminating and land-destroying, truck drives through pristine forest over clear streams against blue skies."

Spike stared at her. She didn't know what was more impressive about Jane's statement, its content or its form. "Yeah. It's like that. Exactly."

Jane grinned. Then continued. "There's a complete disconnect. It's as if they're utterly oblivious to the contradiction between ..." she searched for the accurate pairing, "the medium and the message, no, the appearance and the reality, the action and the consequence—"

"Or they *are* aware of it," Spike suggested, "and they're just using whatever sells."

"Feminism sells?" News to her.

"Superficially. The appeal to equality, power ..."

"Ah. Well, I suppose that's encouraging ..."

"Or not. What'll happen when Beyoncé's fans discover she was right about the end, but horribly mistaken about the means?"

"Mistaken *about* the means or mistaken that there *is* a means? To that end."

"The latter."

They imagined fun-femme feminists becoming radical feminists. En masse.

If only.

Then, since Jane had finished her pain au chocolat—her first one—she beckoned their waiter and ordered more tea.

"I think we also have to blame Miley Cyrus," she eventually said. "'I like to have sex, so what?' is not a particularly feminist message."

"Not because it's pro-sex," Spike added, "but because it's not anti-patriarchy. It's not anti-women's subordination."

"Yeah, when did being pro-sex become feminist?"

"I don't know. But 'The new feminist is in control of her sexuality!'" Spike mimicked one of the women who had been at the SlutWalk.

"Well, that's certainly better than *not* being in control of her sexuality," Jane said. "And come to think of it, it follows rationally from having reproductive rights—access to Plan B, for example."

Spike nodded. "It's exactly what we thought in the 60s and 70s when we got the Pill. As I tried to say. But—"

"Maybe a lot of women have just overgeneralized the 'choice' part of feminism."

Spike agreed. "Simply put, not all choices are feminist."

"Exactly. I know it's considered unfeminist now to blame women, but we *do* have agency."

Again, Spike agreed. "We're not children. Or idiots."

"Isn't that redundant?"

Spike narrowed her eyes at Jane. Whose choice not to have kids was surely one of her better ones.

"And it's unfeminist to believe otherwise," Spike continued. "If we expect one group of men, the more mature—let's just say—to speak out and take action against another, the rapists, then we ourselves should do the same. We should speak out against women who are complicit in our subordination. Who *choose* to be complicit in—"

"But choice is complicated," Jane protested. "That's what makes consent, and coercion, complicated. That standard view is that consent is assent that's capable—referring to cognitive capacity, informed—one understands the consequences, and voluntary. But to be voluntary, a decision would have to be totally free of pressure—physical, psychological, social, economic."

"So are you saying that true consent is impossible?"

"Yes. At least sometimes."

Spike thought about that as she finished her pain au chocolat. "You might be right," she eventually said. "At least with regard to sex. Just listening to the radio all day, which many people do, is like ingesting a constant-release aphrodisiac. Every song, every *line* of every song, is sung with a moan or a whimper—"

Jane nodded. "Miley Cyrus has become the norm."

God help us. They stared at each other.

"Okay, we need a moratorium on sex," Spike declared. "Until we stop that shit."

"We could bomb the radio stations. The recording studios. L.A." Jane thought then that maybe she'd been hanging around Spike too long. Or maybe just long enough.

"Sometimes though," Spike backed up a bit, "consent, and coercion, is pretty simple, isn't it? I mean, coercion is shutting the fuck up because otherwise he'll kill you. Coercion is allowing yourself to be assaulted by your live-in partner because—*if*—that's the only way to feed your kids. Coercion is doing something because your drink was spiked."

Jane took a bite of her chestnut cream pain au chocolat. Oh.

"But wearing make-up on a daily basis just because it's convention? Reddening your lips, putting a flush on your cheeks?

Pushing up your breasts, baring your legs all the way up to your crotch, wearing heels that arch your back? In short, making yourself *sexually* attractive, sexually *attracting*, for *a day at the office*—just because it's convention? That's not coercion. That's stupidity."

Jane took another bite.

"Why *wouldn't* men think women are always sexually available? That's the way they present themselves!"

And another.

"And then they get pissed off when they see them as sex objects," Spike shook her head in disbelief.

Jane licked the last bit of chestnut cream off her fork. She noticed then that the forks, and the spoons, were just as florid, just as elegant, as the chairs and table.

"Of course, the greater problem is *that* it's convention. Women are *expected* to appear sexually attractive, attracting, as a matter of routine."

Jane nodded. "'Femininity is the behavior of female subordination.' Sheila Jeffreys."[17]

And on that note, they ordered dessert.

"But beauty—"

Spike knew where she was going. "There's a difference between attractive and *sexually* attractive. At least, there *should* be. It's just that because men dominate art and advertising, the two have been equivocated. By *them*. No doubt because to them *everything* is sexual. In fact, if it's not sexual, it doesn't exist."

"You're right," Jane sighed. "If you really just want to use your body as a canvas for beauty, you'd wear funky gold glittered hiking boots, you'd paint an iridescent rainbow across your face, you'd do a hundred *other* aesthetically interesting things ..."

---

17 http://www.theage.com.au/victoria/radical-feminist-sheila-jeffreys-retires-after-24-years-at-the-university-of-melbourne-20150522-gh7g1c.html

Spike nodded. "And only when men *don't* see us as *Hooters* will the woman who's a Walmart sales associate be considered for a managerial position."

"I dunno ... You're back to thinking appearance matters. We know that women in full-out nun regalia get raped. So it would seem that appearance *isn't* a motivating factor for rape. Well," she qualified, "unless the man had issues with nuns ..."

Spike squinted at Jane. Clearly, Jane had issues with nuns.

"In any case, quite apart from rape," she continued, "I thought we established that no matter how we look, just like no matter what we do, men don't, won't, take us seriously. Certainly not seriously enough to consider us for a managerial position."

"Yeah," Spike sighed deeply as she leaned back in her chair. "You're right. Damned if we do, damned if we don't. So what's the point?"

Their waiter brought their dessert. Spike had ordered profiteroles. Mainly because of how they sounded. The word. Not the profiteroles themselves.

Jane had ordered a Chocolate Volcano. It came on a plate drizzled with chocolate syrup, and there was a puff of real whipped cream on top. When she put her fork to it, thick chocolate lava oozed out of the cake. And "Oooo ..." oozed out of Jane.

Several slow minutes later, Jane resumed. "So okay, let's say women *do* give up their push-up bras, their high heels, and even their make-up."

"Like we did in the 70s." And look at what didn't happen, Spike added to herself.

"What if men *then* say that any woman who simply bares her ankles is asking for it. Or bares her *face*. We all walk around in burkas then?"

It was a good point, Spike thought. It got to the root of the matter: why should men's problems determine what women should wear? And wasn't that the point of the SlutWalks?

"Okay, but here and now, is it really too much to ask *not* to present yourself as bait? *As a matter of routine?*"

She turned the plate of profiteroles full circle, considering her options.

"You can easily avoid letting your butt and boobs hang out," she added. "You *can't* easily avoid exposing your face. Assuming you want to have peripheral vision. And breathe."

"Wait a minute," Jane said. "I thought you *supported* Gwen Jacobs[18] and the repeal of the shirtless laws. Now you're saying 'Cover up!'?"

"No! Yes! I don't know!" Spike groaned and mentally threw her hands into the air.

A thoughtful minute and one profiterole later—the classic pastry cream one—she tried to sort through her apparently inconsistency. "I *agree* that women should be able to wear whatever they want. That they should be able to go wherever they want, alone, even at night. That they should be able to get drunk if they want. I agree that telling them otherwise diverts attention from the real cause of the problem, the men who rape."

"Which is why, for one thing," Jane interjected, "reporters should use the *active* voice. Instead of 'A woman was raped last night,' they should be saying 'A man raped a woman last night.'"

"Right. Good. But—" Spike bit into the next profiterole. The caramel cream one.

"Remember Twisty's List of Shit Women Do To Confuse Dudes Into Raping Them?"[19] Jane licked the last of the chocolate lava off her spoon. "They're drunk. They leave the house. They're girls."

"See and that's the thing," Spike waved the third profiterole in the air. Chocolate cream. "If you live in a country overrun by morally-challenged muscled-up idiots who think you're just a walking receptacle for their dicks, you *shouldn't* go out alone, especially at night, you *shouldn't* get drunk—"

---

18 http://www.cbc.ca/news/canada/women-s-topless-court-victory-20-years-later-1.1026403

19 http://blog.iblamethepatriarchy.com/2013/03/18/spinster-aunt-curls-lip-at-the-afterschoolspecialization-of-steubenville/

"'Should' in principle versus 'should' in practice. Theory versus advice."

"Yes! If you do any of those things, is any consequent assault deserved? No. But should it have been anticipated? Yes." Satisfied, Spike took one, then another, bite of the profiterole, finishing it.

A moment later, she continued. "SlutWalk organizers don't think through the male over-dependence on visual signals. The gawkers and hecklers who typically undermine the event should be expected. The inability of men to process verbal messages, even those just a few words long, in the presence of so-called 'fuck me' heels should be expected.

"And given men's inability to pick up on subtle cues and/or their refusal to understand the difference between yes and no, let alone yes and maybe ..." She waved another profiterole. No idea what kind it was. But it was the last one.

"Maybe when men can handle a sexually charged atmosphere without assaulting— Maybe when *other* men *do* speak out and take action against the rapists, one way or another— It's no coincidence that there are close to 400,000 samples of DNA evidence that remain untested[20] and therefore inadmissible in court." She bit into the profiterole. It was— Actually, she had no idea what it was. Kind of nutty, kind of creamy. Cashew cream? Almond cream? No matter. It was good. Very good.

"But here and now," she said a few moments later, "given our culture, given men, if a woman is wearing 'fuck me shoes', she can hardly complain when someone fucks her."

Jane raised her eyebrows. "No, that can't be right."

They both stared out the window for a bit.

"The civil rights movement had lots of white people accompanying black people into white-only places, didn't it?" Jane asked.

"So, what, it's hopeless until some men help us out?"

---

20 http://www.huffingtonpost.com/2014/05/29/house-approves-additional_n_5412475.html

"No, that can't be right either," Jane muttered.

They stared out the window again.

"It's one thing to just go without a shirt on a hot summer day and another to wear a push-up bra halter top," Spike tried again, backing up a bit. "SlutWalk comes across as advocating our right to tease. Which is not only immature, it's legally uninformed."

"The provocation defence."

Spike nodded.

"But the provocation defence stinks," Jane said. "Apart from using 'an ordinary person' as the standard for determining whether the act in question was sufficient to deprive one of self-control—as opposed to 'a reasonable person'—because in my experience the ordinary person is a walking miasma of unacknowledged emotions and unexamined opinions, most of which are decidedly *un*reasonable ...

"Apart from that, it puts the blame back on the woman: 'It's her fault; she provoked him.' Which is ridiculous! Even if we assume that so-called slutty attire *is* a promise of sex, 'You promised!' isn't a sufficient justification for assault, let alone murder!" Nailed it!

"As Lucy Reed Harris[21] points out," she added reinforcement, "a flagrant display of cash in public may well precipitate a robbery, but in *that* case, the law doesn't hold the victim responsible!"

"I didn't say it was a *justified* defence," Spike protested. "I just said SlutWalks seem ignorant of the fact that provocation *is* available *as* a defence. You'd think, if they *were* aware of that, they wouldn't *encourage* provocation."

"Oh. Okay."

There was more staring out the window.

"So the SlutWalk message shouldn't be that we can dress however we want," Spike ventured, "but that we aren't sexually available to everyone. No matter what men might think. For whatever reason they might think that." The more she added, the more she doubted. So she shut up at that point.

---

21 http://chicagounbound.uchicago.edu/uclrev/vol43/iss3/7/

"But isn't the message *supposed* to have something to do with appearance?" Jane asked. "Didn't some police officer say that if women didn't walk around looking like sluts, they wouldn't be raped? Isn't that what *started* SlutWalks?"

They considered that.

"So he mistakenly equivocated an invitation to sex with an invitation to violence?" Jane asked, eyes wide.

They stared at each other then. It all made perfect sense. If men equated the two.

"Remember that scene in that movie?" Jane asked a few moments later.

"Yes."

Jane grinned.

"A man shouts at a woman, a woman who'd had the nerve to have sex with someone besides him, that she was a slut. And then with the impressively circular logic of the incurably stupid, he rapes her to prove his claim. The distinction between having sex and being raped being apparently too subtle to understand."

"Or being nonexistent in his mind."

Jane nodded.

"And speaking of going shirtless," Spike said as they got up to leave, "remember that woman, post-bilateral-mastectomy, who was barred from swimming in a public pool unless she wore a bathing suit top?"

"Yes ..." Jane had yet to figure that one out.

"That proves that it's not about covering up. Or whatever. It's about maintaining sex-differentiation. Because the patriarchy, men's power over women, depends on it."

She pushed her chair back toward the table.

"So focusing on appearance, as SlutWalk does, is a red herring," she'd reached a new conclusion. "A huge distraction from the real issue."

"Which is?" Jane wasn't sure at this point.

"Apart from the systemic subordination of women by men? That men rape women."

"So instead, we should have a Kill the Rapists walk."

"Or just a Kill the Men walk."

Their waiter met them at the cash register.

"C'est quatre cent cinquante-six dollars et soixant-cinq cents, s'il vous plaît." He smiled.

Jane smiled back as she handed him her credit card, letting him know that her French wasn't *that* bad.

"Merci," he took the card.

"Je prie pour vous."

"So," Spike asked once they were outside, standing on the sidewalk, "'best ever pain au chocolat'?"

"Well, no. We went over that this morning, remember?"

Spike groaned.

"*Probably* best ever." Jane grinned.

5

For a while on the following day, they passed not much of anything, and Spike thought about heading to the secondary, more scenic and more full-of-interesting-places-to-stop-at, highways. There must be *something* worth seeing or doing on the way from Montreal to Paris.

"Let's go to Boston," Jane said. After just five minutes of googling.

"Before or after Paris?"

"Monday. There's this place, Chantal's. It's a restaurant, but every Monday they have an all-you-can-eat chocolate buffet. Twenty bucks a person."

"Really?"

"Isn't that cool? An all-you-can-eat chocolate buffet!"

"Boston it is. Find us an interesting route though," she added.

"On it ..."

Almost as soon as they'd turned onto a secondary road, a cigarette butt flew out of the driver's window of the car ahead of them. A minute later, the plastic lid of a cup. Jane had her phone ready when the empty Timbits carton came flying out.

"You've got the license plate in focus?"

"Yup."

"Gonna send the picture to the OPP?"

"Yup. No—what's the OPP in Quebec?" She googled.

A balled-up napkin came out next.

"That'll cost him, what, five hundred dollars?"

"A thousand."

And then an empty cup.

"It boggles the mind, doesn't it?" Jane said. "They throw their shit out of their cars, their boats, their spaceships with such ... *ease*. Do they think it just vanishes into thin air? It's like they have no concept of context. No concept of attachment. Their perception of their independence is so ...."

A not-yet-empty KFC carton hit the road. Spike swerved unsuccessfully to miss it.

"And yet they're able enough to see their vehicles as extensions of themselves," Jane reconsidered.

"Maybe it's because they're so visually oriented," she suggested a moment later. "If the garbage they tossed overboard floated on the surface of the lake ... Though it's amazing what they don't see even when it's right in front of them."

A plastic bag danced through the air narrowly missing a landing on their windshield.

"Or maybe it's an expression of contempt. For the other. Men don't *set down* their garbage. They always *toss* it."

Spike nodded. "'Look at me, I don't give a fuck.'"

"So, what, caring about others is for sissies?"

"So is cleaning up after yourself. That's what Mom does. Mom's a woman. So to pick up after oneself is emasculating."

"That sounds right. We do know that most littering is done by men."[22]

When the tv came flying out of his window, Spike leaned on the horn, sped up beside him, and forced him off the road.

"What's your problem?" The man shouted as he got out of his car, slamming his door shut.

"*You* are my problem!" Spike shouted back, as she too got out. Jane continued recording as she went around behind him, casually reached in, and extricated his car keys.

"The world is not your private dump!" Spike said. "Whatever made you think it was?"

---

22 http://www.litter.vic.gov.au/about-litter/littering-behaviour

"What?"

"You're tossing your garbage out your window like you expect someone else to come along and clean up after you. What are you, two?"

"What?"

"What do you think happens to all your shit?"

"The animals'll get it, don't worry about it."

"Since when do animals eat cigarette butts, plastic, cardboard, and paper? And frickin' tvs? The cardboard's going to take a couple years to decompose, and the plastic's going to sit where it landed forever."

"Well, unless he goes back and picks it up," Jane said, off-hand.

"Yeah. Why don't you do that?"

"Fuck you!" He got back in his car and, as they drove away from him, discovered what was missing. Besides part of his brain.

"Did you notice the little Canadian flag flying from his antenna?" Jane asked.

"I did." Spike sighed. "Canada produces more garbage per person[23] than any other country in the OECD. And that's not counting all the shit that flies out of car windows.

"We are second worst when it comes to nitrogen oxide emissions, we are second worst when it comes to sulphur oxide emissions, we are second worst when it comes to greenhouse gas emissions, and we are dead last when it comes to volatile organic compound emissions.

"We consume more water per capita[24] than every other country except the States, and we use more energy and generate more pollution to produce a given amount of goods and services than almost all of the other countries.

---

23 http://www.conferenceboard.ca/hcp/details/environment.aspx
24 http://www.davidsuzuki.org/publications/downloads/2010/OECD_
Report_Final.pdf

"Korea's doing better than us. Not to mention Japan, Sweden, Norway, Finland, Denmark, Switzerland, Austria, Luxembourg, Belgium, the Netherlands, the UK, Ireland, France, Spain, Portugal, Germany, Italy, Greece, the Czech Republic, Australia, New Zealand, and Iceland."

"You've got these things memorized?"

"I do." She sighed. "For all the good it's done."

Jane stared out the window.

"We are hogs," Spike summarized then. "We are stupid, don't-give-a-damn pigs. We're the ones to blame for so much of this climate change—the heat waves, the floods, the droughts, the high food prices. Our fault."

Jane thought about the little flag. "Is it Canada Day?"

"No."

"So ... he just doesn't know, what you know, or he does, and he's a hypocrite—"

"Or he hopes that proclaiming patriotism will absolve him of any and all asshole behavior."

Close to noon, they pulled up to the customs booth at the border—Jane was thinking it was a toll booth, and so had started thinking about cookies—and several guards rushed out of nowhere to surround their car. They were in full military apparel. Worse, they had guns. Pointed at them.

"Put your hands where we can see them!" One of the guards commanded.

"What the fuck?" Spike said, raising her hands.

"What did we do?" Jane said at the same time, also raising her hands.

"Could you please put away your guns?" Spike said through her open window. "Men with guns make me nervous."

"Women with guns make us nervous too," Jane added, quick to take back possible offence.

"Passports."

"Profiteroles."

Jane gave Spike a look.

"Present your passports. Do it now!"

"I had them ready, but they fell onto my feet when I raised my hands," Jane said. "I'm going to reach down—"

"Keep your hands where we can see them!"

"But I can't do that *and* present our passports. They're mutually exclusive actions," she explained.

Spike gave Jane a look.

The guard opened Jane's door, reached in, the barrel of his gun just inches from her face, and retrieved their passports.

"Proceed to the guardhouse. Slowly."

They drove the twenty meters to the guardhouse, guards with their guns drawn escorting them on all four sides.

"Exit the vehicle."

"Can't do that without my left hand disappearing from view," Spike said.

"Exit the vehicle! Do it now!"

"What is this guy's problem?" Spike turned to Jane, who had already opened her door. Apparently. Because she was on the pavement, lying on her back, feebly waving her limbs.

"What the hell are you doing?"

"Jordan's dog does this all the time. Whenever it meets an alpha dog."

"Really?" She stared at Jane for a few moments. Who looked more like Kafka's beetle than a surrendering puppy. "The dog has no spine."

One of the guards cocked his big gun, the sound of metal fitting into metal loud and decisive.

"The dog's still alive."

Spike slid out her door onto the ground, rolled to belly up, and began as well to wave her arms and legs. Feebly.

"'Course she does it when she meets beta dogs too," Jane said, still feebly waving her arms. "*Any* dog, actually. The dog has no spine."

"Stand up. Slowly."

They both did so.

"Proceed into the building." He gestured with his gun.

"When they make us fill out forms," Jane said, "and they *will* make us fill out forms, where it says 'occupation'? Don't put *independent activist*, okay?"

"*Philosopher*'s going to be just as suspect."

"Right. Okay, so we're ..."

"Secretaries!"

"Yes! Perfect!"

"Okay, and after they make us fill out forms?" Spike asked.

"Chocolate. Specifically, chocolate chip cookies."

"We're on our way to Boston," Jane was singing. Two hours later. "... to eat all the chocolate we can eat. We're on our way to Boston, to eat all the chocolate we can eat ..."

"If only your high school could see their valedictorian now."

Jane grinned. They drove in silence for a bit, having never seen Vermont before. Plus, they'd stopped at the first Walmart they'd come to after the border and were delighted to discover that Walmart sold Mrs. Fields chocolate chip cookies. By the pail. Jane was quietly working her way through it.

They never did find out what the hassle at the border was all about. And had given up speculating. Men, territory, guns—it was bound to be irrational. Or at least necessary only because of other men. With territory and guns.

A mile later on a relatively busy part of the highway, they saw a tall woman at the side of the road. Presumably hitch-hiking. Presumably, because she was using both thumbs. And facing the wrong direction. And doing something worthy of employment at Monty Python's Ministry of Silly Walks.

"Okaaay ..." Spike said as they passed her.

But a hundred meters later she signaled, slowed, pulled over onto the shoulder, then started to back up, carefully keeping in a straight line. Jane looked at her curiously.

"I have to know."

Jane nodded. She understood. Completely.

"She didn't look drunk."

Jane agreed.

"Or drugged."

Jane agreed.

"She's going to get hurt," Spike added, as if further justification were necessary.

As soon as Spike got close enough, Jane rolled down her window. "Do you need a ride?" she called out.

The woman lurched to their car, giggling. Several vehicles whizzed by.

Jane looked over at Spike. "Stoned?"

"Maybe." But ... not exactly.

"Are you all right?" Jane asked, then repeated, "Do you need a ride?"

The woman did a dipsy-doo.

"Get her inside," Spike said, looking nervously in the rear-view mirror. A couple transports were in the distance, approaching quickly.

"Yeah."

Jane got out, opened the back door, and bundled the woman inside. The first transport sped by, creating a mini-tornado.

"I'm Jane, "she said, turning in her seat to face her, "and that's Spike." The second transport shook the car.

The woman laughed uproariously. Jane and Spike were confused, but since the woman's laugh was so very infectious, they ended up laughing as well.

"And your name is—"

The woman continued to laugh.

"It's almost like hiccups," Spike said. "Maybe she's getting too much oxygen?"

"But it's too *little* oxygen that makes you light-headed."

"Well, maybe she's an extraterrestrial. And what do *we* know about alien physiology?"

"Right. That's gotta be it."

Even so, Jane put the last chocolate chip cookie into her mouth, then passed the empty pail to the woman. Or whatever. Who had no idea what to do with it. So Jane took the bright red pail, put it over her mouth, and breathed in and out. She gave it back to the woman. Who did what Jane had done. And stopped laughing.

Spike carefully eased back into the highway traffic.

Half a minute later, the woman, or whatever, took the pail away from her mouth. "Thank you," she said. "I was at one with the universe. It was purple."

"Okaay ...," Jane replied, then tried again. "What's your name?"

"Xrrmrvnbnvdl."

Spike glanced in the rear-view mirror. "Okay, but your friends just call you 'X', right?"

X erupted into laughter again. She put the pail over her mouth again, quickly.

"Mmm. Chocolate fumes."

Both Jane and Spike grinned. Jane handed X one of the many chocolate bars they'd also bought at the Walmart. She managed to eat it with the pail over her mouth. Jane was impressed.

"Where were you headed? Can we give you a ride home?"

X took the pail away from her mouth. "You can do that? In this vehicle?"

"Hey!" Jane said, then turned to Spike, "What's that supposed to mean?"

Spike shrugged.

X burst out laughing again. Jane reached into the back and put the pail completely over X's head. It had been a jumbo-sized pail of cookies. X stopped laughing. And didn't seem at all concerned about sitting there with a red pail over her head.

"Where do you live?"

"Grmphflg."

"Sorry?"

"Grmphflg," X repeated, more loudly. "In the Zbixschik star system."

Jane and Spike look at each other.

"Did she say star system?" Spike was ready to believe.

"Sorry," Jane said to X, "we don't know where that is."

"MapQuest it," Spike said.

Jane stared at Spike.

"Hey, I know some geeks. It's not inconceivable—"

So Jane looked up Grmphflg on MapQuest.

"Some of them have a very warped sense of humour," Spike continued. "Get it? Warped?"

"Yeah. Ha-ha."

After a moment, Jane announced, to Spike, "MapQuest doesn't seem to have a 'Beyond Earth' option. Gee." She turned to X. "Can you tell us where Grmphflg is?"

"Well yeah," X said. "I know where I live. But I don't know where *you* live. I was out for a drive and got lost. So I stopped here to ask for directions."

Jane and Spike looked at each other again.

"You stopped here. To ask for directions."

X suddenly went ... inanimate.

"Is she— Did we just kill an alien? With an empty pail of Mrs. Fields Chocolate Chip Cookies?"

The considered the ramifications of that for the Department of National Defence.

"I think she's just fainted," Jane said. Though her body looked more stalled than limp.

"Do you think that when she wakes up, she'll say 'Take me to your leader'?"

"God, I hope not. We wouldn't, would we? It'd be too embarrassing."

"Not as embarrassing as it would've been a couple years ago."

"True."

They were silent. Waiting for— Well, they had no idea what they were waiting for. X's metamorphosis, perhaps, into neon green lizard with iridescent fuchsia wings. Or an ottoman covered in corduroy.

"I hope she doesn't ask about the meaning of life," Jane said.

"Yeah, we don't really have the answer to that one worked out yet, do we."

"The answer? I don't even have the question worked out. I understand 'What's the *purpose* of life?' Even though I don't think it *has* a purpose, because purpose implies intentional design. But what does 'What's the *meaning* of life?' mean? Purpose and meaning are two different things. 'What's the meaning of "persnickety"?' That makes sense. Words mean things. Even an action might mean something. And, as we recently confirmed, appearance might mean something. But how can *life mean* something? It's not a signifier, not a symbol. It just is."

"Maybe you should take the pail off—"

"Oh yeah."

Jane reached back and lifted the pail off X's head. With a great intake of air, X came to. Jane and Spike waited, with great anticipation, for her next words.

"Can we stop somewhere? I have to pee."

"So let's try this again," Spike turned to X once they were back in the car. Jane was driving. "You're from—"

"Grmphflg."

"But you don't—but *we* don't know where that is."

"If I knew where this was," X said, "I could probably figure out how to get back."

"This is Earth," Jane said, playing along.

"Doesn't sound familiar."

"They wouldn't call it Earth," Spike said to Jane.

"Oh. Right." Then she looked pointedly at Spike, clearly saying 'You're *buying* this?!'

Spike pulled her tablet out of her knapsack, turned it on, found a map of the solar system, then showed it to X.

X shook her head. She didn't recognize it.

"Try the Milky Way," Jane suggested.

Spike zoomed out and showed the screen to X again.

X shook her head again.

Spike zoomed out again. And showed the screen to X once more.

"I must have *really* taken a wrong turn."

"Ya think?"

Spike glared at Jane.

"Maybe we can find a library," Spike suggested a minute later, "show her some star charts or something."

"Okaaay." There would be star charts online somewhere, but Jane was ready for another pit stop. "Get directions to the nearest one," she nodded to Spike's tablet. "Here on Earth," she said redundantly. Or not.

While Jane made inquiries at the front desk, Spike and X glanced at the books in a nearby cart that were waiting to be shelved. X picked up a *Curious George* book and started to flip through. She burst out laughing. Then she picked up Stephen Hawking's *A Brief History of Time,* flipped through, and laughed even more. Spike grinned.

"So they don't have any star charts," Jane said, joining them at the cart, mildly distracted by X's laughter, seeing which book she'd had in her hands, "but they have several first-year astronomy texts. You might recognize something," she said to X.

"Okay." She set Hawking back onto the cart. Beside *Curious George.*

Jane led the way to the astronomy stack, scanned the books, pulled out one hefty text and then another and then another, putting all three into Spike's waiting hands. They went to a nearby table and sat down.

"Why don't you just flip through and see if anything looks familiar?"

They watched as X flipped through, stopping at the photographs of various star systems here and there, but apparently not recognizing anything.

"Where the hell *am* I?" She closed the third book with some finality. "Look, if you just gave me your coordinates—"

"Our coordinates?"

"Well, not *your* coordinates, though that would be just as useful. I meant the coordinates of this planet. Earl."

"Earth."

X didn't register the correction. "If you gave me the coordinates, I could figure out how to get home. It would take me some time, it's not that easy, but I could do it."

"What coordinates?" Jane asked. At the risk of appearing like an idiot.

X looked at her like she was an idiot. "The space-time coordinates. The coordinates of Earl's location on the space-time continuum."

Jane and Spike look at each other.

"I don't think we know that," Jane said.

"Well, not *us* we, but—" Spike felt oddly obliged to defend—

"No, I meant 'we' as in 'us Earthlings'," Jane clarified.

X looked incredulous.

"You don't know your coordinates? How can you not know your coordinates? It's where you live. You don't know your own address?" X looked pointedly at both of them.

"Well, it's not a problem if you've never left home, is it?" Jane said.

"You've never left home? How old *are* you?"

"Look, it's getting late," Spike said a moment later. "What say we find a hotel for the night, and then come up with a plan."

"Good idea."

They left the stacks and headed back for the door.

"You know," Spike said to Jane, "I used to have an uncle named Earl."

"Oh yeah? What was he like?"

Spike thought about it, then shrugged. "He was a man."

6

They pulled into a parking space near the hotel's front office and got out of the car. In the space next to them, some guy was saying good-bye to, presumably, his wife and young son. A taxi had pulled up behind a parked SUV.

"Now, you be a good boy and look after your mom until I get back," the man had bent down to look eye-to-eye at his son. The little boy nodded. Satisfied, the man stood up, tousled his hair, and started tossing his luggage from the SUV into the taxi. The woman, clearly *Good Housekeeping* meets *Cosmopolitan*—an ironic, if not downright disturbing, combination—held onto her son's hand.

Spike stopped, one hand resting on the knapsack strap on her shoulder, the other casually getting her phone out of her pocket. Jane and X stopped with her, Jane holding her travel bag and laptop, X holding two pizza boxes with a couple bags perched on top.

"Are you retarded?" Spike asked the woman.

"I beg your pardon?"

"I'm just wondering why you need a child to look after you."

"I don't." She tightened her grip on her son's hand. In case the crazy lady made a grab for him.

Spike turned to the man. "Then why did you tell your son to do just that?" She knew damn well he wouldn't've told his daughter to do just that.

"What?" He didn't have time for this.

"Do you think your wife is retarded?"

X looked sharply at Spike, then at the man and woman. There was a weird look on her face. Shock? Disgust?

"No, of course not!" The man didth protest too much.

"The problem is," Jane began to articulate Spike's concern—one of Spike's concerns, "the boy will over-generalize. He'll grow up to think that every woman needs to be looked after by a man."

The two of them stared at her blankly. Three of them. Though X's stare wasn't exactly blank.

"Which word didn't you understand? 'Over-generalize'?" Jane asked. "'Problem'?"

The woman pointedly ignored her. She gave her husband a quick peck on the cheek, then tugged her son away, back toward the safety of their hotel room. The man got into the taxi, and it drove off.

"Is it any wonder," Spike said as they continued on their way to the office, articulating her other concern, "that somewhere between five and fifteen, when a boy realizes, when it registers, that his mom is female, and retarded, she becomes subject to contempt or dismissal?"

They entered the hotel lobby, which was dotted with guests coming, going, and/or perusing the tourist pamphlet display. X looked on with attentive curiosity as Jane and Spike checked them in. Once the process was completed, the young man hurried around the counter to take— He stopped, confused. None of them had a suitcase he could carry. Especially not a suitcase that only he, a slight man who had never worked out in his life, could carry.

"Down the hallway, on your right," he said, then put his hand on the small of Spike's back, applying a bit of pressure.

She stopped. And stared at him. "Are you *steering* me?" she asked loudly.

Everyone within hearing distance turned to look. Which meant everyone in the lobby.

"What?"

"Do you think I'm a frickin' *car*?"

"What? No!"

"Then what's your hand doing on my back?"

He couldn't say.

"I'm not blind."

He stared at her with a look of dull incomprehension.

"I don't need you to guide me to the hallway."

"Actually, even if she *were* blind," Jane added helpfully, "she probably wouldn't need you to guide her to the hallway.

"But—"

"I don't need you," Spike stated. Baldly.

But he still didn't get it.

"He'd probably try to grab your hand if the two of you were running away," Jane said as they walked down the hallway. Which they'd managed to find all by themselves. "And they think they're the rational ones. Women can run faster if they can use both arms."

"Maybe that's the point."

Once they were in the room, which they'd managed to find all by themselves, Jane announced wearily, and unnecessarily, "Shower, pizza, chocolate. Not necessarily in that order," she added, grabbing a chocolate bar out of one of the bags on her way to the bathroom. Spike set the two pizza boxes beside the tv, opened the top box, took out a slice, grabbed one of the cartons of chocolate milk out of the other bag, then claimed the bed Jane hadn't dumped her stuff onto. X helped herself to both bags, then flopped awkwardly into the armchair in the corner.

When Jane came out of the bathroom, she took another chocolate bar from the bag. The last chocolate bar. Wait, what? She saw then that X had indeed helped herself. Okay, so they knew *something* about alien physiology. That is, if—

"So," Spike said to X conversationally, "if you're not from around here—" Jane groaned, Spike grinned. "—why can you speak English?"

"It came with the brain."

That stopped them both in mid-bite.

Spike eventually queried, carefully, "What else came with the brain?"

"Neural access, sensory inputs, motor control—" X got up to get a piece of pizza and fell flat on her face. "Not very much motor control."

They waited until she'd gotten back up.

"And where did you get the brain?" Jane played along.

"It came with the body."

Of course it did. Jane got up to get a slice of pizza. And one of the cartons of chocolate milk. She handed the third carton to X. Then she asked, not sure she wanted to know, "Are you using someone else's body?"

"No. Not exactly. Sort of. Yes."

"Okaaaay..." Jane said, thinking maybe X lived in some sort of quantum reality. Well, if—

"If I merged when the other person was alive, that'd be wrong. And if I merged when they were dead, that'd be ..." she seemed to search for the word, "yucky."

"So ... what else is there?" Spike asked.

"The time-space between. Duh."

"Oh yeah. The time-space between." She took a big bite of her pizza. As did Jane. They chewed slowly.

"And the oxygen thing?" Jane asked, still trying to establish evidence for or against believing X.

"A byproduct of the merge."

"Ah."

She drank some of her chocolate milk, thinking, thinking ...

"Okay, so if you're using—merging with—someone else's body, and brain," Jane said, "what makes you think you'll be able to figure out our time-space coordinates. Chances are, you haven't got a genius in there."

"You're definitely right about that," X grimaced. "But it's got a lot of unused RAM."

That took a couple seconds. "Gray matter?" Spike asked with some excitement. "You can access the gray matter?"

X turned toward her, a look of horror slowly spreading across her face. "You— Can't? This—" she flipped a finger at her head— "This is all there is?"

"Duh." That was Jane.

X set down her slice of pizza. "Oh."

She reached for the bag of chocolate bars. It was empty. She reached for her carton of chocolate milk. It too was empty. Wordlessly, both Jane and Spike passed to her what was left of their own cartons. She drained them. By drinking them. The chocolate milk, not the cartons. A moment later, she got up and went into the bathroom.

"Good thing we met her on this side," Jane said.

Spike had the same thought. "Would've been impossible to get an illegal alien across the border." They both started to giggle.

"Hey, where's your ship?" Jane called out. "Isn't it a 'smart ship'? Can't you just set the GPS or whatever—"

"It doesn't work anymore," X called back. "At first I thought I'd entered a quarantined area ..."

"We're quarantined?" Jane called out, then turned to Spike. "*That's* why no one's visited us yet!"

"Maybe Earth is a penal colony," Spike mused.

"Or a mental asylum. Maybe the human species originated somewhere else, or is at least flourishing somewhere else, and they shipped their defectives here. Its stupid, its morally challenged, its beauty-blind ..."

"But what about evolution?" Spike said. "We developed here."

"Oh yeah."

"Plus, it doesn't explain us."

"Maybe we were supposed to be the guards," Jane suggested. "Or the doctors."

"Maybe it's an experiment, and we're the researchers."

"Or the control group."

"But then I realized," X continued, coming back out of the bathroom, "that I dinged a chunk of garbage coming in. You've got a lot of shit floating around your planet— What's that all about?"

Jane and Spike exchanged a look. That said 'Earl'.

X returned to her chair, and picked up her unfinished slice of pizza.

"So what's your planet like?" Jane asked.

"It's almost exactly like this," X replied. "But completely different."

They wanted to hear more, but X looked tired. Well, she'd had a long drive.

"I'm going to make a chocolate run," Jane announced after a few minutes of nothing.

"How fast are you going to make it run?"

She groaned. "Want anything? Other than?"

"Actually, I think I'll come with," Spike said, getting up. "Oh."

They looked at X. Neither of them wanted to leave her alone in the room. Hard to say why, exactly. "Would you like to come with us? To the store? For chocolate?"

"Okay." X got up. Then fell down.

They entered the corner store that was just across from the hotel and started wandering around. They liked corner stores. Especially the un-franchised ones. You never knew what you might find.

Jane held up a fly swatter. One of the old rubberized ones. They worked so much better than the new plastic ones, being far more flexible, enabling a far quicker SLAP! At only $1.99, she chose two. A yellow one and an orange one.

"We do heroic things to save three whales caught in the ice," Spike had found the newspaper display and was scanning the headlines, "and then continue to pour dioxin into their living room."

"Jordan's dog has no sense of cause and effect over time either," Jane commented.

"'God said we could live here!'" Spike paraphrased another headline. Then anticipated the 'story' that followed. "'Nuh-uh, God said *we* could live here!'" She continued the 'conversation' with talking hands, looking from her left hand to her right. "'Maybe *your* God said you could live here, but *our* God — *the* God — said *we* could live here!' 'First of all, *our* God *is the* God; second of all, he told us *first!*'"

A few moments later, she found the chips aisle.

"No Barbecue Chicken."

"The vegetarian said sadly."

"Can't help it," Spike replied. "Love the flavour. And the salt. And I'm pretty sure no chickens were harmed in the making of."

"There's Pulled Pork," Jane pointed.

"Really?" Well, they made Buffalo Wings chips, so, she supposed, Pulled Pork chips wasn't such a stretch. 'Course, they also made Cajun Squirrel and Crunchy Frog chips—that's two different kinds—but she didn't know that. She chose a jumbo-sized bag.

They took three one-litre cartons of chocolate milk out of the refrigerator at the back, and then found the chocolate bar aisle. Or, rather, they found X in the chocolate bar aisle. She'd already eaten two. Was everything free on Grmphflg? Or was X an extraterrestrial delinquent? Jane scanned the selection then put several—many—basically one of each—into the basket she'd gone back to the entrance to get.

A young couple was at the check-out ahead of them. Coffee, popcorn, some button batteries, and some Tylenol. The woman got out her wallet. The man protested. "No, I'll get it."

"Oh. Okay. Thanks."

"Don't do that," Spike said.

"What?" the young woman turned around.

"He's not paying for your stuff to be nice. He's doing it to express his superior status. He's underscoring your need for him, your dependence on him."

"No, it's okay," she smiled. "He *is* just being nice." She smiled at the young man then. "Ryan's one of the nice guys."

"Oh yeah? See how nice he is when you insist on paying for *his* stuff. He's got a car? Offer to pay for his gas next time."

"Mind your own business!" the young man said without even turning to look at Spike.

"I am. This *is* my business. What you two do affects me. It contributes to, determines, the fabric of society. The society *in which I have to live,*" she emphasized.

To no avail.

Once back in their motel room, the three of them settled again into their claimed spots, each with a chocolate bar and a carton of chocolate milk. Spike edited the SlutWalk video Jane had made as well as the one from the hotel parking lot—pity they hadn't gotten the concierge thing—then uploaded them to YouTube, then turned on the tv. Reluctantly. Because they were going to watch tv *in the middle of a First Contact?*

But X didn't seem interested in conversation. She did seem interested in the bubbles of her Aero bar. Fascinated, in fact.

Spike started surfing, but stopped almost immediately at coverage of a track event. The women's hundred was about to be run.

"You wouldn't know by looking at her," the sportscaster was saying, "that she's a housewife and mother of three."

"And that's important why?" Spike muttered, mostly to herself. Because the sportscaster sure as hell would never hear her. Even if she screamed it into his ear.

They watched in silence as he called the race. The housewife and mother of three won in 10.7 seconds.

"The men's hundred is next. And as for Lamar—"

"You wouldn't know by looking at him that he looks after his own house and is a father of three," Spike said.

Jane nodded to the sportscaster. "Do you think he doesn't know what he's doing or just doesn't care?"

"Either way, he shouldn't have the power he does."

"Why don't they just compete according to height and weight?" Jane asked. "Instead of sex?" She wasn't into sports, never watched them, and hadn't considered the question before.

"Because then women would win."

"Seriously?"

"Yeah. I read that somewhere. Maybe not the sprints, but ... *The Frailty Myth*?"[25] Spike tried to remember. "*The Stronger Women Get, the More Men Love Football*?"[26]

"That's the actual title?" Jane was delighted, and started googling right then and there. She could do it one-handed.

"*Your Inner Cheerleader,*" she murmured a few moments later.

"No, that's not it," Spike said.

"What do they win?" X spoke up. All her bubbles were gone. "If they win."

Jane and Spike looked at each other.

"Nothing, really," Spike confessed.

"Not a new car, not a trip to Paris ..." Jane happily began to highlight the irrationality of sports competition.

"Because a few hundredths of a second isn't a significant differ-ence?"

"No, because winning the competition, beating everyone else, is all that matters," Jane replied. Pity so many women got suckered into that, she thought.

After another bit of surfing, Spike stopped at the Emmys. Or the Oscars. Or something.

"And why are there separate categories for men and women in *this* case?" Spike wondered aloud, surprised that *she* hadn't considered *that* question before.

X stared at her. Why would they be in the *same* category?

"Because otherwise women would *never* win," Jane suggested. Which, come to think of it, would be a reason *for* not-separate

---

25 by Colette Dowling
26 by Mariah Burton Nelson

categories. "Women almost always play characters in supporting roles, so they could never really compete with the leads."

"But it's the acting that's being judged, not the characters."

"You think people can distinguish between the two?" Jane asked.

"Hm."

"Even if they can," Jane said, "women wouldn't be able to compete. With the men in their leading roles," she clarified. "They wouldn't be able to fully demonstrate their acting ability, because their characters are always so one-dimensional."

"Maybe you're right," Spike said. "None of the other categories are sex-segregated—director, writer, cinematographer, composer ..."

"Though," she added a few minutes later, "most male leading roles are pretty one-dimensional too."

"Good point." Jane reconsidered her hypothesis as Spike tried to find something worth watching. She flipped past the ads for cars, the ads for trucks, the ads for perfume, the ads for volumizing and colour revitalizing shampoo ...

Suddenly X jumped out of her chair. Okay, she quickly staggered out of her chair. "You let *men* have *guns*?" Spike had paused at a newscast.

Jane shrugged. "They're the only ones who want them."

"Well ..." Spike ventured a correction.

"But—" X was flabbergasted. And terribly upset.

"They hardly ever kill people," Jane said, hoping to calm her. She saw Spike's look.

"You need to get a licence first," Jane tried again. "But that's really easy." She'd seen Spike's look.

"Mostly they kill each other." Okay *that* one was true. "And mostly in organized events."

"You mean you organize an ... *event*," X hesitated over the word, "during which men kill each other—for your entertainment?" She was appalled.

Jane and Spike were intrigued.

"No," Jane said a moment later, "the event is organized for national defence. Though," she had to add, "usually the nation's people don't really need defending. They aren't at risk of attack. And even if they were, there are far better ways to deal with such a threat. Trade embargoes, for example, and even before that, refusal to lend money, though I'm not really sure how that works ... I know they talk about the national deficit all the time and about how China actually owns the States, because they own their debt, which is why, I guess, they don't have to worry about being invaded by China, because they've already been invaded ..." She was rambling. And she knew it. But she couldn't help it. Simply put, war was impossible to explain. "Even infrastructure damage is a viable alternative. Though, now that I think about it, that may just result instead in a long, painful death—" she trailed off.

"It's more a matter of defending the nation's *interests*," Spike put her out of her misery.

"Which means what exactly?" X was still upset.

"Access to cheap oil." Jane said, having apparently recovered her ability to be concise.

X frowned.

Spike switched the channel. Gunsmoke was on. She switched again. Men in Black. Again. Terminator. Again, and again, and again. Lethal Weapon, Magnum P.I., Rambo, Homicide Hunter, Die Hard, Luther, Dirty Harry, War Dogs, Black Hawk Down ... Forty-seven channels. And in every last one of them, guns.

X just stared.

"Most of this is just make-believe," Jane said. Lamely.

"Why?"

"Because," Spike said, "men kill each other for their *own* entertainment."

7

S o," Spike said to Jane in the morning, "I think we should try to find someone who knows about this stuff. We go to a university somewhere, find a professor, knock on his door, and just ask."

"'Excuse me,'" Jane mocked, "'could you please tell us the time-space coordinates of Earth?'"

"It might work."

Jane considered that possibility. "In Boston?" she asked. Hopefully.

"Could do," Spike replied. "What's in Boston? Princeton? No, MIT!"

"And Harvard!"

"Well, there we go!"

X came out of the bathroom. She looked ... stressed. She hadn't slept much.

"We're thinking we could take you to MIT or Harvard to find someone who can help you get home," Spike said.

"You would do that for me? Thanks!" Relief transformed her face. "Can we go now?" she added.

They made a quick stop on their way back out to the highway, to fill up on gas and chocolate.

At least it was supposed to be quick. It should have been quick.

There was a work crew in the corner of the parking lot, repairing a sewer drain. Or something. Hard to say, really, since most of them were just standing there. Watching as Spike filled up the gas tank, then blatantly staring as the three of them walked from the car to the convenience store.

One of them hooted and howled. "Oooh, three little hot ones!" he called out, fanning himself.

"Fuck off!" Spike said, and they kept walking.

"What's a matter, can't you take a compliment?"

Spike stopped at that. As did Jane. X didn't stop so much as cower.

"You were paying us a compliment?" Spike said with disbelief, her phone already recording. "Okay, let's go with that." Because addressing his implication that she might not be able to 'take' something would be beyond him. "Do you often call out compliments to people?"

The construction worker nodded, grinning.

"Yeah? Okay, when was the last time you called out to compliment a man, for anything?"

He didn't answer.

Jane added, "When was the last time you called out to compliment a woman for, say, some specific ability?"

He didn't answer.

"See, we didn't think so," Spike said. "You weren't *really* paying us a compliment. In fact, this isn't about us at all. It's about *you.* You might have *said* 'She's hot!' But what you really *meant* is 'I'm horny!'"

Some of the other men grinned.

"And given that sexual desire seems to induce a state of temporary idiocy—we all do really stupid things when we're horny—" she paused, no doubt remembering something, something really stupid, "it's not particularly encouraging that the male half of the species, case in point," she nodded at the man, "actually *brags* about being in a constant state of sexual readiness."

The crew had become blank-faced.

"Or maybe," Spike had a thought, "you didn't mean 'I'm horny!' but 'I'm gay!'"

"What?" the man was alarmed. "No— I'm not gay—" he frowned exaggeratedly and looked nervously at his buddies. "It's just that you *are* hot, and I just—"

"Why else would you need to proclaim *in public, loudly* and *frequently*, that you find women, *any* and *all* women, sexually attractive?"

That shut him up.

"You know, you're right," Jane said once they were in the store. Oddly enough, she hadn't heard Spike make the 'You're gay' point before, when she engaged with men who hooted and howled. Probably because her engagement was usually limited to pepper spray. An appropriate response to being put in one's place as solely a sexual object. "They hardly ever call out when they're by themselves. But he probably isn't gay," Jane said, as the three of them stood in front of the chocolate bar display.

"Perhaps not," Spike agreed easily, putting a couple peanut butter cup bars into the basket Jane had in her hand. X followed suit with half a dozen Aero bars. She wasn't following the conversation. She'd tried, but had given up. It made no sense to her. "But he's clearly insecure about his heterosexuality. And that's okay, but he shouldn't use us to deal with it. We're not in therapy together."

Jane agreed, of course.

"You know, I was just reading something the other day," she added another layer to their ongoing conversation, "about how women are expected to be walking aphrodisiacs, because otherwise men may not feel sexual desire, and since they define themselves as sexual, and so in terms of felt sexual desire, their identity depends on our sexual attractiveness." Jane picked out a couple chocolate bars with almonds. Then added one of each of another half dozen. X followed suit. Adding two of each. Of another half dozen.

"No wonder they demand it."

"And feel free to tell us, also, when we're not hot enough."

Spike thought about that. It made sense.

"Admittedly, it's a pretty pathetic way of defining oneself," Jane conceded. "I have a hard-on, therefore I am."

"Yeah, well. *Homo erectus.*"

A couple hours later, they pulled into a high-altitude rest stop slash scenic view. Belatedly, they saw the tour bus parked on the far side of the small building. The place was crowded, therefore, and everyone wanted their picture taken with the mountains in the background. No, that wasn't quite true. Every man wanted to take a picture of a woman with the mountains in the background, and every couple wanted a stranger to take their picture with the mountains in the background. Neither Jane nor Spike had any desire whatsoever to have their picture taken with the mountains in the background. Hard to say what X wanted since she nearly walked over the edge off the cliff.

They gave her a lesson in Gravity 101. By throwing a small rock over the edge of the cliff.

"Oh."

They wondered what else *didn't* come with the brain as the three of them got in line at the restrooms. Because surely there was gravity on … her planet, right?

"It's a fascination with the technological, isn't it," Jane returned to the easier issue, noticing that it was mostly men who were taking the pictures. Certainly they had the bigger, more complicated cameras.

Spike considered that. "You could be right. I was thinking of dogs pissing on every tree they pass."

Jane considered that. "Could be both."

X was still considering what had happened to the small rock.

The line moved slowly. Those who designed public restrooms didn't seem to realize that fewer stalls-only fit in a given space than stalls-and-urinals. Or that for several days each month, women needed to do something a little more time-consuming in those stalls. Because heaven forbid they make women's restrooms *bigger* than men's.

By the time they'd used the restrooms, the tour bus had left and an old station wagon had pulled in. A family got out, the older son in uniform. It was something they didn't see very often in Canada. Pictures were taken. Of everyone with the mountains in the background. They watched, horrified. Because the young man, the soldier, was smiling.

"It's like he has no idea he may come back a mess," Jane commented sadly. "Physically, psychologically. Didn't he read *All Quiet on the Western Front*?[27] Didn't he see *Born on the Fourth of July*?[28] *In the Valley of Elah*?"[29]

"He's *already* a mess," Spike said. "Why else would he be smiling about going to another country to kill people?"

X opened her mouth. Then closed it. She was confused. Still.

"Or maybe he's just been suckered in by the ads," Jane suggested. "Courage, honor, glory. Those *are* praiseworthy virtues."

"The six weeks of being taught how to load and shoot an assault rifle should've been a clue."

"Yeah, but he probably thinks he'll just be killing the bad guys."

"Failure to imagine. Failure to anticipate."

"Failure to think," Jane summarized. "And his PTSD will be the price he pays for his philosophical irresponsibility."

"Yeah. And *when* did guilt become a psychological disorder?"

"Although I hesitate to discourage anything that increases the likelihood of men getting killed," Spike decided to pursue the matter a little more once they were back on the road, "if we want

27 https://www.goodreads.com/book/show/355697.All_Quiet_on_the_Western_Front
28 http://www.esquire.com/entertainment/movies/a29207/born-on-the-fourth-of-july-25-year-later/
29 http://www.cinemablend.com/reviews/In-the-Valley-of-Elah-2582.html

to decrease war, we should make being a soldier as expensive as being a mother."

"Go on," Jane replied, intrigued.

X opened an Aero bar. Correction. *Another* Aero bar.

"Well, the physical risks are already comparable. We just never hear about pregnancy-induced embolisms, strokes, convulsions, and comas. And the nausea, backaches, headaches, and chemical changes are just ... dismissed. Because ... women. They're just exaggerating ...

"But I'm thinking about the financial and career costs," Spike continued. "If she stays at home, a mother loses at least six years' experience and/or seniority. And if she doesn't, she loses a significant portion of her income, to pay for full-time childcare."

"Unless someone else supports her," Jane interjected.

"Exactly. In which case she loses her financial independence. What if the situation were similar for soldiers? How many men would enlist if they lost six years of seniority? If the experience they gained was considered just as nontransferable to the workplace, just as useless, as the experience gained by women as they raise a child? If they had to depend on their wives to pay for their food and shelter, to buy them their guns and bullets?"

"That would be so ... emasculating!"

"Exactly."

"They'd have to kill her too!"

Okay, not where Spike had been going.

"We can send a man to the moon," Jane commented a while later, "but we just can't figure out how to keep peace."

Jane's reference to a moon caught X's attention, and she started listening carefully. Besides, she had no more chocolate bubbles.

"Because it's not about intelligence."

Jane looked over.

"It's about competition. *That's* the primary motivating force. Competition's the reason we *can* send a man to the moon *and* it's the reason we *can't* keep peace."

"Ah. And if competition's so primary," Jane picked up the thread, admittedly with a bit of déjà-vu, "it's probably hardwired. Which means they can't help it. And if that's the case, we'll never achieve peace. Simply put, they love fighting too much."

X nodded.

As did Spike. Worldwide, over three million dollars a minute[30] was spent on the military. There were about twice as many military personnel per person[31] as there were doctors per person.[32]

"Did you know that male mice learn to run a complex maze when the only reward is the opportunity to have a fight?"

"Really?" Jane looked away from her then, and out the window.

"And as for fighting *as a soldier*," Spike continued, "there's the noise and the action and the chance to be a hero. They *love* war."

Jane nodded. "The death and destruction doesn't register."

"Or they like that too," Spike said. "Otherwise they'd use paintball guns. Or tranquilizer darts. Laxative darts!"

"No, *not* a good idea!" Jane objected. "Guess who'd have to do the laundry!"

"Oh, right."

"Nurses who risk their lives to *save* someone are given the medal of honour," Spike commented a few moments later, "whereas soldiers who risk their lives to *kill* someone are given the medal of honour *with valour*."

"Of course."

X stared at Spike. Then she stared at Jane. Then she put the Mrs. Fields pail over her head.

----

30 https://www.thestar.com/news/world/2016/04/05/global-military-spending-rose-to-nearly-17-trillion-in-2015.html
31 http://www.nationmaster.com/country-info/stats/Military/Personnel/Per-capita
32 http://www.nationmaster.com/country-info/stats/Health/Physicians/Per-1,000-people

"And the rape," Jane circled back. "Don't forget the rape. It's another reason men love war."

"What rape?" Spike asked with mock denial. X had the same question in her mind. But without the mock denial. "That's just ethnic cleansing!"

"Oh yeah. I forgot. And yet if the kid stays with the woman, she's going to raise it. According to her own ethnicity. So if they were serious about cleansing, they'd just kill the women."

"Not nearly as much fun."

"Well it would be if they raped them first."

X opened her mouth again. Then closed it again. She was confused in a completely different way.

"So why don't they just castrate the men?" Jane wondered a moment later. "Wouldn't that be a more effective way to obliterate an ethnicity? Given the belief that it's biological," she qualified.

"Probably against the rules."

"Ah."

They thought about it. "What about when they rape the women on their own side?" Jane asked. "*That's* not ethnic cleansing."

"No, that's just an enthusiastic spillover of violence and aggression," Spike said sarcastically. "You know, they just get carried away."

"Shooting someone twenty-five times when doing so once achieves the intended result is getting carried away. Forcing your penis into someone's vagina is … significantly different from pulling a trigger."

"Is it?"

X had the distinct impression she was missing something. Some critical piece …

"Maybe they rape the women, the *enemy* women," Jane clarified, "because the women are the enemy's property. Rape as a property crime. Like keying the other guy's car."

"No, that can't be right," she said a second later. "If they wanted to destroy the enemy's property, they'd just kill her."

"Rape is conquest," Spike suggested. "*That's* why they do it."

"Then why don't they rape the men?"

"Oh that's definitely against the rules."

X gave her head a good shake. There must be something wrong with the interface. Had to be.

"But," Jane persisted, "if war is really about—or if you really *think* it's about—defending your loved ones, or even your resources, your land, your water, your oil, wouldn't you do whatever is necessary? Wouldn't you 'fight dirty' if that's what it takes?" She'd never really thought about the rules of engagement before. "Rules apply to civil interactions and games. War is neither."

"Are you sure about that? That it's not a game? For men?" She hadn't been talking about the rules of engagement. Per se.

A mile later, Jane had another idea. "Rules give the impression of fairness, decency, civility. They make war permissible!"

Spike nodded. "You should read *The Gender Knot*. Allan Johnson. Best analysis of men and war I've ever read. 'War allows men to reaffirm their masculine standing in relation to other men.' That's why they don't want women in the military. Their presence would change the meaning of war."

"And that's why they rape the women on their own side." Jane sighed. "It affirms their masculine standing in relation to other men." She sighed.

X banged her head against the window.

"It really does boggle the mind, doesn't it?" Jane said several miles later. "Soon after the Cro-Magnons, somebody tried armed aggression as a conflict resolution technique and it didn't work. Then someone said, well let's try it again. And it didn't work. Let's try it again. And again. And again. There is a not-so-fine line between persistence and a mental disorder. Isn't there?"

"Yes," Spike replied, "but war isn't really meant to resolve conflict. It's meant to boost business. And, of course, egos."

"You really believe that one guy declares war—implicates an entire nation, millions of people, in disaster and tragedy—just to one-up another guy?" Jane asked. Then reconsidered. It did fit with what Spike had said earlier.

"And to think that all along we've been shouting that the personal is political ..."

A few minutes later, Spike returned to Jane's not-so-fine line. "Back when the Russians had enough whatever to kill every American twenty times, and the Americans had enough whatever to kill every Russian forty times, they figured America was ahead."

Jane nodded. She'd read the metaphor circulating at the time. Two people are in a sealed room standing in three feet of gasoline. One has 10,000 matches. The other has 20,000 matches.

"Which comes back to ..."

"Men are mentally ill. As a norm."

"Speaking of which ..." Jane was googling. "Ah. Here it is. This is from the Training Center for Subversive Warfare: 'Torture must be kept clean, it must not be carried out in the presence of those with sadistic tendencies, it must be carried out by some responsible person, and above all, it must be humane.'"

"'Humane torture.' Only a man ..."

"You have wars on your planet?" Spike half-turned to ask X. They'd never quite gotten to the question the night before.

After a moment's thought, X replied, "We don't have soldiers." It was the quickest way to answer the question.

"No armies? What we could do with an extra $3.2 billion dollars a day ..."

"You have *no* fighting on your planet?" Jane asked X. "Not for land or food or water ...?

"We have enough. Land, food, water."

"And that's because you do something special to unlimit the space, right?" Spike suggested.

"No, it's because they do something special to limit the population," Jane said, then turned to X. "Right?"

"You can't do that?" X asked with disbelief. "You can't limit your population?"

"Apparently not," Jane said, turning to stare out the window.

8

It was time for lunch, so Spike pulled in to the next pizza-by-the-slice place. While they waited in line, Jane watched the newscast on the tv mounted high in the corner, Spike studied the menu, and X — hard to say what X was doing.

"Hey, maybe that's what the soldier guy was going to," Jane said. "The air show."

"An air show?" X turned eagerly to look, expecting perhaps a dazzling choreography of rainbow sparkles and aurora ribbons. And seeing instead fighter planes and nuclear missiles.

"An air show consists of demonstrations that glorify our ability to kill," Spike summarized, seeing her surprise.

X stared at her for a moment, then said thoughtfully, "Nope, never would have guessed that one."

They all watched the clip in silence.

"'Performers'?" Jane said with incredulity. "They actually call them *performers* now?"

"Like in a circus. 'Hey, kids, let's go to the air show!'" Spike mocked. "'The F-117 will be there! It can carry up to 5,000 pounds of bombs! Wow, eh?! It was the F-117 that destroyed Iraqi water purification, electrical, and sewage treatment plants, killing 500,000 kids just like you! Pack a picnic lunch, Mum! Let's be part of the magic!'"

"I can't *believe* the disconnect."

Fifteen minutes later, they'd finished their pizza and were back in the car.

"Chocolate is good," X said from the back seat, happily sipping her second little bottle of Rolo milkshake.

"Should be one of the main food groups." Jane was happily sipping one of the same.

Spike had opted for the Crispy Crunch Milkshake. Because it wasn't. Couldn't be.

"It's not?" X asked with disbelief.

"You're kidding," Jane turned to face her. "Seriously?"

X nodded. "Calcium, B12, iron, copper, magnesium, potassium. Flavonoids! Endorphins!"

"It's interesting that men don't like chocolate," Jane noted.

"That's why beer stores and liquor stores outnumber chocolate stores by ... a gazillion."

"Yeah," she replied, sadly, "but where I was going with that was their physiology must be— Well, we *know* it's different ..."

Spike glanced in the rear-view mirror at X. "Why did you choose to merge with a female rather than a male?"

"I chose to merge with a human. I wanted the most intelligent species."

They both spurted milkshake out their noses.

"But," Jane said once she'd recovered, "why a female human being instead of a male human being?"

X was silent. For a very long time.

"Males are human beings?" she finally asked. "You consider them the *same species*? As you?"

Spike and Jane were silent. For a very long time.

Finally Spike spoke. Sotto voce. To Jane. "Should we tell her *now* how we reproduce?"

"Or later," Jane said cheerily.

"Didn't feel like it," X continued, shaking her head.

Again, Jane and Spike were silent.

Then Jane asked. "How did it feel?"

"Scary. The emotions— It kept going from hysterical to flat then back to hysterical. And untidy. Whose idea was it to put their stuff," she gestured to her crotch, "on the outside?"

"Such an underutilized advantage," Spike muttered.

"I also tried a dog."

"Oh yeah?" Spike grinned. "How did *that* feel?"

"Fun!"

"Must've been a lab."

"Why do you think they're the same species?" X was genuinely curious. Not to mention appalled.

"We have the same chromosomes, except for one." Jane typed quickly, then raised her laptop to show her.

"But the one that's different," X pointed to the Y chromosome, "is missing a piece. It looks broken. Like something just ... fell off."

Spike grinned.

"But that wouldn't necessarily indicate a different species," Jane said. "Would it? Couldn't it just indicate stunted growth or arrested development?"

Couldn't stop grinning.

"Was it always this way?" X asked.

"Actually, now that you mention it ... I read something about the Y chromosome degrading over time," Jane googled away. "Here it is:[33] 'Currently, the Y chromosome is a train wreck of about 45 surviving genes. Some geneticists count 27. These hangin'-on-by-their-pinkies-genes are primarily devoted to sperm-making. The rest of the Y chromosome is a wasteland of meaningless repetition. This rate of repetition is between 99.94 and 99.997%. Scientists were shocked by this repetition, and at first, could not distinguish one male from another—not even from opposite ends of the planet.'"

Spike was choking on her milkshake.

"So doesn't not sharing all the same chromosomes make you different species?"

"No, it just makes us not clones. I think. I don't know." Jane googled. Then stopped and just stared out the window.

---

33 http://trustyourperceptions.wordpress.com/2013/09/01/dudesare doomed1/

"What'd you find?" Spike knew that stare.

"The chromosomes of humans and chimps[34] are more similar than those of female humans and male humans."

"Seriously?" Spike looked over at her. Almost pulled off the road to see for herself.

Jane nodded. "They're identical, in fact, except that two of the chromosomes, separate in chimps, are fused together in humans."

"And yet we consider *them* a different species," Spike articulated the obvious. "A less evolved species." She started grinning again.

"It would make sense, wouldn't it," Jane said, thinking about male humans as a separate species. "Their body hair, their coarser features, their greater brute strength, their greater tendency to fight and flight—"

"Their fascination with loud noise, their fascination with movement— You know, frogs don't even *see* something unless it moves."

"Their posturing. Their tendency to inflate."

"A balloonfish can actually double its size."

"Their obsession with territory," Jane continued, intrigued by, but ignoring, Spike's *Animal Planet* flashbacks. "Their lack of verbal skills."

X was listening. And nodding.

"Their limited emotional development, both perceptive and expressive," Spike offered, "their stubborn resistance to acquiring any self-knowledge, a resistance manifest in a disdain for all things psychological."

"Their inability to appreciate beauty."

"Their poor social skills, in that their social interaction is almost exclusively limited to competitive interaction."

Still nodding.

"No wonder they like dick flicks so much," Jane said then. "A single dick flick has it all: action, noise, big heroes, big guns, territorial conflict, at least one high-speed chase—"

---

34 http://genetics.thetech.org/ask/ask257

"And dialogue consisting mostly of grunts."

"Though," Jane said a few moments later, "I recall seeing a photograph of three flirty Hooters waitresses and in the same shot a bespectacled woman in nondescript clothing, quietly carrying a sign about reproductive rights. Talk about two different species."

"Speaking of frogs," Jane said, another few moments later, "remember that guy in Taiwan, in some sports stadium, who dropped his kid in order to catch a ball?" Jane asked.

"Yeah. So if ever a kid ever comes flying through the air, he'll be our man!"

Jane grinned. Not where she'd been going.

"I was thinking about the way the media framed it. First, the commentators chuckled. About a child being dropped."

Spike glanced over. Since when was Jane concerned about the welfare of children?

"Second, they chuckled in a 'boys will be boys' way. As if men's immature, irresponsible behavior is inevitable.

"Then there were the giggling comments about his wife's 'death stare' and how 'he's gonna get it now!' What is he, twelve?"

Spike nodded. She remembered the coverage Jane was describing.

"Lastly, there were endless snickers about how he was going to be sleeping on the couch. A child is dropped, and the big concern is that he won't have sex for a while."

"Not to mention that whole marital dynamic," Spike interjected. "If he's good, he gets sex; if he's bad, he doesn't."

Jane nodded. "Where are the men wincing at the implication that their wives are their mommies? Where are the men confronting this guy and telling him to grow the fuck up? Furthermore, if dropping a child in order to catch a ball isn't a wake-up call, to men, to question and reject their conditioning and/or to recognize and resist their biochemistry, I don't know what is."

"And I can't help pointing out," Spike added, "that if it had been a woman who'd dropped her child in order to catch a ball, they'd be hauling her ass into court and taking her kid away."

"What I don't get," X said a few moments later, having been busy thinking, very busy thinking, and not about frogs, "is that picture you showed me? Of the chromosomes? At the very least, wouldn't you consider males to be mutilated human beings?"

Good thing Spike had no milkshake left.

"Or mutated human beings!" Jane resumed googling. "Listen to this. It's from Brian Sykes,[35] one of the world's leading geneticists: 'The human template is female. Men are genetically-modified women. We can tell this because there are still a few genes on the Y-chromosome which have recognizable counterparts on the X-chromosome … pointing to a distant common ancestry. Maleness … is a mutation.' Men *are* mutants," Jane summarized.

X nodded.

"Okay," Spike said, "but can I still think of them as morons instead?"

"Can be both."

"Agreed. Tell us more."

"According to Sykes," Jane obliged, "up to a half of a man's sperm swims in the wrong direction, due to anatomical abnormalities."

Once she'd stopped laughing, Spike said, "In that case, I'd go so far as to say *deformed* human beings."

X nodded again. "So why do you make deformed human beings?"

"We don't exactly 'make' deformed human beings," Jane replied after a moment or two.

"Sure we do," Spike said.

---

35 http://www.nytimes.com/2004/06/08/science/a-conversation-with-bryan-sykes-is-genghis-khan-an-ancestor-mr-dna-knows.html

At the same time X asked, with incredulity, "You reproduce by mitosis? Involuntarily?"

Spike looked at Jane, waiting for her answer.

"No, it's voluntary ..." she answered in Jane's silence.

"Not always. Not exactly."

"Always, and exactly, on the part of the males," Spike said.

"You still— *Rut*?" X had figured it out. "But *why*?"

"Good question."

"Can't you clone yet?" X asked.

Jane simply passed her laptop to her.

"Alien meets Google," Spike said to her, grinning. "This should be good."

A short moment later, X burst out laughing. Jane turned around and Spike glanced in the mirror. X turned the laptop for them to see. Dogs bodysurfing down snow-covered hills.

"Why did they name it Dolly?" X asked. Half an hour had passed. She had found the link to Dolly Parton, but still didn't get it.

"Because they didn't foresee that their discovery would become headline news and make them look like snickering eight-year-old boys," Jane suggested.

"Because they didn't realize they *were* snickering eight-year-old boys," Spike countered.

"They also didn't realize how insulting they were being."

"Or maybe they did."

Jane continued anyway, for X's benefit. "They see women not as people, let alone colleagues, certainly not ever superiors, but only as sexual parts—" she stopped then and looked out the window. It was all just so ... old.

"So *that's* why you can't limit your population!" X exclaimed, having thought it over. "No wait, you *have* connected rutting with having babies—"

"Well, half of us have," Jane said dryly.

"'You're *pregnant?*'" Spike mimicked Everyman. "'But, how can that *be?*'"

"You haven't figured out how to rut without having babies?"

"We have, but—"

"Some of us think it's a duty," Spike said with disgust. "To have babies."

Jane nodded. "Women who ask to be sterilized are accused of wanting the pleasure of sex," she grimaced, "without the responsibility."

"Like men don't do that every frickin' minute."

"Reproduction is the default mode. No one asks why you *want* kids. But they all ask why you *don't.*"

X was puzzled. "But can't you—the smart ones among you— can't you *insist?* For the other ones?"

"Most of us also think it's a right," Jane explained. "An inalienable right."

"A god-given right," Spike simplified. Not at all.

X was amazed. "*Why?*"

"Another good question."

"Don't you see where that's gotten you?" X demanded.

"Yes," Jane said tersely, "we have. Some of us."

"The smart ones among us."

"Seventeen babies at once?!"[36] X had discovered that humans *had* figured out IVF.

Jane turned to Spike. "Did you know that the Royal Commission on New Reproductive Technologies, which was created by the federal government to consider, among other things, the ethical implications of NRTs in order to make policy recommendations," Jane paused, "had no ethicists on the panel?"

---

36 http://worldnewsdailyreport.com/usa-mother-gives-birth-to-17-babies-at-once/

"I did not know that, no."

"It was made up of a private practitioner in internal medicine, two lawyers, a sociology professor, a lecturer in *religion*, and a director of the Office of the *Catholic* Family Life Archdiocese. That is to say, *two* of the six were affiliated with religion."

"The Lord works in insidious ways."

"But you don't clone yourselves?" X wanted to make sure. Because ... seventeen!

"No, reproducing by cloning," Spike explained, "instead of by rutting," she grinned, "is a sin."

"Actually, rutting is also a sin," Jane interjected.

"Only when you do it with someone who doesn't own you."

"True."

"Because," Spike turned her attention back to X, "*God* created us. Cloning would be playing God."

"But IVF isn't?"

"Apparently not." Spike easily conceded the irrationality. Of those who believe in gods. Gods created us. In their image.

"There are quality management programs for making cars," X was still googling away.

"There are," Spike saw exactly where she was going.

"Cars are more important than people?"

"Apparently so."

"But," X was still trying to make sense of it, "if women still incubate, why don't you just abort the deformed ones?"

"Yet another *very* good question."

"Google China and its one-child policy," Jane said. Seething just a bit. It took just a moment.

"You're aborting the wrong ones!" X cried out.

"A lot of women think we need men," Spike explained, anticipating another anguished 'Why?'

"But that's not true! *Is it?*" X couldn't imagine why it would be.

"No," Jane said emphatically. "As soon as the male becomes extinct, parthenogenesis will kick in. It's actually the male genes that prevent parthenogenesis now."

"Really?" Spike asked. "Good to know ..."

"But you weren't talking about reproduction, were you?" Jane asked Spike a short while later. "You just meant that women think they need men in general."

Spike nodded.

"What for?" X was truly perplexed.

Ignoring the question, because, really, they had no answer, Jane continued. "In fact, women like us, independents, are severely ostracized," she said. "And/or insulted—"

"Man-hater! Dyke!" Spike illustrated.

"Patronized—"

"You just wait, dear, some day you'll find *your* prince!"

"Pitied—"

"You just wait, dear, some day you'll find *your* prince!"

"Considered immature—"

"Isn't it about time, dear?"

"Dismissed, ignored—"

Spike stopped with the illustrations to clarify another point, "And I didn't mean just that women think they need men *personally*. They think we need them period. All of history tells them so. Because it's all about men. *Only* men. So they get the message that without men, we'd just up and die. They have no idea what women are capable of. Women's history has been, if not erased outright, buried so deep it takes a lot of digging to find it."

"If a woman is unattractive," Jane added, "she just won't make the front page. No matter how impressive her achievement. Whereas unattractive men are on the front page all the time."

"Quite apart from the habit of men to take the credit for women's work."

"Then again," Jane had retrieved her laptop and was busy googling, "not quite as much digging as it used to take. Still. Most women don't know that it was a woman who discovered HIV. And stem cells. DNA. Pulsars. They don't know that two women built the first solar-heated home. In 1947. They don't know that it was a woman who invented car heaters. Fire escapes. Life rafts. The medical syringe. Refrigerators. Wifi. Square-bottomed paper bags. Central heating. Kevlar.

"And—" she paused for effect, nodding to a place just off the highway on their right, "ice cream."

"And here we've been blaming testosterone," Jane said once they were in the car again, thinking back to the chromosome issue. She took a lick of her chocolate brownie ice cream cone.

"YOU LET THEM HAVE TESTOSTERONE?!" The top scoop of X's chocolate-dipped chocolate fudge ice cream cone almost fell off. Clearly men were not the only morons here on Earl.

"We don't 'let' them have it," Jane said. "They just ... have it. I mean naturally."

"Some more than others," Spike added. She bit into her bubble gum with chocolate swirls ice cream cone. "Hey, maybe that's part of the deformity. Maybe that sick little Y chromosome somehow leads to the production of way too much testosterone."

"So the 'normal' male human being is living with an overdose of testosterone? Interesting."

"You know," Spike mused, "most 'normal' men *are* just a few degrees away from the steroid-crazed guys we hear about."

"It does make sense," Jane agreed. "No, wait, haven't men *always* had 'too much' testosterone? Look at history."

"Well, when did the Y start deteriorating?"

"IT'S A TOXIN!" X shouted. *Clearly* not the only morons.

"So there are morons on the loose all over your planet," X said a long while later, still trying to understand—

"Yep."

"Morons with testosterone."

"Yep."

"So what do you use for protection? Personal containment shields?"

"No," Spike sighed. "We use those." She nodded to a passing billboard. On which ultra-thins with wings were assured to provide women with full protection day and night.

"And the morons are in charge." Still trying to understand—

"Pretty much."

"Morons with testosterone."

"Yep."

"Why? I mean how? How is it that the deformed ones are in power? How do they *keep* power?"

"They keep it exactly *because* they *are* deformed. Because they're willing to do anything to get and keep power. Lie, cheat, kill. Individually and collectively."

"What if women just refused to replicate? Refused to keep producing them?"

"They'd kill us," Spike said. "And force whoever was left."

"For women to get into power," Jane said, "we'd have to kill all the men."

"And the eighty percent of women who support them," Spike added, "emotionally, socially, even physically—by feeding them, clothing them, and cleaning up their messes. All so they have time to rule the world."

"How long for the remaining 3% of the Y to disintegrate?"

"Longer than we've got probably."

"What we need is a male-only plague."

"Something gradual," Jane agreed, "so we can learn what we need to know to take over. How to manage the solar cells, how to repair the sewage system ..."

"Actually, there are probably enough of us already who know whatever we need to know."

"You may be right. Even back when I was teaching, women made up almost 50% of the math and science students. Close to 20% in engineering and computers."

"In Canada alone, that would translate into tens of thousands of women."

"I wonder if someone has already invented a male-only plague," Spike turned to Jane several miles later. "The women who discovered HIV, DNA, and stem cells—are they still alive?" she asked, not very ambiguously.

"And if it were spread through PIV ..." Jane mused at the poetic justice.

"INHIBITORS!" X practically screamed. Reasonably enough. "Why don't they just take inhibitors?" While they were speculating about a plague, she'd been googling. "You've *done* the research. Males with testosterone inhibitors don't rape, don't kill, don't fight nearly as much—"

"Yeah." Jane sighed.

"And still—?"

"And still." Spike sighed.

"They like their testosterone," Jane shrugged.

"That's part of what makes them morons."

9

Hey, let's find a place that sells used electronics," Jane suggested, a laptop-deprived hour later. "X should have her own laptop. Or tablet. Or something."

"Okay."

They were still a couple hours from Boston, but sure enough, as they approached the next town, they saw a mall with a Future Shop.

"Do they carry refurbished items?" Spike wondered out loud.

"If they have an in-store repair shop, they might. Or they might have a sale ... I thought Future Shop was just in Canada though. *And* recently bought out by BestBuy."

"That was Future Shop. This is *The* Future Shop."

"Ah."

They pulled into the large parking lot, then headed to the store. Once inside they wandered up and down the aisles, looking for the laptop section. X glanced at the items they passed without much interest.

"Hey," Spike nudged Jane. "Doesn't that guy look exactly like Sheldon Cooper?" A tall, thin geeky guy was holding two boxes in his hand, reading the fine print on one and then the other. "Remember that scene in which he agonizes over X-Box One and X-Box Two or something?"

"Yeah. And Amy—" she broke off. "You know, I've started fast-forwarding through the Sheldon-and-Amy scenes because they've just become too sickening to watch. I mean, she's intelligent, she has a Ph.D. in neurobiology for godsake, and yet she stays in a relationship with Sheldon Cooper. The most infantile, the most arrogant, the most selfish person ever. How low does her self-esteem have to be for her to think she can't do better?"

"Maybe she can't," Spike said as they turned into the next aisle. "Eliminate the 99% who aren't as smart as her. Of those, eliminate the ones who are already married. Then eliminate the ones she's not likely to ever meet. *Is* there anyone left?"

"Why does the guy have to be as smart as her?"

"You think she'd be happier with a Zack?"

"No." Jane thought for just a moment. "I think she'd be happier with door number three. A life lived alone is far, *far* better than a life intertwined with someone who ignores you, who belittles your interests—he thinks neurobiology isn't as important as theoretical physics, who belittles your achievements—he failed to acknowledge let alone congratulate her publication in a major journal, who knows what you want—romance, sex—because you've come right out and told him—and still doesn't give it to you."

Spike hadn't thought about it quite as thoroughly as Jane had, but given the litany, she had to agree. "Their relationship *has* become pretty emotionally abusive."

"It has. And need we ask who it is, exactly, who finds that entertaining?"

They turned into the next aisle.

"Who is Sheldon Cooper," X spoke up, "and why are we in an antique shop?"

They discovered that The Future Shop did not sell refurbished laptops, and that all of their 'on sale' laptops were high-end, expensive bells-and-whistles stuff, but also that Computer Tech, a nearby repair shop, would probably have what they wanted.

"Hi there, we're looking for a used laptop," Jane said to the guy behind the counter. Mike, his name tag said.

"I've got three at the moment," he set them onto the counter. "All refurbished to be fully functioning."

"This one," X pointed. "What options does the telepath interface have?"

"What?"

What? Spike and Jane turned to stare at her.

"It doesn't have a telepath interface," Jane recovered first. But oh wouldn't that be cool, she thought.

"Retina-recognition?" She turned from Jane back to Mike.

"Nope."

"Oh. Wave-control then?" She fluttered her fingers.

"Nope."

"I have to *touch* the screen?"

"Actually, touch screens are available only on the tablets," Mike said.

"And their screens are much smaller," Jane added. Mike obliged by putting a couple of his second-hand tablets onto the counter.

"Voice activation?" X asked. She was trying to remember her computer history course. Surely she wouldn't have to keep using a physical keyboard for input! She'd thought that Jane's laptop was just an heirloom or something.

"If it has Windows 7 or later, you can load a voice activation program onto it, yes."

"But if you're googling in the car," Jane said, "that could get ..." Annoying, she thought.

"Hm. How big is the holographic projection for that one?" X pointed to one of the tablets.

"Um, it doesn't have holographic projection. None of them do." Mike was starting to get the idea that X wasn't from around here. Or now.

So Jane and Spike were starting to get nervous.

Jane nodded then to the three laptops and asked about battery life, processing speed, and RAM. Operating systems and loaded programs. Price. She made a decision, made the purchase, and the three of them left. Before X started asking about quantum nanobots.

Next, they stopped at a convenience store and replenished their chocolate bar supply. Convenience indeed.

Back in the car, Spike glanced in the rear-view mirror to X, who was googling away on her new laptop. It was red. And shiny. She liked it.

"So what do you do?" she asked. "Back home, I mean."

A full minute elapsed. "Can you be a little more specific?"

"For a living. Your job."

"Oh, I'm still retired."

"But— Aren't you—" she and Jane looked at each other. "That body's only about twenty-five. How old are you? Really."

"Twenty-five."

They exchanged another look. "People can retire at twenty-five on your planet?" The 'still' hadn't registered.

X opened another browser tab. "Well, that's stupid," she said to the screen, then to the front seat. "If you wait until you're sixty-five to retire, you'll be too old to do all the stuff you want to do. We're retired between twenty and forty, then we work between forty and eighty. By then, we've had twenty years to do everything we want, so—"

"But a lot of jobs— Aren't you—" Spike tried again. "I mean, at eighty, well, even at seventy—"

"Sixty—" Jane corrected.

"Robots," X had understood their point. "Besides, ten hours a week leaves you a lot of time to recover."

"*Ten* hours a week*?*"

X busied herself at her laptop again.

"*Forty* hours a week? What needs to be done on this planet that takes seven billion people forty hours a week each—"

"Well, not *all* seven billion—"

"No, she's right," Spike said. "When I think of all the time I saved when I stopped peeling potatoes and ironing bedsheets."

Jane laughed. "You've never peeled a potato or ironed a bedsheet in your life!"

"And you can support yourself on ten hours?" Jane asked X.

"Yes. It's more than enough to cover food, water, and chocolate."

"You have nine nuclear reactors and fifty nuclear warheads on the ocean floor?" she asked with disbelief, having returned to the first browser she'd opened.

Spike groaned. She knew what website she'd found. Frankly, she was surprised it was still up. "They were naval mishaps."

"Mishaps?" Jane asked. Had the *military* reclaimed *that* word?

"And a nuclear bomb fell out of a U.S. bomber and landed in a Carolina swamp," X was reading aloud. "And it hasn't been found yet?!"

"Yeah, you'd think the localized proliferation of two-headed alligators would've been a clue."

Jane snorted.

"And this country dropped four plutonium bombs on another country—*by mistake*?!"

"Oops."

"I have to ask," Jane asked, "four at once or on four separate occasions?"

"You chose a site for a nuclear power plant that was two miles from an active fault line," X murmured as she read, "and the blueprints for the reactors got mixed up, so the earthquake fault supports were installed backwards."

"Yeah," Spike sighed. "We are *so* ready for that anti-matter stuff."

X looked up, horrified.

"And those were just accidents," Spike said a few minutes later. In case she didn't find the *other* website. "We can do much better when we try."

Jane waited.

"Some guys at the Rocky Flats plutonium plant intentionally dumped toxic chemicals into a creek. At the Fernald plant, it was 167,000 pounds of uranium by-products. And Daniel Maston, an assistant operator at the Point Lepreau Station, spiked the cafeteria's juice cooler with tritiated heavy water from the reactor. Apparently he said—and I quote—'I don't have a good reason. I just did it. Maybe it was a joke.'"

"Geez," Jane said, "who needs to worry about terrorists stealing uranium when we have men working at our nuclear plants? Where was their supervisor?"

"Busy cheating on his Nuclear Regulatory Commission Operating exams. James Floyd. Supervisor of Operations at Three-Mile Island."

"You've conducted over 1,900 tests of nuclear weapons," X had continued browsing.

"Yeah, you'd think we'd get it right after, say, the first couple hundred."

Jane thought maybe it was a good thing they *hadn't* gotten it right.

"And we still haven't figured out what to do with the leftover stuff," Spike said. Before X discovered *that* little fact. "We have enough radioactive waste to contaminate all of the Earth's lakes and rivers. Twice. Canada alone has enough to stack a six-foot-high pile along the TransCanada Highway from coast to coast."

"We don't know what to do with the stuff," Jane said, asked, just to be sure, "and yet we keep making it?" Logic 101, she thought.

Spike nodded. "We tossed some of it into the ocean. But apparently it doesn't just dissolve. We launched some of it into outer space. But now the insurance companies won't cover our space shuttles for collision. We buried some of it in containers. Containers that clearly won't last as long as the stuff itself. And we used some of it to build schools. Call it recycling."

Jane looked over at her to see if she was joking. She was not.

"It is remarkable, isn't it," Jane observed a few miles later, "that we still exist. I mean, even more remarkable than Leonard Cohen getting the Male Vocalist of the Year Award."

"You can change the facts?" X asked with surprise a little while later, as she continued to google, bing, and yahoo about Earl.

"I wish," Spike sighed. Deeply.

"The Ministry of Truth can," Jane muttered. "Why do you ask?"

"There's a box here that asks 'What is this animal?' It gives four options and says to vote. So the animal will be whatever gets the most votes?"

Jane turned. "You're on the weather network website, right?"

X nodded.

"That feature should be called 'Test your Knowledge' and should invite site visitors to *indicate* the right answer. Not *vote for* the right answer. To *vote* means to express your preference as part of a *decision-making* process," she added. In case X didn't know. The interface with the brain seemed a little ... unreliable. Either that or things were, as she'd said, almost exactly the same but completely different on ... wherever.

"So it makes people *feel* like they're engaged with the world when they are so not," Spike didn't check weather websites. "Lovely. It instills a false sense of I'm-making-a-difference."

"And along with relentless requests for feedback and the ubiquitous 'Like' feature," Jane continued, "it makes people think their opinion—their uninformed, off-the-cuff opinion—is valuable. When it is so not."

After a moment, Jane continued, "Once the question was something like 'Did this summer feel longer, shorter, or the same as other summers?' And site visitors were invited to 'View the results'. What self-respecting adult *cares* or is even *curious* about such a thing?"

"Not the point, I'd guess," Spike said. "Such a question takes our attention off the *causes* for such changes. Do you really think their use of 'vote' is just a careless mistake in diction?"

"Do *you* really think it's that purposeful?"

Spike reconsidered, then sighed. "No, probably not. More likely, some twenty-something idiot with a Business degree and an entry level position in marketing thought up the idea as a way to increase visitor traffic to the site. Which is no doubt his entire job description."

"And he's ill-equipped to consider the consequences of his ideas."

"He's not being paid to consider the consequences of his ideas."

Jane turned back to X. "*Real* voting typically occurs when we elect our members of parliament. For government."

"And they do it like this?" X nodded to her laptop.

"No," Jane replied. "You have to register. You have to be eighteen and a citizen—"

"Which usually means you just happened to be born wherever—"

"And then you go in person to cast your vote."

X thought about that. "You don't have to take a test?"

"No," Jane sighed. "Any idiot can vote."

"And their vote counts as much as ours," Spike added.

"And that's the problem with democracy. It's just an appeal to the majority."

"And the trouble with the majority," Spike paraphrased Cockburn, "is it keeps getting worse."

Plus," Spike said after a moment, "when they ask us to vote, they don't specify whether we're to vote for what we think is best for the world at large or what will be best for us personally. So some of us do the former, but most, I'd guess, do the latter."

"You know, you're right!" Jane hadn't thought of that before. "If everyone voted in their own self-interest, then at least the outcome would satisfy the majority. Well, no," she reconsidered, "if there's more than two options, it would satisfy only the largest sector. Which could, of course, be quite a minority."

"As it is," Spike said, "the people who think of the greater good, and vote accordingly, *never* get their own interests met."

"Assuming their own interests never coincide with what they think is for the greater good."

Spike nodded. "Which, at least in the short-term, is probably a plausible assumption."

"Do *you* have to take a test? On—"

"Grmphflg." Spike grinned.

"Of course!" X replied. "You have to pass a test, proving you understand the issues and are aware of the relevant facts."

"But don't the people running for office manipulate your understanding of the issues and your awareness of the facts?" Spike was curious.

"How? Everything is in a ... SuperGoogle. Ranked by truth and value, not by popularity." She'd figured that out, Spike realized, impressed.

"But who decides what's true and valuable?"

"Those with expertise on the matter. Someone like ..." X quickly googled, "your Minister of Energy would decide on Energy matters."

Jane and Spike looked at each other.

"The Minister of Energy doesn't actually know anything about energy," Jane said.

"The Minister of Energy isn't likely to have a degree in Physical Science," Spike clarified. Not at all.

"Probably doesn't even have a Bachelor's in Science."

"Probably didn't take Science past grade ten."

X stared at them.

Reluctantly, they gave X a primer on government.

Then a primer on politics.

After a long pause during which they both wondered why the two seemed inevitably connected, X said, "So politicians do things because of the votes they want to get? Rather than getting votes because of the things they do? And your leaders follow, they don't lead."

"Yup," Jane said cheerfully. Then came back to an earlier point, "*And* they follow the lowest common denominator."

"In theory," Spike corrected. "Usually they follow the money."

"How does it work on Grmphflg?" Jane asked.

"Not many people run for office. It's a lot of work. And a lot of responsibility."

"But also a lot of power."

"Not so much. Because of the voting."

"You have referenda? A referendum is—"

"Of course. On all the big decisions."

"And *no one* manipulates your understanding of the issues and your awareness of the facts?" Jane asked. "SuperGoogle aside, is there no politically motivated advertising?"

"What's advertising?"

Once they were in their room for the night—Jane had found a relatively inexpensive hotel just outside Boston— and were waiting for their pizza, Jane worked on her novel, Spike edited and uploaded the wolf whistling video, and X practised sitting down and getting up. At least that's what they thought she was doing.

Five minutes later, Spike turned off her tablet, but before she found the remote, Jane had closed her laptop and opened the night stand drawer. "And tonight's surprise is," she held the paperback aloft, "*Alas, Babylon.*"

She read from the back cover, "'When a nuclear holocaust ravages the United States—'"

"How serendipitous," Spike noted. Ambiguously.

"Oh, we've got to read it," Jane settled onto the bed with it. "Author Pat—Patrick—Frank was a government consultant."

"An inside view. Should be interesting," Spike agreed.

"'A man who's been shaken by a bomb knows what it feels like,'" she read the opening sentence.

"And a woman doesn't?" Spike asked. "Is he saying women are never in bombed areas? Or they are, but for some reason, they don't get shaken by them? Or they do, but they nevertheless don't know what it feels like?"

Undeterred, Jane continued, but skimming, and summarizing. "Chapter one introduces Florence. Who gossips." She flipped ahead a few pages. "She doesn't design state of the art mp3 players ..." she muttered to herself, "and she certainly isn't looking for the cure to cancer .... She gossips." That's pretty much all there was to Florence.

"'However,'" Jane read, "'if your sister was in trouble and wired for money, the secret was safe with Florence.' Only if *my sister* was in trouble?" Jane asked pointedly. "What about me?"

"Author Pat—Patrick—Frank clearly didn't even *imagine* the *possibility* that *women* might read his book."

"And 'in trouble'?" Jane wasn't done. "Being pregnant, having a life begin to grow inside your body— That's not being 'in trouble'."

X stared at her.

"It's either amazingly wonderful or incredibly devastating. But it's not being 'in trouble'," she practically spat the words.

Oh.

"'But if your sister bore a legitimate baby,'" she continued reading, "'its sex and weight would be known all over town.'"

"You sometimes give birth to *fake* babies? How? *Why*?" X was perplexed.

Both Jane and Spike sighed. Neither one of them wanted to explain this idiocy.

"'Illegitimate' is what they call babies when they're born to women who aren't married."

"Married to a man," Spike clarified.

"Because men alone confer legitimacy to life." So the gods speak.

"Just by squirting?" X was truly perplexed. "But the baby develops inside the woman. Right?" she appended the question. Just in case.

"And *that* they alone confer legitimacy on life," Spike had been thinking, and had come up with a new insight, "might explain why they feel they have the right to take it so often, so capriciously."

"Yes!" Jane exclaimed. "That, coupled with the gross underestimation of what's involved in its creation, as indicated by the phrase 'in trouble'! If men were the ones to be pregnant, maybe they wouldn't ..." she trailed off. Because they so capriciously blew up all sorts of things they themselves had with great effort made.

X stared at— Nope. She just stared.

10

Next morning, they carried on to Boston. Specifically to MIT or Harvard. And, of course, the all-you-can-eat chocolate buffet. Probably not in that order.

"So what'll it be, MIT or Harvard?" Spike asked as they approached the city. But not feeling particularly optimistic about either of them. Which is why they decided on the chocolate for 'after'.

"I think MIT. Aren't they more specialized in the sciences? Harvard makes me think law, politics, business."

"MIT it is. Got directions?"

"On it." Jane busied herself at her laptop.

"The guys at MIT are gonna love her," Spike said, remembering X's response to Hawking's book.

X adjusted the pail she was wearing.

They slowed as they drove along the river, looking at the interesting architecture of the campus. Eventually, Jane saw an information kiosk in the middle of a pedestrian-only square off to their right. Spike turned, and turned again, but they couldn't seem to get any closer to it. And there didn't seem to be anywhere to park.

Spike turned to X. "Can we just drop you off? We'll circle around and—"

"There's probably a map on the kiosk," Jane said, "so you just need to figure out where the Astronomy building is. Or Physics. Or whatever."

"Then I find someone and ask for Earl's coordinates?" X asked. It came out muffled.

"More or less," Spike shrugged, than looked over at Jane. "We wouldn't know what else to do—"

"Except you should ask for *Earth's* coordinates."

"Just explain who—no, wait," Spike corrected, "don't say who you are or where you're from."

"Right. They'd never believe you."

Actually, they might. If she left the pail on.

They thought for a moment, then Spike turned to Jane. "We can't let her go by herself."

"But by the time we find somewhere to park—"

"So we go to the chocolate buffet first."

"But it's all-you-can-eat!"

"So we do this tomorrow."

"That works."

Half an hour later, they entered Chantal's restaurant. Their awed silence suggested they had entered a place of worship. Which of course they had.

"Oh wow," Jane said.

"I had no idea," Spike said.

X just grinned.

There were almost a dozen artfully presented sections around the perimeter of the room, each presenting a different category of chocolate, and, in the center, a huge display of chocolatey desserts. Yes, there was soft music, there were interesting paintings on the walls, and there were comfortable chairs set at larger-than-expected tables. But there were almost a dozen sections around the perimeter of the room, each presenting a different category of chocolate, and, in the center, a huge display of chocolatey desserts.

They paid at the cashier, hung their jackets at one of the tables, then went back to the entrance. They each took an empty tray and assorted cutlery, and then approached the first section. It was marked "Chocolate Covered". There were chocolate covered raisins, chocolate covered peanuts, chocolate covered cashews, chocolate covered almonds—

"Chocolate covered pecans!" Jane exclaimed. "I said years ago, they should have these at the bulk store!" She took one of the little dishes, conveniently nearby, and filled it with chocolate covered pecans.

"Do you see any chocolate covered cranberries?"

Spike scanned the table, then pointed.

"Yeah, no, I don't mean like chocolate covered raisins, I mean like cherry chocolates. You know, like in a box of chocolates? With the syrup and everything?"

Spike continued to scan the table. "There!" She pointed again. They were between the chocolate covered section and the truffles section.

Jane took one and popped it into her mouth. She moaned.

"Laura Secord has *got* to make these." She took several more and added them to her chocolate covered pecans. Her little dish runneth over. Already.

Spike took a few chocolate covered cashews, several different truffles, then moved on a little.

X trailed behind. She'd opted for the one of each method. And the eat-as-you-go method.

"Oh."

"What?" Jane mumbled, because her mouth was full.

"Chocolate covered chocolate chip cookies. Still warm."

"No."

"Yes."

They each took several, Jane choosing the soft, Spike, the chewy, and X, the crispy.

The fondue section was next.

"I've never really been a fondue person," Spike said.

"Me neither," Jane said. "Still, we have to try something ..." She speared a mandarin orange slice, then, after considering all her options, dipped it into a pot marked 'Coconut Chocolate'. Spike waited, eyebrows raised. "I could *become* a fondue person," Jane announced.

They moved on to the ice cream section. Jane scanned her almost-full tray.

"Let's come back and do this one last."

"Agreed."

"Though we could get a milkshake now," Jane changed her mind, seeing that X had discovered the make-it-yourself milkshake machine.

X made herself a chocolate chili shake. She did a little dance while her milkshake was shaking. At least they thought that's what it was. Jane mixed a cherry chocolate cream milkshake and Spike went with a chocolate cheesecake shake.

The fudge section was next.

"No surprises here," Spike said, scanning the selection.

Jane had already taken a chunk and popped it into her mouth.

"Except that it's quite possibly the best fudge I've ever tasted. Try the chocolate mint one."

Spike took a chunk, tried it, took another, then moved on.

To the hot chocolate section. Empty cup in hand, she looked at the labeled array of insulated pitchers, then chose the nutmeg hot chocolate.

"Oh, Jane, you've got to try this," she said after just a moment. "It tastes like pure table cream. With melted semi-sweet chocolate."

Jane took a sip from her cup.

"Oh wow. That's *exactly* what it tastes like." She poured a cup of cinnamon hot chocolate.

"Hot chocolate!" X merrily cried out, pointing to the *next* section. Jane and Spike looked on with amazement as X took an empty cup from the stack and reached for the ladle sitting in a vat of melted chocolate.

"Oh   my   god."

An exquisite hour later, Spike nodded to the center of the room. "Are we ready for dessert?" In context, the word lost definition. Besides which, Jane was *always* ready for dessert.

The three of them started circling the island, with newly empty trays. Almost immediately Jane saw the vat of chocolate cake batter, and beside it, a vat of chocolate frosting. She filled a little dish of each. "I've always said this is the way chocolate cake should be eaten!" she grinned.

They circled and circled, each time adding something incredibly decadent to their trays. Chocolate Walnut Torte. Ten-layer Chocolate Butter Truffle Cake. Chocolate Cherry Fudge Pots with Whipped Cream, Coconut, Walnuts, and Marshmallow Cream. Once their trays were full, they headed back to their table.

"We have to go soon," Spike licked her spoon. Another exquisite hour had passed. "They close the chocolate bar for dinner."

"No!" Jane cried. "I'm not done!"

She looked at her still/again full tray, glanced around anxiously, then flagged down a passing waitress.

"Excuse me, can you pack this to go?"

"I'm sorry, we can't do that for the buffet." She turned to leave before Jane could grab her arm.

"But I can't possibly finish it all by— When do we have to go?"

"Well, now," Spike said, looking at her watch, and standing. She gently pulled Jane to her feet.

"No!" She started to shovel in the chocolate.

X followed suit.

"Brownieth!" Jane mumbled with alarm. "We haven't found the brownieth yet!" She turned to X for help. "Go find the brownieth!"

X found the brownies. They were very good.

"Jane, we have to go."

She ignored her.

"Jane— Step away from the chocolate."

She had started to wrap some of her desserts in napkins, but most of them were deliciously gooey. Just as she was about to put the mess into her pocket anyway, Spike tugged her from the table.

"Juth a minute—" She was chewing vigorously.

She started to wrestle Jane to the door. "We'll come back."

"But it'th only on Mondayth."

"I meant we'll come back another Monday."

"No we won't," she swallowed. "We can't," she took a bite of whatever was in her left hand. Added a bite of whatever was in her right hand. "We're in Bothton."

"We'll move here."

That possibility stopped her.

"Yeah? Promith?"

They were at the door.

"Why not?" Spike replied. "We should be able to not get a good job here just as easily as in Toronto."

"I thtill think they should have let uth taken a doggy bag," Jane grumbled from the passenger seat, her mouth still full. She stared helplessly at her seat belt. Her hands were also still full.

Spike leaned over to strap her in, then checked to make sure X was with them. "Doggies can't have chocolate."

She swallowed. "You know what I mean. No reason they couldn't offer take-out. For a price, of course."

"You would've paid," Spike agreed as she started the car then eased out of the parking lot.

"I *would've* paid. Anything."

She took another bite of what was in her left hand. Then a bite of what was in— "THTOP! We didn't *thay* that! We didn't ask if they *thold* the thuff! *Ath* take-out!"

Half an hour later, Jane triumphantly set three large bakery boxes into the trunk of her car. No matter that she'd spent more than— Actually, she refused to do the math. She was just so very glad they took credit cards. Spike set two additional boxes into the remaining space. It was a small trunk. But it was now a trunk full of chocolate.

X got into the back seat. With three more boxes.

Jane hadn't googled a hotel for the night. Which was just as well, because now they had to make sure it had a large fridge in the room. So they sat in the car, while Spike found something nearby. Because both of Jane's hands were otherwise occupied.

An officious young man dressed in a suit looked up pleasantly as they entered the hotel office to check in.

"Good evening, Ms.—"

"No," Spike said. Sighed. She reached into her pocket and gave her phone to Jane, who, after quickly wiping her hands, started recording.

"I beg your pardon?" The man looked nervously at Jane.

"Don't call me 'Ms.'"

"I assure you I was only trying to be polite."

"Polite? Seriously? What does 'Ms.' mean?"

He didn't get what she was after.

"'Mr.' and 'Ms.'," Spike explained, "mean 'male person' and 'female person'. Or 'penis-person' and 'uterus-person'. How is it polite to refer to someone by their sexual anatomy?"

The man had no answer.

"Furthermore, why should what sex I am be part of my name? A mandatory prefix, no less!"

He'd never thought about it.

"Especially when it's so very unimportant. I mean, *I* don't define myself by my uterus." She turned to Jane. "Do you?"

"Never."

She turned to X. Never mind.

"So, Mr.—or should I say *Dick*head—" she looked at the nameplate on the counter, "Davis—"

"Yes, how can I help you?" He hadn't gotten angry. Incredible patience or incredible stupidity?

"A room for the night, please."

"One with a large refrigerator."

"Certainly. If you'll just fill this out."

He presented a clipboard, on which there was a registration form.

"So, Dickhead Davis," Spike switched to buddy mode, and started filling out the form, "your boss make you wear a suit and tie?"

"No," he replied, smiling, "it's my own idea. I find people give me a little more respect when I wear it. It gives me authority."

"Oh yeah? Think it'd work for me? If I wore a tie? I'd like a little more respect. And authority."

The man laughed. Good-naturedly. Okay, stupidity it was.

And they both hated stupidity. So did X, probably, given her earlier comment about the brain she was using.

Spike passed the completed registration form to him, along with her credit card. Jane's was probably maxed out. And anyway, it was her turn. He processed the payment, then gave her the receipt, along with the room key card. Then he came out from behind the counter, walked to a display of brochures beside the counter, and started picking out a few. Spike met him there and reached out to grab his tie. He was so surprised, he didn't resist. Jane grinned. She knew what was coming.

"Take you long to do these knots?"

"Yes?"

"They tighten, don't they."

Quick as a flash, she had him noosed against the wall, having used the heavy-duty stapler that had been sitting on the counter. Which Jane had helpfully put it into her outstretched hand.

"You know, it's the damn suit," Spike said as, two bakery boxes in hand and knapsack slung over her shoulder, she negotiated the door to the staircase. "That makes people ... give way," she clarified. Years ago, she'd noticed that as soon as her brother had started wearing a suit coat and carrying an attaché case, everyone suddenly thought he was— Well, not the person he'd been just the day before. Suddenly he was perceived as a mature, responsible adult.

"I know," Jane's two bakery boxes were more difficult to manage with her laptop and travel bag. But not as difficult as deciding which chocolate bits and pieces to bring into the room and which to leave in the car.

"Did you know that suit coats have padded shoulders?" she called back to Jane. "Makes 'em look broad-shouldered. Subliminal suggestion."

"Surely it's more complicated than that."

"I don't think so. If business wore a dress ..."

She'd seen it happen again and again. Boys taunted girls, she began a mental list as she made her way up the stairs, and did cruel things to animals. They were rude, forever demanding to be the center of attention, and they kept getting into fights with each other. In high school, they became socially awkward, struggled with the material, and developed a fascination with sports. In university, they used pick-up lines and other lies to impregnate women, seemingly unaware of the magnitude of consequences. In the lecture hall, they were always so full of self-importance, so full of themselves, despite getting consistently lower grades. So how is it, one had to ask, that they become our supervisors, our MPs, our CEOs? Why do we think they suddenly become worthy of that power, that responsibility? When do we think that magical metamorphosis happens?

When they put on a suit. It's like a magic coat.

"You mean if women dominated business?" Jane trailed. That would be interesting, she thought. As it was, business was so *very* male. The obsession with competition, hierarchy, rank, power over. What would happen if, instead, business consisted of a network of co-operative ventures, each seeking to better the whole? And the obsession with size. The mergers, the acquisitions. They're always talking about new opportunities for growth. They never talk about cancer.

And, she carefully turned on the landing and started up the next set of stairs, whenever a man introduces the matter of morality, questioning, for example, whether it's right to do whatever it is that's about to be done, he's accused of 'going soft', as if ethics is for women. Or he's accused of being a 'boy scout', as if ethics is for children. Ethics presumes caring, and real men don't care. Qualification: they care only about their status, their position in the scheme of things. And because their sons are extensions of themselves, they care about them, *their* position in the scheme of things. But caring about strangers? Strangers are other; the other is the competition. Ethics is something for priests to worry about and we all know priests aren't real men. They're celibate for god's sake.

"No, I mean literally," Spike said as she reached the fifth floor. And waited for Jane. It was Jane who'd insisted on taking the stairs. As if a few flights of stairs would compensate for her chocolate binge. "If men started wearing dresses, and high heels, and make-up, their authority would disappear. Because who could take them seriously then?"

Jane thought about that. She had to admit that she had trouble taking a woman seriously if she was wearing make-up. It was like trying to take a clown seriously. Ditto for wearing a dress and high heels. 'See my legs? See my painted toenails?' It was such a mixed message. 'I want you to know I'm sexually attractive while I talk about social justice.'

"But wouldn't dresses, and high heels, and make-up just become the attire of authority then?" That had happened again and again in history. As soon as men did something, the something became important. "Men used to wear dresses. The pope still does."

Spike considered that as she leaned against the heavy door to hold it open. "Yeah," she finally said, sighing, "and if they were shorter than us, suddenly small would be compact and efficient. And big would be sloppy and ungainly."

"And having someone look down on you would be a good thing."

"X?" Spike called out down the stair well.

"Coming!" She was walking up the stairs backwards. Who knew why.

Jane put two of the four bakery boxes into the fridge, because it was, of course, a small fridge, carefully set the other two boxes onto the narrow table along the wall, set her laptop onto one of the beds, then headed for the bathroom with her travel bag. Spike found the delivery menus. X found the chair in the corner.

Half an hour later, they were happily munching on double cheese, mushrooms, pineapple, olives, and sun-dried tomatoes. Spike flipped on the tv.

"Why is he so angry?" X asked, a few minutes later. "All she said was 'no'. It's not as if his thing will shrivel up and fall off. Will it?" Given that the bit of Y chromosome had fallen off, she thought it a reasonable question.

They grinned. But it was a good question. Why *does* that 'no' make men so angry?

"They're infants," Jane suggested. "They think they're being denied something they're entitled to. So it's the anger of an injustice."

"But there's *a lot* of injustice they don't get at all angry about."

"True. Okay, so maybe their anger is instinctive, pre-programmed by that damned selfish gene. The one that insists on replication. No that can't be right," she reconsidered, "because they have sex even when they're HIV positive. Which defeats the instinct."

"Just another way they'll kill to have sex," Spike muttered.

So instinct is irrational, Jane didn't have to articulate the obvious conclusion. Okay, no surprise there. Despite what the evolutionary theorists might have us believe about natural selection and survival value.

Spike changed the channel. A woman expressed her all-consuming desire for longer lashes. An impossibly perfect-bodied woman. In terms of fuckability. Spike wondered when women were going to start amputating their legs.[37]

She started surfing, then stopped at a rerun of *Grey's Anatomy*.

"None of the women wear dresses in *Grey's Anatomy*," Jane observed. She liked *Grey's Anatomy*. "And so many main characters, surgeons every one of them, are women. Actually the women outnumber the men."

"And yet, Owen gets the position of Chief. Richard, then Derek, then Owen."

"You're right," Jane sighed. "And Bailey's been there longer than him."

"And Sam gets to be team leader in Ed's absence," Spike recalled a *Flashpoint* episode. "Not Jules. Even though, like Bailey, she has more seniority. And is just as competent. More so. She can shoot *and* she can negotiate a crisis."

"Yeah." Jane took another bite of her pizza. "It doesn't help that she's black," she added. "Bailey. And short."

Spike nodded.

X got another slice of pizza. Without falling down. She'd given up on their conversation after— Well, honestly, she hadn't even tried to follow. Her brain was still a bit chocolate-soaked.

"Hey, did you see that documentary about men who get leg lengthening surgery?" she asked then.

Spike shook her head.

"It's very painful. What they do is break the legs, then set them a bit apart, forcing the bones and tendons to heal a bit longer. Then they do it again. And again. If they're very lucky, they can gain three inches."

"That's insane."

Jane nodded. "When one of the men was asked why he chose to undergo such a drastic and excruciatingly painful procedure, he said something like 'Do you have any idea what it's like to go through life as a short person? To not be able to reach stuff on the

---

37 http://www.generationterrorists.com/boston-legal/107.html

upper shelves in grocery stores? To not be able to drive trucks because you can't reach the pedals properly? To sit in a chair and not be able to put your feet flat on the floor? To have people always looking down at you? Do you know what that's like?'"

"Um, yeah."

"Oh but that's different," Jane grinned. "We're *supposed to* go through life inconvenienced. Feeling subordinate."

"Which is the *real* problem. The *real* reason these guys get the surgery is so they can take their rightful place *over women*."

Jane nodded. "The man actually said, 'I'll be a better father and husband.'"

"Yup. Sure you will," Spike muttered. And started on a second slice of pizza.

When a commercial came on, she started surfing again.

And stopped at a rerun of *Flashpoint*. What were the odds? Ed was questioning Greg's suitability as team commander. 'Should I get you a dress?' he said, and they both laughed.

Jane and Spike stopped in mid-bite and stared at each other.

Spike turned off the tv.

"Okay, that was freaky," Jane said.

"And they *laughed*. Did you notice that?" Spike was livid. "They both frickin' laughed."

"I think it's also because business has this 'social good' thing going for it," Jane said a short while later, as she helped herself to one of the lovely bakery boxes. Apparently not done with their earlier discussion. Or their chocolate.

Unlike X. Who seemed ... asleep? In the chair. Mostly.

"Business is good for the economy," she continued. "It creates jobs. It provides us with much needed goods and services."

"Right," Spike muttered, also taking something delectable from the box. "Business 'provides' jobs the way people 'provide' labour. It's an economic exchange! And those goods and services? They don't exactly *provide* them either; they *sell* them."

"I know that, and you know that," Jane settled back onto the bed, "I'm just sayin'—"

"You know, men say women take everything personally," Spike continued, back on the other bed, "and dismiss them because of it, but they do the same thing. What are 'vested interests' but *personal* interests?"

"You're right," Jane turned to her. "I've never thought of that before ..."

"If people object to a change in zoning bylaws that will probably lead to more traffic because said increase in traffic will destroy the peace and quiet of their neighbourhood, they're just expressing their own personal interests. Okay. But when the guy who runs the gas station says the change should be approved because it'll be good for business—*his* business—he's *also* just expressing his own personal interests. So why should his opinion, his desires, his *interests* count more?"

"Because he has all that *money* invested in his business? And money talks?"

"Okay, so he spent a lot of money expecting a certain future," Spike conceded. "But so did all the people who live there! When they bought their houses, enrolled their kids in school ..."

Jane nodded. Spike was absolutely right.

"It sounds so respectable, doesn't it?" Jane observed. "'Vested interest,'" she rolled it around on her tongue as she looked out the passenger window. "It brings to mind a three-piece suit with a watch on a chain."

"Instead of a red-faced infant with drool on its bib."

"You know," Jane said, a few moments later, a few lovely bites later, "that's why men are so good at politics and government."

Spike gave her a look. "Have you looked *around* lately?"

"Yes, no, I mean— Remember when you thought about becoming the Green Party rep?"

"Yeah ..."

"And you changed your mind because you realized you didn't know anything about being a party rep, let alone being a member of parliament? You realized you were completely unqualified—"

"Never stopped any man," Spike muttered. "Remember that journalism study?[38] Men always consent to be interviewed, whereas women often decline, saying they're not authorities on the subject."

"Yeah ..."

"Every man thinks he's an authority on the subject."

"True, but my point—" she paused. She'd momentarily forgotten her point. It had gotten mixed up with Spike's point. Oh yeah. "My point is that they're so good at politics and government—and maybe *everything*—" Oh. Wow. New point. No, just bigger point.

Spike glanced over, still waiting to hear her point.

"Because it's *all* just personal!" Nailed it. "Politics and government and *everything* is just vested interests and scratching each other's back to meet those interests. And *men can do that!*"

"Ah."

"If anything had anything to do with principles, with justice, or good, or right, they'd be lost, hopelessly incompetent."

"And you know, because you taught all that stuff—principles, justice, the good, and the right—to business students." In addition to Critical Thinking, Jane had taught Business Ethics. "And they all failed."

"Yes. They did." Jane allowed herself a grin, then continued. "They're not very good with abstract thought. Though I imagine *most* adult men can't define 'good' or 'right' any better than a ten-year-old."

"To be fair, neither can most adult women."

"True, but they're not the ones making decisions for the planet."

Spike conceded that point.

"But my point," Jane circled back, "is that they *are* good at getting what they want. Which is, usually, just money. Or status."

---

38 http://www.informedopinions.org/why-women-decline-interviews-and-how-were-trying-to-change-that/

"Life is so much easier when you don't worry about ethics," Spike agreed. "Or truth."

"And when the shit hits the fan, they're good at covering their asses because they're so good at bullshitting."

Spike nodded.

"And hiring decisions!" Something else fell into place for Jane. "It's easy! Just hire someone you know! Deciding which of a hundred applicants is the *best*? *They* can't do that!" she scoffed.

"That's why merit isn't rewarded in the workplace."

"It isn't even *recognized*!" Jane looked at her as *that* piece fell into place. "They can't *tell* when A is better than B.

"Because," she explained, "it's the C students who major in Business."

"And *that's* why men get *ahead*," Jane still wasn't done. "*That's* why they're promoted into positions of power and authority. I used to think it was because— I used to think it *wasn't* because women competed and lost, it was because they didn't compete at all. Men, on the other hand, have been competing since birth. They see everything in terms of competition, in terms of win/lose. Every action, every gesture, every word is measured in terms of 'Does it put me one up or one down?'"

Spike nodded.

"In fact, men are genetically predisposed to hierarchy: fetal masculinization of the central nervous system renders males more sensitive to the dominance-related properties of testosterone. Steven Goldberg. *Why Men Rule*. They can't help themselves. They have to play King of the Castle.

"But women don't think that way. In fact, since infancy, *we've* been *co-operating*. We see everything in terms of helping others. 'How does it affect my status?' simply isn't a question we ever ask."

"Because women are exempt from status ranking. To put it bluntly, we don't count."

"So even if we *did* compete, we wouldn't stand a chance. Not against men who've been doing it since birth.

"But," Jane continued, "if merit isn't even *recognized*, then getting ahead can't possibly be about being the best person for the job, the most qualified, the most experienced at what the job requires. It can't *be* about competing. So it's not that women lose or don't even—"

"It's about who you know," Spike was right there. "Who you can bullshit to get what you want."

"And women can't know who they need to know. Because who they need to know is a man. And women can't know men that way."

"There's only one way a woman is allowed to know a man."

"*And* they've been *bullshitting* from birth." Would never *be* done. "That's the *way* they compete with each other: they fake it, they exaggerate, they cover up.

"They even see dating in those terms. They try so hard to 'say the right thing'. Which is defined as whatever will get them what they want. Which, in that case, is sexual access. They don't want to get to know the other person. They don't want to just enjoy being with the other person. They want to score, they want to win. So, yeah, say whatever you have to say, do whatever you have to do.

"And if you accuse them of insincerity, of lying, maybe even of manipulating, they get such a blank look on their face. They've been bullshitting so much for so long, *they believe their own bullshit.* They don't even *know* it's bullshit."

A moment passed. Which was long enough.

"That's why they're so *convincing* when they're lying about themselves, their skills, their accomplishments. They *themselves* are convinced. They really believe they're that good. After all, they've been saying so all their lives."

A few seconds later, Spike spoke. "Your cv is just a plain statement of your experience and abilities, isn't it."

Jane nodded. Because her mouth was full.

"A man's cv would include a bunch of bullshit about said experience and abilities."

Jane's eyes widened. They'd been *lying*— Even on paper? While she'd been naively telling the truth?

"It's expected."

"What?" No. But yes. Of course.

"That's the way the system is set up. By them. *For* them.

"A man's cv would also include," Spike continued, "a proposal for how to improve the university, or at least the department, based on research of the university's strengths and weaknesses."

"I wouldn't *presume!*"

"Exactly. And men presume all the time. To know better. To give their unsolicited opinion. Their unsolicited advice. And so by comparison ..."

"I look uninterested, unenthusiastic, uncaring ... But if they—the university, the company, whatever—if they wanted that, they should've asked!"

"See, right there. That's the difference. Women wait to be asked."

That stopped them both. Not because it indicated women's passivity. Or, not just— Asking implied that consent was important. So the fact that men *didn't* wait to be asked ...

"But it's more than that," Spike continued after a moment. "Men just ... know. It's common knowledge in their peer network." By any other name.

Jane sighed. If she'd known—

"It wouldn't've mattered," Spike knew what she was thinking. "Those unwritten rules you know nothing about are for men only. If *you'd* included a proposal for how to improve the university, you *would've* been considered presumptuous."

Jane considered that, then nodded. So her life—well, at least her employment history—*wouldn't've* been different. Had she known.

"And as for *keeping* those positions of power and authority," Jane picked up the thread, admittedly without her earlier enthusiasm, "they're masters of telling others to do their work for them. Women get so much less done because they do their *own* work."

"We don't delegate," Spike agreed.

"Because we're the ones work has always been delegated to. And we know it feels like shit. To do someone else's work."

"Quite apart from the fact that we probably don't even *apply* for half the positions men do," Jane said a moment later. With no enthusiasm at all. "Not just because we think we're unqualified, but also because men see the power of the position. Women see the responsibility. And so decline."

"Besides which," Spike pointed out, "if they have kids, they already have enough responsibility." Then added, "Funny how that doesn't apply to men."

"Hm."

"I thought it was the B students who major in Business," Spike had circled back.

"No, the B students major in the Humanities and the Sciences."

"Then what do the A students major in?"

"Whatever they want. But they're girls. So once they graduate, they disappear. Just like Dale Spender[39] said. Decades ago."

---

39 in *Women of Ideas and What Men Have Done to Them.*

11

Okay, so let's try this again," Spike said the following morning. They were sitting in a no-parking zone in front of an administrative building, four-way flashers flashing.

"We'll let you out here," she said to X. "Go inside, ask for directions to wherever you need to go—"

"Ask for directions to the Astrophysics building—" Jane had done some googling.

"Yeah, that's good, then find a professor and—"

"Just say you'd like to know the space-time coordinates of Earth. Say you're doing a research paper or something," Jane suggested.

Spike nodded. "In the meantime, we'll find a place to park, or just keep driving around, and meet you back here at," she looked her watch, "eleven."

"Can you tell time?" Jane thought to add, as Spike took off her watch and gave it to X. "Our time?"

"Yes." X looked at the watch. "Eleven is when both hands are on the eleven." Duh.

"No," Jane said, "it's when the little hand is on the eleven and the big hand is on the twelve."

"It would make more sense the way she said it."

"Yeah. It would even make more sense if the *big* hand were on the eleven."

When they finally got back to the front of the administrative building, having gotten hopelessly lost on the way from the parking lot they'd found, X wasn't there.

"What time is it?" Spike asked.

Jane looked at her watch. She wouldn't say.

"Is the little hand past eleven?"

"The little hand is past twelve."

"Oh. Do you think she was here and then left?"

"*Left* left? I hope not." Jane realized it was true as soon as she said it. There were so many questions she hadn't yet gotten around to asking. Couldn't say why, really.

"Let's walk around a bit. Maybe we'll see her."

They headed toward the largest cluster of buildings. Went completely around it. They crossed a grassy area and headed toward and then around another cluster of buildings. As they rounded the second corner, they saw what looked like a small riot in the distance. Intrigued, and fearing the implausible, they approached. As they did so, it became apparent that there were two factions fighting each other. They could see dramatic gesticulation. They could hear inventive name-calling. Even from the side that was in full clerical dress.

"What the—"

X emerged from the fray, walking quickly.

"Hey!" Jane called out. "X!"

X heard Jane's voice, looked around, then saw them. She broke into a run, tripped and went sprawling. She got up and resumed walking, quickly, with great restraint, and even greater concentration.

"What happened?" Spike asked.

"I tripped!"

"No, I meant what's that all about?" She nodded to the riot.

"Oh. I couldn't find Astrophysics. But I found Psychology. Then I found Theology. You people are— I thought if the theology people met the psychology people, a lot of their questions would be ... not answered, but ... dissolved. So I arranged a meeting. A faculty meeting. But I didn't know so many of them would be—"

"That's not a faculty meeting."

The theologians were lobbing white lab rats at the psychol-ogists. The psychologists were prostrating themselves, wagging their bare asses at the theologians.

Jane disagreed. "It sort of *looks* like a faculty meeting ..."

"Remember Milgram?" Spike asked Jane as they watched. Finding it surprising, and intriguing, but mostly entertaining.

"Of course. 65% of the participants—all of them men—turned a knob to electroshock a stranger whose agony was in plain sight."

"There was a similar study done with monkeys," Spike said. "13%."

Jane turned to her. She hadn't heard about the second study.

"So I'm just wondering where on the evolutionary scale ..."

"But you're assuming that willingness to hurt others without good reason is an indicator of less evolved species," Jane said. "I don't think bugs and worms—"

"Well it certainly isn't an indicator of a more evolved species."

"Agreed."

"It's an indicator of mental illness."

Been there.

"Okay, so we're still looking for Astrophysics?" They'd found a kiosk.

"Yeah. Or Astronomy or Physics ..."

They scanned the map for a few moments.

"'Earth, Atmospheric, and Planetary Sciences'," Jane read out. "That sounds promising."

"And it's ... ?" Spike glanced at the map, then looked around at the buildings. Uniformly grey and rectangular.

"Here," Jane grinned, pointing to the map.

"Ha ha."

X peered at the map. "I saw that building before, but it's not where we are."

Jane looked at her for a full minute, opening her mouth twice to say something, then deciding not to. The first thing was 'No shit, Sherlock.' The second was 'There must be significant differences in our conceptual understanding of time and space that preclude a meeting of the minds." It was the thought of appending "Literally" that made her close her mouth.

"No, but we can get there," Spike said.

"Really?" X was excited. "How?"

Jane knew then why she hadn't yet asked all the questions she'd wanted to.

Spike studied the map again, got herself oriented, then pointed off to the right. "It's over there, I think."

"I wonder why they don't make coloured concrete," Jane murmured.

"Because men are afraid of colour."

X stared at Spike with disbelief. Then confusion. Because if that were true ...

A few minutes later, they entered the Planetary Sciences building and approached the first open office. It was a general office, staffed by a receptionist.

"Hi," Jane said. "We're looking for someone—a professor—"

"Name?"

"We don't have anyone in particular in mind. We're looking for someone who knows about the space-time continuum."

"That'd be Physics."

"Oh. Okay, thanks. And that's ..."

"Out, left, third building on your right. Across the concourse."

"Got it, thanks."

They left.

They entered the Physics building and again approach the first staffed office.

"Hi," Jane said, "can you direct us to the office of any professor who knows about the space-time continuum?"

A harried clerk peered through the piles of reports and books sitting on her desk, ran her fingers through her hair, then said, "That'd be Planetary Sciences."

"We just came from there," Spike said. "They sent us here."

The woman looked pointedly at her desk, and then at the many bursting archive boxes stacked haphazardly on the floor. "I assure you, no one here knows about space or time."

"Hi again," Jane said to the Planetary Sciences receptionist, a little frustration in her voice. "Physics says our question is Planetary Sciences."

"What was your question about again?"

"The space-time continuum." A little more frustration.

"Hm. Try Philosophy. Metaphysics."

"No," Jane put her foot down. Metaphorically. "We are *not* going to Philosophy." Both feet actually. Dug them in good.

"Why not?" X asked.

"Because Philosophy is useless. Half of Philosophy is just infant science, and half of it is just infant psychology. And as for what's left ..."

"Which is clearly not math—" Spike grinned.

"What's left?" X asked.

"Ethics. And no one's interested in doing the right thing," Jane said. "And Epistemology. But no one cares about *knowing*, it's much easier to just *believe*. You don't have to *justify* faith. With stuff like, oh, I don't know ... *evidence*!"

"So don't go to Philosophy." The receptionist didn't really care.

"I was appalled when the term 'evidence-based' found its way into our vocabulary," Jane continued as Spike tugged her away from the receptionist's desk. "On what else would one base knowledge claims and policy recommendations? Wishes, dreams, and sugar plums?"

"Let's just walk around," Spike suggested once Jane had completed her commentary about the many deficiencies of human rationality, "and see who's home."

They wandered through the building, looking at nameplates and open doors, peering in to see if anyone was sitting at a desk. At the fourth office, on the second floor, Spike stopped.

"How about this guy?" She nodded through the half-open door.

"But he's a mutant!" X exclaimed.

"Yeah, well."

"They did invent the light bulb," Jane pointed out. Conceded. "And the printing press. CD players."

"Go figure."

"How?" X asked.

"What?"

"How do you want me to figure— What is it you want me to figure?"

"Never mind."

"Okay. So I should ask this ... moron?"

"Yeah," Spike said, grinning. "Go ahead. Make my day."

X stepped into the office. "I need to know Earl's coordinates on the space-time continuum."

Spike and Jane quickly walked in behind her.

"Excuse me, Professor Donaldson," Jane said, "we're sorry to bother you, but we were wondering—"

"We sort of have a bet going," Spike took over. "She doesn't think you know Earth's coordinates on the space-time continuum," she nodded to Jane, "and I think you do. And we're wondering if you could just settle the bet for us."

"Sorry to disappoint, ladies," he didn't even look up. Nor did he bother to say anything further.

"So what does that mean," Jane said, cutting off Spike's response to the insult. "You *don't* know?"

"It means I don't have time for this."

"So you *do* know?" she pressed.

"Let's say I don't," he smiled, charmingly, he thought, then went back to his work.

"The continuum!" X prompted, in disbelief. "Space? Time? Quantum mechanics? *Relativity?*" she added with some desperation.

Then, as he continued to ignore her, "Don't you know *any*thing?!" Okay that did it.

"Look here!" Professor Donaldson said, full of pompous anger.

"String theory!" X continued. "I read that you—some of you—think the universe has 11 dimensions. It's more like 11,*000*, but your theory might be enough—"

"I don't know who put you up to this," the professor had gotten up and was trying to shepherd them toward the door, "but I've got work to do."

"Did he just *dismiss* us?" Spike looked at Jane. Not moving toward the door.

"But I need to know—"

"No, you don't," the professor said. And actually pushed them out of his office. "When you can figure out Fermat's last theorem, maybe I'll have the time, but until then, thank you very much, good-bye ..." He closed the door behind them.

They left the building in silence, a silence full of rage and disappointment, but once they were back outside, Jane turned to X. "You said there are 11,000 dimensions instead of 11?"

She nodded.

"So, what, some genius got the decimal in the wrong place?" Spike laughed.

They started to walk back to the car. At least, that's what they hoped they were doing.

"What's Fermat's last theorem?" X asked.

"A sort of benchmark for genius," Jane replied. "Fermat was some brilliant mathematician who left a cryptic comment in the margin of his notes, saying he'd finally figured out the solution to some problem."

"But no one's been able to figure out what his solution was," Spike added.

"Actually, someone did," Jane recalled. "Oh my god, that wasn't *him*, was it?" She stopped, flipped open her phone, and googled. "Here it is. Solved by Andrew Wiles."

X looked at the screen.

"Yeah ... that works," she said after about half a minute. "But there's a much simpler solution."

It took a second, but then they both stared at her. "You figured out Fermat's last theorem?"

"No," she snorted. "We learned it in school. Of course, we don't call it Fermat's last theorem—"

"What grade?"

"Five."

"And how old are you in grade five?"

"Five." Duh.

"Can you write out the simpler solution?" Spike asked.

Jane provided pen and paper. Never leave home without. X obliged. Spike took the paper and marched back into the Planetary Sciences building, Jane right behind, X a little left of right behind, straight to Professor Donaldson's office. She didn't bother to knock. She just stomped into his office and slammed the paper onto his desk. He turned from putting a book back onto his bookshelf.

"What the—" He glanced at the paper. "My dear, this isn't the—" Then he sat down, as if all the air had been sucked out of him. Spike and X left. Jane lingered to see a bit more of his reaction, to see the *conclusive* evidence she'd been looking for since, well, since they'd met X. The gravity thing had almost convinced her, but that was an absence of critical knowledge. She'd been wanting to see—what she now saw. She left as well. A little a-tremble.

"But this *could*—oh my god—" He ran after them.

Understanding finally what had happened, X turned and gave him the finger.

"That come with the body too?" Spike asked.

"No, I learned it from the morons in Psychology. Or maybe the ones in Theology."

"Okay, so now what?" Spike asked, once they were back in the car.

"We try the university library," Jane said. "Surely it will have better, newer, books than any public library."

"But first," she opened the snack pack—the snack *box*—she'd insisted on bringing, "we have some chocolate."

They decided to go to the Harvard library instead of the MIT library. Because.

Besides, it was only seventeen minutes away, according to MapQuest.

"You ever notice that women pair with men a couple years older than themselves?" Jane asked lazily, looking at all the couples she saw in the first ten of seventeen minutes.

Spike nodded.

"I always thought— My mother told me that that was because women mature two years earlier, so dating and marrying a guy a couple years older would put you at the same maturity level."

Spike snorted.

"Yeah, that's what I'm thinking now."

"It's because the man being older maintains the illusion of the man being wiser," Spike said. "Same reason, essentially, for insisting he be taller."

"Yeah, but it's as much the woman who insists on that."

"It is indeed." She sighed.

A couple blocks later, Spike suddenly pulled over, got out, and reached under her seat for the roll of black duct tape that had been left there by MacGyver. Jane and X watched, Jane recording on her phone, as she walked up to the yellow school crossing sign, studied it for a moment, then put a skirt on the taller figure guiding the young girl.

12

An hour later, in the middle of the afternoon, they stood in the middle of the Harvard campus, trying to determine which building was the library.

"I say that one," Spike pointed.

"Looks good to me," Jane started walking toward it.

X followed.

They entered the building and approached the entrance turnstile. Spike went through first, but got stuck. Jane tried the turnstile next to her and also got stuck.

X hung back.

"You have to insert your student card," a library attendant at the desk on the other side called out.

"But we're not students," Jane said. "We don't want to borrow any books. We just want to—"

"Doesn't matter. Access to the stacks requires your student card."

"It also requires my tax money," Spike said. "And you've already got that."

The attendant ignored her.

"How about an alumni card from another university?" Jane asked, reaching for her wallet.

"Nope."

"Can we become community members or something? Apply for a guest pass just for the day?"

"Only current students and faculty of Harvard are allowed access to the library. Sorry."

"Can't we just become students of Harvard?" X asked, bewildered.

They both heard the attendant snort.

But only Spike gave him the finger.

"We really need to replace that gesture," Jane said on their way out.
"Yeah."

"So now what?" Jane asked as they stood some distance from the entrance. She was out of ideas.

"Now we improvise," Spike said, suddenly feeling in her element. "We haven't been temps for nothing."

"Right! There's got to be another entrance. The one that lowly office and cafeteria staff are supposed to use."

They started to circle the building.

X followed.

Around the second corner, they saw an unmarked door in the distance.

"What do you think?"

"I think it's worth a shot."

Spike walked up to it boldly and pulled on it. It was locked. She returned to Jane and X.

"Locked. Card key."

"Okay, so we wait for someone to come by—"

"—and we casually walk in as if we belong."

They waited. Eventually, they saw a man approach from afar; it looked like he was heading for the door in question. So Jane headed for the door as well. Spike waved good-bye to her in case the man had seen them standing there, then tugged X in the opposite direction. Jane rushed up just before the man opened the door.

"Hi," Jane said.

The man nodded coldly and started to get out his card key.

"I'm a temp? I'm supposed to report to Linda?"

"In the middle of the afternoon?" he was suspicious.

"Yeah, there's a reason I'm a temp," Jane said cheerily. Ambiguously.

"There is no Linda here."

He started to open the door.

"But I'm supposed to report to Linda."

"Are you sure you're at the right building? Didn't they give you a card key?"

"No, I think that's one of the things I'm supposed to see Linda about. This is the library, right?"

Jane tried to nudge her way in as he opened the door, but he nudged her out.

"Sorry, you really should call your temp agency again. They've given you the wrong instructions."

He entered the library and closed the door behind him. Jane returned to meet Spike and X, who had started to walk back.

"That didn't go so well."

They saw a woman approach the door.

"Let me try," Spike said and headed toward her, quickly.

"Hi, are you Marilyn?"

"Marilyn? No—"

"I'm from the temp agency. They said I should report here, I think, to Marilyn."

"They got us a temp? Hallelujah! We are *so* overloaded. I don't know a Marilyn, but come on in, Audrey will surely know."

Spike entered the building with the woman.

"Now what?" X asked Jane.

"I don't know. Let's wait here. Hopefully, she'll come back out and let us in."

They waited. Then shared the oversized chocolate brownie ball Jane had put in her bag.

They waited some more. While they shared the chocolate apricot mini cheesecake X had put in her pocket. Jane marveled that it had remained unsmooshed.

After about twenty minutes, the door opened and Spike poked her head out. She waved them over. Jane and X hurried to the door, then slipped inside.

Spike held a finger to her lips, then whispered, "The offices are right around the corner." She pointed to a nearby elevator. They quickly walked to it, pushed the 'up' button, and waited anxiously. The elevator doors opened and they got in.

"How are we going to find the stacks without being seen?" Jane asked. "Or stopped?"

The doors opened before Spike could answer. They got out, walked cautiously to a corner, peeked around, then pulled back quickly. They hurried back into the elevator.

"The place can't be that small that everyone knows everyone. We just have to look like we work here." They looked pointedly at X.

The doors opened again, and they got out again.

They walked down a hall, Jane and Spike nodding impersonally to a woman they passed.

"Hello! We work here!" X called out confidently.

They hustled her into the women's washroom. Which was, fortunately, close by.

"Don't say anything!"

"Just do as we do!"

"Well, no, not exactly as we do," Spike qualified, anticipating that X would mimic them exactly. "Just— Never mind."

When the coast was clear, they entered the hall again. They saw another elevator, its door open.

"Might as well," Jane said softly to the question implied by Spike's glance. "No stacks here."

At the next floor, the door opened and a woman got in.

"You look lost," she said pleasantly.

"Am I ever!" X said. "I took a—"

"Yes we are," Jane quickly interrupted. "We're trying to find the stacks. We're still in the library building, aren't we?"

"Yes, you are. But you're in the administrative wing."

"Ah."

"How the hell did we get here?" Spike asked Jane.

"Don't you remember?" X said. "We—"

"If you could just—" Jane suggested.

"The stacks are at the other end. You'll have to go down to the basement, through the tunnel, then take the elevator back up to level four. That'll take you to the main entrance."

"Thanks!"

The woman got out at the next floor. Spike pushed the button for the basement.

They got out of the elevator, found and walked through the tunnel, then got into another elevator. No problem.

Just as Spike was about to push the button for level four, Jane said, "Wait. We don't want to get out at the main entrance."

"Right. So we'll try ..." She pushed the button for level seven.

The elevator doors opened and they saw stacks. They gave a shout of victory and got out.

"Okay, now we need to find a computer, to access their catalogue."

Spike pointed and they walked toward the computer sitting on a high table at the end of one of the stacks. Jane started working at it, ignoring the sign that demanded she display her student card.

"Hurry," Spike said, seeing someone with a cart of books coming their way.

"Okay, physics books are QC. Astronomy is QB."

"That should do it?" Spike asked X.

X shrugged. She was beginning to understand less and less of what was going on. And she hadn't understood much to begin with.

Spike led them back to the elevator where there was a map on the wall.

"P to R is on the sixth floor."

They took the stairs down a floor, wandered through the stacks, looking for QC and QB. They paused at the end of an aisle near a window.

"This is nuts," Spike said. "The Ps jump to the Rs. Q is still between P and R, isn't it? How can a whole section be out?"

It suddenly dawned on Jane. "It's not out. We're in the wrong library."

Spike did a mental head slap. Well, it had been a while.

A group of three students, all young men, happened to pass by.

"Hey, can you guys tell us where the Science Library is?" Spike asked.

"Which one?" the tall, dark, and handsome one asked with disdain.

"Whichever one has physics and astronomy books," Jane said, ignoring the attitude. She'd gotten good at that. While teaching. Assholes like this.

Once their focus was on Jane, Spike walked around behind them.

"That'd be the Gordon McKay, wouldn't it?" the pudgy one asked.

The tall, dark, and handsome one shrugged, eager to move on. No fuckables here.

"Or maybe the math library?" the bespectacled one offered.

"They'd put math, physics, and astronomy all in the same library?" the pudgy one asked.

"Probably not, wait a minute ..." The bespectacled one pulled a book out of his knapsack and started flipping through. An orientation book! Jane wondered where he'd gotten it. "You want the Wolbach," he said after a few seconds. "It says here it's got astrophysics, that's what you're looking for, yeah?"

"Yeah," X said, "because I got lost and—"

"Yes," Jane said. "Wolbach. Okay, thanks."

"Any idea where it is?" Spike asked casually.

"Don't know, don't care," the tall, dark, and handsome one said, utterly bored. And already half way down the hall.

The bespectacled one consulted his book again, then looked out a nearby window. He pointed. "That way, I think."

"Okay, great. Thanks for your help."

As soon as the guys moved on, Spike went through the wallet she'd lifted and pulled out a student card. "Bingo!"

"Tell me that belongs to the asshole of the group."

"Indeed it does," she grinned, looking at the card. "James T. Asshole. Aka James T. Bleckh. Seriously. B-L-E-C-K-H."

They started to walk towards the stairs.

"Thing is," Spike said, "it's photo ID. And I don't think any of us look much like Bleckh." She vomited the word.

"Well," Jane replied, "no one's going to be standing at the door checking our ID, right? It's a library, not a pub."

So five minutes later, after a brief planning session, Jane entered the Wolbach library, swiped Bleckh's student card through the slot at the turnstile, and headed to the stacks, looking for QB or QC.

A few minutes later, she carried five heavy texts to a study carrel next to a window. She put the books down, then opened the window. She looked out. And saw nothing.

"Yoo-hoo!"

Nothing.

"Yoo-hoo!" She tried again.

Spike and X rounded the corner.

"Yoo-hoo? Seriously?"

Jane ignored her.

"First one coming down."

She dropped a book out the window. Spike picked it up and gave it to X.

"Anything in there?"

X flipped through the book, quickly, then slowly, then quickly ...

"Sort of."

"Got another one like it?" Spike called up.

Jane let another text drop out the window. It hit X. She crumpled to the ground.

"Geez, Jane, you've killed the alien again."

Spike attended to X, who, after a moment, recovered consciousness.

"Purple again?"

"Ecru. It was awful."

"But you're okay now?"

"Yes." She sat up then, and briefly flipped through the book that had knocked her out. She shook her head. They assumed that meant it wasn't helpful either.

"How about this one?" Jane dropped another book. But not until Spike had her arms out and ready.

"They're all too old," X said. "Doesn't the library have *current* books?"

Spike checked the publication date. "Actually, this *is* current."

"Oh."

"Well, the publication date might be current," Jane called down, "but— Gotta go!"

She ducked back inside quickly.

A library attendant walked toward Jane, who was suddenly paying great attention to her texts, totally engrossed in reading and making notes. The attendant gave her a suspicious look, then moved on. Jane waited a moment, then left.

Back outside, she turned the corner to see Spike looking up.

"Yoo-hoo," she grinned.

"We're not going to find what we need in there," she explained when she got to them. "By the time a book gets published, it's already five years old."

"Oh. Right." It had been *quite* a while.

"We need to look for journal articles instead of books."

"But journal articles take a while to get into print too."

"Good point. Okay, so how about pre-prints?"

"Worth a try."

They sat down right where they were, backs against the wall, and Jane went to work on her laptop.

"Ah." Then a moment later. "Of course."

"Got one?"

"No. 'Access is restricted to current students and faculty.'"

"But—"

"Right! Hang on," she pulled Bleckh's card from her pocket. Entered the student number.

"Ah. Of course."

"He's a business student," Spike anticipated the problem.

Jane nodded. With access only to the *Business* library.

"Okay, let's think this through," Jane said, spooning something lovely into her mouth. The three of them had gone back to the car and were now having a late afternoon chocolate picnic on a grassy field somewhere on the Harvard campus.

"How do you get a student card? You apply to a university, get accepted, show up, register at the Registrar's office. Then you go to Finance, pay your tuition, and they give you a receipt. Then you go to AV to have your picture taken, then a couple days later you go back and pick up your card. Happen that way at your university?"

"Pretty much. Though I think our cards were mailed to us. Or made while we waited. I don't remember going back to AV. But," she added, "there's a lot I don't remember ..."

"Okay, so we need to intercept at the Registrar's—"

"No, at Finance— We don't want to have to pay tuition."

"Right. Like we could anyway. Here."

The busied themselves with chocolate.

"Okay, where were we?"

"We intercept at Finance—"

"Right, we get three receipts marked paid, for female students, then just walk on over to AV."

"Or," Spike had an idea, "we go to AV and say we're from Finance and need to pull a few cards for students whose cheques have bounced."

"That's good. That'd be quicker. Probably boxes full of cards waiting to be picked up by students."

Spike looked at her watch. "So we try that now and if it doesn't work, you'll be a temp for Finance first thing tomorrow morning?"

"Why me?"

"You look more office-y."

Half an hour later, close to what they thought would be closing time, which they thought would work in their favour, Jane walked into the Harvard AV Department with a piece of paper in hand.

"Hi, I'm from Finance?" she said to the man behind the counter. "They sent me over to pull cards? For students whose cheques have bounced?"

"Sure, let me see."

Just as he reached out for the bogus list, Spike and X bounced in.

"Hi, is this where we come to get our pictures taken for our student cards?" She and X crowded the man. "'Cuz they told us over at Registrar's—"

"Yeah, I need to see—"

Jane edged around the counter. "Want me to do this while you're ...?"

"Sure, they're alphabetical, left to right."

"Are we in the right place?" Spike grabbed back his attention. "Took us forever to find AV. Actually I didn't know what AV stood for at first, but it's Audio Visual. That's so cool—"

"Yeah, yeah," the man cut her short. "You got your receipts?"

"What?"

"You need to pay at Finance first, bring your receipts, *then* I take your pictures," he started to turn toward Jane.

"We have to go where first?" Spike repeated.

"Finance. It's right beside the Registrar's building."

"And the Registrar's building is ..."

Jane left the room, calling back a feeble, "Thanks."

"Didn't you just come from the Registrar's?"

"Oh yeah. Do you remember where we just were?" Spike turned to X. What? "When?"

The three of them sat on a bench a respectable distance from the building that housed AV.

"Any luck?" Spike asked.

Jane fanned through the few cards she'd had to grab blind, then slumped in defeat.

"What?"

"Only one's a woman."

"Well, that'll do," Spike said. "You can go in by yourself, print out a list of possibilities, come out and show X, then go back in and get what she needs."

"A black woman," Jane clarified.

They both looked at X.

"What?"

"You're black."

"I am?" She looked at herself, then at Jane and Spike. "You're right!" She stretched out her arms to bask in their blackness. "Nah nah!" she taunted.

Spike and Jane looked at each other. Did that come from the X or the brain that came with?

"So *you'll* have to go in," Jane said.

"Go in where?"

"This is so *not* going to work."

"It's worth a try," Spike said.

"Okay, but we can't go back to the Wolbach."

"Do we need to? I mean, wouldn't the computers in all of the libraries have access to the same databases?"

"Maybe," Jane said.

"Okay, so we just pick another library."

X kept stretching out her arms, turning them one way then another. She pulled up her t-shirt to look at her lovely black belly.

"A busy one so no one will notice her."

Jane pulled out her laptop and got to work.

"Okay ..." she thought aloud as she worked, "we should probably not send her to the Islamic Seminary Library ... The African-American Reading Room?"

"Might have just one computer terminal. I can't see Harvard having a very large collection of African-American anything. How about the other Science library that guy mentioned … the Gordon McKay?"

"Yeah … Hey, there's a Physics Research Library!"

"Bingo."

"Oh wow," Jane said. "It has its own site *and* it has a list of 'Preprint Servers'. X, take a look at this."

X leaned over to look at the screen.

"What's a 'Google Sholar'?"

"No, that's—Oh look. Harvard doesn't know how to spell 'scholar'."

Ten minutes later, they were standing near the front door of the Physics Research Library.

"Okay, so you select one of the databases I showed you," Jane said to X, "and from there you can probably enter specific search terms. Like 'space-time continuum'."

"Or 'Earl'!"

"This is *so* not going to work."

"If you get stuck," Spike said, "just ask one of the sholars for help."

A few minutes later, Jane and Spike were peeking through a ground level window. They saw X swipe the student card at the turnstile and pass through.

"So far, so good."

Next, X went to the bank of computers conveniently near the entrance and sat down in front of one. She placed her student card in the holder attached to the monitor, admiring once more the blackness of her arm. And then her other arm. And then—

"Good thing she's not wearing shorts."

She put her hand on the mouse and made a few experimental moves with it, following the cursor on the screen. And then she began to search for what she wanted.

"Still good."

After a few moments, she began to laugh. The library attendant looked over to her with moderate interest.

"Should we get ready to intervene? Distract?"

X continued to erupt into laughter every now and then. People around her began to stare. She looked around, then spotted a stack of paper beside a printer. She got up, grabbed a sheet, fashioned it into a funnel, and put it over her mouth and nose, looking like a unicorn whose horn had slipped. She stopped laughing and continued working.

"Oh," Jane said. "I thought she was laughing at—"

"Me too."

"Excuse me, do you have a pin I can borrow?"

Jane and Spike exchanged a look of confusion. That matched the look on the face of the student she'd asked.

X turned to another student. "Excuse me, do you have a pin I can borrow?"

"A PIN!" Spike suddenly realized. "She probably needs a PIN number to print!"

"You know that's redundant, right?"

Spike stared at Jane.

"Just sayin'."

X stood up then, in all her horned glory, and said to the room at large. "Does anyone here have a pin I can borrow? The computer says I need a pin."

The attendant gave her his full attention then and walked over. "Can I be of some assistance?"

"Yes, the computer says I need a pin. Do you have a pin?"

"Are you a student here at Harvard?"

"That's it," Jane said with defeat.

"Hang on," Spike hoped.

"Yes. I have a Harvard student card. Look." X pointed to the card. The attendant looked closely at the card, then at X, still unicorned, then back to the card.

"He's white ...."

"So they all look the same ..."

He plucked the card from the holder and walked back to his station.

"Hey, I need that. Moron!"

"Nope. You're right. That's it."

A Security Guard showed up almost immediately. "Would you please come with me?"

"Do you have a—" She saw the gun he had belted to his waist. Fortunately, she also saw Jane and Spike waving frantically at the door.

"Wait, I see my friends at the door. Maybe they have a pin."

X quickly walked to and then through the door.

"So I guess there's no point in doing the Finance temp thing tomorrow," Spike said. They were back in the car and on their way. Away from Harvard. X was pretty much emptying the snack box.

"Not unless students are assigned an access PIN by or before Finance."

"Unlikely."

"So, what," Jane tried to think it through, "after they take their letter of acceptance to the Registrar's office, and get proof of registration, then take that to Finance, and pay, then take their proof of payment to AV, and get a student card— Do they then have to take their student card to the library to get an access PIN?"

Spike shrugged.

"Maybe it's like credit card PINs," Jane suggested. "You assign your own PIN when you activate it. In which case, there's no way ..."

Spike looked in the rear-view mirror to X, sitting dejectedly in the back seat. The snack box was now indeed empty.

"Did you come close to getting what you need?"

"No. I don't think you people know your space-time coordinates."

"That's a distinct possibility," Jane said.

"I'm never going to get home."

Jane thought that was also a distinct possibility.

"Can't you just phone home?

"No, I need the area code and number of where I'm calling from," X said. "Which is—"

"Earl's coordinates."

The hotel they'd been in the night before had no rooms available for that night, but they found another one close by. Just as inexpensive. With a small fridge. They'd made a point to ask about that.

Jane did some tasteful redistribution of the boxes in the trunk, then carried into the hotel just one box full of the most-susceptible-to-heat chocolate delectables. Spike and X followed with the stuff they'd need for overnight. X had become increasingly quiet, and Spike wondered if all the chocolate she'd had had sent her into a state of semi-hibernation.

Jane put the box lovingly into the fridge.

"Don't let me forget about that tomorrow morning!" she said to Spike.

"As if."

"Hey, my *Boston Legal* thing finally happened!" Jane said. She and X were googling. Spike was surfing.

"How appropriate."

Jane looked at her.

"We're in Boston."

"Oh. Yeah." She grinned.

"You should contact the guy's lawyer, send him your script!"

"He probably already has a defence."

"Yeah, but you had some excellent media bites. 'What kind of society encourages its boys not only to *pretend to kill* people, but also to *have fun* while doing so?'"

X looked up momentarily from her laptop. Then surfed with a bit more urgency.

"I wonder whether parents would be as blasé if their son as repeatedly put his arm around someone's throat and swiped a piece of stiff cardboard across it?" Spike mused. "Clearly deriving pleasure from doing so."

"They would, if the Earth's rotation on its axis suddenly changed direction and people became rational," Jane muttered.

"It can *do* that?" X said. She almost choked on her chocolate Oreo streusel.

"No," Spike assured her. "It can't. Can it?" she glanced over at Jane.

"No, the polarity changes every now and then, but that doesn't change the direction of rotation. I don't think." And *nothing* would change people's irrationality. *Ever.*

"We'd feel it slow down, wouldn't we? Because it couldn't just suddenly change, could it? We'd all fly off— Then again, we don't feel the rotation now, so maybe we wouldn't feel it if it changed direction ..." Spike trailed off. She'd actually never thought about this before.

Jane resumed googling. As had X.

The room was silent for several minutes.

Except for a music video Spike had happened to stop at: "'If she ever tries to fucking leave again, I'm a tie her to the bed and set this house on fire ...' 'Just gonna stand there and watch me burn, but that's alright because I like the way it hurts ...'"

She changed the channel. An ad urged her to get rid of her split ends.

"Hey," Jane suddenly turned to X with excitement, "why don't you contact— Go to the NASA site. N-A-S-A. Salstein looks like he might know ..." She turned back to her laptop, "No, wait, he's into atmospheric stuff. That wouldn't be helpful, would it ..."

"No, but this NASA group ..." X sounded hopeful.

"No," Spike said firmly, turning off the tv. "We're not taking you to NASA."

"But they have space ships," X said, exploring the site. "Ugly space ships, old space ships, but—"

"Doesn't matter."

"Right, because I have my own space ship, but wouldn't they *know*? The coordinates? They'd *have* to know! Wouldn't they?" She clicked on the 'Earth' tab. No space-time coordinates there. She clicked on the 'Solar System and Beyond' tab. No coordinates there either.

"If they did know the coordinates, they probably wouldn't put them on their website." Jane had guessed correctly what X was doing.

"Why not?"

"Because the purpose of the website is ... Never mind."

X found the 'Contact Us' option and sent a short, to-the-point, query.

Jane looked for a 'Chat Now' option. A representative would be with her in thirty seconds. Sixty seconds passed. Then ninety seconds. When thirty seconds had become five minutes, Jane thought that either NASA knew nothing about the time-space continuum or they knew a lot.

"I think my laptop died."

"What?" Jane got off her bed and went over to X, sitting in the room's chair. The screen was black. Then it filled with gobbled-gook. Then it went black again.

"What did you do last?"

X told her.

"See?" Spike's voice rose several notches. "She asked about Earth's space-time coordinates, and they wiped her laptop. *Now* will you agree that we're not taking her to NASA?"

13

They decided that the Goddard Space Flight Center—they hadn't known that NASA had ten different centres—would be their best bet. MapQuest said they could get to Greenbelt, Maryland in about six hours.

"We'll have to stop somewhere to get X another laptop," Jane said as they headed out of the hotel parking lot.

"Yeah, why don't you find something at a couple hours from now. We'll be ready for a break by then."

"Sounds good."

"So," Jane turned to X a short while later, "what's it like on—" She changed her mind. They'd asked that question already. "Are people happy on Grmphflg?"

"Usually."

"Do you have art, music, dance ...?" Jane tried again.

"Yes."

"Is there any violence? Attacks, assaults ..."

"Sometimes."

"What do you do about it?"

"Call Animal Control."

Spike snorted with delight.

"But she's right, isn't she?" Jane said a few moments later, knowing exactly what Spike had been imagining. "I mean what if a wolf attacked and seriously injured a human being?"

"They'd shoot it on sight. No questions asked."

"There'd certainly be no murmurs of a misunderstanding."

"And if it happened every nine seconds,"[40] Spike said, "and packs of wolves roamed the streets at night—"

"They'd organize a hunt and kill every one of them. Whether it had blood on its paws or not."

They considered this.

"Wolves would be extinct by now."

They drove on for a while, then Jane asked another question.

"Is there any poverty?"

"No. We have enough of everything to go around. We make sure of it before. And befront."

Right. Before. And befront.

"Is there any pollution?"

"No. We don't put poisons into our water. Or our air. That would be stupid."

'Nuff said.

A couple hours later, Spike took the exit to a small town that apparently had a computer repair shop. They couldn't see it on their drive through, so they decided to park, then walk along the main street, looking for it. X followed behind, forlorn, clutching her shiny red laptop to her chest.

"Maybe it's gone out of business," Jane said.

"Maybe. Though you'd think everyone here would have some sort of computer needing repair from time to time."

"Maybe like small appliances, it's become cheaper to just buy new than repair."

"You girls look lost," a man passing by had stopped. To help. He thought.

---

40 http://www.tomdispatch.com/post/175641/tomgram%3A_rebecca_
solnit,_the_longest_war

X opened her mouth, but Jane tugged her along, and they kept going.

But Spike turned back. Of course she did.

"You were talking to us?" she asked the man. "There's no way we look under eighteen."

"What?"

"She means we're not girls," Jane said. "We're women." If they had a dollar for every time they had to assert their adulthood ...

"Don't get your panties in a knot, it's just a figure a speech."

"No, it's *not* just a figure of speech!" Spike said angrily. "When you call us girls, you infantilize us. Why do you do that, do you think?"

"What?"

"In all fairness," Jane said to Spike, "you *did* ask two questions there."

"Good point." She turned back to the man. "Why do you do that?"

The man walked away.

"I would've gone with the other one first. Logically prior and all that."

"To his credit," Jane muttered as they carried on, "he didn't call us crazy or bitches."

"'To his credit'? It's gotten to the point that we *praise* men when they *don't* insult us?"

Jane considered that. "It's telling that they're not offended by how low we set the bar, isn't it."

"I mean, if he changes a diaper, he's father of the year," Jane continued a moment later. "If he dusts or vacuums the apartment once in a while, we're impressed. And if he writes a manuscript that's an incoherent mess, full of spelling and grammar mistakes, and missing references left, right, and center, it gets published. After someone else cleans it up for him." Jane had clearly been such a someone else for a while.

"And actually," Spike said a few moments later, "he *did* insult us. Told us not to get our panties in a knot. Which implies that we were *unduly* upset. He thus dismissed our legitimate concerns."

Jane considered *that.* With some embarrassment. "We're insulted so often, we don't even notice it half the time."

"You know," Jane said, as they crossed the street to head up the other side, having gotten to the end, apparently, of the town's business district, with*out* finding the computer repair shop, "when 'girls' is used to refer to *all* female people, *real* girls remain undifferentiated, which enables men to interact with them without shame."

"You mean to fuck them."

Jane nodded. "If adult females were always called women, then it would be quite clear when men—not boys—were having sex with girls."

"You mean fucking them."

Jane nodded again. "Maybe only men who don't want the distinction to be made call women 'girls'. They don't want people to know when they're engaging with actual girls.

"I mean fucking them," she added.

"I think you're assuming too much consciousness," Spike said a few moments later. "I think people do it because it's convention. To infantilize women."

They found the shop halfway up on the other side. A young couple was at the counter, speaking with the repair guy. X started to wander around the small shop, looking at the various bits and pieces on display. Jane and Spike stood near the counter, waiting. And listening. And, yes, after a moment, recording.

"I think it's the graphics program," the woman explained.

"It's the RAM," the man disagreed. "We need more RAM."

"I can check both when I take a look," the counter person said pleasantly.

"But we're paying you for your time, right? So I think you should look at the graphics program first."

"You know," Jane said quietly to Spike, "I've changed my mind about 'I think.'"

"Descartes was wrong?"

"No, Tannen was wrong. Or whoever it was who said it was a hedge that only women use."

"You think men use it too?" She grinned.

"No, men don't use it."

"Because men don't think." She grinned even more.

"No, because women are correctly aware of their status as subjective beings, whereas men are not. Or pretend not. Women thus correctly qualify their claims as opinions. Men, by omitting that qualifier, present their claims as facts. They thus presume objectivity, omniscience."

"The arrogance!" Spike pretended surprise.

The couple's conversation continued. Jane's observation was spot on.

"*That's* why—remember that scene in *The Good Wife*?" Spike asked. "With that judge who insisted that the lawyers in her court preface all of their comments with 'I think'?"

"Oh right! I'd forgotten that!"

"The guy, Will, so clearly thought she was being ridiculous—"

"Of course he did. That omission is the quintessential, absolutely critical, male lie. It's how we come to consider them as authorities. About everything. Their refusal to consider their thoughts as opinions indicates a refusal to accept the possibility that they're incorrect. Particular shame on male epistemologists for this," she added.

"Or maybe," Spike was thinking out loud, "the absence of the 'I' is simply the denial of, the failure to take, responsibility. Compare

'Your postal code is indecipherable' to 'I can't read your postal code': the first, without the 'I', doesn't even *consider* the possibility that the fault may rest with the reader."

"Hm ..."

"So in either case," Spike suggested, "we should start telling women to leave off the 'I think'. They'd be granted more authority that way."

"No, I think we should start telling men to *add* the 'I think'. *That's* the epistemologically true version."

"But—" the young woman made another attempt.

"Let's face facts—" the young man interrupted her. Of course he did.

"Are you implying I'm *not* 'facing' 'facts'?" the young woman replied. "That I've been, to this point, too *cowardly* to face facts?"

Spike grinned.

"No, I—"

"Then why did you say that?"

"I just—"

"Just what?"

He stared at her. Because, hey, sometimes that worked.

"You just said it without thinking," Spike jumped in, "and it's just one more thing you say that puts other people down, presumably to put you one up. Say *that*. 'I constantly put other people down by not thinking about the words I use.'"

The young woman nodded.

The young man glared at her. Because when staring doesn't work—

"Say it!" the young woman insisted.

"What? What do you want me to say?" He protested helplessly.

Jane groaned. "No, don't do that. Don't pretend she's making some unreasonable request."

"And don't just say whatever you think I *want* you to say!" the young woman added.

"Yeah. Get real." Spike grinned at the retro that tumbled out of her mouth.

"Can you do that?" the young woman asked pointedly. Proving that the retro was apparently still relevant.

The man didn't respond. He was thinking. He was thinking three against one. No fair.

"Why is it so hard for so many men to just say what they really think?" Jane mused aloud once they were back on their way. It was clearly not the first time she'd asked that question.

"Because they don't know. They are supremely unaccustomed to introspection." Clearly not the first time Spike had given that answer.

X had her own questions about men and was busy googling for answers. On her new, old, so very old, laptop.

"Or maybe it's because the truth is irrelevant. 'What do you want me to say?' really just means 'What lie will work here?'"

Spike considered that. It fit with their obsession for competition, which would require strategy, manipulation—

"And then they're surprised when the relationship doesn't last," Jane said. "I mean, if they've gotten their girlfriend, or their wife, by saying 'the right thing'— Do they really think they can keep up the ruse for a lifetime? Do they really think women won't figure it out one day? Won't realize that they've been, basically, bullshitting since day one?"

"Hey, while you're here," Spike glanced in the rear-view mirror at X in the back seat, "is there anything you'd like to do or see? We've been focused on the immediate problem, but we can take a couple days to get to Maryland, make a couple side trips ..."

"Okay." She didn't sound too enthusiastic.

"Why don't you google for some ideas?" Jane suggested.

"Okay." Not enthusiastic at all.

Spike settled in for a couple hours of driving. Jane opened her laptop.

"Going to work on your novel?"

"Actually, no, I'm going to start a new book. A translation dictionary."

"Like 'What do you want me to say' means 'What lies will work here'?"

"Yes. And 'I have a right to'—"

"—means 'I want to'."

Half an hour later, X looked up from her laptop and broke the pleasant silence. "Are there morons *everywhere*?" They'd told her as much a while ago, but still ...

Spike nodded. "Actually, a moron-free space is illegal now."

"Well, we fought to make men-only clubs illegal, so I guess ..."

Spike glanced over sharply. "There's a huge difference between banning women from university and banning men from the Michigan Womyn's Music Festival."

"Yes, but not a huge difference between the festival and the clubs."

"True." Spike sighed.

"And anyway, it wasn't men who insisted they had a right to be at the Festival, it was transgender women. Who are men," she added quickly. They'd had this conversation. Part of this conversation.

But Jane was in the mood for the rest of it. After all, six hours to Greenbelt.

"The problem is a stunning lack of clarity. The word 'woman' should identify only one's sex. A woman is a female adult human. In which case, transgenders should call themselves trans*sexuals*."

"Which is impossible," Spike said. "Because to become female, they'd have to replace their Y chromosome with an X chromosome. And/or get ovary, uterus, and vagina implants, as well as breast implants, complete with milk ducts. And/or estrogen injections.

"And if testosterone—the amount that males typically have— poisons the brain, probably rewiring it, permanently—" Spike paused. They hadn't actually considered this, before. "Then they'd have to get those injections before they hit puberty."

Jane nodded. "To become trans*gender*, on the other hand, they merely have to cross the gender line. 'Tomboys' are transgender. 'Sissies' are transgender."

"You and I are transgender."

X was googling 'trans*species*'.

"To some extent," Spike qualified. "I don't think one can ever completely escape one's gender conditioning. It starts so early and is so ... relentless."

Jane agreed. She stared out the window for a while, then took their discussion into a slightly new direction. "What's more interesting than *what* they are is *why* they are. I mean, transpeople keep saying they were born into the wrong body, that they *feel* female, but how do they know? It's the bat problem."

Spike glanced over.

"You know," Jane continued, "Nagel's 'What is it like to be a bat—for the bat?' Even females don't know what it's like to feel female. We may know what it's like to have a uterus, because the damn thing hurts every month, but in general? We know what it's like to feel healthy only after we've been sick. The only way we'd know what it's like to feel female would be if we'd actually had the experience of feeling other-than-female."

X googled. And found Batman.

"It's too bad no one's doing a study," Spike commented. "The MTFs who take estrogen, the FTMs who take testosterone—they could tell us first-hand what it's like, what effects those chemicals have. On their personality, their emotionality ... It would be only anecdotal evidence, from a skewed sample, and it would be difficult to untangle the social influences, but still."

Jane nodded. Then had a new thought. "Quite apart from, if they already 'feel like a woman inside', why do they get estrogen injections?"

"Isn't the estrogen to change the outside? From the inside? Doesn't taking estrogen reduce their muscle mass, their body hair...?"

"Okay, but if their outside is male, and their inside is male, on what grounds do they *feel female*?"

"Their brain."

"But brain is part of body," Jane said. "If chromosomes and chemicals wire the brain, their brains are also male."

"If. And even if, do the sexual chromosomes and chemicals have a *dominant* effect? I mean, enough, proportionally speaking, to make the brain 'male' or 'female'?"

Jane nodded. "In any case, I think most of the time, it's not that they feel female or womanly or feminine, it's that they don't feel male or manly or masculine. They don't fit the social construct."

"Welcome to our world."

X had found Spiderman.

"And, but, if people don't fit the social construct, then shouldn't the *social construct* be changed?" Spike asked pointedly. "Transgenders *reinforce* the gender dichotomy. You're in a male body, but you'd really like to wear lavender chiffon and spend the day baking cupcakes and arranging flowers? Just do it!" She grinned at her Nike reference.

Jane nodded. "If we had more people with the courage to just do what they wanted to do, regardless of what others think they should do, based on their indefensible notion of a sexual dichotomy based, in turn, on physical appearance— If we had more people who were willing to stand up to the consequent taunts and ostracization, maybe eventually the taunts and ostracization would disappear."

"Or maybe they'd get themselves killed," Spike sighed. "It's not 'just'. It's way more dangerous to be a sissy than to be a tomboy."

"Yeah." Jane sighed too.

"So maybe," she had another new thought, "becoming trans is a way to cross gender lines without that risk. An MTF leaves the man's world altogether.

"Which would explain," she continued, "why they cling to being women, to being *perceived* as women, as if their lives depended on it."

"That would explain their wardrobe choices," Spike agreed.

"The *why* is intriguing," Spike said a short while later, "but the *what* has policy implications. For example, *should* they—whatever they are—have been allowed at the Michigan Festival?"

"Well, women who've had hysterectomies and/or bilateral mastectomies would be allowed. So it's not about being female per se. At least," Jane qualified, "female defined by the other-than-chromosomes biological stuff. It's about having lifetime of gender conditioning. So, no. Because MTFs don't have that. So they don't 'get it'. So their presence would ruin the empathy-based solidarity. Same reason you wouldn't want a bunch of non-alcoholics at your AA meetings."

"So we're saying nurture trumps nature?"

Jane thought about that.

X googled 'AA' and found small batteries. Which were *huge*.

"You know," Spike said a while later, "they've even insisted on being hired at women's shelters. If they had *any* sensitivity at all, if they could stop thinking about themselves for one goddamned minute—"

"If they were *really* women—"

"Yes!" Spike glanced over. Jane had nailed it. "That's exactly why answering the question of whether MTFs are women is a no-brainer for those of us who've been women all our lives. MTFs make demands, not polite requests. They are quick to resort to insult, threat, aggression. They compete. They dominate. They convey a sense of entitlement that *none* of us has *ever* had. They don't take 'no' for an answer. They scream WHO THE FUCK ARE YOU TO KEEP US OUT, WE HAVE A FUCKING RIGHT TO BE HERE, TO GO WHEREVER THE FUCK WE WANT!"

Spike stared at the road ahead of her, then added one more thing.

"If it quacks like a duck."

X googled and found a site that enabled her to make a cat quack like a duck.

"Then again," Spike said a while later, "maybe we *should* treat MTFs like women. Let's pay them less for work of equal value, let's deny them promotions they deserve, let's mock or ignore their contributions to society—"

"Hang on," Jane was searching her bookmarks. "There was an excellent comment like that made at Femonade's website… Here it is."[41] Jane read it aloud. "'So, I say to MTFs … if you want to be considered a woman, act like one. Sit down and shut up. Understand that your opinion doesn't count. Be sensitive to everyone else's feelings, respect them, accommodate them. Don't assume you know more than anyone else. In particular, don't assume you know more about sex and gender than second-generation feminists and radfems; they are Ph.D.s (in fact, many of them *have* Ph.D.s) when it comes to sex and gender, and no man *of any kind* comes close to their level of understanding.'

"And as evidence for that last bit—and I think this is where you were going, she says 'They lost many of [their] privileges when they started identifying as women, but rather than recognizing that this is because of sexism, they decided it was because they are trans. Why? Because, being male, they knew fuck all about sexism.'"

---

41 https://factcheckme.wordpress.com/2009/11/16/the-fallacy-of-cis-privilege/

Spike nodded. Had been nodding throughout, in fact.

"Remember that scene in *Tootsie*?" Jane asked then. "The look on Dustin Hoffman's face when his suggestion was just so utterly ... dismissed. Not just not taken very seriously, but not even really heard. They really should have done a lot more with that."

"They should have made a whole different movie. With that."

"It makes you wonder," Jane mused a moment later, "I mean, if the men who want to become women understood *anything at all* about sexism ..."

Spike agreed. "It's no surprise that twice as many MTFs as FTMs commit suicide. I haven't read very many accounts of transition, but in most of those I've read ...   It's as if they had no idea that they were voluntarily becoming a member of the sexed subordinate class. So no wonder, on top of everything else, they can't handle, are broadsided by, the sudden and almost complete disenfranchisement ..."

"Yes! So maybe they're screaming so loudly not because, or not *just* because, they're men, but because they've just jumped into a pot of boiling water. The rest of us, *real* women, have had a lifetime to get used to it."

"Poor MTFs," Spike said, with no sympathy whatsoever. "They thought they were going to be such special little princesses. What a shock real life must have been."

"Then again," Jane reconsidered, "you've read about people who say their leg, or whatever, isn't their own and they want it amputated? They'd rather go through life crippled, disabled, than deal with the disconnect."

Spike looked over at Jane. "What a brilliantly apt analogy."

They took an exit, stopped at a convenience store—X insisted they get some Tootsie Rolls—then carried on. Jane resumed googling, to answer X's miles-ago-asked question.

"So where oh where can we find women only?" she mumbled to herself. "Women's studies classes!"

"No, remember what happened[42] when Mary Daly wanted her classes to be for women only?"

"Oh yeah. Cooking classes?" But as soon as she said it, she knew that was a no as well.

"You know," Spike said, "I'm all for men cooking—I'm all for making *everything* sex-*un*aligned—but what bothers me so much is that when they started cooking, it suddenly became so frickin' *important*. So important it's being *televised*. They have to have people *see* them cook."

"You're right. Wait, you watch cooking shows?"

"Once. By accident. A surfing accident." She grinned.

"Ah. But you're right. When women did the cooking, it was no big deal: some were good at it, some not; sometimes it was a chore, sometimes a joy; it was an art and a skill, yes, but they didn't make a show—a *show*—of it."

"And my god, the drama!" Spike said. "The chefs scream with indignation at their minions, they rush around with such urgency making sure every sprinkle of cinnamon is just right, because, well, it's so frickin' important. And they call *us* drama queens."

"I doubt Julia Child ever did that," Jane agreed.

"She wasn't competing. She *gave away* her recipes, didn't she?"

"*That's* why! The drama. Men turn *everything* into a *competition*! In fact," Jane was thinking, "*So You Think You Can Dance* and *The Voice*—is that what it's called?—and all the stupid new reality shows—they're *all* competitions!"

"Probably intended to increase the numbers," Spike said. "Which increases the sponsorships. The price of the ads. Television is just a vehicle for advertising."

"But at least in the first case, I doubt the intended audience was men. So either the women are watching it *in spite of* the competition or male producers have turned us all into competition addicts."

---

42 https://debradeanmurphy.wordpress.com/2010/01/11/mary-daly-and-women-only-classrooms/

"Or a lot of women like watching men compete." Spike didn't think very much of a lot of women.

"Actually," Jane said a while later, "maybe the intended audience of *So You Think You Can Dance is* men. At least *now.* Have you seen it lately?"

"No."

"It's become pornified. I swear, nine out of ten dances are hypersexualized. In costume, in movement— No doubt due to the increased viewing of porn by men. Who then expect women, and girls, to be like that. Which then makes women, and girls, think they need to be like that ..."

"Or maybe it's the growth hormones they put in the food chain," Spike said. "Girls—maybe boys too—are experiencing puberty at eleven now, aren't they?"

"Hm. I wonder if anyone has done a study comparing vegetarian kids with meat-eating kids, with respect to age of onset."

"That would be interesting."

"Or it could just be what the producers want," Jane said a few moments later. "I did read an explanation that said something like girls dance totally differently than boys. Which, of course, is nonsense. If they do dance differently, it's only because the choreographers insist on it. Strength, balance, coordination, musicality, skill—none of that is sex-specific."

"I think my all-time favourite dance was Kanumura's 'Bohemian Rhapsody' audition piece," Spike thought back to one of the earliest seasons.

"Mine too! And it was asexual, wasn't it. Another good one is Mandy Moore's 'Boogie Shoes' which was, despite the gendered costumes, pretty much just fun movement to the music."

"And look at the language change," Jane said, going back, but moving forward. "Women are cooks, but men are *chefs.* Chefs have more status than cooks."

Spike nodded. "The same thing happened with bank tellers, remember? In reverse. When men were bank tellers, the job was important, it was a position of some status; once women started being bank tellers, it became much less important."

"But food preparation was important before. Doing it the wrong way can be fatal. Literally."

X read the label on her Tootsie Roll. And wondered how syrup came out of corn.

"Which makes it even more irritating that the recognition of importance didn't occur until *men* started doing it.

"And the truly stupid thing is that they've made the *trivial* aspects of it important. People don't die if the cinnamon sprinkle isn't just so."

"Right," Spike said. "And since they *aren't* focusing on the legitimately important aspects, the aspects with *intrinsic* importance, they have to *manufacture* importance. And making something into a competition is a way to do just that, a way to make what they're doing *seem* important."

"That assumes we think competition per se is important."

"Competition determines status."

"Ah."

"So *not* cooking classes?" X asked. Her Tootsie Roll was gone.

14

A couple hours later, they decided to take another break, in a small town that had a dog park. That was what X wanted to see. Or do.

When Jane pulled into the parking lot, they immediately noticed the wedding-in-progress at the church across the street.

"In the middle of the week?" Spike was surprised.

A rented limo, polka-dotted with Kleenex pom-poms, had just pulled up, and three bridesmaids, each in cupcake, were helping The Bride extricate herself from the back seat, while the Father of the Bride escorted the Mother of the Bride into the church.

"Is that a Hallowe'en Party?" X asked.

They looked at her, startled. She knew about Hallowe'en parties? And didn't know about weddings? There was *so much* in common between the two ...

"No, it's a wedding," Jane said. "They're getting married."

"And the costumes?"

"They're playing The Little Princess and Prince Charming."

"Just for the day," Spike clarified.

"I've never understood why women get married," Jane commented as they sat in the car watching. "Voluntarily. Though I suppose the squealing and jumping up and down when he asks her should be a clue."

"There are social incentives."

"Yeah." Marry a man and your status increases. By association. Mrs. Archer gets taken more seriously than Judy.

"And economic incentives."

"Yeah." Even if you weren't a kept woman.

"But most of all, getting married is getting happy-ever-after. Who wouldn't want that?"

"But domestic violence—*domestic* violence," Jane practically spat the euphemism, "is the leading cause[43] of injury to women aged 15-44." More common than automobile accidents, muggings, and cancer deaths combined. "One in five[44] women is severely beaten during the course of the marriage. Half of those[45] are beaten when pregnant, often kicked in the abdomen." She'd done the research. As every heterosexual woman should. "One-third[46] of the women who are murdered are murdered by their husbands. And yet," she said, with a deep sigh, "over eighty percent[47] of all women get married. It boggles the mind."

"Yeah well, our capacity for delusion is legendary."

The Bride was out of the limo.

"Still, all the congratulations—more squealing and jumping up and down—it's not like she's won a Nobel Prize. It's not an *achievement*."

"But it *is*. If you look at it as a rite of passage. It's like all those wilderness vision quest things. If you survive, they have a ceremony, they celebrate you, call you an adult, give you a new name—"

"Mrs." She snorted.

X googled rites of passage. "'The Vanuatu go bungee jumping with vines wrapped around their ankles,'" she read aloud. "'The objective is to come as close to death as possible.'"

"See?" Spike grinned. "Same thing. Exactly."

"No, wait, we're mixing it up. If the wedding is the celebration ceremony, then the rite of passage should come *before*, not *after*.

---

43 http://www.clarkprosecutor.org/html/domviol/facts.htm

44 http://www.ncadv.org/learn/statistics

45 https://www.bestbeginnings.org.uk/domestic-abuse

46 http://www.huffingtonpost.com/2014/10/09/men-killing-women-domesti_n_5927140.html

47 http://www.citylab.com/work/2014/09/not-married-the-odds-that-you-never-will-be-are-higher-than-ever/380686/

What has the woman survived? To be celebrated and accorded adult status via marriage?"

Spike thought about that. "Bars and roofies?"

A silver SUV pulled up behind the limo, and several late-arriving guests rushed out and up the steps, past The Bride and her cupcake entourage, disappearing into the church.

"It's the kids."

Jane waited.

"That's why women get married," Spike said. "In our society, you have to become a kept woman in order to have kids. There is no stronger, no more complete, trap into subordination. True, nothing says you have to become dependent on a *man*, but you have to become dependent on *someone*. If not for wanting to have kids, women wouldn't have to marry."

"And once there *are* kids," Jane continued that line of thought, "you're stuck. You can't have an income of your own, so you *are* dependent. So you *have* to cater. To the man. Who was it who said 'Family is female extortion'?"[48]

"And unfortunately, said catering becomes a habit, a *generalized* habit. Married women start catering to *every* man."

Jane thought about that. "We may be confusing cause and effect."

"Maybe," Spike conceded. "In any case, it's almost impossible to unlearn what you've been doing, how you've been thinking, for twenty years—two to three kids' worth of time."

"So in countries in which there's state-provided daycare, do women get married? Do *they* become doormats to their husbands?"

"Good question. No? Or at least not as often? Which would explain why there *isn't* state-provided daycare here. Men would lose their live-in maids and prostitutes."

"Also explains why men keep making more money than women. If women made more than men, *men* would be the dependent ones. *They'd* be the ones staying at home, looking after

----

48 http://trustyourperceptions.wordpress.com/2013/09/01/male-bullshit-stories-god-how-it-is-and-daily-dudeplots-part-iv/

the kids, catering to some *woman.* And putting their heads in the oven."

From the back seat, X was looking at Jane, then Spike, then back at Jane, trying to follow, trying to *understand,* the conversation. Like a dog who knew it should be a tennis ball going back and forth. Not an octopus.

"But why do so many women *want* kids?" Jane wondered aloud. "None of the women I've known wanted to be nursery school teachers when they grew up.

"Sure," she conceded, "there are a few years there where your body is pushing you to replicate—"

"*Damn* those selfish genes—"

"But really, it's not that hard to ignore. If you think about it. If you think about actually spending the next twenty years *being responsible* for the kids. Ah." She'd answered her own question again. "Their heads are full of sugar plum pictures, of rosy-cheeked babies and tiny little booties."

"Like getting married," Spike suggested, "having kids is perceived as a measure of adulthood. You aren't really grown up until you're married with kids."

"Go figure. It seems to me you aren't really grown up until you can recognize you've been force-fed contradictory crap all your life."

"An added attraction for women," Spike said, "is that for once in their lives they get to be an authority. If only to their children. I remember something *Jean Baker Miller*[49] said: a woman who has power over herself doesn't need power over others. Flip that and ..."

"No doubt a factor for men as well."

Spike nodded. "In addition to a live-in maid and prostitute, marriage gives him authority. Over the wife *and* the kids."

"Furthermore," Spike continued, "you don't even need any training to be good at it. Being a parent. All you need is love." Of course, her voice dripped with sarcasm.

"Hm."

---

49 *Toward a New Psychology of Women.*

Jane continued to consider various reasons for having kids, grasping for something more ... fundamental. And then she had it. "I wonder if most people are simply too unimaginative or too lazy to make their own lives worthwhile. So they have kids. That's their contribution to society."

"Genetic replications of their deepest deficiency. Gee, thanks."

They watched as The Bride tottered up the steps, leaning heavily on the Father of the Bride who had come back to get her. She may as well have already been crippled.

"If getting married were just a five-minute civil court thing—" Jane didn't finish. Didn't have to. "No hype, no— What we have to ask is why weddings *are* so hyped."

"Because otherwise women would see marriage for what it is and run the fuck the other way."

"We don't see a *Today's Groom* magazine at the checkout," Jane noted, ambiguously.

"Women need more brainwashing than men," Spike suggested. "They're clearly getting the short end of the stick. Any woman who makes it to thirty kid-free and husband-free realizes, if she thinks at all, that she's got the far better deal."

Jane nodded.

At every step, the three cupcakes struggled with the bride's train, which was attached to the bride's veil. Which, if it moved, would surely undo half a day at the hairdresser's.

"Plus," Spike said. "Consider the oxytocin. I think a lot of women realize, eventually, that their children make them vulnerable, that their love holds them hostage. So many things they would do—"

"Like leave—"

"If it weren't for the children."

The party had reached the massive oak doors at the church's entrance.

"But I wonder how many women realize that their imprisonment, that love, is, to a not insignificant degree, physiological," she finished her thought.

"Sex, pregnancy, childbirth— It all increases your oxytocin level," Jane agreed. "Breastfeeding is like mainlining."

They continued to stare. Helplessly.

"We need an intervention."

Spike looked at Jane. Jane looked at Spike. They grinned at each other. Then got out of the car, sprinted across the street, and up the stairs.

X ran after them. Because— Actually, she had no idea why. For the octopus, maybe.

Or— She caught, remarkably, the already-recording phone that was tossed to her.

"JUST SAY NO!" Spike shouted as they raced up the aisle. Not bothering to keep time to the funereal version "Jesu, Joy of Man's Desiring." Hm. Spike glanced at the organist. Kin?

She shoved the Father of the Bride aside— After all, he was *giving* her away. Of course *selling* her would be worse, but the point was that he was acting like she was his to give. He was acting like he owned her.

Then they each grabbed an arm, backed The Bride away from the altar, and started dragging her down the aisle. Kicking and screaming.

The Mother of the Bride fainted. Denied the chance to relive the worst mistake of her life.

"Don't take that first hit!" Jane followed Spike's lead, "You'll feel so happy[50] all the time, and you'll just *love* your sweet little baby—"

"But that'll be the oxytocin[51] talking!"

The Bride kept kicking and screaming.

"Plato's Cave," Jane thought to herself, as encouragement, and continued pulling. "And you'll want to do nothing but look after it, and that's fine for five or six years—"

------

50 http://www.ahaparenting.com/ages-stages/pregnancy/oxytocin-pregnancy-birth-mother
51 http://www.psychologicalscience.org/media/releases/2007/feldman.cfm

"No it isn't," Spike interjected, "it's a supreme waste of a good human being who could be, instead, trying to stop the fossil fuel industry."

The bridesmaids followed their bride, trying to maintain wedding decorum for all of five seconds, at which point they just started bashing Spike and Jane over their heads with their bouquets. And screaming.

"Ouch!" And kicking.

The audience, the congregation—the audience watched from the pews.

"But when she's ten or fifteen or twenty," Jane had to shout to be heard, "she'll hate you. Or at least not need you."

"You could have another and another, sticking your head up your vagina like an ostrich—"

"But eventually you're going to have to face not just the empty nest syndrome, but oxytocin withdrawal. And that'll be long after Prince Charming will have left you for a body *not* stretched and sagged by childbirth. Half[52] of all married couples end up divorced, you know that, right?"

"The other half just couldn't be bothered."

At the first sign of disruption, the priest had frozen, hands outstretched with a paternal benevolence that seemed to consecrate the shenanigans. He now recovered, folded his hands into his vestments, and simply waited.

"Thing is," Spike shouted, "by the time the oxytocin kicks in, it's damn near impossible to see that you've made a mistake. By then, you're addicted."

"And apparently it rewires the brain. Permanently."[53]

"Which is why people can smell a mom from a mile away."

The Bride was still kicking and screaming. One pretty white satin shoe came off. It lay gleaming in the aisle. The other shoe came off a few steps later.

---

52 http://www.divorce.usu.edu/files/uploads/lesson3.pdf
53 http://www.attachmentparenting.org/support/articles/art chemistry.php

Seeing the shoes, two of the groomsmen raced down the aisle. They started bashing each other with their newly acquired weapons, because, hey, FIGHT!

Geez, Jane thought. Oxytocin addicts on the one hand, testosterone addicts on the other hand. They deserved each other. She wavered for a moment.

"It'll change your personality, as any drug does," Spike continued, valiantly.

Jane decided to stay the course. "You'll become affectionate, caring, you'll want to nurture, not just your own kids, but *everyone.*"

"You'll become obnoxious."

"Because you'll think you *can.* Nurture everyone," Jane clarified. "You'll think you know best. And like any addict, you'll insist you're happy, you'll think you're doing well."

"But the rest of us will see what a one-dimensional idiot you've become!"

One of the flower girls finally decided to break rank. She raced down the aisle, having ditched her bouquet and hiked up her dress to reveal jeans ending in running shoes. "Take me with you!" she cried out to the two of them. "They'll make me do the Macarena!"

Spike looked back and saw herself, at twelve.

The organist, who, once The Bride had reached the altar, had segued into "Another One Bites the Dust," returned to "Jesu, Joy," but in a delightfully rollicking style.

"When all is said and done twenty years from now," Jane kept trying, "you'll have done *nothing* with your life. Sure, you'll have raised a couple kids. Yes, it's hard work. But what was the point? The best you'll hope for is that *they* get married and have kids. And then you'll die."

"Utterly exhausted, floating belly up in the water."

"People say it's 'the circle of life' as if it's inevitable, and a good thing. But can't you see that the circularity is pointless?"

They'd reached the foyer, the—sanctuary? No, that would be too ironic.

The Father of the Bride finally caught up with them, having tended to his wife first. He took a swing at Spike. She dodged, and his fist slammed into the wall.

"Bitch!" he screamed, exhibiting a confused notion of causality, Jane thought.

The Bride tried yet again to get away, but Spike had unknowingly stepped on the train. They all heard the tear.

In the great and sudden silence that followed, the Bride stared at Spike with a sort of dull incomprehension—

And then she screamed. "This dress cost $5,000!"

Jane and Spike were stunned. Five thousand dollars for a dress? A dress you'd wear only once?

Well, it was a magic dress. Clearly, it had cast a spell.

Because the woman ran back to the altar. *Ran. Back.* Like a bedraggled but still besatined sheep to a slaughter.

Jane shouted after her, trying one last time, "The word 'wife' first referred to women who were captured, after the invasion and conquest of a neighbouring tribe, and brought home to be slaves. 'To have and to hold' is in fact a legal expression used to transfer possession of a piece of property!"

Halfway back to the altar, The Bride switched from screaming at Spike and Jane to screaming at Prince Charming. Who, everyone had noted, had not come to her rescue. Probably because he saw no threat in two women. Even if they were, as The Bride was shrieking, wicked bitches.

Spike also tried one last time. "A year from now, you'll be singing 'Did I shave my legs for this?'"

The organist broke into Deana Carter's song, and Spike flashed her a broad grin.

Back in the car, the two of them slumped, utterly defeated. What does it take?

Suddenly Jane remembered the chocolate in the—

"X!" They'd forgotten about X. They got back out of the car and looked around with alarm.

"There!" Jane pointed to a park bench on the church lawn. X was sitting with the defected flower girl.

"Hey," Spike said conversationally as they approached. She took the phone X held out to her. Yes! A full ten minutes!

"We've been talking," X said proudly. "I asked Star to tell me everything she knew about weddings."

"Yeah?"

"She says they're stupid."

With regret, and an argument for a license to parent, they insisted Star return to her mom and dad.

And then they headed across the road to the dog park. Actually they headed to the attached puppy park. Into which X enthusiastically climbed.

"I get why men want to get married, but why do they agree to have kids?" Jane said once they back on the road and out of the city, since she clearly wasn't done yet with the intervention, or at least the analysis. As soon as the phrase was out of her mouth, she answered herself. "If 'have kids' was replaced with 'look after kids', they wouldn't. The men." Been there.

Spike nodded, accepting with an unspoken 'thanks' the mint cheesecake chocolate cup Jane had picked out of the box for her. She herself had chosen crème brûlée chocolate cup. "Having kids is just symbolic for them. A *real* man has a wife and kids. End of story.

"Well," Spike added, "not completely end of story. Not only are the wife and kids automatic subordinates, they act as his own personal audience."

"Both of which explain why he doesn't just leave," Jane said. "I mean, if he keeps getting so angry at her that he keeps hitting her, you'd think he'd just get a divorce."

"It would seem," Spike again added, "that men *need* to hit. Need to hurt. A man's wife and kids also act as his own personal punching bag."

Jane stared out the window. "What is *wrong* with them?"

X opened her mouth to reply, but decided instead to just take a big bite of her chocolate chip cookie dough chocolate cup.

"Or maybe," Jane had a new thought, "maybe most women *don't* really want kids, but become pregnant anyway, because sex is defined as intercourse, and then claim, smiling, that they wouldn't have it any other way, they love their children because—"

"That's the oxytocin talking."

"So those new mothers who *don't* fall in love with their babies?" Jane hadn't thought of this before, but of course it made perfect sense. "The ones who want to throw them out the window because they're crying all the time?"

Spike anticipated. "Maybe their brains didn't produce enough, or perhaps any, oxytocin. Maybe post-partum depression is just oxytocin deficiency."

"And the assurance that the labour will be worth it, that you'll forget all about the pain as soon as you see your baby, as soon as you hold your baby— All true."

"Because of the oxytocin."

"Which they get more of if they have a vaginal birth." And then she had another new thought. "Which is why women who intend to give up their babies for adoption or who are surrogates should have caesareans! It would *reduce* that drug-induced attachment and make it easier to follow through with their plans." And yet another new thought. "Why doesn't any medical professional tell them that?!"

X took another chocolate cup from the box. It was a brownie batter marshmallow cream chocolate cup.

A few minutes later, Jane circled back. "You know, I've never understood it when people, women mostly, accuse me of being selfish for not having kids. *They're* the ones who are being selfish."

Spike agreed. "Having kids is an excuse to remain self-absorbed. Because kids serve as ego extensions. While appearing to be just the opposite."

"They use them as excuses to get what they themselves want. Better pay, better housing … Because after all, they've got kids. They act as if kids, their kids, have the right of way."

Spike nodded. "And why should someone else's spawn take priority over me? I'm more important than a baby-Barbie. A pre-Barbie. A limited-resource-consuming Barbie who will in all likelihood take more than she gives back."

"The right of way for innocence is highly over-rated."

Spike thought about that.

"And we're not selfish," Jane made an important distinction, "we're just self-centered."

"And there ain't nothing wrong with that."

"You're right," Jane said. "In fact, most people should be a little *more*, no, a *lot* more, self-centered. They should pay more attention to themselves, to what they believe, what they think, what they do. Instead, they're so busy paying attention to other people."

"Which is why they do stupid stuff. They haven't taken the time to think about it."

"Because they don't *have* the time," Jane added. "Or the energy."

"Because they did stupid stuff. Like have sex. The kind that makes new human beings."

They both sighed. It was such a pedestrian reason for the status quo.

X sighed too. There were no more chocolate cups in the box.

"And what's immature about wanting to live your own life? What's *mature* about living your whole life *for someone else*?

"They resent us," Spike said. "That's all."

Jane thought about that, and quickly came to agreement. "Because we didn't get sucked in to the wife and mother thing. Because if they'd thought about it as clearly as we did, they would've realized they *didn't* want to spend their lives looking after someone else. Husband. Kids."

"We're a reminder that they didn't think about it. And whenever they see us doing whatever the hell we want, whenever the hell we want, it reminds them. That they can't. They *envy* our marriage-free kid-free lifestyle."

"So why do they keep telling us how much we're missing?" Jane asked.

"Because the alternative—facing the truth, that they have given up their entire lives, for others, others who turn out to be all-too-ordinary—is too damned depressing."

"Ah. So of course they glorify it. Their devotion. Their sacrifice."

Jane stared out the window.

"Though," she added, "they *are* right to say that once we have some of our own, we'll change our minds. Because—"

"That'll be the oxytocin talking."

"Which is also why they don't get that when we—those of us who are oxytocin-free—when we say we don't like kids, we mean it. We *really* mean it."

Pity there were no more chocolate cups in the box.

15

You know, I'm still uncomfortable with this," Spike said the next morning. They were in a hotel room, in Greenbelt, eating breakfast. Double cheese, olives, and sun-dried tomatoes. X was googling Greenbelt. Because she had not seen a green belt yet.

"What if they take X to— Where does the military keep the aliens?" Spike asked.

Jane googled 'Where does the military keep the aliens?'

"Area 51."

"What if they take her to Area 51? We'll never get her out again!"

X googled Area 51. And fainted. Or whatever.

"Yeah, but NASA isn't the military," Jane protested.

"Then why did the President of the United States nominate, and the U. S. Senate confirm, a *Major General* Charles Frank Bolden as *Administrator*?"

Jane considered that. "Point taken."

They noticed X then. "Should we get the Mrs. Fields pail out of the car?"

"No, isn't that for when the universe goes purple?"

"Right. So is this like when it went ecru? Like outside the library?"

"White." X had recovered.

"You okay now?"

"Yes. Maybe." She resumed reading, while Jane and Spike reconsidered their plans.

"What other options do—"

"Are they *all* morons? At the Goddard Space Flight Center?" X interrupted, having seen nothing but men in all the pictures at the website.

"Yes. Maybe. No," Jane replied, "PR is probably staffed by women. Because we're the ones with good communication skills."

"Which is why first contact teams are all male."

"You know, it's weird that they don't prefer women astronauts," Jane said. "We're better at co-operative living. We're less volatile. We're smaller. Which means we'd need less oxygen, less food, less room ..."

"They probably don't want to go," Spike said. "Women. Into space. Would *you* want to spend several months in a studio-sized apartment with a bunch of other people? *Never* able to go outside?"

X looked up from her laptop. Confused by the analogy.

"Only men are deluded by the sales pitch of glory and honour and adventure," Spike continued. "They don't actually think about the trip, the day to day living experience. It's just like having kids. The *idea* appeals to them. They don't actually think about the reality."

"Okay, so how about just you and I go?" Jane suggested a few minutes later. She'd started on dessert. A slice of chocolate cashew pie topped with chocolate whipped cream. "X can stay here."

"Okay," Spike said, then immediately changed her mind. "No, not here." She turned to X. "You should go somewhere else—"

"I can wait at—"

"No, don't tell us!" Spike clapped her hands over her ears and starting humming. "If we know," she shouted, "they can torture us until we tell them!"

Jane stared at her. Then gently tugged her hands away from her ears.

"And if we *don't* know," she shouted at her, "they can torture us until we die!"

"Right. Okay. She could go wait in the park." There was one conveniently, and surprisingly, situated across from the hotel.

"But the mutants—with testosterone—and guns—" Being with Spike and Jane had been, she now realized—

"If one comes toward you," Jane suggested, "just—run away!"

Spike glared at her. X would likely fall flat on her face if she tried to do that.

"I could take one of those ultra-thins with me."

"Yeah. No." Spike didn't bother explaining. "You'll be okay." More okay than if she came with them. But more okay than if she stayed in the hotel room?

They decided that she'd go to the park, but sit on the bench that was both across from their window and close to the road where passing motorists would see ... anything. And when she saw them return, she was to wait for their 'All Safe' signal—they'd open and close the curtains three times—before coming back. They gave her one of the hotel key cards, and made sure she knew how to use it. Then they gave her some cash. And made sure she knew how to use it.

"Take a book and—" Halfway to the nightstand drawer, Spike stopped. "What do we have in your trunk?"

Jane thought. "Nothing, really. I mean, nothing really ..." Flattering? Remotely comprehensible to an extraterrestrial?

So Spike opened the drawer. And laughed. "Here." She handed X a copy of *Planet of the Apes*.

"'Non-employees visiting on official business should pull into the parking lot,'" Jane read off the website as they approached the Center, driving along Good Luck Road (seriously), "'park their vehicle, and obtain a security pass from inside the Main Gate building. Visitors *not* on official business should *not* enter the Main Gate.'"

Spike turned onto Greenbelt Road and entered the Main Gate.

Nothing happened. This was NASA, after all.

They parked, then entered the nearest building. Grey concrete. Of course.

"Name?" The uniformed man at the Security Desk barked.

"Spike Dubrey."

"Jane Smith."

"Name of the person with whom you have an appointment," he clarified, irritated.

"Oh, we don't have an appointment," Jane confessed. "We just want to ask a question."

"The Visitor Center is on ICESat Road." He reached under the counter, then handed them a brochure.

"But we have just the one question," Spike said. "It would be quicker if you could just tell us. What are the space-time coordinates of Earth?"

The man finally made eye contact.

"That's classified."

"Well, duh," Jane replied. "*Everything*'s classified. Pens are classified. As writing instruments. Writing instruments are classified as physical objects. What's it classified *as*?"

He stared at her.

"I think he means it's secret," Spike said.

"Oh. 'Classified' isn't a synonym for 'secret'," she told him.

The man furrowed his Neanderthal brow, confused. "It is here."

"Oh." First contact was going to be a disaster. *Official* first contact.

Jane stepped away from the counter and made a call. She returned in just a few seconds.

"Ellen Armstrong," she said. "We have an appointment with Ellen Armstrong in Media Relations. She's expecting us at— Now."

Spike looked over, surprised. Jane whispered an explanation. "I told her I was a freelance journalist. Working on a story titled *Earth Bad, Space Good*."

But before Ellen Armstrong could come down to meet her guests, two other men showed up. The one in the lead was tall, trim, relatively handsome, and well-groomed, with a full head of hair greying at the temples. A cookie-cutter Dean, CEO, President. They were never short, or overweight, or bald. The one trailing him, the one wearing a lab coat rather than a tailor-made suit, was short, overweight, and bald.

"These two?" the first one asked the Security Guy, in a voice stern with authority but somehow also conveying a buddy-to-buddy camaraderie.

The Security Guy nodded.

"I'm Dr. Arthur Ingles, Vice-Chief of Operations," he said, smiling with charm. "May I ask why you would like to know the space-time coordinates for Earth?"

"I'm doing a research paper for a course I'm taking," Jane launched into the explanation they'd used at MIT, "and —"

"I see."

"What's the Euclidean space perspective?" the other one asked.

Jane didn't know.

"How do displacement currents work?"

Jane didn't know.

"Okay," Spike jumped in, "you've got us, she's actually helping her sis—her brother with a research paper. That's why she doesn't—"

"I see. Kindly tell your brother to send his request through the proper channels." Dr. Arthur Ingles, Vice-Chief of Operations, started to walk away. Not smiling anymore. The other guy followed.

"Wait!" Jane called out. "I don't have a brother. We're really here just to settle a bet. She thinks you *don't* know the time-space coordinates of Earth, and I think you do."

"Good day, ladies."

As soon as the two men rounded the corner out of sight, a woman approached from the other direction. She was taller than she would have been without her heels, trim, attractive, even with the make-up, and had well-coiffured hair. She was wearing a burgundy skirt suit, little pearl earrings, and a matching pearl necklace. Not even her assistant's assistant would be short or overweight. Let alone bald. Even if she'd had chemo.

"Hello, Jane Smith? I'm Ellen Armstrong. If you'd just follow me ..."

Jane followed Ellen. Spike followed Jane.

"You're lucky to have gotten an appointment on such short notice," Ellen was saying amiably as she led the way to her office.

"Yes, and I really appreciate—"

Spike reached out and yanked her into the restroom they'd just passed.

"The Goddard Space Flight Center was established in 1959," they heard Ellen start to deliver a speech she'd probably delivered a thousand times, "and is named after Dr. Robert H. Goddard, a pioneer in modern rocket propulsion ..." She wouldn't even notice they were gone until she stepped into the elevator.

Jane stared at Spike, waiting for an explanation.

"If Dr. Arthur Ingles won't tell us the space-time coordinates, Ellen Armstrong certainly won't."

Jane considered that. "Good point. So what do you propose, see if it's written on the— Actually ..." She opened the door of the first stall and started reading the graffiti. *What was the worst day of your life? / Every day, struggling with an eating disorder. / I promise you, although I don't know you, you are beautiful, you deserve your health. ... Stay away from Evan Dellott. / And Mike Lane. ... I'm independent, but sometimes I just need someone to hold onto and tell me it's okay. / It's okay. ... Question everything. / Why?*

"We should check out the *men's* restroom."

They left the women's room and ducked into the men's, fingers crossed and excuses ready. All clear. Jane opened the door to the first stall. *Fuck gays. ... Pussy's gonna die. ... Beer-shits.com.* The rest of the wall was covered with drawings. Mostly of huge penises. And huge breasts.

They exited the restroom and—

"There they are!"

—were instantly surrounded by several men with huge guns. And probably small penises. And, probably, medium-sized breasts.

Fifteen minutes later—five floors, two elevators, and three hall-ways later—they were escorted into a small room. It had no windows.

"We're never getting out of here," Spike paced the room.

"Don't be silly. There's no toilet in here."

Meanwhile, back at the park ...

Dave or Leroy or Carlos or Abdul saw her sitting on the park bench, nice as you please. He started walking in her direction with the dog. A big, goofy, St. Bernard of a pup.

X saw the dog and ran toward him.

Wow, Dave or Leroy or Carlos or Abdul thought, this really *does* work.

No, toward the dog, you moron.

"And what's *your* name?" X asked, crouching.

Damn. He'd forgotten to ask.

Didn't matter. X had already found out. Boris.

"So, are you from around here?" the moron asked.

"They have to let us make a phone call, right?" Jane asked.

"And just who are we going to call?"

"Alan Shore. We need Alan Shore."

"No, I'm from Grmphflg." Fortunately, X had her face buried in Boris' furry neck when she said it. "I just stopped here to ask for directions. I got lost," she explained. It was okay. Boris was there.

"Oh," the moron smiled, "where did you want to go? I'm pretty good with directions." I need to be able to find my way back to my cave after I've killed a mastodon.

Right. You wish.

Also, I need to know where my territory is exactly so I can defend it.

Right.

I tried pissing on a few trees along the border, but I can't smell my own urine.

Pity. Everyone else can. And everyone else *did* that time you pissed against the wall of that building. That building that had several washrooms right inside. None of which would have had a line-up.

"Oh, really?" X was surprised. "Can you tell me the space-time coordinates of Earl?"

"What?"

"So why didn't the guy tell us the coordinates?" Jane asked. From her comfy position on the floor in the corner of the room. Spike had claimed one of the other corners. "Because knowledge is power?"

Spike snorted.

The moron stared at X playing in the distance with Boris. Was he supposed to join in? No, that wouldn't be cool. But— This wasn't working quite the way he'd anticipated.

After a very long twenty minutes, a woman entered the room. Lab coat, pants, no heels, no make-up, no jewelry. Hair, though. Uncoiffured.

"You're the ones wanting to know the space-time coordinates of Earth?"

They nodded, getting up off the floor.

"Hello," she said, pleasantly. "I'm Dr.— Alice. Would you please come with me?"

"No. I mean, where to?" Spike was suspicious.

"It's okay, you're safe with me."

"How can we be sure?"

The woman thought for a moment. "I think you've met an old professor of mine. Professor Donaldson?"

Okay, but—

"A bit of a moron?"

Jane's eyes widened. Spike's narrowed.

Still—

The woman thought a bit more. "Have you seen much of Greenbelt yet? There's a fantastic dessert place on Bellamy Street. They have the best chocolate malted cheesecake. They serve it with a scoop of fudge frosting."

"Lead the way."

X chased Boris. Boris chased X. The moron sat on the bench.

"So why didn't the guy tell us the coordinates?" Jane asked Alice as they followed her through a couple tunnels—tunnels?—out to the parking lot.

"He doesn't know, right?" Spike suggested. Heaven forbid a man admit he doesn't know something.

"Right."

"Because that information's above his classification level, right?"

"It would be, yes."

X and Boris tumbled together down a hill. The moron got up and left.

"What did she mean by 'It *would* be'?" Jane and Spike were on their way back to the hotel. Alice had given them the address of the dessert place, and they were to meet her there. She'd smiled with barely contained excitement when she'd said she'd get a table for four.

"Because she should have said 'It *is*'," Jane continued. "I mean, if someone actually *had* the information. Right?"

Spike kept driving.

"Maybe she was just using the conditional tense as, you know, a sort of polite version of the declarative tense," Jane continued. "And not to indicate an epistemological possibility rather than an actuality."

Spike kept driving.

Once back in their room, they looked out the window to the park across the road, but didn't see X. They opened and closed the curtains three times, then looked out again. Still no X. A few anxious moments later, they saw her come into view, running— more or less—across the grass. A big goofy St. Bernard was chasing her. She was laughing. Suddenly she turned and chased the big goofy St. Bernard. The St. Bernard laughed. Then the dog turned and zoomed off in the other direction. Must've been called. X turned and headed to the bench that was across from their window and close to the road. They opened and closed the curtains again three times. She noticed, waved, and headed to the hotel.

It took her several minutes, and just as many wrong turns, to find their room.

But once there— "Did you get the coordinates?" she asked. *Planet of the Apes* in hand.

"No, but we're going to go meet someone now," Spike said. Happily. Or at least hopefully. "And— We're going to take you with us."

"Not a moron?"

"Don't think so."

"Okay."

16

As soon as the three of them entered the café, Alice stood and waved them to her table at the side. The café was surprisingly spacious, nicely lit, with pastel chairs set at boldly coloured tables.

"Hello," she said, extending a slightly trembling hand to X. "You must be—"

X looked uncertainly at Jane and then at Spike.

"It's okay," Alice said. "Alice makes sure the place doesn't have any bugs, and none of the NASA men come here. Ever. Desserts ... chocolate ... you know."

Jane mentally slapped her forehead.

Spike nodded a 'go ahead' to X.

"I'm Xrrmrvnbnvdl."

"I'm honoured to meet you, X." She almost bowed.

"Please, sit," she gestured to the chairs.

A woman immediately came to their table.

"Hi, Alice, this is X."

"Holy shit! Really?" Alice looked at— Alice. "I am *so* delighted to meet you!" She smiled broadly at X. "And to have you here at my café, it's just— Holy Shit!" She turned to Alice again, as if to confirm that this was indeed—Holy Shit!

"We'll have your chocolate malted cheesecake— All round?" Alice asked her guests. They nodded. "And four cups of hot chocolate."

Alice left with their order. Muttering. Holy Shit.

"I thought *you* were Alice," Spike said, confused, when the woman left.

"I am, sort of. We're all Alice. It's like ... a secret password."

"I see." Spike did not see at all. But first things first.

"So can *you* tell X the space-time coordinates?"

"No."

"But—"

"I don't know them."

X slumped in her seat, understandably disappointed.

"But—"

"No one at NASA does. We've made sure of it."

"I see." Again, she did not at all see.

"So ... the information's *not* classified?" Jane was having trouble keeping up as well.

Just then, four women came into the café, saw Alice, paused, then tentatively approached their table.

"Hi Alice, Alice, Alice. Alice."

They nodded to Alice, but didn't look at her. They were staring at X.

"This is X," Alice said. Part of her face wanted to break into a Boris grin. The other part remembered that she worked at NASA.

The four women smiled, nodded politely to X, and murmured variations of "Holy Shit!"

"Every Alice within a hundred miles will come," Alice said apologetically to the three of them. "I hope you understand."

"Sure." They understood nothing.

There were a few starts and stutters and silences, then the four women left.

"So," Spike said, trying to recover ... something ...

"The two of you must want to talk," Jane said, looking at Alice and then at X and then back to Alice. "You must have lots of questions—"

"No," Alice said firmly. "I don't want to know. Anything. We're not ready for it. Any of it."

X looked relieved.

"In fact," she hesitated, then decided to continue, "that's why— There's a bunch of us—"

"You're sabotaging their work!" Spike suddenly got it.

Alice nodded. "It started with nuclear weapons. With the Women of Alamo. The wives of all of the men at Alamo. They were the first Alices. They were physicists, mathematicians, engineers, all under deep cover. They tried to stop the discovery, but ... failed. Obviously. As a result— Well, you know your history, I imagine."

They nodded. Though apparently they *didn't* know their history.

"It's really tricky," Alice continued, explaining. "You have to be very careful about the errors you introduce. Not only so they're not noticed, but the physics, the math ... you could make it worse."

"So you're all— You've been— For almost a century—" Spike struggled with the magnitude of it. And with the relative futility of her own efforts.

"So you're intentionally handicapping yourselves, because of *men*." Jane had gotten up to speed. She sighed. Deeply. What else is new.

"We *could* know the coordinates," Alice hastened to say. "By now. Well," she clarified, "not me, but Alice. And Alice, I think ... But it's just too dangerous."

"So you could help X figure them out?" All was *not* lost. "So she could get back home?"

X hadn't followed much of what had been said, but she sat forward eagerly again when she heard Jane's question.

"Probably. Again, not me, but—" She broke off, but then the words gushed out as she leaned forward and looked at X. "That would be the most exciting thing any one of us would ever do in our entire lives!" Her eyes shone.

"That said," Alice slumped back in her chair, "we won't. We can't. I'm so sorry, but we're all too closely connected to NASA. It's too great a risk. You understand?" She begged X to understand.

And by now, yes, X did understand. She sighed so deeply she deflated. Not literally. Just— She'd have to figure out the coordinates on her own. Somehow. Or figure out another way ...

Two more Alices entered the café and were introduced to X.

"Hi, X, I'm so— I'm—" More starts, stutters, then silences.

It was painfully clear that every Alice who entered the café was so very eager to ask ... everything. And yet—

It was a *Groundhog Day* of The Saddest First Contact ever.

Alice brought their cheesecake and hot chocolate.

"So how did you know about us?" Spike asked, once she'd had a bite of cheesecake. "I mean, to begin with?"

"Professor Donaldson was one of my profs at MIT. He sent me an email, gloating about how there was another nutcase just like me who thought there were 11,000 dimensions— I'd noticed the mistake on the original paper. And had corrected the guy."

"How'd that go over?" Jane asked.

"How do you think?" Alice grimaced.

They both nodded.

"Still, you did land a job at NASA," Jane said, with envy.

"As a research *assistant*."

"Even so," Spike said. "Dr. Jane Smith here is an office temp."

Alice had the grace to blush. "Point taken."

"Donaldson blathered on and on about the three of you asking about Earth's time-space coordinates," she continued, "and solving Fermat's equation in a different way, and I thought if you're legit, eventually you'll find your way here."

"But how did you know we *had?*" Jane asked. "Found our way here?"

"Oh, Alice hacked into the security system at the Main Gate. We've been keeping an eye out."

"Ah."

A few bites later, Spike suddenly had an idea. An awful idea. "The Challenger disaster—"

"No, that was them all on their own," Alice assured her. "The O-ring— That would have been too obvious. Though," Alice hesitated, then continued, in for a penny, "if that hadn't happened— You don't want to know what they were *really* going to do. So Alice, on board—"

Suddenly a dozen Alices came crashing through the door, and over the next five minutes, all of the Alices who had already been, returned, bringing more Alices with them. They busily, noisily, happily went about hanging streamers from the ceiling, rearranging all the chairs in the café, clearing space at one end of the room and hanging a black drop sheet, with an iridescent 'Welcome' across the top ... Five minutes later, they invited X, with great ceremony, to take the front row center seat for a series of performances.

First up was a performance on a light synthesizer. "That's what I call it," Alice, the designer, explained, "because it synthesizes light, much like a sound synthesizer synthesizes sound. And like someone who uses a sound synthesizer, I can compose and then perform a piece. Or I can improvise."

X looked very interested, so she continued.

"Instead of controlling pitch, the various keys control the location of the light projected onto the wall." She demonstrated, first pressing a high note, or key, and then a low one. A single point of light appeared first high up on the black drop sheet, then it appeared near the floor.

"Ah!" X's eyes danced.

"The harmonies control the colours." Alice played a few chords in different major keys and then a few in minor keys. In the first case, vibrant reds and oranges appeared, and in the second, muted purples.

"And instead of controlling volume, key pressure controls intensity." Again, she demonstrated.

"I control the form of the light with various sliders, knobs, and what have you..." There were murmurs of admiration and wonder all round as various shapes flickered and floated across the black drop sheet.

Then, she stood ceremoniously. Everyone was quiet.

"I've titled this piece 'Welcome' and dedicate it to you, X." They found out later that she'd composed it over the course of the last couple days, anticipating, hoping for, this very moment.

She took her seat at the synthesizer and began. Splashes of light sparkled, changing colour as they moved, glittering, across the black ... then a single flame of light rose up, and up, stronger and stronger ... aurora borealis intensified into existence, filaments becoming ribbons ... they swirled slowly, some touching the flame, some wrapping around the flame ... they twirled more quickly ... then gradually dissolved away ... X was enthralled. The piece lasted a full ten minutes. And it was over far too soon.

Next up was a dancer. Not a pornified jazz dancer, not an anorexic ballerina on foot-deforming toe shoes, but someone reminiscent of Margie Gillis, who defied all expectations and achieved extraordinary expressiveness with her large, athletic body. Alice danced in silence. It was incredibly striking. And incredibly moving.

Next up was a piece from one of the suites for unaccompanied cello now known to have been composed by '*Mrs.* Bach'. Anna Magdalena.

After that, someone read poetry. The imagery was so fresh, so engaging.

Spike thought with shame that they should have been taking X to concerts, poetry readings, theatre performances, art galleries, museums— Well, maybe not the latter. Last time she went to a museum, she'd noticed that almost every woman, in paintings in which there *was* a woman, was either half-naked or with a child. And certainly every Broadway musical in New York ... Truth is, they'd have to search long and hard to find what they were experiencing here and now.

Next, one of the women performed a vocalize, her rich alto voice warming everyone to the core. With its humanity.

Lastly, an Alice did a short stand-up comedy routine, ending with "Why did the ET cross the road?"

"To get back to the future!" Someone called out.

"Why did the ET cross the road?" she asked again.

"To phone home!" The antiphonal coda continued.

"Why did the ET cross the road?"

"Same reason she crossed the rift—to get to the other side!"

"Why did the ET cross the road?"
"Shut up, Wesley!"

There was food (a lot of pizza) (and even more chocolate), drink, laughter, smiles, pleasure, delight, surprise, celebration. It became The Partiest First Contact ever.

Eventually a bit more space was cleared and a violinist launched into an energetic reel. Spike grinned when she recognized the Irish Rovers' "Wasn't that a Party?"—it was in there somewhere, but the accompanying musicians were improvising over it, elaborating on it, doing something, something *more*, with it ... The women formed a circle, and a simple pattern was established that everyone could manage, but that left space for the more skilled among them to ornament, to embellish. X found herself in the center of the moving circle, dancing in a way that can only be described as Silly-Puppy-Meets-Butterfly.

In the lull that followed the end of the dance, X asked Alice to play another piece on her light synthesizer. As soon as she managed to blink away her tears, she did so. The first movement opened with a night sky of infinite black... ruby stars appeared one by one, and then when the sky was filled with twinkling stars, the rubies turned into amethysts, a small galaxy here, a small galaxy there, the changes making a path, winding through the dark. The second movement was multi-coloured moonlight on water, gleaming, glimmering, shining, shimmering. The third movement was fireworks, choreographed purely for the visual aesthetic, without the ... noise. The light burst across the black, in silence, it rained down, it fountained up, it tumbled into lightfalls. Everyone sighed with such ...

To live, to be, *without the noise.*

The three of them returned to their room in a sort of emotional black hole. The party had been fun and uplifting, but the meeting with Alice had been, ultimately, depressing. They'd eaten; there was no need to order out. They'd already opened the nightstand drawer. Spike stood in the center of the room, turned on the tv, and started clicking.

They watched an old news clip, wherein men set the oil wells in Kuwait on fire.

"Don't you *need* the oil?" X asked.

"Yeah." They didn't even try to explain it.

Spike clicked a bit more, stopping at a weather report.

"'Acts of weather,'" Jane repeated the weatherperson's words with incredulity. "Not, like, 'acts of humanity.'"

"Because we had nothing to do with it," Spike said sarcastically.

"And of course we don't want to blame someone's god."

"Will any records be broken this month?" the commentator asked with some excitement.

"It's not the frickin' Olympics," Spike said with disgust.

"It's like he thinks breaking a record would be a good thing," Jane said with disbelief.

An image followed of an impossibly huge chunk of ice breaking off and crashing into the Arctic Ocean. It was a dramatic image. But not for the reason the producers had in mind.

"Once, on one of the weather websites," Jane said, staring blankly at the image, which was being replayed over and over, "the 'Photo of the Day' was a huge iceberg, floating freely, and—"

"And the caption read 'Does anyone else see a face in the iceberg?'" Spike had seen that too. In fact, it had been a turning point for her.

"You know, *since* that's begun," Spike nodded to the tv, "and it's all inevitable from this point on, I've been thinking that we *should* go ahead and start chunking off the ice for fresh water."

"Before it drops into the ocean and melts away," Jane understood.

"Then I thought, why bother. Since it *is* all inevitable from this point on."

Jane glanced over. There was something in her tone—

"The point of no return is two degrees,"[54] Spike said flatly.

---

54 http://globalwarming.berrens.nl/globalwarming.htm

"Which is 440 parts per million carbon dioxide. We're at 404, last time I checked.[55] And increasing at 2.1 per year."[56]

Jane nodded. "I read that we'll get there by 2017.[57] *Rolling Stone*—well, Holthaus[58]—says we're already there."

"Either way, we've pretty much closed that door. Even if greenhouse gas emissions—and I'm including the methane from cows, the meat industry is as much to blame[59] as the oil industry—Even if all our greenhouse gas emissions stopped overnight, the concentrations already in the atmosphere would mean a global rise of at least one degree. Given everything we've already done, we're certain to reach 1.5 degrees."

"Certain?" She knew it, but she didn't want to believe it.

Spike nodded. "Nothing short of a suspension of the laws of cause and effect will save us now."

"You don't think a few geniuses will find solutions?" Jane asked a short while later. Clinging to ... hope.

"I think a few geniuses have already found solutions. Light rail transit instead of SUVs. A way to neutralize radiation.[60] Solar panels and wind turbines instead of fossil fuels. Hell, some teenagers in Africa have figured out how to make six hours of electricity out of a litre of pee.[61]

---

55 https://www.co2.earth/

56 https://www.co2.earth/co2-acceleration

57 http://www.washingtonpost.com/blogs/wonkblog/post/when-do-we-hit-the-point-of-no-return-for-climate-change/2011/11/10/gIQA4rri8M_blog.html

58 http://www.rollingstone.com/politics/news/the-point-of-no-return-climate-change-nightmares-are-already-here-20150805

59 http://www.scientificamerican.com/article/the-greenhouse-hamburger/

60 http://nuclearwaste-theroyprocess.blogspot.ca/2005/12/to-all-late-dr.html

61 http://makerfaireafrica.com/2012/11/06/a-urine-powered-generator/

"We also have the soapstone stove, which can heat and bake all day with half an armful of wood. We have high tech incinerators with energy recovery and pollution controls. We have cars that can get 77 miles per gallon, and fridges, air conditioners, photocopiers, light bulbs, computers, ovens, and dryers that use one-fourth the energy of current models."

"Hm. Don't recall seeing any of those at Walmart."

"Exactly."

"Pay attention to the insurance companies," Spike added, as if Jane needed more proof. "Note which exclusions they start inserting into their policies. Refusing to insure for damages and injuries resulting from nuclear accidents will be the least of it."

"So why isn't the rest of the world boycotting us?" Jane wondered aloud. "Telling us they won't buy any of our shit until we get our act together?"

X googled 'boycott'.

"Better yet," Jane added a moment later, "Why aren't the scientists doing something? I mean other than publishing their papers in journals that only a dozen other people read?"

"Good point. You'd think that if they can figure out how climate is changing, they can figure out how to use a gun."

Okay, not where she was going.

"Instead of organizing their international conferences," Spike elaborated, "they should be organizing international coups, in which they take politicians hostage until the fuckers make the right decisions."

A commercial interrupted, *preempted,* the report. Of course. Because getting our whites whiter was more important. Never mind that we're getting our whites white with *dioxin,*[62] one of the most toxic chemicals known.

---

62 http://articles.baltimoresun.com/1991-02-20/features/1991051144_1_dioxins-paper-products-paper-mill

"Did you know," Spike continued, "that when Rachel Carson's *Silent Spring* first came out, a reviewer[63] for *Time*"—X looked up from her laptop—"called it 'unfair, one-sided, hysterically overemphatic, an emotional and inaccurate outburst'?"

"Perhaps it was just an oversight that she wasn't burned at the stake."

"Species are becoming extinct at 1,000 times[64] the natural rate. Probably exactly what she said. Or close to. They simply don't have time to adapt to the changes. And of course most people, being idiots who didn't pay attention in high school biology and haven't read a book since then—"

"Not that they read a book then—"

"Don't realize how much we depend on a lot of those species. Bees, for example. They pollinate 70%[65] of our crops."

"I wonder how those people are explaining the increase in food prices."

"Well, it's mostly the fruits, vegetables, and grains that are increasing in price. Not so much Cheetos and Twinkies."

"Are people still eating Cheetos and Twinkies?"

X googled Cheetos. Found cheetahs.

She googled Twinkies. They didn't look at all twinky.

"And," Spike nodded to the tv with even more disgust, "'*extreme* storms'."

"It sounds like 'extreme sports'."

Spike nodded. "Once I saw a spot called 'This week's wildest weather!' As if we're all on a fun safari."

Jane nodded. They watched for just a bit longer.

"They've turned the death of our planet into entertainment." Spike said it quietly.

She turned off the tv. It was the least they could do.

And, apparently, the most.

---

63 http://www.environmentandsociety.org/exhibitions/silent-spring/personal-attacks-rachel-carson
64 http://web.mit.edu/12.000/www/m2015/2015/climatechange.html
65 http://www.bbc.com/future/story/20140502-what-if-bees-went-extinct

"Do you really think scientists should take hostages?" Jane asked a short while later.

"I don't know. The Nuremburg principles say that an individual has not only the right, but the *duty* to interfere with his or her government when it is preparing for a war of aggression or a crime against humanity.

"But when Katya Komarisuk did just that—she's the one who 'decommissioned' Navstar, the weapons computer required for a nuclear first strike—she wasn't allowed to explain her motives or introduce any expert witnesses at her trial. She couldn't even *say* 'nuclear missile,' 'first strike,' or 'international law.'"

"Could she say 'shafted'?"

A few minutes later, Spike addressed the elephant in the room.

"So, what next? Do we try another *professor*?"

Jane slowly turned away from the blank tv. She'd just realized something. "No. It's not the profs, it's the *students* who are cutting edge! We need to find a doctoral candidate! Or a post-doc!"

X googled post hoc. They could find something before it was done after? That sounded promising.

"A conference?" Spike suggested, but Jane was ahead of her, already googling.

"Okay, there's an APS conference coming up at Caltech. Can we get to California in a week?"

X looked at them. Stunned. Jane saw it.

"In my car," she qualified. "Since it's all we've got." She stuck out her tongue at X for good measure.

Surprised, delighted, X stuck out her tongue back. Then, realizing what she'd just done, became fascinated with the fact that she *could,* in fact, *do* that. She stuck out her tongue again, grabbed it, and laughed.

As Jane was MapQuesting, Spike had an idea. "What if, instead of just attending the conference, we have X do a poster session? To attract the kind of people she needs to talk with."

"Like some kind of code!" Jane got it. "So only those doing research into the space-time continuum will stop. Or even understand. X, are you following us?"

"Nobnth."

"We might need to be students to register ..."

Jane was already searching ...

"Well?" Spike said a few minutes later.

"There's a place called Everything Chocolate near Caltech."

"And?"

"And a chocolate truffle shop."

"And?"

"And we can attend the conference and even present a poster session as independents. But we have to be members of the APS, and we have to register for the conference."

"Make it so!"

17

We put tons of carcinogens into our food, water, and air," Spike said, as they passed a billboard urging them to join the Relay for Life, "and then spend millions of dollars looking for the cure for cancer. Oh where oh where could it be."

Jane had stopped working on her novel and her dictionary an hour ago and was looking out the passenger window.

X was in the back seat reading *Formulation for Observed and Computed Values of Deep Space Network Data Types for Navigation.* She'd discovered Google Books. And, apparently, a way to access the brain's RAM.

"Remember what you said about Plan B?" Jane said. She'd done a lot of thinking after their conversation the previous evening. "So even when we *have* good ideas, or solutions, we can't get them out there? I mean 'we' in general."

Spike nodded. "Or they get out there and then economic or legislative barriers suddenly and oh-so-mysteriously appear that make it impossible for anything to be done with them."

"Yeah. And remember that Nancy Kress novel? *Beggars and Choosers?*"

Spike nodded again. "Someone just *gave* it away, and still."

"So the problems aren't technological," Jane said. "They're psychological, philosophical, sociocultural."

"Which means," Spike saw where she was going, "the solutions have to be psychological, philosophical, sociocultural."

"Which means we *are* screwed."

"Though," Spike said, "there are entire institutes doing research into conflict resolution alternatives. I've read articles like 'What Would Peace in the Middle East Be Like?' and 'Demilitarization and Prospects for Democracy.'"

"Don't recall seeing the Coles Notes versions of those in *Chatelaine.*"

"Like you read *Chatelaine,*" Spike snorted.

"Even so," Spike conceded a moment later, "it doesn't help that over half of our planet's scientists and engineers work for the military."

"And the other half work for Pizza Pizza."

X googled Theodore D. Moyer. *He* didn't work for Pizza Pizza. He worked for NASA. And the California Institute of Technology. Wait— He could be at two places at once? She kept reading.

"CFCs and the ozone," Jane gave the example foremost on her mind. "It took us 10 years to figure that one out, another 20 to do something about it—"

"'Wear sunscreen.' Good one."

"So what *is* the point?" she continued. "I mean if we're so fucked up that even the solutions to the problems—   It used to be, for me, 'Quick, live, before you die.' Now ..." she paused. "I think it's become 'Quick, live, before we're over.'"

Spike had to agree. Now. No matter how many outrageous acts and everyday rebellions she'd staged, nothing ever changed. Not really. Not in any way that mattered. It was like bashing her head against a jellyfish.

X kept reading. The book was surprisingly good. Despite having been written by a moron.

"And it's even worse than that," Jane said. She'd also done a lot of googling. "In some cases, there *are* no solutions. Every CFC molecule we put into the atmosphere *will* get heated by UV. Which *will* make each chlorine atom break away. Then each chlorine atom *will* react with an ozone molecule, taking one of its oxygen atoms, turning it into O_2 instead of O_3."

Spike nodded.

"Add the increase in CO_2 and you *will* get an increase in air temperature. You have to. And that *has* to lead to an increase in ocean temperature, both of which *have* to lead to the melting of the Arctic ice, which unquestionably increases the temperature even more because of the change in heat reflection: white snow reflects heat better than dark water. Add the methane that will be released, and the conveyor belt in the ocean *will* stop. Because the water on the top won't be cold enough anymore to sink."

Again, Spike nodded.

"We can't change the laws of science," Jane said. She'd come to the same point Spike had made. "That chain reaction is as inevitable as a long line of dominoes tumbling over once the first one is tipped. End result?"

"We will fry to a crisp," Spike said. "Unless we drown first. Or, because of distribution inequities, starve. Or die of thirst. Unless we're in the path of one of those thrilling extreme storm events. 'Course, we could just succumb to an infectious pandemic that, due to changing vectors, we won't keep ahead of ..."

"So by the time 'the point of no return' gets into the news—"

"We'll be long past it."

Jane nodded.

"It took real talent," Spike re-purposed Chomsky's comment about Brazil, "to create a nightmare on a planet as favourably and richly endowed as Earth."

X stopped reading. The Orbit Determination Program could be used to navigate a spacecraft "anywhere in the solar system." *Could* be used. Not *can* be used. Besides, she didn't want to go anywhere in 'the' solar system. (Did Moyer think there was only one?) She wanted to get *away*—far, *far* away—and just as much awhile—from *this*, solar system. She wanted to go home.

"Though," Jane said a few moments later, "I did read that the hole in the ozone is expected to heal by 2050.[66] Thanks to the Montreal Protocol."

"Which is why we don't hear about it anymore," Spike said almost as a reflex. "The news has to be exciting. It has to be about *problems,* not solutions."

"You're right," Jane said, recalling 'the news' of the night before. And, actually, every 'news' program she'd ever watched. "It's all accidents, pain, injury, death. Big fights, little fights, old fights, new fights. And football."

"Which is really just pain, injury, and little fights."

"So it's no wonder people don't— I mean, first it was all about acid rain. In the 70s, remember?"

Jane nodded.

"Then CFCs. Then CO2. Then methane. The media manufactures—no, *manages*—crises. When we get tired of one, they let it go, and give us another." Been there.

"They probably do that," she continued, "because they've met my students. And understand their attention spans."

"They *created* your students. *And* their attention spans."

"Either way, people get the idea that everything will be all right," Jane saw where Spike had been going. "Life is like the tv shows they watch every night."

"Every single night," Spike interjected for emphasis.

"Everything works out in the end."

"In half an hour. An hour, tops."

"Do you think that's because we thrive on conflict? Well, not *us* we," she corrected herself.

"Maybe. We do feel more important when we have problems."

---

66 http://www.smithsonianmag.com/science-nature/ozone-hole-was-super-scary-what-happened-it-180957775/?no-ist

"Ah. The attraction of addiction," Jane said, making an interesting connection. "When you have a *need*, an urgency, one has importance, one is significant."

"Hm." Spike had never seen the Munchausen element of addiction before. Now that she did, she made another interesting connection. "Maybe that's why everyone 'watches the news.' It's a Munchausen by proxy thing."

Jane got three chocolate bars out of their bag—they'd finished off the last of their bakery boxes the day before. She handed one to Spike and another one, the Aero bar, to X.

"Soon we won't be able to get chocolate anymore." Jane bit off a chunk of dark mint chocolate and let it melt in her mouth, slowly.

"We're no smarter than frogs," she said a few moments later, "sitting in a pot of water that's gradually coming to a boil."

"Oh we're much smarter than frogs," Spike objected. "We're the ones heating the pot. How clever is that?"

Within five minutes, they passed a McDonalds. Of course they did. Then a Burger King. Then a Wendy's.

"Cheeseburgers[67] are responsible for *half* our greenhouse gas emissions," Spike grumbled. "And we don't need a genius to tell us how to solve *that* problem."

"So what do you think," Jane said, "start with a bang, end with a whimper? Will people just quietly kill themselves or will they freak out, party hard, and destroy everything not already destroyed?" And why would they do that, she wondered as soon as she'd said it. Why would they destroy what little is left ...

"Neither," Spike said. "They'll be watching tv. Probably some new reality tv show."

---

67 http://www.huffingtonpost.com/neal-barnard-md/cowsnot-coalare-the-real-_b_5526979.html

Jane grimaced.

"But you'll finish your book? The novel? Before then?"

She nodded. Then said, sounding like a BBC program, "Clearly these are the final moments of our species. And it is imperative that we understand just what the fuck happened."

Spike grinned. "So read to me what you wrote this morning."

Jane opened her novel-in-progress. Then paused. For drama.

"It was a relatively dark and stormy night. If a train was traveling east at 1.43 gazillion miles per hour and another train was traveling west at 2.65 gazillion miles per hour ..."

"At some point, we need to get a new credit card," Jane said, when, on the second day, they'd stopped for gas. She'd gotten out of the car to go into the convenience store while Spike filled the tank. X said she'd wait in the car. "We should go to an airport."

Spike glanced over, confused.

Jane explained. "Isn't that where they have people accosting strangers and urging them to sign up for one? I think that's how I got this one ... When I went to that philosophy conference."

"Really? Okay."

Once inside, Jane selected a number of chocolate bars to replenish their supply, then approached the counter. Just as she started to get out her credit card, a man entered, pushed right by her, and grunted "Pump 4."

The attendant looked at his meter. "Sixty dollars."

"Excuse me—" she spoke up. Then remembered that some animals couldn't hear sounds above a certain frequency.

Once back on the highway, Jane started flipping through the newspaper she'd purchased. God knows why. "'Violence in our society'," she murmured. "It sounds so ... *inclusive*, doesn't it?"

She didn't need to say that over 90% of all violent crime was committed *by* men—that the gangs were made up of *men*, that the bar brawls were fought by *men*, that the corner stores were held up by *men*, that the rapists were *men*, that the muggers were *men*, that the drive-by shooters were *men*.

She didn't need to google to know that a man is about ten times as likely as a woman to commit armed robbery, nine times as likely to commit murder, and almost six and a half times as likely to commit aggravated assault. Thirteen times as likely to commit fraud, eight times as likely to commit vandalism, seven times as likely to commit arson, four times as likely to commit offenses against children, and twice as likely to commit forgery.

"Did you know that it's routine[68] for police to receive extra training and to have more of them at events that attract large numbers of men?" Neither was needed at events attended by large numbers of women. "How can they be, why are they, so ethically-challenged?"

It was a rhetorical question, but Spike decided to answer anyway. "For starters, we stunt their emotional growth. From day one, we encourage outright denial: big boys don't cry. They don't cuddle and hug either. So hurt, pain, love, and affection are— Not cards in the deck they're playing with.

"We also stunt their social growth," she continued. "Competition over cooperation. Self over others."

"Well," Jane clarified, "not *us* we." The whole situation was an argument for parent licences. Mothers raised the kids. Ergo, women had the power. Given such a pervasive and monolithic culture, maybe not *a lot* of power. But surely some ...

"And apart from all the nurture stuff," Spike added, "nature." 'Nuff said.

"Hm. No morality, no emotion, no empathy, excessive self-interest— Isn't that the definition of a psychopath?"

Spike stared at Jane. "It is indeed." She'd thought of men as mentally ill, in one way or another, but she'd hadn't— To be male, to be a man, is to be a psychopath.

---

68 http://radicalhubarchives.wordpress.com/2011/07/

"I really like June Stephenson's idea,"[69] Jane said a few miles later.

Spike waited.

"You know, about having men pay extra on their income tax. To cover all their shit. Prisons are expensive to maintain, and we have to feed and clothe all those prisoners. Then there's the expense of the police forces and courts that get them there. And the emergency services that take care of all the gunshot wounds, the knife slashes, the broken jaws ..."

"Then there's all the environmental stuff," Spike got on board. "They're the ones driving the gas-guzzlers with the high emissions. They're the CEOs dumping toxic waste, clear-cutting forests, damming rivers, drilling and fracking for oil ..."

Jane nodded.

"And you know, that door's been opened," Spike continued, "by the insurance companies. Men, young men in particular, pay higher premiums. Since they're such lousy drivers,[70] compared to us. Almost three times the accidents and driving violations."

Jane nodded again.

"But most of their shit is done before they're even old enough to *pay* income tax," Spike continued working through Stephenson's idea.

"So their parents should pay. Five thousand a year, annually, until the boy turns eighteen."

"Might decrease the number of male births."

The thought about that for a while. Dreamy smiles on their faces.

They decided to stop at an electronics store to see about buying a GPS. On the one hand, it would make their cross-country trip easier, but on the other hand, they suspected, it would make it more boring.

---

69 *Men Are Not Cost Effective.*

70 http://www.statisticbrain.com/male-and-female-driving-statistics/

"Let's see how much they cost," Spike said. "If we don't like using it, we can always turn it off." Spike glanced at the billboard they passed, wishing they could turn *it* off. It was one of those animated boards. And it informed them that Gillio was a girl's best friend. Spike had no idea what Gillio was. But the almost-naked woman looked pretty orgasmic about it. Maybe it was a laundry detergent.

Jane googled and found a Best Buy that looked pretty accessible.

They took the exit, drove to the parallel service road full of mini-malls, then parked in the Best Buy lot. X said she'd wait in the car. Again.

Once in the store, they found they needed a GPS unit to find the GPS units.

"You girls need help finding something?"

"WE'RE NOT *GIRLS*, GOD DAMN IT!" Spike shouted at the young man who had appeared. It didn't help that he couldn't've been more than twenty-five. Which meant that even men *younger* than them thought they were— "IF WE'VE SAID IT ONCE, WE'VE SAID IT A MILLION TIMES: WE   ARE   ADULTS."

He stared at them with total incomprehension.

Jane tugged Spike away before she slugged him one. "Actually, *we* may have said it a million times, but— I think most women like being called girls."

Spike thought about that. And conceded that that was probably true.

"It's hopeless," she said.

A mile later, when it was clear they were lost, Jane said, "And speaking of Plan B," she grinned—it had been a while, but the idea of parent licences put Plan B back into her head, "it doesn't help that we're dumbing down. Only the smart people are using contra- ception. Intelligent women don't want to spend their lives looking after other people. They'd rather be doing research, writing books, composing symphonies. Natural selection is not intelligent design."

"Hey, that's really good. 'Natural selection is not intelligent design.' You should put that in your novel."

It took a just a second. "No wait, it'll sound like you're advocating divine design. Which is *also* not intelligent design. You could put *that* in your novel."

Jane made a note. Two notes.

"And speaking of Plan B *and* dumbing down," she one-upped herself a few miles later, "I remember reading *Freakonomics*, in which Dumb and Dumber present the *astounding* connection between access to abortion and crime: twenty years after Roe v. Wade, the U.S. crime rate dropped."

"Astounding indeed," Spike laughed. "That men are so surprised by that."

"Exactly! I mean, how clueless *are* they? About the power, the influence, of parenting, about the effect of being forced to be pregnant, to be saddled with a squalling baby you do not want, on an income you do not have, because you've got a squalling baby you do not want ... What did they *think* would happen in situations like that? The women would get 'Mother of the Year' awards for raising psychologically healthy adults?"

"What *I* find surprising," Spike said, "is that access to abortion isn't related to infanticide.

"Pity," she added a moment later. "Given the *Freakonomics* boys."

"Oh, this is interesting," Jane said a few minutes later, googling to pass the time. "A group of video gamers, no doubt cognizant of Anita Sarkeesian's work,[71] have designed some games in which the *men* get insulted, humiliated, beat up, and raped by the *women*."

"And? Did they get it?"

---

71 https://feministfrequency.com/

"'These are supposed to be video *games*, bitch!'" Jane read one of the responses. "'Nothing fun about this!'"

"Guess not."

They started worrying about X third day on the road. She didn't want to go anywhere, see anything, do anything. She didn't want to talk. *And* she didn't want any of the chocolate bars Jane had bought. Not even the Aero bar.

She often went—not purple, ecru, or white ... Grey, they suspected. Or at least beige. She wouldn't say.

And what could *they* say?

X might never get home. And she knew it.

She might have to spend the rest of her life on Earl.

And she knew it would be nasty, brutish, and short.

On the fourth day, they stopped for gas again.

"Hang on," Spike said, as Jane headed into the convenience store. "I'll go with you. Stretch my legs a bit. X?"

She shook her head.

A few youngish men lingered at the entrance. "So ... you girls travelling alone?" the one with his pants half way to his ankles asked.

Spike counted to ten, while she reached into her pocket to start recording, then said, "Does it *look* like we're travelling alone?"

"Well, yeah."

"Then you need to have your eyes checked," she said. "I'm travelling with her, and she's travelling with me."

"Ergo," Jane summarized helpfully, "neither one of us is travelling alone."

He laughed. "You know what I mean," he said in a sort of cajoling voice.

They did. And it was so incredibly insulting.

"I was just thinking maybe you'd like to give me and my bro a ride. We could have a little fun."

"Take the bus." Jane said, heading into the store.

"Not interested." Spike said at the same time, following her.

"Oh," he nodded knowingly, "You're like that."

Spike stopped. And turned. "Like what?"

"Into each other. But that's cool," he smiled.

Oh well, good to know she had the man's approval.

"Not really fair to be batting for the other team, but 's okay."

"Did you know," Jane said casually once they were back on the road, "that an Islamic woman must be accompanied by a man whenever she appears in public? Otherwise, she is subject to torture."

"Otherwise?"

Jane grinned. Spike made a note to herself to splice that tidbit into the video—well, the audio—she'd later upload.

Once they'd finished the top layer of the box of chocolate-covered cherries they'd bought, Jane asked, "Remember that guy who killed himself because he couldn't get laid?"

"*After* killing six other people. Yes."

"Didn't *he* say something about how it wasn't fair?"[72] Jane asked.

"He did."

"I wonder what definition of 'fair' he was using."

"The one that says every man is entitled to at least one woman."

"Yeah. I wonder where he got that idea."

"I remember a movie," Spike said a short while later, "some apoca-

---

72 http://fusion.net/story/5741/elliot-rodgers-frightening-manifesto/

lyptic thing in which there aren't enough women to go around."

"Interesting phrasing."

"Yeah. And that's exactly how they phrased it. So they figured it was only fair that each of the women make themselves available to every man."

"Of course. Only fair."

About five miles later, Jane said, "Hey, I've got an idea for a sci-fi movie! A plague kills all the women on Earth except five, who manage to escape infection. On these five depend the continuation of the human species."

"And when the men find them," Spike anticipated the plot, "it takes all of fifteen minutes to rape them to death."

"It would be a very short sci-fi movie."

"It used to be that men just killed their girlfriends or wives," Jane gazed out the window. "Now they kill any woman who don't provide sexual service.

"And I can't believe I said 'just'.

A minute later. "I also can't believe I used to think education was the answer."

"Yeah," Spike said, "the whole 'No means Yes, and Yes means Anal'[73] thing at Yale kinda refuted that, didn't it."

"Okay, *what?*" Spike said with exasperation. They were in their hotel for the night, waiting for their pizza to arrive, and Jane was reading the surpris-du-soir from the nightstand drawer. Well, not reading, exactly. She was flipping through it, irritation escalating with every page.

---

73 http://scholarlycommons.law.northwestern.edu/cgi/viewcontent. cgi?article=7410&context=jclc

"Four sentences in, the guy," she looked at the cover, "Steven Barnes, describes a woman as 'a small wiry brunette'."

"Seriously? Does anyone actually identify women by their hair colour anymore? That's so ... 1940s."

"1998."

"I stand corrected. The tradition of objectifying women lives on."

"Not only that—" she broke off suddenly, looking into space. "You know, those are *made-up* words. Brunette, blond, redhead. Made up specifically *to* categorize us. *According to our hair colour.* As if all women with brown hair are what, interchangeable? Because we are so completely defined by the colour of our hair? A definition is supposed to indicate the essential properties of a thing," she said.

"Not only that," she returned her attention to the book, "but he had to mention her size. She's a '*small* wiry brunette'."

"But of course. If she's going to be the heroine, she has to be small. Did he say how large her breasts are?"

"No, but he said the man is 'enormous.'"

"Of course he is."

"Reverse it," Spike suggested a moment later, "and read it aloud."

Jane obliged. "'The man, a small, wiry brunette with an ugly bruise on his left cheek, wore a yellow unisex utility uniform. The woman was enormous, but barely conscious.'"

They— No, they didn't quite laugh.

Jane flipped ahead a hundred pages. It took that long for a second woman to be introduced. And she had "an oval face framed by a cascade of small soft blonde ringlets."

"*Ringlets*?" Spike asked, amazed. Because, well, 1998.

"And in case we missed it," Jane read on, "'Her habit of peering out from behind them sometimes made her resemble a mischievous *child* peeking through a fence.'" Jane looked up from the book. "And that's why the only male writer I read is Robert J. Sawyer."

A few pages later, Jane almost shouted, "And she *nibbles* on dry wheat toast!" She ripped the book in two. With her strong hands.

"Who's it published by?"

Jane checked. "Tor."

"It's science fiction?" Spike was stunned.

Jane nodded, then slumped in defeat. "Which means that they can't even *imagine* a world, a possible future, in which women exist just as ... people. With goals and objectives, dreams and desires, interests and abilities, that have nothing to do with sex."

"Or them."

Ten minutes later, they discovered the motel had Netflix, so they watched an episode of the Swedish drama, *The Bridge*. The women weren't especially attractive. The men weren't angry all the time. The hierarchy was mostly irrelevant. Marriage and kids, was an issue, or non-issue, for men and women alike.

Jane was delighted.

"In Sweden, tv shows have to pass the Bechdel test,"[74] Spike said.

"Cause or effect, I wonder."

---

74 http://jezebel.com/sweden-introduces-new-movie-rating-system-based-on-the-1459696241

18

On the fifth day, they passed close enough to an airport to make the detour.

"Do you want to come in with us?" Jane turned to X. "It'll be fun."

Spike stared at Jane. "How can huge buildings full of thousands of stressed out people be fun? The air will be *saturated* with anxiety, impatience, frustration, anger, and boredom—"

"Every airport has a Godiva."

X chose to wait in the car again.

"What if she—"

"She can come live with us."

"Okay, good."

As soon as they entered the terminal, they were approached by a Walmart greeter—a senior citizen whose pension was inadequate, or gone, whose job it was to provide directions and thus decrease airport users' stress. An excellent idea. In theory.

"Good afternoon, ladies—"

"I am *so* tired," Spike interrupted, clearly stressed, now, "so very *very* tired of being labeled by my sex."

He stared at her. He had no idea what she was talking about. But her tone indicated that she had taken offence—

"Young lady, I assure you—"

"Ooh, a twofer!" Spike exclaimed. Then helped him out. "Labels *describe*, and, therefore, *conscribe*, people. Labels determine what you can and cannot do. Labels determine how others respond to you. Or whether they respond at all. And I'm just so frickin' tired of my *sex,* my supposedly *inferior* sex, being my label."

He still had no idea what she was talking about.

"Wait for it ..." Spike murmured to Jane, as they stood there waiting...

"My dear, I—"

"And there it is!" She high-fived Jane, then moved on.

Or not. Not quite. She turned back.

"Excuse me, old man, can you tell us where the credit card people hang out?"

As soon as they'd moved on, they were approached by a (self-identified) (and proud of it) born-again Christian. They were ready. Oh so ready.

"Have you heard the Word of God?" the rosy-cheeked woman asked, ready to deliver said Word of God.

"No," Jane said, as Spike started recording, "but I've read it."

That stopped her. More than Spike's cellphone being pointed at her.

"And it's not very good. The plot's incomprehensible, the characters unlikeable, and the themes quite disturbing."

"Jesus loves you!" A non sequitur if there ever was one. Too bad Jane wasn't still teaching.

"Okay, Miss Jesus-loves-me-this-I-know," Spike said, "If God's so smart—and he is, right?"

The rosy cheeks went up and down.

"Okay, why didn't he arrange any advance publicity for the resurrection? Why didn't he lend one of the apostles a videocam or send someone from *The Times* back to Bethlehem. I mean, geez loueez, your national spelling bee gets better coverage!"

"... Thy will be done ..." She'd gone into prayer mode. It was the fallback subroutine.

"*You're* doing God's will?" Jane responded. "God appointed *you* executor of his will? Then for *sure*, I'm not following him."

Spike broke out into a twangy version of Mac Davis' "It's hard to be humble ..."

"Did you tell them about The Great Flood?" another born-again Christian had come to the still-praying woman's rescue. Oddly enough, also rosy-cheeked.

"That's the one where the water rose 15 cubits and covered the mountains?" Jane asked.

"Yes!" she replied, so pleased that Jane knew.

"One cubit is about a foot and a half," Jane said, "so let me see ... 15 cubits would be about ... 25 feet."

"Those are some awfully high mountains." That was Spike. "And *your* god created those?"

"... Pray for us sinners ..." She'd gone into prayer mode as well.

"Speaking of which," Jane said, "we're all born as sinners because Eve ate from the tree of the knowledge of good and evil, right? That is, because she developed a morality. And that's bad because *why*?"

They continued walking, passing several waiting areas in which people were watching tv.

"That's new," Spike commented. "Isn't it?"

"What?"

"Putting tvs in airport waiting areas. Forced indoctrination in a—" No, an airport wasn't a public place. And in any case, forced indoctrination in public places wasn't new. Advertising.

"I was angry!" the man on the tv shouted. He'd just thrown something, or maybe someone, against the wall.

"Oh well then," Spike commented, as they watched. "That's okay. The *man* was *angry*."

Jane nodded. "No wonder they get angry so often. It's a get-out-of-jail-free ticket."

"Not only that," Spike said. "An angry man is more of a man than a calm man, let alone a fearful man or a grieving man. Real men must control their emotions, or, better, not have any. Remember?"

"Well, except for anger," Jane pointed out the obvious contra-diction. She so enjoyed doing that. "And it's just a little ironic to allow a defence of emotion," she was thinking of the provocation defence, "to those who pride themselves on not being emotional."

"Well, except for being angry."

They watched for a few moments more, as the man went into a full-out tantrum.

"There's nothing worse than not taking a man seriously," Jane commented. Not idly.

"Except taking a man seriously."

Five minutes later, they turned a corner into what must have been the waiting area for a flight to Disney World. Dozens of kids were running around—actually, a good number of them were waddling around, something fried and sugared in their sticky hands—

"CUNT!" a little boy screamed at Jane as he rocketed by.

"I believe that children are our future ..." Spike intoned Whitney Houston.

"She wanted to put in a rock garden!"

"What the hell is a *rock* garden?"

Half an hour had passed. Jane and Spike were standing in the middle of nowhere, trying to figure out where they would be most likely to find the credit card people. Failing that, where the credit card people would be most likely to find them. A pair of men clearly on a business trip were standing nearby. And speaking loudly. Which kinda went without saying.

"And I know we've got to do *something* with it, but ..."

"A *rock* garden?"

"Exactly. So I says to the wife, you can't do that!"

"'The wife'?" Jane looked at Spike.

"*You* know," Spike said. Because she did. "It's like the maid, the nanny, the cook, the butler—"

They listened for a few moments longer, Spike recording, as the men talked about, commiserated about, their wives. Their indefinite articled, no-named, and thus indistinguishable and interchangeable, wives.

A few minutes later, the middle of nowhere suddenly got very crowded, so they headed to the nearest bunch of chairs until the hurricane of people passed. A man wearing baggy pants and a baseball cap was sitting, legs spread wide, in the middle seat of a five-seat row. No one sat, could sit, on either side of him. Without rubbing up against him.

Spike carefully set her knapsack on top of the garbage can at the end of the row, her phone peeping out of the outer pocket. She then claimed the second seat of the empty row directly across from him. Her legs spread out wide. Jane did the same in the fourth seat. Together they took up all five seats. The man stared at them. They stared back. Well, Spike stared back. Jane was having a little trouble. Her legs kept wanting to close.

Almost immediately another man on a business trip, coat over arm, cellphone to ear, approached.

"Excuse me," he said to Spike. Then kept talking on his phone.

She ignored him.

"Excuse me," he said again, nodding downward.

"I heard you the first time."

"I'd like to sit."

"That's nice."

He blustered, then finally said it. "You're taking up too much space!"

"So's he," she nodded to the guy across from them. "Why don't you go say 'Excuse me' to *him?*"

The man looked at the baggy pants and baseball cap, then hurried away.

Spike kept staring at the man. He kept staring back. Didn't know what game she was playing.

Finally she said, "Go ahead. Tell me your package is so big it's uncomfortable to sit with your legs together."

"You know it, babe!" he broke into a grin.

"Show me."

"What?"

"Prove it. Show me those big boys you're so proud of."

"Proud of," Jane added, as her legs slowly crept together yet again, "even though you have no influence whatsoever over their size. Which means your pride is misplaced."

"What?"

"Go on," Spike insisted. "Isn't it okay when women show a bit of boob and a bit of butt? So show me a bit of ball!"

"Bitch!" He got up and stormed off.

They watched him leave.

"Ever notice how quickly men can go from 'babe' to 'bitch'?"

"Faster than the speed of light."

A minute later, after Jane made a note for a new entry in her dictionary—"*Bitch!* means *Waa-aa-ah!*"—they both heard it. The sound that so completely *defines* airports and airplanes around the globe: a wailing, nay a bawling, *squalling* baby. They turned and saw a woman take a seat in the row behind them, then jostle the infant, trying desperately to make it stop crying.

"Can't you shut that up?" A man wearing a so-called muscle shirt was sitting across from the woman.

Spike got up, surreptitiously adjusted the angle of her knapsack, then sat in a seat a couple down from the woman. She faced the man who'd spoken. Jane followed.

"Go ahead," she said to the woman. "'Shut that up'" she quoted the man as she stared at him. Then she added to the woman, in case it wasn't clear. "Do what you have to do."

The woman hesitated for just a moment, then popped out a very large breast. The infant latched on immediately. And, of course, stopped crying.

"You can't do that here," another man objected, with prim and proper righteousness. "This is neither the time nor the place."

"The baby's so hungry it was crying," Spike pointed out the obvious. Pointed out what *should* be obvious. Even to men. "So this is *clearly* the time. As for the place—"

"She should go to the ladies' room," the man said.

"Washrooms are where people go to piss and shit. How is feeding a baby remotely similar?"

"Oh!" Jane raised her hand, "I know! Ask me!"

"If she insists on doing it in a public place, she should use a bottle," yet another man spoke up.

"Why should she do that when her breasts are so full of milk they hurt?" Spike said, glaring at the two women who *weren't* speaking up.

"Plus it's better for the baby," Jane added.

Spike thought of the PCB-contaminated breast milk of Inuit women, but decided not to confuse the issue.

"Besides," Jane had a thought, a daring thought, "if you don't like it, leave. Why should *she* be the one to have to go somewhere else?"

"Yeah!" One of the women finally found her voice. The other one at least nodded.

"But this is a public place!" the 'Shut that up' man finally spoke again. "What she's doing is private!"

"Agreed. So why don't you stop staring and give the person a bit of privacy."

It sounded so different with 'the person' instead of 'the woman'. So different it shut him up.

"He's just jealous," Jane said in the silence. Since the other two men *had,* in fact, left.

Spike raised her eyebrows.

"*He* wants to do that," she explained.

His face reddened.

"No, I think he's embarrassed."

This time Jane's eyebrows raised.

"He's getting an erection."

At that, he stood up and quickly walked away. While he still could.

They resumed their wandering, keeping a look-out for the credit card people. For someone with a clipboard, approaching people with a sales pitch.

What they saw instead was the man in the so-called muscle shirt, ostensibly getting something from the vending machine, but in reality flexing and posturing for a group of nearby young women.

"Isn't it odd," Jane observed, "that the men who seem to value women the least spend the most time trying to impress them?"

They both stared at the man. And the young women. Who were, tragically, impressed.

"Excuse me, can I interest you in one of our SuperSavings PointsPlus MaxReward credit cards?"

"Why, yes, you can!" Jane turned eagerly to the young woman with a clipboard who had gently tapped her on the shoulder.

"We have a limited time offer of no interest for six months."

"Six months?" Jane turned to Spike. "*When* will we reach 450ppm?"

"What's the interest rate *after* six months?" Spike asked.

"Oh, all of our interest rates are competitive."

"Yeah, but competitive with what, the grades we got in university?"

Jane had already filled in the application form.

"Thank you," the woman took the clipboard back and made sure all the critical boxes had been filled in. "You should get your new card in the mail within seven to ten business days."

"Oh." Hadn't she gotten it on the spot last time? "But I need it now."

"Well, we do have an introductory card. It comes with a limit though, of $1,000—and you can't increase it. It's intended just to—"

"I'll take it." Jane did a little happy dance. She couldn't help it. Because ... chocolate.

"Yeah, I'll take one of those too," Spike said, wondering how the bank, whatever bank it was, could stay in business.

"Can I get two?"

"Sorry, only one per person."

They wandered around a bit more in case any other credit card companies were giving out introductory cards. And in case someone sold wigs and fake mustaches.

At some point, by accident, they found Godiva's. Jane couldn't decide between the Ultimate Dessert Truffle six-pack and the Ice Cream Parlour Truffle six-pack. Good thing by then they *each* had *five* new credit cards.

Six-packs in hand, they headed for the exit.

Jane suddenly stopped. Spike bumped into her.

"What?"

"Did we leave the car windows open a bit?"

"It's an old car. The windows open by—"

They hurried.

On the sixth day, when they stopped at a gas station to fill up, they managed to meet their objective, achieve their goal, fulfill their tiny, *tiny* dream, without incident. That is to say, without being infantilized, sexualized, ignored, or otherwise insulted. Probably because they'd been able to pay at the pump with a credit card. One of their five new credit cards.

On the seventh day, they stopped at a store to get Bristol board, markers, and whatever else they might need for X to participate in the poster session at the conference. X waited in the car. Again.

They heard the man from two aisles away. Which gave Spike lots of time to get her phone out.

"We're getting this one, and that's all there is to it!" the man shouted angrily.

They also heard the woman trying to get a word in.

"But I don't think it prints colour, and—"

"So what if it doesn't print colour?! It's a good brand, which means we won't have to come back next week to get another one! You get the other one, and we'll be back before you know it, I guarantee it!"

Had to be husband and wife. The rut was deep. Well-gouged.

"But when I do my Christmas—"

"You never look at the big picture, and you never consider the cost of things! This is a good printer, I'm telling you, and it's not going to cost an arm and a leg. It holds 500 sheets of paper."

"But my cards aren't paper, they're—"

"You're not listening to me!"

Jane and Spike glanced at each other with— Well, no, not really with disbelief.

"The cartridges last for a long time," he said slowly. As if talking to a child. "They're easy to replace. It has a thirty-day warranty, and we can extend that if we want."

"But if it's not going to—"

"Will you just for once shut up and listen?!!" he shouted.

"Talk about the kettle calling the pot black," Spike shouted too, when they were one aisle away.

That stopped him. For just a second.

"You stay out of this," he shouted back. "I'm sick and tired of hearing you women yammer on and on so's a man can't get a word in edgewise!"

Jane and Spike stared at each other. Okay, now it was with disbelief.

"And every time someone tries to say something, you interrupt!"

Nothing more was said, by anyone. Which, Jane was dying to point out, refuted his claim. Conclusively.

Jane found a hotel that was relatively close to Caltech. It was more expensive than anything they'd stayed at so far, but hey, they *each* had *five new* credit cards. Unfortunately, they got to Pasadena at rush hour and it took forever to get to it.

"How about a little smile," the middle-aged man at the reception counter said as they approached to check in, "it can't be that bad!" He reached for the registry.

"What do you imagine I should be smiling about?" Spike asked. She was tired, but not that tired.

Well that stopped him. The implication that there's supposed to be a connection between facial expression and felt emotion.

"Knowing what I know about political corruption, big business subsidies, and population growth rates," the list tumbled out with no trouble at all, "I'd have to be an idiot to go around smiling all the time."

He just stared at her.

"Do you say that to men?" Spike asked.

"What?"

"Do you ask men to smile?"

"Well, no, I guess ..." he trailed off.

"You guess what?"

He didn't say. He didn't know.

"I suggest you not ask another woman to smile until you figure out why you don't ask men to smile."

"But he'll *never* be able to figure that out!" Jane protested.

"I know." She smiled.

"Shouldn't we help him?" Jane asked, as if Timmy had fallen down the well again.

"No."

They settled in, then ordered room service. Because hey, they were in a hotel that *had* room service. *And* they had five new credit cards. Each.

Once they'd replenished themselves, they got X set up at the desk in the sitting area—yes, they had a room with a sitting area! with a desk!—and tried to explain what she should put on her poster.

"Pretend it's a summary of a paper you've written," Jane said. "Put the title across the top, then put bits of it ..."

"Maybe divide the poster into four sections, and put a set of equations in each section?"

"Yeah, that'll look good. I mean, real."

X stared at them.

"Make it something that will attract someone who will know how to help you figure out the coordinates."

"Don't make it too difficult," Jane said.

"But don't make it too easy," Spike said.

X stared at them.

"She could write out the easier solution to Fermat's equation," Jane suggested.

"But that doesn't have anything to do with time-space coordinates, does it?"

"Not in *my* universe," X said.

They stared at her.

Spike edited and uploaded her many videos.

Jane made a few new entries into her dictionary:

Case closed. 1. I'm losing.

Don't be so judgmental. 1. Don't judge *me*, just let
me get away with—everything.

Don't be so sensitive. 1. I want to believe that my
actions have no effect whatsoever on anyone.
2. Don't reveal by comparison what a dull-
headed emotionally-challenged thug I am.

X worked on her poster.

After about ten minutes, Jane started flipping through the tv guide that was on top of the flat-screen tv. She wasn't in the mood for channel surfing.

"Hey, did you know there are thirty-three sports networks? *Thirty-three!*"

"And I'll bet every one of them shows almost exclusively men's sports …"

Jane looked up. "Can you imagine thirty-three networks showing stuff that—"

"Yeah," Spike anticipated her question. "The shopping channel, the fashion channel, the food channel …"

They decided to watch a movie called *Trust*. They kept the volume low so as not to disturb X, who was hard at work, a box of chocolates by her side. (The hotel had had a gift shop! And the gift shop had had boxes of chocolates!)

Two hours later, Jane and Spike just stared at tv screen. Fourteen-year-old girl meets sixteen-year-old boy online, falls in love (he says all the 'right' things) (she assumes he's telling the truth) (fool), is then told, by him, that he's really eighteen, then twenty, then twenty-five (he continues to say all the 'right' things though), meets him in person, discovers he's more like thirty, agrees to accompany him to a motel room (she's too slow to adjust her beliefs, her opinions) (because that's hard) (even harder to do quickly) (and it requires admitting she was a fool), where he rapes her. He posts pictures of the rape online. Unable to deal with it all (that she was a fool, that she was raped, that he put it online, *and* that people dismissed it all), she tries to kill herself. Bad enough that it was just one more male-predator female-victim movie. But—

"They made it all about the dad," Jane murmured, then looked over at Spike. "The closing scene ..."

Spike nodded. Close-up of dad, devastated by his inability to protect, his inability to avenge— Being comforted. *By his daughter.* Said *fourteen-year-old girl.*

"Sex trumps age and relationship," Spike summarized with a sigh. "Woman comforts man. Instead of adult comforts teenager or parent comforts offspring—"

"Not to mention *non*-rapee *non*-suicidee comforts rapee-suicidee."

"Are those even words?"

"They are now."

"And where's Mom in all this?" Jane asked a moment later. "I mean she's also the girl's parent. So parental responsibility is also hers. This should have been written, directed, produced, as a mother-daughter story. *She's* the one who empathized with the whole experience. No doubt she knows it just as easily could've happened to *her.* At fourteen."

Spike turned off the tv in disgust. "They always find a way to make it about them."

19

Jane, Spike, and X entered the busy lobby of the Caltech conference center. It looked like university lobbies everywhere, with its shiny floor, its tasteful portraits and photographs on the beige-grey-cream wall, and its trophy case. And, for now, its swarming academics happy to be important for a few days. X clutched the poster she'd prepared, a pad of graph paper, and several sharpened pencils. They approached the registration table, under which huge banner hung, welcoming everyone to the American Physics Society Spring Meeting.

"Hi, I'm Jane Smith," Jane said to one of the three smiling undergraduates staffing the table, who immediately started flipping through her files.

"Spike Dubrey. And wipe that smile off your face."

She looked up, startled. "But— I'm happy! Being here is such an exciting opportunity ... I get to meet all these brilliant minds ..."

"Yeah, well," Spike said, knowing that that would soon change. Being happy. Thinking this was an exciting opportunity. To meet all those brilliant minds. "When you smile," she explained, "you just endorse your unimportance. As a bonus, when women *don't* smile, all hell breaks loose. Google the smile boycott by the New York receptionists."

"Actually," Jane turned to Spike, "it's not on Google. Anywhere." She'd looked for it.

"No?" Spike was surprised. And then she wasn't.

"You'll have to get the book by Sally Cline and Dale Spender," Jane said to the undergraduate. *"Reflecting Men at Twice their Natural Size."* The student was making a note. And trying very hard not to smile.

"When you smile," Spike added, "you get kicked in the teeth." She didn't add that when you don't smile, you get kicked in the teeth anyway. Too much, too soon.

The student had by this time pulled out a receipt. She glanced at it, then turned to X for confirmation. "And you are ...?"

"X." Jane said quickly. "X Notovearl."

Spike rolled her eyes at the name Jane had made up for X.

Jane started to stick out her tongue—coming up with that name had taken her a good half hour—then wisely changed her mind.

"Okay," the student said, "so here's your copy of the receipt," she gave the piece of paper to Jane, "and here are your IDs, which you must wear at all times," she picked out their ID badges from a box, "and here are your conference guide," she took three thick folders from a pile.

"And the poster sessions?" Spike asked. "Where do we set up?"

She consulted a clipboard, then looked at X. "Just you? You're the only one—"

"The only one who's lost, yes."

"We're sort of all together," Jane explained.

"No problem. You're at Board #42. Down that hall and on your left."

"Great, thanks."

They put their ID badges on, then headed down the hall as directed. A few moments later, they entered a huge room full of rows and rows of bulletin boards. Not a chair in sight. Or a table, for that matter. The room was relatively full of people setting up or already set up, as well as people already making their way through, looking at the displayed information. They wandered around looking for Board #42. Then they wandered around looking for X.

She'd stopped at Board #18 and was studying it carefully.

The brightly-coloured graphs on laminate had clearly been professionally prepared. Belatedly, they realized that they should've done that. Had X prepare a mock-up, then taken it to OfficeMax or Staples or something.

"Let's get your poster set up first," Jane said, "then you can go around and look at all the other posters."

X started laughing.

"Or not."

They held on to her until they got to Board #42.

"Okay, here we are. We put your poster here," Spike pinned the poster onto the board. It was covered with equations using symbols she didn't recognize, all written with a black felt pen. Geez, they may as well have just gotten her crayons.

"You stand here," she positioned X beside her poster. "You've got your ID badge on, you've got your conference folder and your pad of graph paper, so you're looking all official ... And we'll stand here on the other side," she and Jane positioned themselves on the other side. "And ... we're ready!"

"For what?"

"Hopefully some of the people walking by will stop and ask you questions about ..." Jane looked at the poster. There was a title across the top: *Extension of Calabi-Yau Manifolds into an 11,000-dimensional space: A proposed approach to navigation in the Brane landscape.* "That."

"And you'll be able to figure out who, if anyone, knows what you need to know."

"But don't come right out and ask them for Earth's space- time coordinates."

"Why not?"

"Because you tried that before and it didn't work."

"Oh yeah."

Almost immediately, a few men walked by, showing no interest whatsoever.

A few minutes later, a few more men walked by, showing no interest whatsoever.

An hour passed. Spike had gone on a scouting mission and had returned with a couple chairs from a nearby room. She and Jane were sitting close to, but a little behind, X. Who was still standing, eagerly, beside her poster. A hundred men must have passed by, but not one had stopped.

Another hour passed. Jane had gone in search of something to drink and had returned with three bottles of juice from a vending machine. X was still standing, a little less eagerly, beside her poster. Another hundred men had passed by. None had stopped.

"They're not even stopping to read it," Jane observed. "They see a woman—"

"A *black* woman—"

"And walk right by. Like she's invisible."

"Or can't possibly know anything about ..." Spike looked at the poster, again, "that."

"What do they think, she channeled the poster content from Einstein's ghost?"

Just then a man in military dress stopped and read X's poster. He made a few notes on the tablet he carried. Then he simply nodded at X and moved on.

Spike leaned forward to X, urgently. "Okay, if that guy comes back—"

"Or anyone dressed in a uniform like that—" Jane leaned forward as well.

"Don't talk to them. At all."

"Run away."

"Why?"

Jane sighed. The answer was complicated. "Because he's a member of the military, and—"

"It would be like giving a bus pass to a toddler."

"A toddler with a gun."

"Who's prone to tantrums."

A while later, Jane idly commented, "Lieutenant General Daniel Graham once said that if a one megaton bomb was about to explode and you had the good sense to start walking and get behind a lilac bush, the bomb wouldn't hurt you.'"

"Is that the same Lieutenant General Daniel Graham who was later chosen to be the Senior Military Advisor to the President?"

Shortly after, another man stopped and scanned X's poster.

"What planet are you from?" he simply asked, laughing.

X had opened her mouth to tell him, but he'd already moved on.

It was late afternoon. And it was not looking good. X was slumped in a third chair Spike had scrounged from another nearby room. She and her poster had been ignored. In a rather complete way.

Then two women approached X's board. One couldn't've been more than fifteen and of Asian descent. Tang, her ID said. The other was twice her age and of East Indian descent. Shilpa. They stopped and read X's poster carefully and with intensity. X stood up. Eagerly.

Tang pointed to the 11,000 figure.

"See?!" She turned with excitement to Shilpa.

She then moved her finger, ever-so-slightly hovering, along the equations. She got to the third line.

"No," she said, incredulously. Then read a little further. "Get out."

"It's true," X said.

Tang focused on X, seeming to see her for the first time. She looked back at the poster, reading further still. Then she pointed to a smiley face in the middle of an equation.

"And this?"

"I needed a symbol for—" X showed Tang her pad of paper, "this." The first five pages were completely filled with calculations. Tang studied them, following them, understanding them, and when she got to the end, she broke into a wide grin, uncannily like the smiley face.

"But if— If—" Her hands were making restless gestures. Shilpa handed her a brand new pad of paper and a pencil. Tang scribbled some equations on the pad and showed them to X.

"Ah, but—" X scribbled some equations back.

"Yeah?"

X nodded.

"Can't be." She scribbled some more. Then it was X's turn to be surprised. And excited.

"That's a constant?"

"Of course!"

"In what universe?"

"This one!"

"Really?" X digested this. "Until where?"

Spike looked at Jane. She mouthed "Until where?"

A few moments later, all three of them—Jane, Spike, and Shilpa—were grinning broadly. Watching X and Tang was almost better than watching puppies play.

The two of them continued to scribble back and forth. Jane and Spike were silent with awe and hope. Shilpa kept trying to follow.

"I knew it!" Tang yelped with glee and did a little happy dance. At least they thought that's what it was. Shilpa smiled, as did Jane and Spike.

"Wait a minute. How—"

X scribbled more.

"You're right. You're absolutely right. But then—Oh.   Wow." Tang turned to Shilpa. "Can we keep her? Can we take her home with us?"

X nodded happily at Tang, then looked to Jane and Spike, grinning like a goofy mutt at the shelter who'd just had people ask to adopt it.

"Well, not *home* home," Shilpa said to Spike and Jane. "Hi," she said then, extending her hand and smiling at the time lag of the introduction. "I'm Shilpa, and this is Tang. We're from Stanford. I'm a post-doc there and Tang's still slaving away at her dissertation. Her advisor is a real asshole, he's been holding her back— Excuse me—"

Tang and X had resumed scribbling formulae back and forth. A moment later, Shilpa added something to the conversation they were having.

"Right. That is easier."

Shilpa kept her eye on their conversation, but continued speaking to Spike and Jane. "He keeps telling her she's going in the wrong direction, but the girl's a genius."

"So ... you want to take X back to Stanford?"

"X?"

"Sorry, I'm Jane, this is Spike, and this is—"

X burst out laughing. Gleefully. Shilpa smiled again. So did Jane and Spike.

"No, I think Tang just wants to go back to our room— We're staying at the Westin—"

Tang and X were still scribbling equations back and forth. And Shilpa wasn't quite ...

"To keep working on ... this. With ... X."

"X?" They looked at X. Who was oblivious.

"Tang?" Shilpa tried.

Tang and X stopped then and stared at the others. As if they'd forgotten they'd existed. Which they probably had.

"X, do you want to come back to our room and continue—"

X unpinned her poster from the board and held it awkwardly to her chest, along with her pad of paper and pencils. Tang held the other pad of paper, also close to her chest, and they both stared at Shilpa waiting to follow her. Like two little puppies. Two little incredibly brilliant puppies.

As soon as they were in the room, Tang and X spread out their stuff on the floor.

"So, we need to figure out the values for 11,000 variables?" Tang asked. With more curiosity than despair.

"No, I crossed dimensions—"

Shilpa's eyebrows raised.

"It's sort of like changing lanes— I crossed only five times before I got here. Well, ten maybe. Twenty tops."

"Okay, so we figure out the formula for each one, then test it for your own planet and—"

"Wait, what?" Shilpa hadn't gotten that from the equations she'd seen. But now that it was said openly— She sunk into one of the chairs.

"And if we get the right values, we know we've got the formula right."

"Right," X said. "Then we use it to figure out the values for Earl."

"Earl?" Shilpa asked.

"Earth," Tang explained.

"You know by heart all 20 values for your own coordinates?" Shilpa asked. Impressively up to speed already. And relatively unruffled. Though maybe it hadn't yet—

Again, Tang explained. "It's like knowing your own phone number. With the area code. And the country code. And—"

"Got it. So then when you have Earth's coordinates—"

"Then I can plot my route from here to wherever I was going before I stopped to ask for— Oh. I didn't know where I was going next."

"Maybe you should go straight home," Shilpa suggested. God knows what would happen to her anywhere else. She briefly imagined Tang lost ... in space ...

"Yeah."

Shilpa turned to Jane and Spike then, who were still standing by the door, a little lost themselves.

"What room are you in?"

"Actually, we're staying at the Travelodge," Spike said. Feeling incredibly behind. Everything. "We're not really here for the conference. We're not even physicists." Talk about stating the obvious. "We just came for X."

"We were on our way to Paris," Jane said, clearly clarifying the situation. "Though we'd planned to see a bit of Pasadena while we were here ... There's a place called Everything Chocolate—"

"Oh, that sounds good. Maybe I'll come with you two," she got up. "No," she changed her mind and sat back down, "I should stay here. Why don't you two go and do your thing, and when you're done, come on back. Stay here." She waved her hand at all the space.

"But—"

"We've got a whole suite. Paid for by the university. By mistake." Her eyes twinkled.

"In that case," Spike knew she had Jane's agreement, "okay!"

"Thanks!" Jane did indeed agree.

"Bring me something?" Shilpa asked hopefully. "Of Everything?" she grinned.

So they went back to the Travelodge, got their stuff, and checked out. Then they headed for—

"There it is!" Jane cried out when she saw Everything Chocolate. "Pull over!"

"Can I find a parking place first?"

Two hours later, they knocked on the door to the Governor's Suite at the Westin.

"Hi!" Shilpa said warmly when she opened it.

"Hi yourself," Spike said.

"We brought you some brownies," Jane said. "And a bunch of other goodies."

Shilpa took the first box, set it onto the small table in the kitchenette, and opened it. Drawn by the scent, both Tang and X looked up from where they sat on the floor, in the middle of an organized array of laptops, tablets, an old-fashioned calculator, several pads of graph paper, and even more loose sheets.

"You brought chocolate?" Tang asked.

"The only thing that'll interrupt Her Genius!" Shilpa laughed.

They gathered around the open box. Tang took out a huge brownie that was two inches frosting on half an inch brownie.

"Oh wow. The perfect brownie."

Jane smiled. She'd thought so too. She'd already had two.

Tang sunk her teeth into it. And moaned. X took one as well, then the two of them went back to their calculations.

While Jane and Spike put their stuff in the unclaimed bedroom, Shilpa took a jug of iced tea out of the regular-sized fridge. She refilled Tang's glass, then X's glass, then her own, then poured two new glasses for Jane and Spike and set them on the table.

When they returned to the kitchenette, Jane opened the second box and helped herself to a chocolate cashew cream truffle square. Spike took a chocolate raspberry cream truffle square.

"Thanks," they said, each taking a glass of iced tea, and then looking around for a couple of empty chairs.

"Let's go out onto the balcony," Shilpa suggested, taking a chocolate orange cream truffle from the box.

"Wow," Jane said a moment later, settling into one of the lounge chairs. They could see the mountains, blue in the distance.

"Nice," Spike agreed.

They ate their truffle squares, sipped their tea, and just looked out at the mountains for a few beautiful minutes. It was surprisingly quiet.

"So, it may take a few days," Shilpa licked a bit of cream truffle from her fingertip, "but I think we can figure out Earth's coordinates. Or rather, *they* can. They lost me an hour ago," she smiled. "So I 'done good'!"

"No question!" Spike said, raising her glass in a sort of toast. She had mixed feelings about the predicted success, so she didn't actually say 'That's good news.' Though it was, of course. "So you're a post-doc?" was what she did say.

"Yes. I'd hoped to be tenure track by now, but ..."

"No one's hiring?"

"Oh, they're hiring. It's just— Some guy stole a chunk of my work a couple years ago, and I've sort of floundered ever since."

"What? Really?" Jane looked up from her cream truffle, surprised. That didn't happen in Philosophy. Other stuff happened, but ...

"Really," Shilpa grimaced. "I was stupid. There was a bunch of us at a bar one night ... I'd been invited, finally, and I was so glad to be part of the after-hours group at last— You know, to be able to discuss my work with my peers, and ..."

"A couple months later, you saw your work in someone else's paper." Spike wasn't surprised.

"Yes. I confronted him, but he couldn't understand why I was so angry. It was a very strange conversation. He genuinely didn't consider it theft. I'm sure he would've, if I'd been a man. But as it was, it was as if ... "

"As if we exist *for* them."

"Yes! He seemed to think I was just helping him out, that I was just *giving* him my work or something. I don't know."

"And you couldn't prove it."

"No. I mean I had my notes and everything, but there was no record of our conversation. People thought he just happened to figure out the same stuff."

"Or that you *had* just *given* him your work." Unbelievable.

They traded stories about academia. Jane told Shilpa about some of the things posted on the What Is It Like To Be A Woman In Philosophy[75] website, some of which had happened to her. Spike said that the same things happened in psych departments.

"On top of all the personal shit," Spike added, "women's research, especially if it has anything at all to *do* with women, is considered less worthy, so it isn't published as often. Which means the discipline is ignoring the experience of half the human species.

---

75 https://beingawomaninphilosophy.wordpress.com/

"And when it *is* published," she continued, "it isn't cited as often, so it doesn't count as much for tenure. Many women submit using just their initials, but if only women do that, it's just as much a give-away as their full names. A few journals have implemented blind review and across-the-board initials-only attribution, but ..."

"I would have thought things were better in Science, Tech, and Engineering," Jane said. "I mean women's presence there is so obvious, relative to their presence in the Humanities and Social Science. Hasn't that meant that the discrimination is similarly obvious? And called out?"

Shilpa shook her head. "Women get heavier teaching loads and committee work, so they have less time and energy for research. I think more of our journals have blind review and initials-only-attribution, but women are invited far less often to edit special issues and to chair conference panels, despite being as qualified, and often better qualified, than the men invited. They get tenure far less often. Their starting salaries are often lower, and since increments are based on that, and tenure, the pay gap keeps increasing, as they proceed through their careers."

They stared at the mountains. Not so distant actually.

"Tang wants to get a job at NASA," Shilpa said then. Jane and Spike looked at each other. "I'm thinking it'll be better than academia." Shilpa had noticed the look, but didn't ask. Maybe later. "You ever see the movie *Dark Matter*? The one with Meryl Streep?"

"No ..."

"It's about a young man in a doctoral program, and his advisor ... sabotages—there's really no other word for it—his progress."

"Why? I mean, doesn't it look good when their students *succeed?*"

"The young man had made a discovery that undermined the theory upon which the advisor had built his career."

"Ah."

"What he does is—the advisor—he rejects the young man's dissertation—at the oral defence stage! Just because a few minor mathematical calculations aren't in there! If he'd said earlier that they should be there—and they *needn't* have been there—the young man could have, certainly would have, put them in. As he explained, stuttering, to his examiners ... Embarrassed, humiliated, appalled, confused ..."

"So what happens?"

"He doesn't get his doctorate. As a result, he loses his student visa standing, and then, rather than return home, in disgrace, to work at his father's fruit and vegetable shop or some such, he kills himself."

Again, they stared at the mountains. The huge, hard mountains.

"I'm afraid something like that's going to happen to Tang. It's all that messed up."

"So you've taken it upon yourself to be her mentor, her guardian."

Shilpa nodded.

"So what do *you* two do?" she asked then, changing the subject. "Clearly you're academics ..."

"I work at a fruit and vegetable shop," Jane said.

"We're office temps," Spike corrected. "She's a writer."

"Sort of. And she's an activist," Jane offered.

"Sort of."

"Oh, have you published anything?" Shilpa asked Jane. Perhaps she'd find the time to read it.

"No."

"And I haven't changed anything."

The mountains.

"It's too bad that we can't just have our own universities," Shilpa said a little while later. "If Radcliffe, Vassar, Wellesley, and the others had gotten it together just a bit more—with their funding, and their curricula ..."

"Wouldn't it be great?" Spike agreed. "To have a women-only university?"

"I imagine women would *run* to it," Shilpa agreed. "Students and faculty alike. If I knew how to get the capital ... I don't think we'd have any trouble staying solvent."

"It would be illegal though," Spike said. "Title IX."

Shilpa nodded. "Pity."

"It really is," Jane agreed. "I went to a SWIP conference once—Society for Women in Philosophy," she answered Shilpa's raised eyebrows, "and it was amazing. The difference between it and the APA conference was almost palpable. It was like I was on a different planet. Everyone was smiling, and laughing, and it was all just so ... *easy*. People listened, really *listened*, to each other's papers, and the comments and questions from the floor were ... *constructive*. The authors would actually take notes. It's like the whole conference was some huge cooperative effort to build better conceptual models, to enrich and refine our analyses ..."

Mountains.

"You know," Spike said a moment later, "they criticize the radfem doctrine of separatism, but men are already separatists. How did Kate Clinton put it?" She turned to Jane, unable to remember the comedian's brilliant bit.

"'When women go off together, we call it separatism. When men go off together, we call it Congress.'"

20

Over the next few days, Jane and Spike kept X, Tang, and Shilpa fueled with pizza and chocolate. Spike's tablet was put into service, and a few incomprehensible apps were loaded onto it. Jane's laptop was also put into service, but mostly just to have an additional calculator available.

They also did a bit of sightseeing. One day, they went to the Sequoia National Park. They walked one trail, then another, then another, and felt, as they often did these days, both joy and sorrow, at the majesty, the beauty ... soon to be gone.

They drew the line at driving their car through the Tunnel Log: "The only tree you can drive right through!' the brochure of attractions read.

"Kinda rubs it in, doesn't it?" Spike commented.

Jane agreed. It was a perfect metaphor in the way Spike was thinking.

But there was also something sexual about the tunneling, Jane thought. Which made it a perfect metaphor in that way as well.

Next day, for the contrast, they went to the Joshua Tree National Park. It made them giggle.

Otherwise, they spent their California stay at the beach, swimming in the ocean. Didn't get to do that much in Toronto.

They'd intended to see more of Pasadena, and some of L.A., and Santa Barbara, and Malibu, and all of the other California names they'd heard about all their lives, but they realized quite quickly they'd rather just sit in the sand on their lovely new California beach towels and stare out at the ocean.

Besides, their first attempt at a pleasant drive-around-and-look-see was not pleasant at all.

They'd stopped to stare at one of the houses. They'd never in a million years be able to buy such a house.

"How is it they're so rich?" Jane wondered, not for the first time. "Even if I worked twenty hours a day, 365 days of the year, I wouldn't make anywhere near the *down payment* on such a house. So they must be making a hundred times per hour what I'm making."

Spike nodded.

"Is what they're doing a hundred times more important than what I'm doing?" Jane asked.

"Not if you're a garbage collector."

"Is it a hundred times more difficult?"

"Not if you're a nurse in the paraplegic ward."

"Does it take a hundred times as much training?"

"Couldn't happen in a lifetime."

"Rich people have their millions because they've been paid, by others or by themselves, an unfair amount for their work." Not a new revelation. But one that needed to be said. Again and again.

"Or," Spike suggested, "because they know how to work an unfair economic system that, for starters, rewards risk: the stock market. And, for finishers, counts only cash-generating activities as 'productive'." Spike was thinking about Marilyn Waring's work.[76] Ben, who sits in a nuclear missile silo for eight hours a day waiting for an order to push a button and destroy the planet as we know it, is considered productive. While Tendai, who lives in Zimbabwe and spends eighteen hours a day providing food, clothing, and shelter for herself and her children, is not.

---

76 https://inastrangeland.wordpress.com/2008/04/11/friday-feminist-marilyn-waring-3/

"And *why* do we reward risk?" Jane focused on the first point. Because the second was a no-brainer: it came down to 'We can measure quantity; we can't measure quality'. Or, even more simply, 'We like quantity'.

"Because it's a male thing," she answered her own question. "And males reward themselves for male values."

"Though actually," Spike said, "most of the time, it's *not* a risk. Not really. If the company they start loses *a lot* of money, they can declare bankruptcy. And *other* people pay the price for the risk they took. In the case of government bail-outs, that's us. Paying the price. For the risk they took.

"Furthermore, they're not even risking *their own* money. They probably borrowed the start-up money from the bank. So, again, it's *our* money. Because the bank's money is money they made by *investing our* money.

"And even if *was* their own money, it still probably wasn't."

Jane glanced over.

"It was inherited from their parents. Who probably inherited it from *their* parents. Because you can't *have* that much money to invest simply by working and saving. Even if you work twenty hours a day, 365 days a year."

"All of which is why rich people should have to pay higher taxes," Jane concluded. "*Much* higher taxes. Not because of some sacrifice-for-the-common-good principle, not because of some trickle-down principle, not because of some from-each-according-to-their-ability principle, but because *they don't deserve their money*."

They'd driven on. And passed a swimming pool. Then they passed another swimming pool, larger than the last. Then they passed another swimming pool, larger still.

At swimming pool number six, which was surely beyond Olympic size, Spike pulled over, got out, and screamed through the fence at the people relaxing beside their pool, colourful drinks in their hands.

"You've got a lot of nerve!" she screamed.

They looked up, confused.

"We're running out of fresh water. Planet-wide. And you live within a mile of ocean beach. What the fuck do you need a *swimming pool* for?!"

"Excuse me? Do I know you?" the woman called out. Ever ready to illustrate irrelevance.

"Our swimming pool is none of your business!" the man got up. Ever ready to defend the indefensible.

"The hell it isn't! Your swimming pool means that my friend in Canada will have to sell her beloved home, for next to nothing, because water importation for your fricking swimming pool will lower the water table and make her well run dry!"

"Quite apart from which," Jane added, "given that a swimming pool isn't a necessity and water is a limited resource, it doesn't really make for a just and sustainable society, does it?"

"You know we're way past[77] swimming pools, right?" Jane had asked once they'd returned to their car.

"Yeah." She sighed. Of course she knew.

"Still," Jane had said once they'd gotten back into the car, "it's the principle that counts."

"No. It's not." Spike stared out the front window, her hands on the steering wheel. She hadn't yet started the car.

Jane looked at her, surprised.

"If there were a god and some sort of afterlife, then yeah. But there's just here and now. And what's the point of doing the right thing if it has no consequence whatsoever?" She looked at Jane, begging for an answer.

---

77 http://news.nationalgeographic.com/news/2014/08/140819-groundwater-california-drought-aquifers-hidden-crisis/

Jane was silent. She had no answer. How had she not realized that principle-based morality required a god and an afterlife? Or that is was, in the end, an appeal to consequences. To the good of society, at the very least.

"Draining his swimming pool would make no difference whatsoever."

Jane agreed. But. And the depth of despair in Spike's voice was unsettling.

"So, what, we go with ... morality by arithmetic?" She found the idea repulsive, but if that's what it took to salvage morality. "If a thousand people drained their swimming pools ..."

"No," Spike sighed. "Even then."

"Because we're way past swimming pools." Not because Spike was going over to the dark side.

"Because using only what you need is the right thing to do when taking more than you need means others will have less than they need. But if, say, you take more apples than you need because otherwise they'll just rot on the ground, because the distribution of things is all fucked up, what's wrong with that?

"And because we're way past swimming pools."

So they decided instead to just sit on the beach. They tried to ignore the empty cups and cans and wrappers and cartons they stepped around on their way to an empty patch of sand. (First day, they'd picked them up and put them in the nearby trash can.) (Second day, they would've had to do that all over again.)

They also tried to ignore the fact that almost all the women they saw were almost completely naked (shaved and waxed because they were exposing 95% of their bodies (and women's bodies had to be hairless) (in order to look like little girls' bodies) (so men ...), whereas the men could relax in baggy knee-length shorts and midriff-covering t-shirts. (Of course speedos and no shirts would've been worse. Far worse. Most of the men they saw had *much* bigger bellies than most of the women. *And* more back, arm, and face fat. And yet they seemed blissfully oblivious, remarkably unashamed, of that fact.)

And they tried to ignore the fact that after a mere five minutes, they had to slather on sunscreen. SPF-2000.

But they *didn't* try to ignore the cluster of beach dudes who had just set up their umbrella, cooler, chairs, and towels in front of them. *Right* in front of them.

"Hey!" Spike called out.

One of the young men turned slowly and eventually focused on her. As if he was just now noticing her. Because she was ... old.

"What?" It was his version of deferring to your elders.

"You're setting up right in front of us. There's an empty spot over there." She pointed.

"And there, and there ..." Jane was nothing if not thorough.

"You'll be blocking our view." Spike had to spell it out.

He thought about that. Or not. Because, "You know what your problem is?"

She rolled her eyes. The man was going to tell her what her problem was. Because of course, *of course*, he knew. Despite being half her age.

"We should get something for X," Spike said. They were standing in front of a souvenir shop, which was located right beside the ice cream shop they'd just been in.

"Like a going away gift, you mean?" Jane took a thick lick of her California Chocolate ice cream cone. It was full of nuts and marshmallows.

Spike hadn't quite thought of it in that way, but— "Yeah," she said sadly. And took a bite out of her Surfer Chocolate ice cream cone. The chocolate had a wave of bright blue ice cream running through it that tasted like one of those Mr. Freeze things.

When they'd finished their ice cream cones, they went inside. Jane ran her (clean) hand through the rack of t-shirts. "'I went to Earth and all I got was this lousy t-shirt'?"

Spike laughed. "But once she unmerges, she may not need a t-shirt."

"Good point."

They passed a display of snow globes. In a souvenir shop in California. Did Taiwan know nothing? Well, it wasn't Taiwan's fault. Unless they made their supply a package deal ... She picked one up and shook it.

"Hey, remember that snowflake from the North Pole that Leonard somehow had made into a gift for Penny? *Big Bang Theory?* How about we get X a rock— No a leaf, a few blades of glass, a bit of earth," she smiled, "and put them in a little glass box or something?"

"Might get broken en route."

"Yeah."

They continued to wander through the shop, seeing nothing.

"We can give her a box of Aero bars! A whole *carton* of Aero bars."

"If she's travelling at the speed of light, won't they just melt?"

"They'd still be good," Jane muttered.

They'd circled back to the entrance. Nothing had seemed appropriate.

"Hey, you took a video of Alice's 'Welcome' composition, didn't you?" Jane asked. "On your phone?"

"Yes! That's perfect! She *loved* the light synth stuff. We can put it on a mini flash drive!"

So they found a store that sold flash drives, bought one, then sat on a bench and copied the video from Spike's cellphone onto the drive, using one of the cables also, conveniently, sold by the store.

"Seems a shame," Jane said. "I mean we've got 64GB and all we're putting on is a 200MB video."

They thought about that.

"We could put the human genome on it!"

Spike looked over horrified. "And contaminate Grmphflg?"

Jane thought for just a second and sighed. "You're right. We're a virus."

"Well, not *us* we."

"No, not us we."

On the way back to the Westin, Jane had an even better idea. She opened her laptop and started googling. Spike glanced over.

"Whatcha doin'?" she asked, pleasantly, curiously, fearfully.

"Trying to find Alice." Jane was going through all the staff photos of the Goddard Space Center.

"Bingo!" She clicked on 'Contact' then composed, and sent, an email.

"Whatcha done?" Spike asked, just fearfully.

"I asked Alice to ask Alice if she had a video of the other piece she performed."

"Brilliant!"

The following day, they received a response from Alice, and ten minutes later, the flash drive for X contained not only the video of 'Welcome', but also a video of the other piece, the scores for both of them, and the specs for her light synthesizer.

On the fourth day, they returned to find X and Tang sprawled on the floor, looking exultant. Shilpa was sunk into the chair she'd seldom left for the past three days.

"You've got the coordinates?" Spike asked.

"No," Shilpa smiled, dazed and exhausted, "but the conceptual work is done. All we have to do now is put the numbers into— A really big computer."

X grinned. She was going home!

"And Stanford *has* ... a really big computer? And you'll be able to get access?"

"I'll make sure of it."

Jane swallowed the last big bite of brownie she'd had in her hand. "So ... you're going to take X back to Stanford with you? This is good-bye?" she added, suddenly up to speed.

"Unless you want to come back with us. You're welcome to do so. We've got two other house-mates, but we can make room for a few— No, wait," Shilpa said then, "you drove here, didn't you."

"Yeah, so—" Spike saw it first. "You flew?"

Shilpa nodded. They both looked at X.

Jane articulated the problem. "Can X fly?"

X gave her a look.

"I mean, can you travel on an Earth airplane? The altitude, the speed ..." She was thinking of purple, and ecru, and white ...

X gave her another look.

"Okay, right, stupid me. But what about— No, you won't need a passport. But she'll need photo ID, right? To get onto the plane?" Jane looked at Shilpa and Spike.

"Not for a domestic— No, wait," Shilpa corrected herself, "we *did* have to show photo ID. Didn't we?" She looked at Tang. Tang nodded. "Right ... post 9/11 security changes, racial profiling, whatever. Yeah, she'll need photo ID."

Okay, so that wouldn't work.

"I guess an alternative is that you rent a car and drive back," Spike suggested. "It'll take a bit longer, but ..."

"But if that's safer, that's what we'll do. We certainly don't want her to be detained for suspiciously fake ID."

"Hey," Jane had an idea, "why can't she just— X, where's your ship?"

X looked up from the bubbles in one of the Aero bars they'd brought back, smiling, then suddenly frowning. "Oh."

"You forgot where you parked it, didn't you." Jane did that all the time.

X nodded forlornly. "No, wait!" She suddenly remembered. "It's beside Walmart!"

"Okaaaay ... and that would be where?"

"I don't know," X confessed. Then wailed, "I've lost my ship!"

The four of them considered, then, the elephant in the room. And X's ship being stripped of its hubcaps was the least of it.

"No, wait!" X rummaged in her pocket and pulled out what looked like a car remote. "My sister got me this. I forgot my head once when it wasn't screwed on tightly enough."

Jane, Spike, and Shilpa looked at each other. Tang giggled.

"But you won't hear the—" Surely a starship wouldn't beep— Then she had another thought. "Will you?"

"There's nothing for me to hear. When I press this, my ship hears me. It's a smartship. It'll come get me."

"Cool," Tang said.

"Wait!" Shilpa stretched out her arm to X in alarm. "Let's do that from Stanford," she said to her, then turned to Jane and Spike. "I'm surprised some radar system didn't pick up her entry. If anyone sees the ship on its way here, then on its way back to Stanford ... Though I'd really like ..." she trailed off, grinning.

"Good point," Spike said. Then added, also grinning, "And yeah."

"You could still come with us though," Shilpa said to the two of them.

"It's sort of going in the wrong direction," Spike replied. And would only delay the inevitable.

Shilpa nodded, understanding. "Okay. We'll leave day after tomorrow then," she announced, then explained. "Because tomorrow, we're *all* spending the day at the beach!"

So next morning, late, Shilpa and Tang headed out to get a couple coolers and fill them with food and drink, while Jane and Spike took X to buy a beach towel and a swimsuit—a pair of baggy shorts and a t-shirt—and get a couple coolers and fill them with dessert. They'd agreed to meet at around two o'clock at one of the less populated spots on the nearby beach.

When Jane, Spike, and X arrived, they saw that Shilpa and Tang had already rented a couple umbrellas and a few lounge chairs.

"None of this looks like pizza," Jane said, peering inside the larger of two coolers.

"No," Spike agreed.

The cooler contained potato salad, bean salad, coconut bread, and lots of other things, mostly unidentifiable but begging to be tasted. Shilpa had also thought to include paper plates, cups, and plastic cutlery. The smaller cooler contained several jugs of iced tea and a bag of ice.

Jane and Spike's coolers, on the other hand, contained a great number of boxes of liquor-filled chocolates—cherry brandy, cognac, amaretto, apricot brandy, tequila, champagne. And a box of Malibu Coconut Rum Chocolates. Because.

They'd also purchased several boxes of little chocolate bottles filled with wine. "Who knew?" Jane had said when she saw the cute little chocolate bottles.

After they'd gone for a swim, then eaten their fill, Jane, Spike, and Shilpa claimed the lounge chairs and watched Tang and X play beach volleyball. With something that wasn't a ball. It wasn't even spherical.

"It's weighted in a weird way," Shilpa explained, as they watched them toss it back and forth. "You have to know physics to be able to predict its trajectory ..."

Tang was exceptionally good at doing just that. She seemed always to be in the right place at the right time. X, on the other hand ... She laughed with delight when suddenly at the last moment, the thing swooped out of reach. Again and again.

The afternoon passed leisurely. They swam, they lay in the sun, they sat in the shade, they walked along the sandy beach, and they let liquor-filled chocolates melt in their mouths ... It was wonderful.

But not nearly as wonderful as the sunset. Jane and Spike had never seen the sun set over the Pacific. The world turned gold and orange. It was truly breath-stopping. Not one of them said a word as it slowly brightened then quickly faded ...

But every one of them gasped as three dolphins suddenly arced out of the water, close enough to silhouette against the glowing sky.

It was a perfect moment. And a perfect memento.

The next morning—well, the next noon—they stood awkwardly in the Westin parking lot between their car and the rental Shilpa had had delivered. Courtesy of the university.

"Okay, then," Spike said, "I guess this is good-bye."

The fact of their parting suddenly cut through X's excitement, feverish work, and celebratory glee of the last several days. She was clearly sad, as were Jane and Spike. She got up and went to Jane and Spike, hugging them each in turn, jumping up and down when she did so. Pure Monty Python.

"Thank you. Thank you so much."

"You're welcome," Spike said. "We're glad it worked out."

"Yeah, for a while there ..." Jane added, then quickly concluded, "well, good luck. And here," she gave X the flash drive. "We got you a going-away gift." She explained what it was and what was on it, worrying just then about whether X could access it. Apparently she could, because her eyes widened and she hugged them again. And jumped up and down again. And then fell over.

Tang giggled. X got back up, a goofy grin on her face.

Spike gave Shilpa a 'Take care of her' look. Shilpa nodded.

And then the two of them could only stand there, waiting to wave, as Shilpa, Tang, and X got into the rental.

"Wait!" Jane cried out, then dove into the back seat of their car.

"Oh yeah," Spike said, and gave an explanation to Shilpa. Which was really a non-explanation. Because they'd never really figured it out.

And then they waved good-bye to the extraterrestrial wearing a red Mrs. Fields' pail.

21

She'll be all right, yeah?" Jane asked once they were on the road.

"I think so. Shilpa will look after her."

"I miss her."

"So do I."

"We should've gone to Stanford to see her off," Jane said. In San Bernardino.

"But it might've taken days for the computer to do its thing."

"I keep thinking of questions we should've asked her."

"But Alice—"

"I know, maybe not *those* questions, but ..."

"So where are we going?" Jane asked. In Escondido.

"Back home?"

"You said we'd move to Boston."

"We'd need work visas."

"Oh. Right."

"We should have stayed in California longer," Jane said. They'd crossed into Nevada. "Nice weather."

"California's going to be the first to go."

"You could finish your dissertation," Jane suggested.

"No point. The only jobs are in industry. And they just want to use psychology to manipulate people. Their employees, their customers."

"You know, when I was looking for a job, everyone kept saying 'You're overqualified.' And I said, 'Yeah, well, the jobs I'm qualified for are filled.'"

"By men." Spike got it.

"You could take that guy up on his offer to hire you."

"What guy?" Jane asked with excitement. Had she forgotten a job offer?

"Your neighbour. Remember?"

"Oh yeah." She snorted. When Jane was walking home one day, one of her neighbours had stopped her. He was getting on in years and looking for someone to look after him—do his cooking and cleaning and whatever. Once Jane had recovered from the insult, she'd asked him if he'd asked John, the unemployed IT specialist who lived down the road a few houses. The man was confused. Why would he ask John? Well, why would you ask me? she'd retorted. He'd sputtered. It was obvious, wasn't it?

Yes. It was.

A few minutes later, Jane opened her laptop and started setting up a website titled "And here's something else that would never happen to a man." She intended to post the episode and invite similar posts.

"Why can't we just find real jobs?" she asked. An hour later. "Good jobs. Jobs that pay. Jobs that make a difference."

"Because those jobs are filled."

"Oh yeah."

"You've still got your novel. And your dictionary."

"And I've started another one. *Collected Epitaphs.*"

"Hm. What've you got so far?"

Jane opened her laptop and then <In-Progress-Collected-Epitaphs>.

"'I knew this would happen some day.'"

Spike laughed. "What else?"

"'Help, I've fallen and I can't get up.'"

"I like that one better. What else?"

"'Yeah, but—'"

"We really should get a GPS," Jane suggested. When it was clear they were heading toward Tijuana.

"Tell me again why this isn't considered hate speech." They'd stopped for gas, and chocolate bars, and Jane was flipping through one of the porn magazines on display along the wall. Just above the row of *Cosmopolitan* and *Vogue* and *Whatever*, which, truthfully, had covers that looked pretty much the same. As the one in her hand.

"Hey," Spike, standing beside her, called out to the man behind the counter. "Isn't this illegal?" She nodded to the rack of porn magazines. They were on display, easily accessible in a public— Though, come to think of it, the internet was just as public, just as easily accessible, so maybe the law—

The man shook his head.

—didn't reach Tonapah.

"Even so, you think it's okay to hurt people?" Spike approached him.

He stared at her blankly. Of course he didn't think it was okay to hurt people.

"Then don't sell this shit."

His brain was working ... working ...

"By selling this shit, you increase the likelihood of me getting hurt."

He rolled his eyes.

"The mere fact that you believe porn *isn't* harmful is proof that it *is*," Jane said, joining Spike at the counter, "because such a belief indicates that you're so accustomed to seeing women sexually subordinated, you think there's nothing wrong with it. Such a belief proves that porn has skewed your perceptions so much you actually *believe* the women are enjoying, asking for, whatever it is you see."

If he only had a brain.

"They're *pretending*, asshole!" Spike shouted at him. "They're *acting*. According to some guy's fantasy script. And they're doing so only because they're getting *paid*."

"Considerably more than they'd be paid at any job they'd otherwise be likely to get," Jane added. "Enough to support a couple kids, probably." Which, sigh, they'd probably have.

The man started stocking cigarettes. *Behind* the counter. Because cigarettes are harmful. It says so right on the package. And, therefore, have to be kept out of easy reach.

"Furthermore," Jane continued, because Spike was busy ripping to shreds the magazine she had in her hands, "such a claim also proves you haven't read the research. Compared to those who did not watch porn, men who watch porn are more likely to have aggressive and hostile sexual fantasies, more likely to say that women enjoy forced sex, and more likely to consider women subordinate and submissive. Read Gail Dines.[78] Read *any* of *the studies*[79] that *prove* that exposing yourself to porn increases the likelihood that you'll do what you see."

---

78 http://gaildines.com/

79 http://ldsmag.com/disturbing-new-study-porn-is-linked-to-increases-in-sexual-aggression/

He turned to them. Spread his hands wide on the counter. "It's just the lads having a bit of fun. That'll be $9.99."

"And that makes it *better*?" Spike asked. From over at the rack. Where she was busy ripping up the rest of the magazines. "That seeing women humiliated is *fun*?"

"It doesn't humiliate women. $9.99 *each*."

Jane picked up a couple pieces from the floor. She set them on the counter, then put them together with exaggerated care. Her completed jigsaw puzzle showed a man urinating on a woman.

"We don't mean anything by it. Plus tax."

"And *that* makes it better?" Spike called out. "That you humiliate people so *mindlessly*? Or that women's humiliation doesn't *mean* anything?"

"So we watch a bit of porn. It's a release. No credit cards."

"Like a safety valve?"

"Yes. Otherwise, there'd be a lot more sexual assault. Cash only."

"So," Jane said, "if we want people to stop beating their kids, we should show them lots of pictures of parents beating their kids, with the kids appearing to enjoy it?"

Spike stopped shredding and looked at her, impressed at the comparison.

"Sara Daniels," Jane gave the citation. "*Masterpieces*."[80]

"How can he be so clueless? How can they *all* be so clueless?" Jane was truly amazed.

"Do you think he got our license plate?"

They drove to another store for chocolate bars.

----

80 http://www.bloomsbury.com/uk/masterpieces-9781474218061/

And then to a motel for the night. In Palm Springs.

They really wanted to just go for a slow, relaxing walk—it was a lovely, warm night—but they couldn't do that even back home in Toronto.

"Most attacks are by men," Jane said, thinking of the 21,000 acts of violence against women each week,[81] "but it's not the case that most men attack. We really need *that* percentage."

"Well if nine out of ten men watch porn, and almost all of it shows violence toward women, and studies conclusively show that what we watch influences our behavior ..."

"Nine out of ten *young* men."

They thought about that.

"Males between fifteen and thirty should be quarantined," Spike said. "We should bring back the draft."

A moment later, she had a new thought.

"Most of the men in Palm Springs are old, right?"

So they went for a walk after all.

But just five minutes out, they saw three pre-menopausal men in the distance. They both knew one of them would rape if he thought he could get away with it.[82] One in four[83] had already done so. More than one in four, if some men aren't admitting, let alone recognizing, what they'd done.

So they turned around and headed back to the hotel.

---

81 http://www.msmagazine.com/news/uswirestory.asp?id=15200
82 https://wearawhitefeather.wordpress.com/survivors/rape-culture-statistics/
83 https://thinkprogress.org/what-we-can-learn-from-the-largest-international-study-on-rape-thats-been-conducted-so-far-eb2b549a0ab3#.dhshotdoc

"Changed your mind?" the man behind the reception desk called out pleasantly when they passed by on their way back to their room. Pleasantly.

So they wondered yet again: how is it that so many men have no idea?

There were no videos to upload. Neither of them had recorded the scene in the porn store.

Jane made an entry in her translation dictionary:

> We were just having fun. 1. I don't want to be held responsible for it. 2. We didn't think it through.

Then while they waited for their pizza, they watched tv.

Gunshots. Spike changed the channel.

More gunshots. She looked at her watch, then changed the channel again.

Again gunshots. Again Spike looked at her watch before changing the channel.

Two minutes later, Jane had to ask. "Whatcha doin'?"

"Seeing how long it takes before some guy hurts or kills someone."

Fists. More gunshots. "Better luck next time, loser!" More gunshots. Knives. "When I give you an order, I expect you to follow it!"

Jane waited.

"Forty-five seconds," Spike announced.

"That long?"

"Fifteen seconds before they engage in some sort of competition or display of dominance."

She watched for a few minutes. More gunshots. "Are you threatening me?" More fists. More knives. Still more gunshots. Injury. Pain. Death.

And always a complete lack of remorse.

Jane thought back to, well, everything. "We play with a completely different set of rules, don't we."

"The 'Don't lie, Don't destroy, Don't hurt, Don't kill' set?"

"That'd be the one."

A few minutes later, Spike stopped at a football game, and they watched for a while.

"Do you think they play football because they're brain-damaged or do you think they're brain-damaged because they play football?" Jane asked.

The commentator explained then that charges against so-and-so of aggravated rape had been dropped ...

"And yet they're against women's football because 'they could get hurt'. It boggles the mind."

"They're just lying," Spike said. "About why they're against women's football.

She switched channels.

"It's really time they raise the basket."

"But as it is," Jane protested, "they need to grab onto it on their way down."

"Yeah, but that's just lack of coordination."

"Oh, it's the robot floor event!" Spike had changed the channel again. "And look! He can stand on one foot!"

Jane grinned. "I've never noticed that before. But you're right. Women land back flips on a four-inch beam three feet off the ground, and meanwhile they're proud of holding a front scale on the floor."

"And now to the bar! Singular."

"Again, never noticed that before," she grinned. Again. "Even when they work on two, they're set at the same height."

She turned to Spike then. "How do they manage to make us think they're better than us at everything when there is such clear evidence to the contrary?"

"Hey, there's a new show, a drama, starring not just one but two women ..." Jane was reading through the tv guide, trying to find *some*thing worth watching.

"Be still, my heart." Spike switched to the channel Jane indicated.

While they watched, Jane made another entry:

Stay here. 1. *I* want to be the hero. 2. I don't want you to see me make a fool of myself. 3. My ability to concentrate is so minimal, your presence will make me completely ineffectual.

Within five minutes, one of the women got the life bled out of her by a vampire, and the other one revealed that she was pregnant.

"You know I hate redundancy."

A few minutes later, the pizza arrived. Delivered by a man, of course. Because if women were pizza delivery people, they'd get hurt.

They ate in silence. Because Spike had unplugged the tv and thrown it against the wall.

Next morning they stopped at the first store they figured would carry GPS units. They found the GPS display. They also found a customer service representative. Kyle, his name tag said. He was standing right next to it.

"Hi, can you tell us a bit about these? We've never used one before."

"Well, we carry both the Garmin and the Magellan."

They waited. But nothing more was forthcoming.

Just then, a middle-aged man approached the display.

"Looking to buy a GPS?" Kyle asked the man.

"Yeah."

"Well, the Garmin and the Magellan are pretty much the same, but this particular model has a slightly bigger screen size than the others. It also has free map updates, which is a good thing."

Jane and Spike just stared.

"This one gives you more options with the voice though," he pointed to another one. "And the warranty is longer."

The man nodded.

"All of them come with both car chargers and USB cables, but if you want a wall charger, you have to buy that separately."

"Great, thanks." The man picked one of the Garmins and left.

Kyle was about to follow.

"Wait just one god-damned minute."

He turned. To Spike.

"Why didn't you tell *us* any of that?" she asked.

He looked at them blankly.

"Do you think we're too stupid to understand? Or are we just not worth your time?"

"You didn't ask about any of that," he shrugged.

"NEITHER DID HE!"

"You know, most women would deny that that sort of shit happens."

"Most women are accompanied by a man."

That afternoon, they happened to pass a gorgeous lake—while the GPS was "Recalculating ..."—so they decided to pull over for a while, walk around for a bit, stretch their legs, just sit not-in-the-car for a while.

Soon after, some guys pulled up in a pick-up truck, a boat on the attached trailer.

"Goin' fishin'?" Spike asked.

"Yup."

"What kind of fish do you catch here? They good to eat?"

"Catch-and-release."

"Then what's the point?" Jane asked. Truly perplexed.

"The fish usually dies anyway," Spike added. "No surprise, really. I mean, first you jerk a hook through its mouth—that's gotta hurt, by the way, fish have nerves in their mouths—then you drag it by that hook through the water. Then you let it hang by that hook, in the air, so it starts to suffocate, it starts to jerk and spasm— All that trauma alone reduces its chances of survival.

"But then by the time you throw it back in—and most of the time, you do just *throw* it—like it's garbage or something—by that time, you've removed so much of its slime, it's severely compromised—its slime is its protective coating, you know that, right? It gives the fish immunity to all kinds of shit. That you put into the water."

Both of the men turned their attention then from getting their boat into the water to the women. "You say something?"

They stopped for gas again, and chocolate bars again, and then checked in to a motel. Again.

Once in their room, Spike headed for the bathroom. Jane made herself comfortable on one of the two beds, turned on her laptop, waited until it found the motel's wifi, then accepted the password she'd provided, conveniently written on a card beside the phone, then connected to the Internet.

They discovered, much to their surprise, that there was no pizza delivery. So they got back into their car and drove around looking for, well, pizza. They had to settle for a pub that looked like it might have pizza on the menu.

It did indeed, and while they sat at the bar waiting for their extra-large, with extra-cheese, onions, and olives (no sun-dried tomatoes, no pineapple, no mushrooms), Spike glanced at a newspaper that had been left behind. The Olympics had started. There was a headline in bold about some guy who'd won the silver. And *below,* in *smaller* print, *not* bolded, a headline about a woman who'd set a new world record.

She tossed it away from her in disgust.

"What?" the man nearest her asked. "Your guy didn't win?"

Momentarily torn between responding to the "your" or the "guy" or not responding at all, because why bother, she eventually said, tersely, "Silver medal trumps world record because, surprise, male trumps female."

He stared at her.

Jane nodded to the newspaper. "She could have— Well, I don't know what she could have done because what's better than a world record? And still."

"But he's more important," the man replied, finally getting her point. "Everyone knows him, his name."

"Right. But *why* is he more important? *She* set a new world record."

"Yeah, but everyone knows *him. His* name. So you lead with—"

"Because the editor has made sexist decisions like this all along! If she'd gotten the coverage he's been getting ..." she trailed off. Because women would *never* be more important, would never be *considered* more important, than men.

"Yeah, well, women do sexist shit too."

She turned to him with surprise. He knew the word 'sexist'? And could use it in a sentence?

"That's irrelevant," Jane spoke up, then saw that she had to spell it out. "Whether they do or not doesn't change whether men do or not."

The man got up and headed to the washroom. So his buddy took over. "They sit at home all day doin' nothin', while we're out working to support 'em. Where do they get off?"

Spike turned to him. She did not, note, turn *on* him. "You've got kids?"

He nodded. Amazingly unable to see where this was going.

"And your wife looks after them all day?"

He nodded. What was her point?

"And now it's evening, and you're here? While she's still at home, still looking after them?" Spike expressed surprise, even though she wasn't even a little surprised.

"Okay, so let me get this straight," she kept on. "You made a couple kids, and now you're angry because your wife is just 'sitting at home all day' while you're at work."

"Yeah!"

Spike thought for a moment.

"You *do* know that an infant and a two-year-old—I'm guessing—can't be left alone for eight hours. Let alone eight minutes."

He looked at her as if to say 'Your point?'

"So she *can't* go out to work, you moron! Unless *you're* willing to look after the kids all day."

"Fuck that," he spat.

Spike gave up.

"His brain's broken," Jane said.

When the first man returned, he opened with "Women like you probably think all men rape."

What?

"No," Spike sighed, only partly because their pizza wasn't ready yet, "but I think *only* men rape."

"That's because only men *can*," he smirked and drained the rest of his beer.

"You don't think a few women could overpower you, cuff you face down to a bed, strip you, then shove a bottle up your ass for a couple hours?"

He stared at her.

"What, you don't know that rape is often anal? With a foreign object?"

"A foreign object that's not a penis," Jane clarified.

"What do you think she put in your beer," Spike nodded to Jane, "when you went to take a leak?"

He paled. Only partly because he couldn't remember going to take a leak. Then he tried to make a run for it. Four beer, so he stumbled. Though that could've been because Spike shot her leg out and tripped him. In any case, he went down. She let him crawl out of the bar.

Once back in their motel room, Spike glanced at the tv, then headed for the night stand instead.

"Hey, a book by a woman! What are the odds?"

"One in three,"[84] Jane paused at the bathroom door. "Even though publishers know very well that far more women than men read books.

"'Course," she added, "that doesn't really matter since women read books by men. Men don't read books by women."

"Must think they don't have anything interesting to say. Go figure."

"And," Jane continued, "somewhere around seventy-five percent[85] of the reviews are written by men. Oddly enough, the percentage of the books that *get* reviews, that are written by men, is also seventy-five."

"Well that sucks." Spike was flipping through the paperback.

A few moments later, Jane opened the door and returned to the bed she'd claimed, glancing at the book in Spike's hand. "You know J. D. Robbs is *Nora* Roberts?" She was surprised.

"No, I guessed. Initials." Spike stopped flipping through and turned the book over to read the back cover. After just a moment, she tossed the book onto the nightstand in disgust.

"What?"

She picked it up again and read aloud. "'Roberts is indisputably the most celebrated and beloved women's fiction writer today.' *Women's* fiction. They ghettoized it. Practically *guaranteed* that men won't pay any attention to her."

Jane said nothing. This was not news to her.

"Despite," Spike read on with disbelief, "having more than 145 million copies of her books in print and more than sixty-nine *New York Times* bestsellers to date!"

---

84 http://www.salon.com/2011/02/09/women_literary_publishing/
85 http://www.theguardian.com/books/2011/feb/04/research-male-writers-dominate-books-world

Jane chose an Aero bar for dessert and settled herself onto the bed. "One has to wonder," she said, having wondered already, many times, "what makes her work *women's* fiction? I mean, what *is* women's fiction? Fiction written *by* women? Then Harper Lee's *To Kill a Mockingbird* would be women's fiction. As would be Ayn Rand's *Atlas Shrugged*." She started unwrapping the bar.

"Fiction *for* women?" she presented a second hypothesis. "And what's that, fiction that women are interested in? As if all, or even most, women are interested in the same things. It's painfully clear that not all women are interested even in sexism. Just as not all blacks are interested in racism."

"Is *To Kill a Mockingbird* ever called black fiction?" Spike asked.

"Good question. No." She'd mumbled the answer, since her mouth was full of chocolate bubbles. "Interesting." Also mumbled.

"Proof that sexism trumps racism. Worse to be a woman than to be black."

"Hm. Yeah." She took another bite of the bar, then resumed exploring her second hypothesis. "Robb's *Death* series is about a cop, murder, good and evil, justice. Men aren't interested in these things? Since when? And her *Key* series is about three women, each on a quest. Success means money and power. Of interest only to women? Hardly."

"Yeah, but it sounds like all of her books are *about* women. The main characters are women, yeah?" Spike had nailed the third hypothesis.

Jane nodded. And finished her Aero bar.

"There you go. Men aren't interested in reading about women. Men aren't interested in women. Period."

Jane nodded again. And got another chocolate bar out of the bag. Another Aero bar.

"You ever notice how men's blogrolls never include women's blogs?" Spike said.

"Yeah, Katha Pollitt noticed that too."[86] She took a bite.

---

86 https://www.thenation.com/article/invisible-women/

"Have you considered the possibility that 'women's fiction' doesn't actually *mean ... anything*? That it's just a way to put women in their place? As a member of the subordinate class?"

Jane shuddered at the possibility. That words had no meaning. And took another bite.

"I'm just so frickin' SICK of it!" Spike picked up the book from the night table, tore off the back cover, and flung it toward the wall. It fluttered to the floor just past the edge of her bed.

Jane looked at her in alarm. She'd never seen Spike do something so ... ineffectual.

"I'm tired," she explained, slumping against the bed's headboard. "So ... *tired.* We're going to be forty next year. Which means we've been dealing with this shit— Which means that every day for forty years, every *frickin'* day, we've been subordinated. In one, in *at least* one, of *a hundred* ways. We're sexualized, patronized, dismissed, ignored ... It's humiliating. All of it. Every day. For forty years."

She was near tears. Jane was ... aghast. She'd thought—

"I hate that they work less hard in school, get lower grades, and yet get better job offers. I hate that they're just *given* respect, while we have to earn it. I hate that they're *assumed* to be competent, while we have to prove it. By being *better.* Even as they're sabotaging our efforts. And even *then,* they refuse to accept that we are, in fact, better. I hate that—

"It'd be so nice," she started again, her voice trembling, "to be able to take on a male body once a week. Just for a bit of relief. To be taken seriously for a whole day. To *not* be sexualized, patronized, dismissed, ignored. To not have to fight for everything I've ever wanted. To not have to argue for it, beg for it, and still not get it."

Wordlessly, Jane passed her the bag of chocolate bars.

When Spike opened it, she saw that it was full of Aero bars. Only Aero bars.

"You know," Jane said, yet another Aero bar later, "they should call all of the novels with male main characters 'men's fiction'. And then people would see."

Spike grunted. People would see *nothing*.

They refused to turn on the tv at the next motel.

They refused to open the nightstand drawer at the next motel.

Instead, Jane picked up the newspaper that had been left behind.

"Hey, there's going to be a commission to investigate 'women's issues,'" she read without enthusiasm. "That we have to establish them as 'add-ons' proves that 'issues' are really '*men's* issues'," she added. Unnecessarily.

"And calling them women's issues guarantees that men won't become involved in them," Spike added. Also unnecessarily.

"They own most of the property," Jane said, as she continued to flip through it, "they hold most of the executive positions, they occupy most of the political positions, and they typically don't concern themselves with ethics, which adds to their power, because it makes them free to do ... anything. So," she got to her point, "as long as men are in positions of power over us, we have to ask them for whatever we want. The right to go to school. The right to vote. Equal pay for work of equal value. Daycare centers in the workplace. Contraception.

"And more often than not, they say no. Not because of what we're asking for, but merely because we are women. To be seen acceding to requests by, let alone taking orders from, women is emasculating. Once I asked the guy who lives across from me, when he was doing some noisy work indoors, if he could at least close the window facing me so I didn't have to hear it so much. Easy enough to do. But GOD NO!! He fussed and fumed, WHY SHOULD HE HAVE TO DO THAT?! And yet when Brian down the street made the same request, sure, no problem.

"So the only way we're going to get any of what we want is to somehow just take it. But there are never enough of us to make that happen. We never reach ... critical mass. Because so many of us are wives and mothers, happy to be kept women, too afraid to risk the alternative, or too busy looking after husband and kids."

"How did black people get out from under?" Jane asked a long moment later.

"Men took the helm."[87]

"Yeah. And that'll never happen."

Spike agreed. "Because some men are black. No man is a woman."

"But weren't the men who took the helm white?"

"Yeah. Bros before ..."

---

87 http://www.shmoop.com/civil-rights-black-power/gender.html

22

Let's go out to eat," Spike said after they'd checked in to yet another motel and tossed their stuff onto the beds. "Either the pizza's getting worse or ..."

"Agreed."

So they freshened up, got back in their car, and drove around. Their options were limited: McDonalds, Taco Bell, a Chinese food restaurant that was closed, a pricey-looking steakhouse, and a place that looked like a Casey's or Kelsey's. They pulled into the last one.

The place was louder than they would have liked, but they were able to get a table for two in the corner, far from the men who crowded the bar watching the ubiquitous large-screen tv.

"Oh for fuck's sake, he's playing like a goddamn pussy!"

Not far enough.

"Do you think their tendency to project their voices—regardless of the need to be heard—that is, the importance of their words—"

"They do it to occupy as much air space as possible," Spike replied tersely.

"Yeah. What I thought."

A waitress came to their table.

"Hey there, what can I get you?" she chirped.

"A lower voice," Spike said.

"Yeah, they are kinda loud."

Jane would've used the word 'coercive.' Because the volume forced her to pay attention. To what he was saying.

"No, I meant you. When women speak in a higher register than is actually necessary, they come across as child-like. Trying lowering your voice. To normal."

"Like this?" She spoke in an alto, then giggled.

They ordered garlic cheese bread, vegetarian burgers, and chocolate milkshakes.

"We won!" the fattest guy shouted and high-fived the next-fattest guy beside him. Getting off their bar stools was too much effort, so they didn't do a victory dance.

"Manufactured enthusiasm," Jane observed.

"Misplaced tribal affiliation," Spike added.

A few minutes later, the waitress brought their bread and filled their water glasses.

She tried for a Darth Vader, "Here you go," then giggled again.

Jane picked up a slice of the still warm bread, glanced back to the tv and paled.

"What?" Spike asked her, then turned to follow her gaze.

"It's *19-2*," she said with disbelief. *19-2* was a Canadian cop show set in Montreal. What was it doing on a network here in wherever the hell they were? "And we saw this episode, remember?"

Spike watched for the few seconds it took to recognize it.

And then they were both trying, as quickly as they could, to remember the sequence of the scenes, to figure out whether—

"Let's leave. Now." Jane got up quickly from the table. Spike followed.

One of the only two women in the unit was on patrol, alone, and when she stopped to help a seemingly injured or mentally confused woman crouching in the middle of the road, she was ambushed by three men.

When they were halfway to the exit, one of the men threw her against the car door. Twice. Then slammed her face into it. She crumpled to the ground. They started kicking her, viciously, and then the one with the baseball bat brought it down as hard as he could. On her face. Hopefully she was unconscious by then because what they did next—

They were almost to the door, moving quickly, but not too quickly. Don't attract attention.

The guy with the bat told the other two to pick her up, by her ankles.

"Higher," he said.

They held her higher, spreading her legs like a wishbone.

And then he swung the baseball bat again, this time smashing it down as hard as he could into the V of her pelvis.

Jane and Spike were through the door.

They heard the men cheering as they raced to their car. *Cheering.*

Spike had her keys out. Get inside, lock the doors, get the hell away. Get inside, lock the doors—

"Lock your door!" Jane sputtered as she locked her side, then twisted in the passenger seat to reach into the back, still hearing the men's cheers.

Spike locked her door as well, reached into the back—

"Got it?"

"Yes!" Spike put the key into the ignition, hand shaking—

"Okay GO!" Jane screamed then, losing it, and Spike sped out of the parking lot, turned right on the red light, and drove. Kept driving.

Jane looked out the rear window. No one seemed to be following them.

Not a word was said. For a full minute. Then two. Three.

They were busy replaying what had just happened. Someone must have made a DVD of that particular episode and—

"Do you think we're safe h—" The 'here' sort of dissolved into a puff as Jane saw Spike's dark look.

They were back in their motel room. Still shaking. Jane, with fear. Spike, with rage.

"WHAT THE FUCK IS *WRONG* WITH THEM?" Jane screamed a few moments later, huddled on the bed.

It was a question that needed to be asked. Betty McLellan, psychotherapist, observed[88] *years* ago that even with all the evidence we have that something's not quite right with the male of the species, there is impenetrable resistance to focusing on men's behaviour and asking, essentially, that question.

Though 'not quite right' is a bit of an understatement. Given.

"What the fuck is wrong with *us?*" Spike corrected, tightly, still pacing.

"Their psychopathology clearly comes from testosterone poisoning and/or the Y chromosome, and yet we don't prescribe, let alone require, chemical castration and/or genetic re-engineering.

"They're clearly subject to the herding effect and the pull of nocturnal predation, and yet we don't limit their freedom of association or impose a curfew.

"To be a man is to scorn empathy, and morality, and self-control. It is to feel, and *be*, entitled. To everything. It is to embrace competition above all. Conquest is pleasure. Destruction is beautiful.

"And yet we continue to raise our boys to *be* men."

Jane was impressed with Spike's articulateness. Must be the rage.

"Well, not *us* we," she replied.

Spike paced for a few moments longer, then sat down heavily. She'd made a decision.

"Why do they do what they do? Because they can. Because we let them."

"Well, not—"

"*Us* we."

Next day, three hours away, somewhere in Texas, or Oklahoma, they parked in front of Guns 'R' Us. Though they could've gone to Walmart.

---

88 https://radicalhubarchives.wordpress.com/2011/06/01/guest-post-betty-mclellan/

"It's probably owned by Toys 'R' Us," Spike said, as they stared at the store. They'd expected a bit of a hole in the wall, but Guns 'R' Us was, apparently, a thriving and upfront business. Probably even in the top ten of Fortune 500.

Jane nodded, making no move to get out of the car.

"It's legal to use force proportional to the threat perceived," Spike turned to her. "Who's to say the guy who tells you he just wants to have a little fun doesn't end up raping you? And who's to say he isn't HIV-positive? Considering his sexual proclivities, it's quite possible. Which means he could be killing you. So you have a legal right to kill him. It would be self-defence."

Jane raised her eyebrows. That didn't seem right.

"Google it."

She did. She went to one site. Then another. Then another.

"You're right," she said. "In theory."

Still, she didn't move.

"In practice ... You're reluctant only because men have monopolized the legitimate use of violence."[89]

Not only.

"We've tried polite request. For a couple centuries. We've tried rational argument. For a couple centuries. It appears the only language they understand is power, force, threat, fear—"

Jane nodded. Then followed her inside.

The guy behind the counter wore a three-piece suit that covered most of his tattoos.

"What kind of guns can we get here and now?" Spike asked.

"If I've got it, you can have it," he passed a form to each of them.

"We just have to fill this out?"

---

89 https://witchwind.wordpress.com/2013/05/19/spot-the-man-behind-the-man/

He nodded. "Then I do a background check. Takes a few minutes."

Seriously? Unbelievable. For Canadians such as themselves.

They started filling in the form. Ever been convicted in any court of a felony? No. Ever been discharged from the Armed Forces under dishonorable conditions? No. Ever been adjudicated as mentally defective? Not officially.

He looked over the forms they handed back to him. "You have to be a U. S. citizen. Or a resident alien."

They thought the latter applied. Given.

"You have a green card?"

Spike shook her head. "So we can't even get tasers?"

"Nope."

"Pellet guns?"

He shook his head.

"*Squirt* guns?"

Jane looked at her.

"We can put acid in them."

Jane recovered quickly. "Won't it corrode the plastic?"

"Good point."

The man was looking at them, just a little horrified.

"What?" Spike challenged. "Men throw acid at women all the time."

"Well," Jane put her hand on Spike's arm, in a June Cleaver sort of way, "not all the time. And," she smiled sweetly, but the tattooed guy beat her to it.

"Not all men."

"No," Spike conceded, "not all men."

And then she screamed the question. "DO WE HAVE TO WAIT UNTIL *ALL* MEN DO IT?"

The man stepped back.

"Isn't it enough that *only* men do it?" she asked pointedly. "Or that *most* men do it?"

The man—

"Oh wait!" Jane said. "I have a green card!" She pulled out the last of her credit cards. It was green.

He walked away then and made a phone call. "Yo, Martha? I got a Thelma and Louise here." He nodded, then nodded again, then hung up the phone and returned to the counter.

"Be in the Hooters lot around one. When the waitresses start coming off shift, ask for Martha."

So around one, they were in the Hooters lot. The waitresses started coming off shift.

"Hi, we're looking for Martha," Spike approached the first one. Who nodded to the woman behind her.

"Martha?"

"Yeah," she looked at Jane and Spike, made a quick assessment, then walked a few metres away from the exit. They followed. "Either of you smoke?"

They shook their heads, then stood with her in silence while she had a cigarette.

Ten minutes later, the parking lot was empty except for their car. And a panel van. Martha walked to the van. They followed, a little nervously. Then watched in disbelief as she pulled off her face. It was like that scene in *Mission Impossible*. She looked—well, she looked like them. Especially when she took off her t-shirt. Because the TripleD boobs came with it.

"It's *all* fake?" Jane asked.

"Men." Martha spat the word. "Can't tell the difference. Or it doesn't matter. Haven't figured out which yet."

They waited for the little orange shorts to go.

"The legs and the ass are mine," she said, grinning. Then added, "You don't get those boobs with this ass and these legs. Or you don't get this ass and these legs with those boobs. If you know what I mean."

They nodded. They did know what she meant. Men's view of the perfect female body defied biology.

Half an hour later, they were loading their purchases into their car: tasers, tear gas grenades, stainless steel squirt guns (filled with acid), semi-automatic pistols (Isla Vista specials, Martha called them), Mini-14 rifles (Montreal specials) (yeah), submachine guns, rocket launchers, various explosives, and an Obi-Wan Kenobi light saber.

"I don't suppose I have to tell you that if you use *any* of this just to injure or even deter, you should be hooded and masked and otherwise untraceable. Because any man you *don't* kill will spend the rest of his life trying to find you. And when he does, he'll kill you just for having had the nerve—"

They understood. Which is why they also bought a couple HooterSuits.

They drove in silence for almost an hour.

"There are places in Germany,"[90] Jane broke the silence, "legal places," she emphasized, "where men can pay to cut women." She'd come across the information while googling the night before. But hadn't quite wanted to believe it. She mentioned it just then as if she needed further justification for what was, what was now, in the trunk of her car.

"It's one of the items on the list," she continued. "Right after fist fucking. Anal fist fucking.

"You can get all you want for a flat rate of $100.

She was babbling. She knew it. She couldn't help it.

"Thousands of men showed up on opening night. Busloads.

"Seven hundred stood in line. Waiting their turn."

"Stop. Just—stop." Spike had broken into a sweat after 'men can pay to cut women.'

---

90 http://www.huffingtonpost.com/taina-bienaime/germany-wins-the-title-of_b_7446636.html

It was a while before either of them spoke again.

"Maybe after Paris, we'll go to Germany."

Next day, a couple hours out—Spike was driving, Jane was working on her *Collected Epitaphs*—the car started making a terrible noise. Then a louder terrible noise. Then no noise at all.

"Shit!"

"Oh that's a good one!" Jane made the addition.

Spike coasted to the shoulder of the road, set the brake, popped the hood, and got out to look.

"Well?"

"I think this will require more than a squirt of WD-40."

Jane flipped open her cellphone. "Tow truck?"

"Yeah."

"Oh. I forgot to recharge."

Spike reached into her pocket.

No signal anyway.

They look up and down the highway. No cars in sight.

"Where are we?" Spike asked. The GPS had stopped shortly after she'd told it to recalculate itself.

She looked around at the uniform landscape. As if that would tell her.

Jane did the same. "I've a feeling we're not in Kansas anymore."

"Walk or wait?"

"People don't stop anymore," Jane observed, "so waiting wouldn't do any good."

"Yeah, but ..."

It was hot. Unusually hot. But, of course, not unexpectedly hot. They had *some* water—

Suddenly a candy-apple-red Porsche-of-a-starship appeared. Out of nowhere. Or nowhen.

X poked her head out of the gleaming vehicle. "Do you need a ride?" She grinned.

"Hell, yeah!" Spike grinned back.

Jane was too surprised to grin. So her ship was okay, she was thinking, a couple steps behind the present. It had cloaked itself. Smartship indeed.

"Where're you going?" She finally managed to say something. Something stupid.

Tang poked her head out the back window and nodded at X. "Her place."

They noticed then that both Tang and Shilpa were squished in the back.

"Is there room for two more?"

Shilpa leaned toward the window. "Oh yeah. There's a couple thousand of us in here already."

Tang giggled. "Just sort of not all at the same time."

"What?"

"Who?"

"Hypatia, Aphra Behn," Shilpa answered, "Simone de Beauvoir, Betty Friedan, Germaine Greer, Robin Morgan, Gloria Steinem, Shulamith Firestone, Andrea Dworkin, Valerie Solanas, Kate Millett, Sheila Jeffreys, Catherine MacKinnon—"

"Rachel Carson," Tang took over, "Barbara McClintock, Ada Lovelace, Jocelyn Burnell, Ruth Wakefield, Stephanie Kwolek—"

"Who's Ruth Wakefield?" Jane asked. As if that was the only name she hadn't recognized.

"She invented chocolate chip cookies."

"Ah." She grinned.

"Marilyn French," Shilpa resumed, "Dale Spender, Susan Brownmiller, Mary Daly—

"Octavia Butler, Ursula LeGuin, Marge Piercey, Charlotte Perkins Gilman—"

"Susan B. Anthony, Elizabeth Cady Stanton, Sarah Grimke, Jane Anger—"

"Jane Anger?"

"She said in the 1500s that men were dicks. Gerda Lerner. Marilyn Waring—"

In disbelief, or confusion, or both, Spike leaned forward to peek inside. And saw Star, the twelve-year-old from the wedding intervention. Spike high-fived her.

Jane also peeked in. And saw Alice. And Alice. And Alice ... And all of the Women of Alamo, presumably.

"But ... X," Jane said, "are you *sure* we can all come with you? I mean, have you checked—before and befront?"

She nodded happily.

Spike looked at Jane. "Well?"

"Can we live on X's planet? Can we breathe its atmosphere? Can we—"

"Not as we are," Rosalind Franklin said. "We'll have to make some minor modifications."

Right. "Such as?"

"Well, X says we'll have to modify our lungs first—"

"I don't think I can," Jane said. She'd gotten behind the present again.

"Normally, you could. You can. X says that testosterone causes part of the brain to shut down—"

The ship erupted with laughter. Cackling guffawing hyperventilating laughter.

Half a light year later, when the laughter had subsided, Alice said "Our working hypothesis is that when we get to X's planet, the rest of our brain will come online, so to speak, and then we'll be able to modify our lungs, and—"

"We probably can't come back," Jane said to Spike. Trying madly to catch up.

"Do we have a reason to?"

"Well," Jane sputtered, "what about our pension funds?" She giggled hysterically. This couldn't be happening.

"You know what they called the first fission bomb made at Los Alamos?" Katya Komisaruk asked.

"Yeah." A baby. And truly, that was proof enough, reason enough—

"A baby boy or a baby girl?" A baby boy. If it was a success.

"The world is going to pieces because of them, and I'm tired of watching," L. Timmel Duchamp added.

"If the history of the Earth were a year,'" someone called out, quoting a metaphor they were both aware of, "life wouldn't appear until March, multi-cellular organisms not until November. Dinosaurs would show up on December 13, and mammals on December 15. On December 31, we'd show up. By late evening, we'd have well-developed brains. And then it'd take us 60 seconds to thoroughly trash the place."

"Well, not *us* we," someone else called out.

"Intelligent life forms change their environment in ways that *enhance* their lives."

"We'll be at five degrees by 2100."

"We—*us* we—can't survive that."

"Earth is an ecosystem. Everything's connected. It's a network of relationships."

"Men aren't good at relationships."

More cackling.

"And they never will be. Because."

"Chocolate's going to go extinct," Spike pointed out. In case Jane needed yet another reason.

"Yeah ... Wait! X! Is there chocolate on your planet?" As soon as she said it, she knew the answer. Hadn't X said it was one of the major food groups?

X nodded. "Every town, no matter how small, has its own bar—"

"Its own *chocolate* bar? We could be chocolate bartenders!" Jane turned back to Spike. Okay, that decided it. They started to get in.

"No, wait!" she cried out again, and stopped. "I didn't get to deliver my John Galt speech! From my novel—"

Spike caught the reference and so knew what it was.

"Leave the flash drive. In case anyone cares."

On second thought, she left the whole laptop.

"Wait." This time it was Spike.

They looked at each other, both suddenly sober with their decision.

"A moment of truth?"
"And an epitaph."
They looked out over the flat land.
"It's over." Jane shrugged. Sadly, helplessly.
"We're done," Spike said. Ambiguously.